AUTUMN BREEZE

I AM A NEW YORKER

By RW Richard, Aka The Romantic Novelist

Amazon's editors' pick for best books of 2015
San Diego Book Awards, Best Romance, 2017

The author thanks Toni Noel for her notes that led to this edition:
2.1, 9/30/15. Any who have bought the 1st edition please contact the author at rwrichard@ymail.com for a free copy of this edition. The cover's insignia reads SDBA which means San Diego Book Awards (as best general romance for 2017).
Published by WEB Press, Carlsbad, San Diego, California.

E-mail your request(s) to rwrichard@ymail.com. Visit the author's blog at http://romancetheguyspov.blogspot.com. The author thanks you for purchasing *Autumn Breeze*.

The author dedicates this novel to the innocents and heroes who died on and because of 9/11 and the brave men and women who fought to keep us safe. The author also wants to thank the Writers Bloc critique group and the local RWA chapter (San Diego) for their professionalism and comradery. Thanks go to the author's dear friend, Kim. Her sixteen-year-old daughter labeled the author, *The Romantic Novelist*. It stuck and the author loves it.

WORKS by RW Richard

NOVELS:

Neanderthals and the Garden of Eden, **A unique take on human and wolf pre-history.**

Double Happiness, **Loosely based on Shakespeare's** *Comedy of Errors.*

Autumn Breeze, **Amazon Books of the Year Award. *San Diego Book Awards Best General Romance 2017. About the aftermath of 9/11, a fourteen year-old genius must avoid deportation by putting a spy and a detective together. Carlos Series, Book 1.**

Angel's Eyes, **A blind colonel is kicked out of the Army. She must now cope with men and disability, but discovers a new talent. Carlos Series, Book 2.**

A More Perfect Union, **Amazon Books of the Year Award, San Diego Book Award Finalist. About the Republican and Democratic nominees for President falling in love. Carlos Series, Book 3.**

NOVELLA:

The Wolves of Sherwood Forest, **A young Robin and Marian save England.**

SHORTS, etc.:

Wings by Christmas **and other short stories and homages.**

BOOK ON WRITING:

101 Tips, Primarily on Writing Male Characters

Author's note: It is a common misconception that no one knew 9/11 was coming. Over the years, various studies—some published, some secret—had addressed the reason the World Trade Center was attacked in 1993 (to make the building fall down), who was behind it (al Qaeda), that planes could fly into high value targets. The Twin Towers remained the prime target. Up to the moment of this story's beginning, many intelligence agencies were working feverously to prevent an imminent attack… There were also a few amateurs who were—for whatever reasons—focused enough to notice things and draw conclusions.

What you are about to read is a fictionalization of various true events (and some yarns) homogenized into one story.

AUTUMN BREEZE
Chapter 1

Tuesday, September 11, 2001, 8:52 a.m., New York University

Autumn could see just fine from where she slouched, thank you. The smoky white and dark gray fingers of the devil painted the higher panes of glass and ruined the otherwise brilliant blue day. The blue day the city died.

She would not cry, but her legs shook a little. Not just because her mom was down there near the twin towers.

Gathering calm she quieted her knee-knocking. Emotion equaled weakness and a barely fourteen-year-old super genius didn't do weak—not much anyway. Conversely, the older girls dressed up to show off their states of mind. She wore a brilliant aura and, well, a cool black jean jacket and matching pants.

Autumn slithered farther down her chair, stretched out her long legs, and pushed Miss Stinky's desk two inches closer to the professor's lectern. Her classmate smelled like a moldy cauliflower. Autumn also wanted a little distance between herself and the we-have-nothing-in-common snob. She could push the desk quietly, yay, because everyone else who hadn't sprinted out of class without permission plastered their snotty noses against the south facing wood-latticed windows. They sobbed like two-year-olds or jabbered on, confused by what they saw.

Autumn wasn't confused. She had predicted the who, what, when, where and how of the attack and told a cop friend. The detective probably ignored the information or maybe her superiors ignored her.

Maybe the whole country overflowed with numbskulls. In any case, for her worried classmates, the attack site measured two miles away. Unless Osama bin Laden wanted to kill the brightest kid in America, they were safe. Good that nobody but geeks read any of her published papers on mathematics because someday, having just made a resolution, she'd destroy the terrorist using probability theory. Somebody else would supply the bullets.

The professor turned away from the window, face twisted with untold pain but telling tears. Out of his fog, he just happened to focus, no stare, at Autumn doing her aloof thing. Normally she displayed a whimsical, puckish face but today the best she could do was vary between melancholy and anger.

Maybe she should have feigned shock and trotted over to the window with the rest of them—to fit in. She did care. Maybe she cared too deeply. Look at what horror just happened and there was more to come. The professor paced back and forth from the window to the door, all the while continuing his penetrating stare. Maybe he hated babysitting. She didn't care about his misunderstandings. She glowered back.

"I've got no direction *here*. You should all go. Check in with your families. Give blood..." He swept his hand toward the door as if shooing away flies. With the phones fluky, how was she going to find out if her mom was okay?

Still locked in a staring contest, she shook her head, chastising the professor. "I was taught to keep on living, which means learning so we might contribute someday and make a better world than the hell outside." Her aunt from Las Vegas had consoled her in this way at her dad's funeral. Auntie Danielle was always right about things, when her dementia didn't steal her wan smile and wit.

"Take a seat, everybody." The professor pondered some great truth, glanced out the window and then dropped his head. The students, some blowing their noses, dragged themselves to their desks. "Our prodigy, the Jeopardy champion, has a point. However, my dear Miss Breeze, we aren't in high school anymore. We can't just stand idly by when we might be able to help. When our hearts are being ripped apart. You hear those sirens? They scream to each of us. Now is not the time for study. Now's the time to help." He boomed, lathering up.

Why was this tweedy professor focused on her Jeopardy fame rather than her Nobel candidacy in math? Maybe he hadn't boned up on her bona fides. Or maybe he talked down to stereotypically know-nothing freshmen. It mattered not. She needed to practice a little humility. She needed to show respect for the dead and dying. She needed friends. It was time to lose the sneer or whatever ugly had taken over her angelic face.

"Sorry, Professor. Just…the assignments would help me."

He scrubbed a weary hand across his face. "I can't think."

"I think Autumn left her heart at home today, professor," smart-ass Joey interjected. But he was smiling at Autumn, as if she were a puppy he wanted to cuddle. Yuck. Those students, who weren't morosely preoccupied, giggled, but they didn't know a thing about her heart.

Left my heart at home, not likely. Her often drunk mother forced her to do everything except her withering business. Mom sat on her medium-sized ass, stroking away on the computer while guzzling a fifth of Jack Daniels. Her e-matchmaking business would not land her a man, and in her drunken state, she wasn't doing any better for her clients. Autumn hoped she could help her mom before it was too late.

Joey Demarco would never need dating service help. He was way too Italian, tall, with thick curly black hair and penetrating gaga eyes. Yes, Joey was more than okay looking, but he was older and what would he want with a skinny girl from Trinidad with microscopic boobs?

Yeah, love. The last person she'd loved, her dad, went to heaven years ago. She was through with love. It only disappointed.

"Shut up, Joey. Can't you see she's hurting?" cute as a pixie Marcie asked. Maybe Autumn had a new friend. But Autumn wasn't hurting. It was more like seething over a disaster that should *not* have happened.

"I was just trying to wake her up," Joey said, with his Brooklyn inflection and attitude flaring.

The professor got back to staring, as if he were trying to figure out how to bottle her intellect. "I wasn't asking for a critique of Miss Breeze. I can see we're all upset, each in our own way."

"Being younger, I guess I'm not used to all this freedom," Autumn said.

The truth? She had an insatiable passion for learning and nobody should get in her way.

"All of you, except maybe our *wunderkind*, have an obligation to help. As I said before, you can start by letting your families know you are okay. But check the news and be careful where you go. A week from now is a different story, hopefully. For next Tuesday's class I want each of you to read the first three chapters of our main text, *Human Society and Culture*, and write at least five pages on how the human society and culture of New York will change: temporarily, permanently, or perhaps not at all. Hint: You can make it personal by citing examples from how your family and friends are coping."

"You expect us to argue from the specific to the general?" Autumn asked.

"I expect both. Class dismissed."

The class started to collect their things and leave.

"And you, my precocious one, can bring me a bucket full of tears as well as an A+ paper."

Autumn's eyes welled. Her first installment. Damn him, well no, darn him, for Satan was loose today and looking for weakness.

"Don't go down there," the professor shouted.

With all the students rushing and crushing, Autumn wedged book bags with Marcie at the door.

They squibbed into the hallway. "Are you all right, baby?" Marcie asked.

"I'm okay, really. I'm just angry that this terrorist attack could happen."

Everyone started talking at once. They rambled on again, over whether it was an accident, a small plane. They railed against war, a very New York University thing. Some predicted nuclear holocaust. Conspiracy theories hatched like baby chicks everywhere. But in the end, they showed concern for the snot-nosed kid in the class. Even Miss Stinky showed she cared by invading Autumn's ears with words of encouragement. They clustered around her as they blobbed down the drab hallway on their way to the racket going on outside.

Somehow, Stinky's aroma wasn't important anymore. Autumn's classmates were loving her and it felt great. She felt like a hotdog being squished by roll, mustard and relish. But she couldn't let them know she actually liked the brand new feeling of having friends, even if they weren't at her level intellectually. If they knew how lonely she was, she'd have no peace, no time to chart her own course to success. Somehow, she'd find a way to help stop the insanity outside. She had to think her mom would come home.

"Yo, too close," Autumn said, swirling her head to sweep the group. Their eyes said stop your bluster, baby. Her cutesy, cheeky face belied her tough-sounding words. She'd get nowhere with this crowd. Or worse…

Joey planted himself in front of her and grabbed her shoulders, which halted the parade. She quivered and downward-dogged her lips. *Way too close, hunky monkey.*

"Listen kid. You're everybody's cute baby sister. We're gonna look out for you whether you like it or not."

He said cute. That's amazing. She stiff-armed his chest and gave him and the mashers a tepid smile.

They all timidly inched onto Third Street because the explosion of noise, primarily unending sirens, scared all the kids for sure. Everyone, not just the students, looked bewildered and mostly kept their mouths closed. As if their voices were stolen, as if no words could be uttered. Had to be collective shock. For Autumn, she tried reflection, which brought her a tiny sliver of serenity. Things were going to change, for the better. Had to.

Oh no, one full no-hiding-it tear is dribbling down. She refused to swipe it.

The mostly blue-jeaned army surrounding her cut right, heading for Thompson.

A frumpy lady in a white dress sat in the middle of Third. Her elbows propped her face, which was hidden behind thick raven curls. Not one of the six cars waiting honked. Autumn's pretty police detective friend leaned over the lady and stroked her hair.

"Detective O'Sullivan. Cha Cha…" Autumn tried to shout over all the noise, but her friend didn't hear.

Autumn and her silent bodyguards lingered at the corner and then started south on Thompson towards the devil's face. Leaving one by one, they chose her to hug. Lucky, huh?

"Which way are you going? Marcie asked.

"I'm not far. I'll be fine." But doubt gnawed at her resolve.

Joey turned toward her and gave her a super serious look. "Listen, kid. I need to call you. Okay?"

"What?" Hands on hips, or lack thereof.

"Physics tutoring. I hate the subject." He shouted over the mournful cries of the continuing army of emergency vehicles heading south. He too was young, sixteen, and had a scholarship. Something stunk here. The boy was up to no good. She knew she was pretty, but go figure with no figure.

"I'll text you Friday, Joey. Get out of here."

He gave her a piece of paper with his cell number on it. "You call me."

"I don't know…" If her mom were safe, she could still use a little extra pocket change.

"We godda help each other?" he asked, choking from emotion.

"We'll talk," She said loud and clear and she meant it.

"I'm going to the chapel. Gonna pray for them." Joey did an about-face and headed for Washington Square and the little Catholic Church at the corner. "Gonna pray for you, too, kid," he boomed back.

Like, totally unnecessary, Joey. She smiled anyway, but Joey was running toward God and missed it.

She continued down Thompson like the unfeeling zombie he thought she was. Yet something else bothered her. How many people were dying right now? No matter how smart she was, people really didn't listen to a kid. Maybe she should have called the press. Maybe she should have marched down to World Trade and told people not to come to work on the 11th. No, all that would do was alert the enemy and they'd pick a different date. Besides, nobody understood. Just like the Tower of Babel, this mess was biblical.

Her stomach twisted. Her head hurt. Fear slapped her face. Irrationally, she felt that her mom was dying or dead. *Monique Breeze might never come home again.* Her mom was a little teary eyed this morning. Acting miserable, in fact, as if she were going to die. Whenever her mom got like that, something horrible always happened. The night before her daddy had died, Monique, crying, begged him to take a day off if he loved her. He loved her but they needed the money. He went to work and never returned.

She had tried to call her mom who said she'd be out all day down there near the towers, a business on West Broadway mom had said evasively. She'd promised not to go in the towers, but nobody, not even her mom, listened to her.

Autumn's cell still wasn't working.

A sweat broke out all over. If her mom really died, she could be deported. If NYU or her relatives in Trinidad found out, she'd be packing. If. If. If. Revving up, scenarios piling higher, she turned around and ran back to find her cop friend and maybe a just-in-case new mom.

Somebody would love her, right? Cha Cha was everything her alcoholic mom could no longer be. They were like big sister, little sister. They shared make-up secrets, did each other's hair, talked of silly boys and one-eyed men. Best of all, Autumn felt like a rookie NYPD officer helping Autumn plan and execute Washington Square community events. Cha Cha'd actually had the guts to tell her that she danced with old farts. They were tight.

Could I adopt Cha Cha? Nope. Dope. I'll make Cha Cha love me enough to call me— daughter. Yeah, and cows can fly. This is way too over the top. My real mom has to be alive.

She amazed herself at the typical kid think invading her 210 IQ genius space. *Emotion over logic sucks.* In spite of being smart, she could be as dumb as the trashcan she had just kicked. She peeked back, a little scared; the smoke had turned into faraway fingers chasing her down the street.

Chapter 2

Detective Second-Class Chastity O'Sullivan—Cha Cha to her friends—worked for the sixth precinct, which wrapped Greenwich and West Village. Its Deputy Inspector rushed what officers and detectives he could spare into community service during the emergency. He split apart teams to more effectively and quickly canvass neighborhoods. The newly assigned officers were to augment the fire department and other services, if possible, and if they did nothing else, keep people away from the disaster site. Other officers, including her partner, headed south to seal off the disaster area, help with the evacuation and risk their lives. Although she'd not likely lose her life today, she knew her work and the work of the team of officers assigned, would keep the city's heart beating.

O'Sullivan approached a distraught woman sitting in the middle of West Third Street, a short block off Washington Square. Other officers were discouraging vehicles from turning south onto Thompson. The officers were instructed to say in so many words, head away from the disaster, park—there'll be no parking tickets today— walk home. Six cars waited politely, if you can believe that, for the woman and officer to leave the street. New Yorkers didn't *do* polite, but God was testing souls today and New Yorkers were the winners, at least some of them.

The constant play of sirens horrified her. Countless people dying. Conjured images of suffering and death, tortured her spirit. She put on her professional face with just a hint of concern and got close to the woman's ear.

"What's your name, hon?"

"I don't know." The woman rocked back and forth.

Dispersed in all the noise, Cha Cha thought she heard someone shout her name. She turned as much as possible, being bent over and all, but saw no one.

She patted the woman's shiny dark ringlets and spoke calmly. "The fire trucks are going crazy on their way south. We have to give them a chance to save lives."

The woman burst into tears. Cha Cha wrapped her arms under the woman's armpits and through to her back, and then contemplated the maybe one-hundred and eighty pound problem. She locked her grip. *Here goes nothing.* Her one-hundred and twenty-five pound frame, five-foot-eight body was made of taut steel. Still, she hoped she'd bend not break.

"Help me, just a little," she said, struggling to pull the woman up.

"I'm so sorry, Officer." Most people didn't recognize rank of men and women in blue, especially women detectives. Didn't matter, she served best with calm dignity and love for citizens, even the scalawags, a favorite term of her beloved, murdered grandfather.

"There's a hotdog vender in the park who's handing out free ones," Cha Cha said.

The woman struggled. Her face contorted and turned a bit red which probably matched Cha Cha's cheeks. Patent leather shoes scraped as her crisscrossed legs pushed up to help the officer. They hugged and then walked off the street, arm-in-arm. The drivers, who hadn't already parked, waved and cheered. As long as it wasn't a Bronx cheer.

Cha Cha caught sight of Autumn, her very young best girlfriend, chess partner, confidante and likely the one who had shouted. The kid turned the corner south onto Thompson with some other undergrads. That girl had predicted this disaster, down to the day. Cha Cha would catch up with her soon. Yes, Autumn had a whimsical and overactive imagination, but what she had said about a team of five young middle eastern men in Vegas in late August made sense. Anyway, Cha Cha had written—Autumn's apparently inspired deductions—up in a full report and then forgotten about it. Until now.

Absolutely amazing.

"No hotdogs for me—I should lose some weight," the lady said, no doubt snapping out of her funk by using a little levity. Who cared about weight when people were dying? But Cha Cha knew the answer. God imbued every living soul with an indefatigable will-to-live and to succeed.

"I just dropped ten pounds swimming." Cha Cha patted her tummy and tried to match her new friend's awakening from a funk, but her stomach roiled. She swallowed a gag.

Oblivious to her discomfort, the woman laughed. "You? Yeah sure." Okay, Cha Cha was a bit scrawny, but once upon a time, B.S—before swimming—she had lost ten pounds. Really.

And right now, the trick here was to focus on the citizen's needs and distract from such things as 'the why' or the atrocities unfolding. The why of this woman's sitting in the street seemed obvious anyway. These horrors were like slamming your head into the concrete sidewalk.

"Do you want to talk about it?"

"My boyfriend works down…" She pointed at the smoke and gasped.

"Fellow officers and firemen I love went down there. I'm terrified for them." Tears welled up in both of them.

"You go, officer. You must have a thousand nuts like me to take care of. I'll be all right."

"Here's my card. Call me anytime, when the phones are working. Or just email me. Okay?"

"Sure. Teresa here, hairdresser for TV and Broadway stars." She offered her card and hand. "A free do, someday."

"Chastity O'Sullivan here, detective without peer." The woman started to laugh but her face soured again by tears. On Thompson at Third, both women heard and shook from the wumph of a new explosion. Smoke trailed from the south side of Tower 1 or 2, hard to tell from their vantage point.

"Go, just go," Teresa urged, shaking her head from side to side.

Cha Cha prayed by some miracle loss of life would be minimal. *Don't take my partner, Lord.*

She hoped all the things her little genius, Autumn, had predicted would not happen. So far, so bad.

Cha Cha turned around at Thompson and took in the horror on the faces of her fellow New Yorkers. Autumn was no longer there.

She had to get to work.

Cha Cha broke into a run west on Third and then zipped south a block later on Sullivan Street. She needed to avoid her usual beat in Washington Square Park. The locals would want to vent, and she couldn't afford to be sidetracked right now. The people on Sullivan might need her help. Besides, her co-op was there. Maybe she'd grab water, later. The air had a slight acrid taste—death—although the sky directly above remained brilliant blue. Even though parched, she'd wait.

"Our Father…" was all she could choke out. She needed to use her actions as prayers.

Pedestrians walked in purposeless directions, obviously disoriented. Some snapped photos. Some leaned out from fire escapes. She handed out seven more cards to concerned citizens before she got to a five-year-old boy with his shirt missing, sitting on the bottom of three steps of a co-op. He was bawling.

She squatted down into a catcher's pose and faced the mop-topped cutie. His big, round hazel-colored eyes dazzled her. Someday, maybe she'd have a family…a little boy, a little girl after this hell passed.

She had been so damn busy. And her dance students—well, they gave new meaning to the graveyard shift. She couldn't think of such things now. End of story. Save lives. Fidelis ad mortem. Mortem. Mortem. Mortem. Another tear rolled for the men and women in true harm's way, which she quickly swiped. Her glorious, goofy foolhardy partner was down there somewhere. She had tried a hundred times; he couldn't be reached by cell.

Composed now. Not really. "What's up, little man?" She pushed up his bangs and her heart broke.

"Up there. My cat won't come down because of the smashed building noises."

"Oh my, what's her name?"

"Sneeze." She'd try to figure the odd name out later if she had time.

"Achoo."

The young boy laughed. Good, she turned his cry off. But what about the flood of tears and grief she held back? She had to hold up.

"Cats are curious, and they love police officers too. So maybe I can get her down."

"He's not a girl cat. Is your gun full of bullets?"

"We are always prepared, but we never hurt cats." Being prepared meant staying in touch with her surroundings—the now gathering crowd of curious souls—even with buildings on fire, a too cute kid and cat proved a temporary panacea for their heartaches. In her peripheral vision and through the mix of crowd and space, she picked up someone coming on fast. Cha Cha tensed her legs.

Autumn ran up panting.

"Please don't go down there. Promise me," she said. "Please."

Cha Cha stood and hugged Autumn. "My job is here in this neighborhood with—"

Autumn wiggled away and looked frantic. "They're both going to crumble."

"Let's hope not." Yes, she had said that would likely happen and yes it was reported. H*ad we all screwed up so bad?*

"My name is Billy," he said and pointed into the tree. "He's name Sneeze. *Named.* I meant named." The boy frowned.

"Very good English, Billy," Autumn said. "My name is Autumn."

"I'm Officer Chastity."

The boy shook their offered hands.

Autumn caught Cha Cha's eyes. The girl wrinkled her nose and twisted her lips. Okay, Chastity was a funny name, but what could this kid know of such things? Of the endless teasing Cha Cha had endured? Easy answer: the super genius with encyclopedic and photographic memory knew everything, just not intimately, in this case. Some better day ahead, they'd get back to scrabble, chess and girl talk. Autumn wore the pink lipstick Cha Cha had given her and taught her to apply properly. They had shopped at Bloomies for her school clothes, this cute black jean jacket and matching pants, just a week ago. Somehow nothing mattered anymore.

Again, an image of her partner flashed before her, this time of him munching on a torpedo sandwich oozing with ketchup, letting it drip on their reports. *Oh God, where are you, sweetie?* Her partner, Detective Jerome Price, had a loving wife and two toddlers, a boy and girl, waiting for him to come home tonight. *Please come home.*

"*Should be a snap.*" Autumn said, dragging her back to the present.

Her young friend was suggesting she stand on Chastity's shoulders and reach out to get the cat. Acquiescing, Cha Cha had her hop on. Then she turned toward the street and asked Autumn to face the co-op and help watch, so that Cha Cha could remain alert and in control as best as possible.

The small thinning crowd gave them room. They used the skinny trunk for balance and then inched across the branch with Autumn crossing one hand over the other. Although the girl was five-five, she didn't feel heavy. Since no fire trucks would stop today, nor should they, and commercial vehicles with ladders were being deflected north, they'd be the heroines for little Billy. Cha Cha spotted a parked black van close to Bleecker Street, but it had no ladders.

Near the cat, Autumn started cooing, calling his name, sweet-talking. The boy chanted Sneeze, Sneeze, Sneeze. The cat liked all this and tentatively used Autumn's slightly bent arm. Sneeze's claws clung to Autumn's black denim jacket like a scratching post. The cat got to her shoulder, but then refused to go any farther. He swirled his tail all over her face. Autumn sneezed, but with both hands still on the branch, she retained her balance. The boy thought that was funny and giggled. *Sneeze, his parents must have a sense of humor.*

A feeling of imminent invasion of her personal space once again put Cha Cha on alert. If she had to drop the kid, she'd catch her. Someone in the milling crowd had gotten too close, but she couldn't see until he or she fronted her. Damn it. Today she just wasn't thinking straight.

"That was a terrific shot. Thank you." A tall, very good-looking, athletically built man clicked away with his camera.

Oh great. She had enough problems with her lieutenant, if this got back to him. '*Officer rescuing cats while New York burned,*' would go the headline and poof would go her career. But right now, she didn't care, and least of all for her harsh boss.

"Here, let me steady you, and you, Miss, can put the cat on my shoulder, but use one hand and hold the branch with the other or at the right moment, I'll reach up." His deep husky voice whispered over her skin.

"Her name's Autumn," Billy said.

The guy stepped up on the curb and invaded Cha Cha's space like a manager facing a ref at a baseball game, but close enough to swap chaw. Normally an idiotic thing to do, but she had her hands on Autumn's legs, not her snub-nose .38 or pepper spray. He hugged Cha Cha, lending support, but it felt like a caress. Something primitive passed between them or at least her. She already disliked this man for allowing her own body to betray her. For not offering his shoulders like any tall, decent man would do.

Why today? What drove a man to hug a woman and stranger? This was creepy.

"You've got one second, mister, to let go of your grip."

"No Problem. Autumn, please hand down the cat." But Autumn was having a hard time gripping the slinky feline.

This couldn't be happening while people were suffering. She'd have a talk with her *very* primitive brain stem, but it wouldn't listen. Her mom had warned her of the day her soul mate would come along when she least expected it. 'A regular miracle and you'll know God's will for you, immediately,' she had said, over chocolate-chip cookies and milk. Soul mate, her foot. *Cellmate* was more like it. Not that she'd be the one in the cell with him.

"Time's up. Move away now or get arrested."

"Just a moment," he pleaded.

Yet, she didn't know how Chemistry 101 worked. But this guy was an entire degree, plus a couple courses in biology. She was going to hell. He hugged harder and then started to untangle, having his way she supposed. She resisted the stupid urge to melt into his hard body, to surrender.

Cha Cha regained her composure quickly. Her partner Jerome's image crossed her mind and she cried inwardly. While many were in harm's way, she rescued cats wrapped in a man's steel grip.

"Step away."

Never compromise her person, of course. She did carry a full complement of weapons ripe for the picking. He could feel her up and run off with impunity. He, at least, was no longer hugging her.

"Please back off, completely."

"Just a moment. The cat is almoooost with me."

He didn't look like the masher type, although from his eyes, he was taking her in, like a display at Horny and Hardart's. Hell, she hadn't had a real one-on-one date for what, seven months? This was not the answer.

Get a grip or rather thank God he no longer gripped. The world was going crazy while a guy and gal and two kids and a cat were trying to live. She was reading way too much into this man's actions.

But she was no gal. She *was* a cop. *Was—if my boss finds out what this civilian did to me, if only for maybe five seconds.*

He had ceased touching her anywhere, but they were still close enough to kiss. His pupils dilated, and with her body in revolt, she was sure she couldn't stop her eyes from doing the same. *Ever fall in love, mister, or do you just take what you want?*

He needed a full interrogation, later. But last she checked lust was not an *arrestable* offense. However, hugging a police officer—well this could be construed as assaulting a police officer— but there was a war going on in her between good girl weighing down her shoulders—or was that Autumn—and shady lady.

If she looked up at her young friend, *he'd* look down into her eyes, and if he had ever read any pop psychology articles, he would know from her lying eyes, that she was interested. Instead of risking eye contact, she focused on the curly hairs peeking out of his twice-unbuttoned gray dress shirt. That only made it worse. When the smell of Ivory soap, mingled with his heady male scent, assailed her…Cha Cha knew she was done for. *Handcuff me.* This guy could even nibble on her ear or squeeze her bottom and then run off. This had to stop, now. Totally pissed, her face warmed with anger and maybe lust. How did she lose control? What about the tragedy? She was about to tell herself off…

Where the hell did he come from anyway?

"We'll manage on our own. I'll get the cat."

"Yes, ma'am, but consider its claws penetrating your scalp or scratching your beautiful face."

"I won't let that happen," Autumn said.

This six-foot-two hunk with curly black hair, sharp gray eyes, dimpled jaw and broad shoulders was just about—no, *was* the most gorgeous creature she had ever been mauled by even if it were only for a moment. Whatever. He was way out of her bony-assed league, and today was the worst day to even try finagling a date or for her to attempt to understand her mom's prediction.

Besides, he was an idiot. Touching a cop could land the perp in the hospital or worse. She'd slap a pair of cuffs on him if she could, but before she could come up with a viable plan b, the cat was in his hand. Still, he seemed to take his time, breathing in her scent. She knew a letch when she spied one.

"Stop it, sir."

"I was trying to—"

"I know what you were trying to do." She pushed her words out through clenched teeth. "Identify yourself and back off farther." She had never lost her cool like this before. Yikes, she was a mess. The waning crowd must have sought respite from their collective misery by focusing on this Punch and Judy show.

"My name's Johnny Lance. I'm trying to freelance a story for the Post or Times. Was heading south when I spotted you two damsels in distress. I'm sorry… I meant no harm."

His lying eyes. He had rested an old-fashioned Minolta on the stoop, an odd choice for a reporter. The gathering crowd was in no mood for stealing his equipment. She hoped.

"Never touch a police officer, again. Are you crazy or dumb…or both?"

"I wasn't thinking. Again, I'm so sorry, Detective ah…"

This grandstander was holding the cat like the *Statue of Liberty* held her torch.

"Chastity." Oh, crap. Why did she give her name? Seething with anger—at him, at her own stupidity, at this tragic day—she tried to stomp her hard boot on his, probably loafers, but he was amazingly quick and she missed. Now she really had physically crossed a line and immediately regretted her display of unprofessional behavior. She'd acted like a civilian, like a *woman*.

She didn't deserve to be a NYPD detective. How many times had she questioned her ability to serve? Her gentle methods of persuasion had served her well when compared to the Clint Eastwoods on the force. This time though, her studied approach to policing failed by a mile. But at least he had backed off and looked contrite.

"Sorry, Detective. I've almost got this furry Houdini secured."

Johnny Lance, if that was even his name, patted the cat now safely on his shoulder, grabbed his scruff and lowered him to Billy. Sneeze scrambled to the ground and ran through the propped-open building door. The boy chased after him. Grinning broadly, Autumn smiled like a sweet cat and dropped into Johnny's outstretched arms. And looking pleased to be cradled. Cha Cha, following up on the shirtless boy, ran after him with Autumn now trailing behind. For some insane reason, Johnny, her personal standup masseuse, quickly overtook them on the steps.

Had to be a stage name, Johnny Lance. He bounded the stairs, muscles flexing. Looking so yummy in gray cargo pants, color coordinated with the cotton dress shirt. *Still, why was he still here?*

They reached the third floor and stopped.

"Hey Billy, where's your shirt?" Cha Cha asked.

"My daddy and mommy work down there." Not really an answer, but in a five-year-old's brain, it made sense somehow.

They all entered the boy's place through a half-opened door and found Billy's probable babysitter watching TV.

The woman started screaming.

Chapter 3

The babysitter, a shapely buxom blonde in too tight pink stretch pants, didn't get up to hug or chastise Billy. She stayed glued on the couch in front of the TV but focused on Cha Cha's uniform. Autumn took the boy and plopped on the couch next to the woman.

Cha Cha would reprimand the screaming thirtyish-year-old woman about not watching the boy, but first she needed consoling for whatever was making her hysterical.

The blonde raised her hands in surrender. Her screaming turned to cries, and then her cries turned into foreign language gibberish. Had to be Russian. Cha Cha's now cooing words wilted like a wounded bird, Autumn patted the woman's hand, but Johnny Lance, the *freelancer* or whatever, calmed the forlorn woman by speaking Russian back. Hmm…this was interesting. Johnny was clearly not who he said he was. Cha Cha trained new eyes on him. She couldn't penetrate the enigma because his body language told no story. He reeked of cool—way beyond that of the toughest journalist. *More like James Bond.*

The Tower tragedies could mesmerize this woman, but her hysteria told a different story. Her fearful, bloodshot eyes darted from Cha Cha's gun to her NYPD cap, and then back again to Johnny. Not once did she look at Billy or smile back at Autumn. The babysitter was obviously afraid of authority.

Cha Cha approached. The numerous bagel-chip crumbs strewn across the sitter's lap jumped like Mexican beans. She was digging at the quick of her fingers. The TV sang a sad song, both Towers afire, and the woman cringed as Cha Cha leaned forward.

Cringing over me?

The woman stressed over their presence, not the disaster. In what used to be the Soviet Union, KGB or other police could grab the innocent or not so innocent at any time for any reason and poof, they'd disappear.

This brought her to the next conundrum.

How innocent was Johnny Lance? This gorgeous gumba was as Italian as tangy Gelato, not Ruskie. Russian was difficult to learn. Cha Cha preferred intelligent, Renaissance men. This man, however, had an agenda, because he hadn't minded mashing her and then turned into a boy scout when he claimed he had work to do.

The babysitter and Johnny's conversation varied, turning from choppy to relaxed to quiet. Then he explained what the woman had said.

"I calmed Lucya down by reassuring her we aren't here to deport her or put her in jail. That we were worried about Billy being outside unsupervised and shirtless. She apologized, said whenever Billy took his shirt off, it meant he was going down the hall to his little girl friend, Charese, in 3B, not outside. Besides, the world was ending, I think she said."

"Tell her thank you and that the world is not ending. And if she promises to keep Billy off the street, we'll leave, and she can stay in this country. Give her my card, please." She could sling a little BS. Because the truth was, she had no idea if Lucya was deportable, and didn't care. Not today. Probably not any day, unless she broke some other law.

"A card for me, too?"

"Nyet," Cha Cha said with a grin to put off his all too flirty smile and inappropriate, bedroom eyes.

She still couldn't wrap her head around this guy. Who was he exactly? Many Russians learned English but few Americans learned Russian. One typical reason for learning Russian involved Cold War spying. But Johnny, the squeezer turned boy scout, maybe thirty himself, well, was almost too young for the Cold War. But he used an old camera. There was a black van, which could have been labeled Government Issue, surveillance mobile. He spoke Russian. Probably just coincidences, paranoia. Puzzles intrigued her. As a detective, she lived or died by solving them. She stole a quick prayer that her partner would get out of the Tower or away from it. *Divert him, oh Lord.*

"Я хотел укусить вашего осла," Mister Lance said, with a devilish smirk.

Autumn let go of the boy and put her hand to her mouth. *She knew what Johnny said*, and from her surprised expression, it wasn't good. This guy, in spite of his immeasurable help in calming the woman, was cruising for a bruising. Later, Cha Cha would ask her young friend for what could prove to be a most interesting translation.

Aha. The babysitter blushed which stopped her tears. She then revved up her chatter with Johnny again. This time her voice foamed to a fuck-me-anytime saccharine sweet tone. It was Johnny's turn to say nyet. Hey, Cha Cha didn't stand a chance. Lucya's knockers would definitely need to be deported.

They said their goodbyes to Lucya, Billy and Sneeze.

Out on the co-op's steps, Autumn leaned over to pick up the camera he forgot and gave it to him. Mostly any other day in New York that old Minolta SR-101 would have been flying down the street in the hands of some scalawag.

"I'm going down to the disaster. I've got to interview survivors."

Well that was brave and foolhardy.

Johnny had to know this was pure folly. Why did he taunt her so? Did he want her to stop him? An officer could—no should— stop him. The woman within her screamed to be free, wanted to hug him until he gave up his foolish desire to be in harm's way. He'd probably announce his intent to disobey her police order or break her hold with one flex, pure uncivil disobedience. Persuasion was her strong suit if she had anything left of her soul to give today.

"You'll be stopped, even with a press pass. Damn it, Johnny, the story is here with me. We saved a cat, helped a little boy, you caught Autumn. Human interest, right? Besides, the buildings are being evacuated because of the risk of possible collapse and increasing fire. Come with me..." she raised her voice to compete with the din of heavy trucks, perhaps the National Guard, "and live another day."

She had little idea about possible evacuation orders, but it made sense and was normal protocol, as best she remembered from some cross-courses with firemen. In any case, the police and heavily armed guardsmen weren't going to let anybody get near the site. In the chaos, sly Johnny could give them the slip. Who would want to run into a burning building anyway? Conclusion: He wanted to taunt her, for reasons unknown. James Bond. Nope, just a stupid fantasy, and of all days to dream like a little girl.

Johnny fake-name Lance presented an unusual mix of stubborn and cooperative, of cultured and bad boy. Without so much as a goodbye to them, he sprinted south as fast as Carl Lewis would. Her heart sunk for all the agony and one more lost soul slipping away from her.

Would she ever see him again? Such a complex and beautiful man. She shook her head; too many tears added to the oversupply that New Yorkers and the whole world were likely shedding.

She'd never fall in love…and really, why did *any* of that matter right now? She should be with her partner. She slung her last tear after the lingering image of him.

Autumn and she turned away. She caught Autumn looking perplexed, but with her arm holding out a hankie.

"It's a hard day, sweetie." She refused the hankie.

Autumn stuck it back in her pocket. "My hankie is pretty wet, anyway."

"Listen, honey. You know Russian, don't you?" They sat on the stoop.

"I read chess books and speak some to an ex-pat chess master in the park. You know, Anatoly." Anatoly, a kindly, down-on-his-luck elderly man, was harmless. If anything, he played the part of part time grandfather for Autumn.

"Yeah—Anatoly. So what do you think Johnny said to me?"

"I don't think he's a reporter," she said evasively.

"You know, I have the same suspicions. Someday, girl, you could be a better detective than Sherlock Holmes, or anything you want to be."

"I don't know yet."

"Hey, sly one. *Please tell* me what he said."

"Well his grammar and tense were screwed up." She put her hand to her mouth again. "Sorry."

"Give the words to me, the way you think he meant them."

Autumn put on her puckish face. "He wanted to bite your ass." Then she plastered on the most disarmingly broad I-just-ate-all-the-cookies smile. Wheels whirled in this kid's high-octane brain over something Cha Cha couldn't fathom. She wanted to squeeze the girl silly, but knew they both had to get going. The thinned crowd, now three adults and two toddlers, seemed in awe of the two cat rescuers or just desperate for distractions. At least they didn't add their New York two cents.

"I'll kick his ass," she whispered in Autumn's ear, "if I ever see him again. *Men*."

"Boys." Autumn placed her hands on her developing hips and did a little Janet Jackson head role.

Nasty, nasty boy. "What made you think he wasn't a reporter?" Cha Cha pressed.

Autumn listed the same suspicions Cha Cha entertained and added that the black van had to have backed illegally onto Bleecker since she saw it speed east at exactly the same time Johnny rounded the corner, plus a three and half seconds for jumping on board.

"The chances it was the same black van are about eighty-two percent." Yep, genius alert.

"Well, okay. Maybe he has a reporter sidekick... I know. I know. Why would the van be parked facing north and why would he walk north away from the disaster just to hug me?"

Autumn giggled. A sure sign a whopper would be delivered. "Because you're so beautiful, and he wanted one last hug before he died."

Cha Cha smiled fondly at her young friend. *Thinking about boys, much?*

"Sweetie, you better get home. We'll play detective soon. We'll go back to our girl talk. I'll make you my honorary partner, next time." That made Autumn smile, but it disappeared too quickly. She looked deep into the girl's eyes and gleaned terror or worry. *But not over the disaster.* Autumn either knew more about Johnny she wasn't telling, or she was wrestling with another problem. Cha Cha would get to the bottom of this as soon as she could.

"I promise you I won't go down there," Cha Cha said.

"Can I call you soon?"

"Tonight, unless I pull a double. As always my sweet friend, anytime you want. If I don't answer, you'll know I'm busy helping another Johnny Lance or little boy."

"I won't bug you. Maybe after things get back to normal I'll see you in the park," Autumn said.

"Are you okay? Your mom?"

"She's fine…I'm fine…Cha Cha." This kid never trailed off when speaking. If anything, it was one run-on sentence after another connected with ands, ifs, therefores, buts. You name it. There was no empty space in Autumn's speech.

"Check in on Monique to make sure." Autumn didn't respond. "I'll see you in the Park, then, someday soon."

For the first time, her young, brilliant friend seemed lost. Shaken. Maybe somebody in her family was down there. Maybe her mom.

"Is your mom okay?"

"Fine." She said with a flat tone, no animation. Her invincible aura missing. They embraced. The girl walked off, head down. The co-op door chose that moment to slam shut. North at Third Street a man tried to pull a baby out of a woman's arms. Officer needed?

Cha Cha rubbed her hands over her weapon belt as an inventory check and broke into a run. What a hell of a day. Worse than the day her grandpapa was executed by a fellow detective.

The day her grandpapa had been shot, she wasn't able to help—being too young. Today, she couldn't help her partner—not being with him, she couldn't help Johnny Lance—too bullheaded. Instead, she rescued a cat. She should just resign. No wonder her lieutenant rode her ass. She was weak.

Still, love for the City of New York and her focused empathy in solving problems should count for something. If only somebody would come along and recognize her value.

Was she suffering a typical case of New York angst?

Surely, the whole city's heart and livelihood wouldn't be tested in the days to come beyond their spirit and abilities. No less her heart or job.

She ran up to the man, woman and baby. Without a word, the man gave the baby to the woman, backed into a tree and started rubbing the back of his head.

Cha Cha stepped up to him. "Are you all right, mister?"

"Yes, officer...I'm sorry, my wife hates me. She wants a divorce but I love our baby girl."

"I don't hate you, George."

Cha Cha remained silent as the couple talked it out over their tears. The man and woman took Cha Cha's cards, promised to enroll in therapy and walked north, their bodies tentatively close, it seemed. Hopefully this couple would not be torn apart and their baby girl would grow in a loving home.

Grandpapa watch over me, the people and the city I love.

Chapter 4

Temporary deputy director of OTTS, Frank J. Lancia, AKA Johnny Lance to a certain feisty cop, had an abhorrent job to do that would rely heavily on his experience as an ex-CIA/NCS covert operative. He was and always would be a spy.

OTTS—over the top secret—was President Eisenhower's pet name for an agency he had personally dreamed up, to investigate and harness, if possible, unexplained phenomena. Eisenhower had mostly responded to the crazy Soviets with their spoon benders, remote viewers and flying saucer fanatics. Nothing much came of it all, from what Frank had ascertained so far, but Carlos, the current Director of OTTS never talked much about the agency's past. The current U.S. president wanted to shut down OTTS. Therefore, biding time and applying their old spy craft, they mostly worked national security issues. There was nothing paranormal about terrorism, unless you believed in hell. Families would wake up; they'd miss sons, daughters, parents, whose only crime was living.

Detective O'Sullivan's background investigation and clearance from any terrorist ties needed to run its course. On the plus side, if she were linked to a terrorist group, why would she divulge the attacks method and date? On the minus side, the information she reported had to have sprung from somewhere—if not her. Carlos and Frank took point on trying to discover Detective O'Sullivan's source, not because there was anything paranormal about the attacks but because Carlos and Frank were the best cloak and dagger boys, the government had at their disposal. Still, something nagged at Frank. He had made a mistake with the pretty detective when he gave her a fake name he should have spent time thinking about. The detective was notoriously smart.

Johnny Lance was probably a porn star's name. It just spewed off his tongue in an irrational moment of being too close to the beautiful detective and ill prepared. Truth be told, he'd been utterly transfixed by that adorable peek-a-boo dimple on her wholesome girl-next-door face. Not to mention that ridiculously plump ponytail of curly brown hair with shimmering red highlights. Oh man, what he wouldn't give to press up against her again, run his fingers through those thick lustrous ringlets and breathe in her sweet womanly fragrance. So badly, in fact, he had considered letting her handcuff him just to spend more time with her.

Not today.

But that's the way God made the male body and soul. He'd drool if he wanted to, even when he had a job to do. Oh God, he loved a woman in uniform, especially with a slim, ladylike figure like hers. Although she was nearly as thin as, but even more gorgeous than a runway model, her muscles flexed like a pro-athlete's.

Next time, a better name, knuckle head. Don't let your silly pickle do your thinking. He forgave himself for not being prepared with a made up name. The disaster had set in motion instant responses, right down to a certain building in Kandahar that would be blown up shortly. America was going to war and it started now.

He had streaked to the corner of Sullivan and Bleecker being careful not to knock down any of the many distraught and aimless. There, half up the corner curb and out of sight from Sullivan Street rested the van with a crumpled trashcan under it. His boss, Carlos, ain't got no respect and wasn't the best driver.

They had to find their coworker, Emily Livaudais. He knew Carlos felt like shit for letting her go to the WTC today. Via her last cell phone call, maybe before the phone died, she had reported following a possible al Qaeda sleeper into one of the Towers. It seemed likely now that the suspect was either unlucky or a patsy. Poor Emily. Her only crime was a belief in ghosts and a love for Frank. He couldn't love back. Therein lay the crime—against her humanity.

So it seemed—both she and the suspect had walked into a trap.

Adrenaline pumping, Frank jumped in the van. "Go, go, go." They squealed off east on Bleecker, leaving the trashcan wobbling its way into the gutter. Then they whipped south down Broadway to the WTC disaster.

"Today you make three mistakes, yes? You never do this." Colonel Carlos Petrovich said.

"Stupid name?"

"*Funny* name. Your first two mistakes were letting sex get in way and not thinking. Number three, my young friend, you spoke Russian—and very poorly." He glowered at him. "What a joke. Your bad judgment pushed O'Sullivan to think like detective. She is no dummy...probably she noticed this fine vehicle and your camera, as well."

It was no use arguing with his boss, who was right, anyway. He hadn't practiced Russian for quite a while. *But give me a break, Carlos.*

"Sorry. Today is the worst day in our sorry lives. I had no time to compose myself."

His sidekick just barrel laughed. Apparently Frank's excuse didn't fly.

Carlos Petrovich, ex-CIA, ex-KGB, was a brilliant analyst and the most feared assassin in the clandestine world. His name seemed foreboding, not very Russian. His Basque mother and Russian father had named him Carlos, as if they were training him to be a jackal, but he looked more like a not too cuddly Russian bear. Someone who could crush a man with ease and relish. Or put a hole in his head.

"This is your camera, Carlos." Frank leaned back and put the Minolta on the carpeted floor by the middle row seat. This banged-up, old camera had caused practically the same argument in Bosnia. It did however take great pictures.

Carlos removed his headset and raised a bushy eyebrow. "Never mind camera. We do not have to die today, and I do not want you to do anything foolish. Even if you are quitting, I still..." He trailed off. Perhaps he had listened to something interesting on his headphone and was mulling it over.

Carlos's little kingdom of paranormal freaks had lost nearly all direct federal funding under the new administration. The new president didn't believe in all that 'razz-ma-tazz' or 'hocus-pocus.' Carlos hadn't helped make his case by hiring any pretty, young woman who claimed to have a paranormal talent. The fortunetellers were the worst. All his boss got out of them were blowjobs, which hadn't taken a soothsayer to predict. Carlos would soon be a one-man show. The stubborn bastard should join him and go back to the NCS full time or to the parent organization, the CIA.

"We've got to find Emily," Frank said, competing with Carlos's earphones.

Carlos gave his sour apple face. "We are busted. That kid—and O'Sullivan—are on to you…and my van. You're going to have to get the bug back off her back before she finds it. Besides, I have enough already on her phones and computers. I just don't know who her informant is." Carlos looked pensive. "Maybe that g—"

"Will do. Keep her from getting into her co-op if necessary until I get back. Okay, boss?"

On their journey to the World Trade Center, they were stopped for the last time a block short. They presented government ID again but were directed west on Barkley. They weaved by the barricades and a clutter of emergency vehicles to West Broadway. They slammed to a stop nearly hitting a fire truck.

"Do not get yourself killed."

"If she's alive, I'll find her. You come to my place for dinner." Frank keyed-in an inter-services query on Carlos's swivel-mounted computer and found out that the upper floors of Tower 2 had some evacuees. If she were alive and in Tower 2, the firemen would have guided her down or were in the process now. If she were high up in Tower 2, it had one top to bottom intact stairwell, which had filled with smoke but was passable according to the latest from FDNY.

"If O'Sullivan's report is correct, both buildings will collapse today. Keep your eyes open for street nooks or doors," Carlos said with worried brow.

They both craned their necks upward. The north Tower, AKA Tower 1, seemed off square at the top and buckled precariously. Would Tower 2, directly south of their position, fall over like a domino? The plane had hit the south wall, so the domino would fall north. If so, they were both dead men. Squished like bugs. Or was it the other way around? Like a lumberjack chopping a tree, wouldn't the top fall toward the chop, that is, south? He knew better than anyone that it was dangerous and foolhardy to be here. But what choice did he have?

"You don't even love Emily."

Okay, his boss had a point there. Frank enjoyed her as a steady girlfriend and nothing more. Nevertheless, he loved her as a person, a colleague.

"Where's your humanity, Carlos? She's one of us."

"It is called insanity, not humanity, even if you love her. Just check evacuee lists and get the fuck out of there, yes? You damn Yankee, pig headed—schmuck." The typical Carlos diversion. His boss was trying not too subtly to detain him, to save his life. But right now, Frank hadn't done enough. Carlos and he had done shit with the OTTS agency, except for one HUMINT channels top-secret report of imminent attack on the Towers, which they had delivered to the White House in August. The president ignored the cable maybe in the same way Detective O'Sullivan's report was downplayed at police headquarters. Too many crying wolf?

"I'll meet you on Sullivan Street at noon."

"I know the girl with Detective O'Sullivan." Carlos said, giving it one last try.

Frank scanned his friend's furrowed brow, twisted smile and mischievous eyes. Instead of taking the bait, he raised a thumb and eyebrows while exiting the van. He sprinted the short block south to Vessey. The ghosts Emily supposedly communed with now walked the streets of New York and he sure as hell hoped she wasn't one of them. Carlos took off in the van, laying rubber. *Couldn't blame him.*

The street scene was oddly void of human voice. The only sounds besides the sirens were the loud thumps and louder pops of falling debris and the crackling of fires.

Nonetheless, he could feel the rescue crews' overwhelming malady of spirit. They were quiet and somber looking, as if to say something to each other—invited bad luck, as if to smile— impossible. All that remained were triage centers, Army, NYPD, FDNY and a couple civilians walking quickly north. Frank had no trouble flashing his government ID as he picked his way closer to the Towers.

In the face of two angry looming monoliths of smoking concrete and steel, he quickly assessed his morning's foolishness. He crossed himself and looked around for somebody to direct him, maybe to admonish him like an errant child.

God no. To his right, maybe a hundred yards off, lay a crumpled brunette, face down circled by blood. It wasn't Emily. She didn't wear dresses. Who was this poor woman? Who did she love? Did she have children, brothers, sisters, a mom and dad, dreams? Was she in heaven?

He shook his head and it hit him. The misery, the absurdity. If he were in Afghanistan now, he'd put a bullet into top suspect's Osama bin Laden's demented, useless brain. Everybody in the intelligence community knew this was his work. It wouldn't be long before the terrorist and his lunatic followers were dead men. Frank gritted his teeth and squeezed off a tear.

A bit dazed, he almost walked into a fireman.

"Brother, you'll have to back off," the fireman said, while clasping Frank's shoulder.

He confronted a deputy Fire Chief with his problem and ID.

"The evacuees are all being interviewed at various sites. I think you can get the collated lists on your computer or call me tomorrow. There's nothing you can do now." The tall deputy clamped harder on Frank's shoulder as if to arrest him. Oddly, they both thinned their lips. For Frank this unspoken gesture between them, seethed with hatred for terrorists. The ones still living would soon join their brothers in hell. The chief twisted Frank's shoulder, turning him.

"Over there to triage. Help them." He pointed and gently nudged Frank.

A deafening roar made them look up at a building that was missing its top floors. Clouds of dust shot out of the middle floors at the speed of millions of bullets. They were going to be peppered to death at least. Tower 2 was crashing down. Straight down?

"Stay here and die." Frank grabbed the older man's hand and forced him to run for the Starbucks door. The Deputy Chief was slower, much slower in his gear. The grains of building overwhelmed them. Frank preferred to die helping somebody than live as a coward.

Barely making it to the door, they were pressed by complete blackness. Pummeled by pieces of what were probably pulverized concrete and God knew what else. Frank groped and found the handle exactly where he had pictured it, thanks to Carlos's advice.

He barely opened the door against the force of the death wind. They wedged into a surreal scene of gawking refugees from the morning's horrors. The crowd froze for a moment in various states of agitation, from red-faced crying to banging tables and cursing. Then they crowded the Chief and Frank.

The lights flickered for a moment. Somehow, this scene made sense. People needed people. Their confusion over the senseless counterproductive acts of terror was palpable.

You do not pull a lion's bob. The U.S. would soon strike back with unimaginable force.

Some others rose. They all cheered, and clapped for the fireman. They needed heroes today. Those civilians surrounding them dusted off a fine gray soot and chalk from their backs, shoulders, head and helmet with their hands. They may have touched human remains. Frank tried to see out the window, but the outside world was as black as the inside of a coffin. Would they all die here?

The Chief tried his walkie-talkie.

"Tower 1. Evac everybody. Over."

"Already issued. Good-bye, William. You and Betty are lousy bridge players. Over."

"Live, you bastard." He didn't say over or out. Just hung his head to hide his tears and went over to the door, which the patrons blocked.

"Get something for the chief to drink," Frank said. A little girl with her mom helped block the door. The baby took the chief's hand.

"My mommy and me are safe, Chief." He bent down and gave her a hug. "Because of you." She poked his chest.

"I have to go help more people, okay?"

The girl fingered his badge, "it's dark now, w-i," and sounded out the letters.

The chief patted the little girl's head. "W-i-l-l-i-a-m. I'll drink the coffee for you. Okay?"

"I can't have coffee. Mommy says it would make me walk on the ceiling." She pointed up where God was. *If God were protecting us, what worse disasters would this holocaust prevent? Nuclear?* He didn't believe God intervened normally. Yet he wished he had, at least this one time. Perhaps, the U.S. reaction to today's horror would eliminate future and possibly worse attacks. For this, he would pray.

* * *

An hour earlier, Mahmoud Ali Abunayyan had jumped down the endless steps in Tower 1, two and three at a time when left-behind briefcases, and other crap, crowds of people heading down, and firemen going up weren't in his way. He was careful not to crash into slower people. He thanked Allah—he looked Greek, with his tall slim frame and curly dark brown hair. Today, he'd call himself Petros Papadopoulos. Today, somebody he had never met wanted him dead.

"Sorry Miss," he said as he lost his balance and accidentally squashed a good-looking maybe fifty-year-old into the stairwell platform wall. She was unhurt. He didn't wait for her to say anything.

He looked back at her before rounding the next staircase. She resumed her slow trek downward. On seeing him, she cocked her head and gave a half-hearted wave, as if to say 'I'm tired. Live, kid. Pray I make it down.' He would pray to Allah for all these innocents.

Firemen continued up in full gear.

He ignored their suggestions not to jump steps, because they didn't have the time to stop him. They could be heroes if they wanted to be. He needed to live.

These men were great, not the crazy jihadists. Killing these people to make some point about Israel was not Allah's teaching. This morning he'd kill somebody if he knew who his tormentor was. Allah would give him strength and maybe supply the means for his enemy's destruction.

Long ago, he had refused to become a suicide bomber. He hated America, because of their imbalanced stance on Palestine and Israel. But, destroying his body was not the Creator's intent, no ticket to paradise, more likely hell. He later went to Harvard. With this education, perhaps he could bring people together. But the jihadists persisted in thinking he'd help in some way to sting the great Satan. He argued with them over the internet. These internet banshees had asked him to take pictures of all kinds of landmarks in

Manhattan. He did, only because his family still lived in Saudi Arabia. They had him by the balls. The building shivered again. He quickened his leaps. This piece of shit construction would surely collapse.

At the sixteenth floor, the building shook again. Then a young lady fell down a flight in front of him. He hadn't pushed her. He jumped three steps at a time, shouting. "Can you walk?"

"I think it's just a sprain and bruises."

"Excuse me. I must touch you to help you."

"Touch away, Sir Galahad," she said with a bittersweet smile.

After deciding her ankle might be broken, he flopped her over his shoulder into a fireman's carry. Then took the steps one at a time but with due speed and the energy of a hundred men. His spirit lifted. He could actually save somebody. Allah blessed him with this angel, her weight but a trifle. Allah's test of courage and humanity made him smile at his walk-down-mates. He was sure of this as a test. She felt like heaven. Dying this way would bring glory to his family and paradise for him.

At the bottom, the Fire Chief pointed the way to an enclosed crosswalk.

"I'll get you a medic."

"Your men are busy. Take care of yourself, Chief. I don't think there are any more coming." He lied to the Chief. He thought he knew what was coming, coming soon. These Towers were built light to help with sway but the construct could also help them fall.

"Nice try, brother." The Chief stayed put, pointing at the covered crosswalk. He shooed them on.

"I can walk," she told him.

"No you won't."

They reached safety and the medics took over. Not long after, the lady he had squashed in the stairwell found him, and squashed him back with a big and lingering hug. He wasn't exactly a hunk. He was tall, worked out and had a young and permanently tanned face, but he was also skinny. This woman looked so forlorn, so lonely, but...

"Glad to see you again," she said.

"I worried about you all the way down. Thank," he caught himself, "God." God was Allah. Allah was God.

One of the Towers came down so loudly he thought his ears would explode. Everything outside the triage center went black. The Chief—must have died—a true hero. Mahmoud couldn't stop his tears for people he hated. His head was twisted silly with opposing beliefs.

Mahmoud vowed to disappear. He was now officially dead. Any dates with either of these women might endanger them and ruin his plan.

After about fifteen minutes, the black turned gray. He could see the apocalypse outside. He got up.

"We haven't checked you out yet," a doctor said.

"I am fine."

"What's your name?" asked the really cute one who had the nicest rear end and legs he had ever held onto.

"Petros Papadopoulos loves you both as God would have it." He gave both ladies a bow and smile. Waving to the doctor, who hardly looked up, he walked out the door into deep ash and a nearly unbreathable mocha air. Yet he could see Tower 1, still standing, weeping smoke. The Chief might live after all, but Mahmoud would have to die figuratively and perhaps literally, if he didn't run north like the wind.

Chapter 5

Not long after Frank left Starbucks, Tower 1 collapsed, spewing a new form of black death in all directions. He ran on the young fast legs that had earned him nicknames like Flash or Streak when he played wide receiver for Notre Dame or ran track. The debris peppered, stung and stabbed him in his back and legs over and over again. Taking too many hits, he dived into a building nook. A man literally flew right by him, then dropped and wedged hard under a car just north of Frank by ten feet.

He barely heard the man scream.

"Help me."

Good, he was alive. Thank God for small favors.

"Hang in there," he shouted back over the hurricane of noise. He felt little pain, but worried for the trapped man.

The black turned gray once again. He rushed to help. Three firemen joined him and they extricated the man. Afterwards, the man revealed apologetically he was trying to get the story of a lifetime. He mucked around for his camera, but it was no longer there. The reporter at least had a story in his head, and a broken leg, which would give him plenty of writing time.

Frank felt disgusted for not doing enough, comparing himself with real heroes, firemen and police. He walked north like all the other zombies. He refused a ride on an Army transport or to request medical aide because he assumed so many more would need help. His only physical problems came from the feeling that he had been stabbed hundreds of times in his back and legs and his lungs labored like a coal miner's last breath. His only spiritual problem was in not nurturing his relationship with Emily. If only he had been closer and said, "Where are you going today?" If only he had singled out, from those who cried wolf on every day of the year, Detective O'Sullivan's outrageous report. Would things have changed?

Emily…she'd come home tonight. He'd hold her tightly. Try to love her the way she wanted.

A fresh westerly breeze cleared his head of uncomfortable thoughts and held back most of the filthy cloud.

In Saint John's Park, he had to stop due to heavy breaths. He leaned on a maple tree trunk and coughed blood mixed with a gray clump. Dizzy, he made his way north. The park swirled around him as if he were in the eye of a hurricane.

Somehow, a big glob of a guy he loved came into focus.

"What the hell," Carlos said, walking quickly from his van.

Frank steadied himself by grabbing Carlos's shoulders. "No Russian bear hugs. What's on me is toxic crap, mixed with the dead. Where is she?" he rasped, before spitting out a wad of phlegm again.

"You should see a doctor."

"After I get that bug back. Where is she?" He gathered resolve and strength to try to speak and walk better.

Carlos shrugged. "She's busy helping an old man find his co-op. You've got time." Carlos handed him eyewash and eye drops, but he refused. "Take it. Do you want to lose your sight?"

"Fuck you, too." Oh, they loved each other all right. It would have been best to approach Detective O'Sullivan without any obvious signs of having received medical aide, but his eyes felt like toothpicks had been jammed in.

After a quick call to his mom—telling her he had no time to talk and wasn't harmed—he then promised to call tonight. He hung up on her frantic worrying. Shit, now she was all concerned. What about the rest of his life? He handed Carlos his government ID, wallet and the NSA cell phone. His boss, ever so diligent, handed him a worn, crumbled business card,

JOHNNY LANCE
FREELANCE PHOTOGRAPHY
ARTISTRY CAPTURED
555-555-1212
JLance@freelance.com

with his picture and a sunrise shot from the Asbury Park boardwalk and a newly minted email and phone number. Nice touch.

"Tuck this into your bottom pocket."

Carlos ripped his top cargo-pant pocket down while he was tucking. "She'll wonder where your wallet went, if you do what I think you are going to do." The burly Russian gave him that, *you're-going-to-fuck-her-aren't-you* look. But he'd do nothing but mourn the dead and dying today. He did not indiscriminately fuck women. He asked first, when he was without a girlfriend. Until Emily's status was known, he still had a girlfriend. End of story.

"We'll see."

He limped north. A strong west to east breeze continued to keep the smoke and crud away from his failing lungs. Thank God, he could breathe. A little later after crossing Spring Street, he spotted his mark sitting on a co-op stoop halfway down Sullivan. She leaned against the railing staring south as if mesmerized, a sandwich bag dangling absentmindedly, an unopened Coke on the stoop. He limped forward. Acting, but not much.

"Chastity."

"Oh my God." Although her egg salad sandwich was wrapped, the smell made his stomach do somersaults. He had forgotten to eat all day, war on. The noisy stomach creatures revolted, insisting he'd live. He went instinctively for a wallet that was no longer there so he could buy something.

"Can I, ah, have…?" He felt miserable attempting to steal the poor woman's sandwich.

"Sure, sure, it's not much. I can't eat, anyway." She glanced south to the disaster, teary eyed. "Too much misery, too much blood."

Was he bloodless? He cared more than he could tell her today. He turned away from her and cleared his throat as best he could. What could he say? She had to have lost comrades. He certainly had. Right now, the pain and death of strangers, innocents, the inhumanity of it all, struck in bold relief to this woman's heart.

"Sorry." He turned away from her and spat.

"Can you eat?" She broke her pickle in half.

He said nothing at first, but took her sandwich.

"I—I'm so sorry I can't explain my behavior. I forgot to eat this morning."

"If I get hungry, I'll eat something else at home."

His eyes constantly teared from irritation—but her uniform, and all it stood for, soothed him. His eyes could have had worse to look at. Sitting before him was vibrant life, maybe his life through her heart. Maybe just gazing upon her would cure his eyes, his soul, his grief.

"Come with me. Let me take care of you." She extended her hand, but he refused until she explained that her only job today was to help the sick of mind, body and spirit for which he had won the trifecta. She broke out into the kindest smile. Hmm.

"I can't be touched."

"Half a kosher pickle?"

His hand trembled when he reached for the pickle. He worried about passing out and not getting the electronic bug back. He would normally enjoy the pickle but it made him gag. Still, maybe all this food going down his pipe would clean some of the crud away from his throat. His entire body would handle the poison better. He didn't know. He wasn't a doctor. In compensation for ignorance, he had a makeshift nurse now and that alone was a taste of heaven if he should die.

"Here, give it back to me." She held out her hand like a teacher collecting chewing gum from a disobedient boy.

When she opened the door of her ground floor co-op, he would not enter.

"The stuff I have on me could take weeks to get out of your beautiful place." Well, from what he could see, it was more strange and modest than beautiful. Maybe it was 600 square feet, like many of these ground floor apartments. Not the normal female lair full of poufy things, although a weird and probably expensive starburst light fixture hung over the light oak kitchen table. The oak-planked floors and red and blue modern-art throw rug were normal enough, but the far end and high windowed wall heading toward a probable alcove bedroom, was all black rubber on the floor and up the walls to the high windows. A mini gym was complete with punching bag where most gals would put keepsakes. He recalled his quick read-through of her history. One John L. Sullivan—the Boston Sullivans and her O'Sullivans were related—was 19th century world heavyweight boxing champion. A picture of him hung on the punching bag frame.

"I'm a jock," she motioned with her hand as if to apologize for the rubber, "and because… Listen, we'll talk. Remove your shirt, shoes and pants, and then you can come in."

He removed his shirt and shoes, hadn't worn socks, didn't believe in them.

"Come on."

"I can't. I don't wear underwear. Someone might see me and then there's you."

"For God's sake, I'm a professional. No, no, no. Wait." She ran off and came back with a ratty towel.

"Do you use this to dry your dog?"

"Don't have a dog, just you." He deserved her wry humor. Besides, he was bleeding, it seemed from everywhere. He didn't expect her to break out a Bloomingdale's beach towel. He'd bark if it would cure her worried look, but when he tried, only a cough came out.

"I'm going to bag and dispose of this stuff and the towel." She had slipped on crime scene gloves. She checked his pockets and pulled out his crumpled card.

"Throw it away. I've got plenty." He said this with all the dead pan he could muster. His energy was slipping fast and the small apartment across the threshold spun around like a carousel at a carnival. He blew in and out three times and regained his strength. In the meantime, her head was down, probably exhausted or embarrassed.

"Throw away the shoes too. I don't want any reminders." He didn't want to state the obvious. His body had been pierced a thousand times with concrete, asbestos, fiberglass, office obliterations and possibly human remains.

"Where's your wallet, cell phone, personal items?"

He put on his best confused look, which was easy, because he was.

"I don't know. My camera…I lost it when I smashed into a Chevy. I lost everything but that stupid card." He mentally kicked himself for overplaying it.

"After you shower, I'll tend to your wounds." She looked exasperated, worried and a little bit ticked. His acting today, around her, would never land him on Broadway.

"Come all the way in."

* * *

Cha Cha didn't know where to begin. He had protested about someone, including her, seeing him naked in her hallway, but she had the only ground floor apartment and her opaque windows were closed. The rest of the floor comprised of storage bins and on the other side of the wall, a Cuban restaurant. The cops-on-ground-floors program got her a great price for this unit, her humble home.

Even though her old towel was large, he fumbled, obviously weak. She could see, well, too much. So much for chocolate and roses. Her throat went dry, this guy was well endowed and his body still gorgeous, even with a checkerboard of welts and digs on his muscled back, and less so on butt and legs. He was losing too much blood.

Towel draped properly now, he treaded across the threshold and onto her oak floor. He looked like a boy in a candy shop while he took in her strange subterranean world, her bat cave. The black rubber floors and walls got his attention.

"You wrestle, box," he rasped.

"Save your breath. Turn left, walk past the kitchen and through the mirrored door. When you get out of the shower, I'm going to go over your body and take out every splinter." She worried about her competence with too many cuts, digs, and bruises, plus his labored breathing. He could go into shock. She kept a complete first-aid kit, which was a little low on normal bandages but had a ton of kid Band-Aids for neighborhood parties and visits by her married cousins. Numerous digs in his back, less so on his legs and what little she saw of his lovely rear, made her call a hospital from her house phone, but the lines were overwhelmed. Her cell still didn't work. But the hospitals were probably too busy, and this had to be a simple job of patch-em-up anyway.

"God bless you. You're my angel."

He sounded drunk. For no apparent reason, she started crying and the tough guy's eyes watered in response. He shook his head as if to say, the horror of this day will never be forgotten, nor would he forget his angel, hopefully. He closed the bathroom door.

"Use the Therapeutic Shampoo. It's good for allergies. It also calms my scalp after swimming. Do it maybe three times, but don't take too long. We have to stop the bleeding."

"Okay."

All she could hear was a man grunting in pain. She realized how much easier and faster it would be to gently wash off the pieces of building in the shower instead of on her bed. Besides the image of that man on her bed was sacrilegious at best, especially today.

She decided to undress, put on one of her college swim team suits and join him.

Chapter 6

Autumn had walked home slowly, stopping to pick up some groceries. She methodically mulled over the strangeness of today's events. The babysitter had been worried about deportation. She harbored the same concerns about herself. But—was that all this was—an irrational fear? So what happened today? Cha Cha was hugged and squeezed by a mysterious stranger with a fake name. The stranger ran off and hopped into a black van. Big deal.

Bigger deal. She speculated: The mysterious hugger of her girlfriend wasn't after the story downtown. He was after the detective for her report about today's attack. A report Autumn had given Cha Cha. Yeah, she passed it on. Boo, she passed it on and the FBI didn't stop those terrorist nuts.

Nuts. Johnny, the U.S. spy, would soon figure out who gave Cha Cha the report. Would Cha Cha tell on her? Nah. Well maybe. Cha Cha loved her country. Her country.

Damn, no darn.

She'd be deported.

But the government was run by fools. Well, this wasn't so strange; it was the way of history. Advance, progress, but kick yourself in the rear, regularly. Then take two steps backward.

She revisited deportation—her *departation.* Using her photographic recall of past events, she speculated her parents had never applied for U.S. citizenship. She peered down Thompson, drawn by a horribly loud thunder. A huge black mushroom hovered over the World Trade Center. Satan had won. A building was down and he'd be busy stealing the souls and wouldn't bother her for a while. The devil should start and finish with the hijackers and leave all those poor people alone.

She froze, transfixed and studied the cloud's changing form. The face of the devil. Time slipped by and the blackness subsided. Tower 2 was gone.

Why was she not surprised? She kissed the gray blob of frightened souls goodbye and ran for her co-op building.

She entered her apartment, backing in to it—face to doorway—in case any spirits were following her, they'd see her face and not enter. Relaxed now, her mind rumbled back to concern number one.

If only she were old enough. If only people had listened to her. What kept them from acting? Someday, she'd find out how she could help best, what kind of job she could get with the government. She'd accelerate her education once again. There was no time left to help, the world was going crazy. But in the meantime, where was her mother? Would she be able to stay at NYU, stay in the USA? What of her only until today friend. She loved Cha Cha. Although her grandparents would treat her lovingly in Trinidad, although she could go to the University of the West Indies, although their beaches were so fun, although grandpa would try to beat her at various card games, her home was here, now.

Maybe she could help the U.S. spy agencies while being educated.

Would this same government deport away one of their finest assets because of bureaucratic incompetence? How could she or anyone change the system? Well, if she could figure out a puzzle or two for them, maybe the government would let her stay.

First things first: Find her mom's records. In her mom's closet lay a safe. Instead of cracking the combination, which would take precious time, she looked in the master bedroom's night table for her mom's ledger. Under "C" for combos, she found the safe code. It didn't work.

She studied the numbers, recalled her mom's many drunken proclamations. "Autumn dear, if ever something happens to me, think backwards to the time the three of us were happy. Your dad, and me, and you. Use that to access all of my accounts." Autumn already was a cosigner on the checking account. Duh, their last time together was her birthday. Six permutations of their birthdays would yield the combo and the most likely order would be dad, mom and then her birthday and there'd be eighteen digits because that's the way her mom wrote dates. She ran back to the safe. Twirled away, left, right, past right to left, six numbers each time. The safe opened. Piece of ginger cake with a touch of lime.

She took four stacks of inch thick papers to the kitchen table and devoured them like a snack. Oh, she should eat something. She grabbed a yogurt and cherry juice squeezy and resumed studying the papers while munching. *Multi-tasking.*

She learned and/or verified:

Neither her mom nor her deceased dad were citizens. Nor was there any documentation that showed they applied for a renewal of a work permit visa. They all could have been deported years ago. But now with the country up in arms and paranoid, they'd kick out all the foreigners who weren't supposed to be here. She'd hack the government computers just to double check on her mom's immigration status, if any.

Pounding keys furiously, she found no government records of Monique Breeze renewing her work visa, or that she was still in the country. Good and bad. Good, they didn't know. Bad, they might find out. She'd have to hack the IRS at some point to find out if Mom paid taxes, and if so, how?

Her mom kept a virtual and real office for her Matchmaking Service, comprised of two employees. God forbid her mom died. She'd have to, unfortunately, fire these people before they figured out they had no boss and she ran out of money. Besides, the business wasn't all that successful. They probably thought a million times about moving on. They'd welcome the request for severance.

As much as she disliked her mom for not being much of a mom, she understood that her mom had been miserable ever since daddy had died. Because she understood, she looked forward to her mom walking through the door and running into a hug.

Back to taking stock. There was another savings account with $14,123.00 in it, leftovers from her Jeopardy win. This wouldn't be too hard to transfer to checking. The amount struck her as way too low, way too spent, way too fast. Her mom hadn't bought Gucci or other expensive things. *Something's wrong.* Still there was enough left for her to use on special projects or maybe a cool new outfit or two if she absolutely needed them. Perhaps another account she didn't know about hid in plain sight. She'd do a thorough search, some other time.

She dug deeper. Her mom was having an affair with a married man. She was no longer pretty because of Jack Daniels slapping her around. Well, pretty or pretty-not, this did explain her absences. With all the bachelors in New York and on her website, a big why smacked Autumn. Her mom used to be smart, not super genius smart. Alcohol stole her IQ. She had hoped to turn her mom around. Make her love her again. She got up, got a drink from the frig and fixated on the front door while she sipped.

Then she backed into the bedroom and neatly stacked everything back into its original order and folders, closed and locked the safe. Next on her agenda was her mom's computer. Everything she tried to open was some variant of the birthdays and their names if there were any passwords at all.

She spied the whiteboard over the desk and sure enough, there was a note scribbled WW, J.C. 8:15.

J.C. must have been a client or someone in the business, not Jesus Christ, her mom wasn't religious. The initials didn't match her boyfriend's. WW could stand for—Windows on the World, the top of the World Trade Center's North Tower.

8:15, of course was 8:15 a.m.

If so, maybe the helicopters could have rescued her from the roof.

She turned on the TV and quickly realized the helicopters rescued no one. Nada. The explanation for another idiocy would have to wait. She clicked off the TV. Commandos could have blown the roof doors. Copter after copter could have rescued small numbers with the commandos demanding order. *If government only had a brain.*

Although her mom treated her more like an ignored girlfriend than a daughter, she still loved the woman who loved her daddy, the woman who through great pain gave birth to her, and the woman at one time through the sweetness of her sober heart held her close, read her nursery stories, bought her pretty things, told her she was a genius. Then Daddy died. The mom she knew disappeared into a bottle of Jack Daniels. Autumn bit her lip and fought off tears. She entered her fairytale melancholy world and pranced back and forth. Alone. Alone. Shit. She couldn't escape reality.

She turned her window air conditioners to inside circulate to keep the disaster crud out of the co-op. Then grabbed the phone and slumped into the couch. Another thundering sound was shaking the building. She didn't need to turn on the TV to find out what happened. If her mom were in Tower 1, she had just died. Tears dripped into her yogurt.

How could she not listen? I had told her not go anywhere near the Towers, and what did she do? She knew how good I was at predicting. Why? Why? Maybe she's punishing me for reminding her of Dad. Crazy. Come back to me, Mommy. I'll stop your drinking. I'll be the strong one. I'll run your business, just get better. Love me like you used to.

Autumn walked over to her giant plush Old English Sheep dog, Julius Caesar, jumped on him and buried her eyes into the soft, fake fur. But she could still see. Her mom reached out when she was falling with the building and said, *I'm sorry, sweetie. Mommy loves you. Please forgive me.* She would. She had to. Hatred slowed people down, made them do crazy things like fly into buildings. She wasn't crazy, at least not yet.

She got up and tried calling her mom but her mom's cell was still not working. There was nothing to do but homework for now. Autumn was overreacting. Perhaps Mom would be home soon. Maybe she could get four years of education down to one. Before they sent her back to Trinidad, she'd have her degree. But a degree in what? Engineering, mathematics, politics?

Surely, the sleeping giant that was the military and all the politicians would unite to go to war on al Qaeda. Yes, people would demand stricter immigration laws. Before doing her homework, she researched on the computer the immigration policies and popular attitudes toward immigration. New York attitudes. Then she furiously pounded away on her keys, penning her first paper on how the events of September 11, 2001 would impact the way New Yorkers—

Someone knocked on the door.

"Who's there?"

"We're with the federal government, Autumn. We have some questions for you," a female voice said.

Oh, shit.

She couldn't escape. If she used the fire escape, someone would be waiting for her, anyway. The Americans were real good about cleaning up messes they themselves made. Maybe all the foreigners were being rounded up right now.

Double shit.

"I'm just a kid. My mom isn't here. Come back when she comes home, maybe around 5 p.m." Of course, her mom should have been home by now.

"You're no ordinary kid, Ms. Breeze. Open the door."

A gruff male voice with a strong Russian accent postulated.

"Don't you know the United States is about to go to war?"

Russian again, the mystery man had spoken Russian. Had the government hired a bunch of Russians to do their dirty work? Did this guy know Johnny Lance?

"Good luck," Autumn responded, pretending not to get their meaning. But despite her outward bravado, she whimpered and then shook. Her world was crashing down already. Maybe this government had some people in it who were smart enough to figure out that they blew it. Big time. Maybe they wanted her help.

"I think you know why we're here."

"Give me one minute." She ran over to the plush dog and put his ears down properly. Then, shivering, she peeked through the peephole. "Show me your IDs, please."

A man and a woman were holding up badges. The guy was the director of something she had never heard of—OTTS—but the woman was from the super-cool NSA, if they weren't fake IDs. If they weren't going to get her into a threesome. If they weren't going to cut her up into little pieces. Mail her back to Trinidad. She peeked again.

The guy was a stocky fellow with a craggy round face and eyebrows that looked like caterpillars. His very curly, deep dark brown hair made him look more like a grizzly bear than a human. Next to him was—oh boy. She looked like the ex-Miss Cherokee Nation. Oh so pretty. These two were not going to harm her, at least not today. They had to have figured out who gave Cha Cha the heads up on the Twin Towers disaster.

She left a tear on her cheek that the fat plushy dog didn't wipe off. Heart pounding, she grabbed her cool, unlatched the door and invited them in.

Autumn scanned the apartment. She, not her mom, kept everything tidy.

Polite, the robust man waved his beefy hand. Lady first. The elegant thin American Indian lady—yep it was her—with high cheekbones, way down, wavy raven hair, wearing a gray business suit, entered, followed by the big guy dressed in faded blue jeans, with muscles bulging from a dirty, probably with the gray soot from the Twin Towers, tee shirt. It read *"I love New York"*. She jumped to the tentative conclusion that he was doing undercover work and his partner was Johnny Lance.

Autumn raised her hand to shake, but the woman blew by the hand and crumpled her into a hug. "I'm so excited to meet the author of *A Revolution in Probability and Statistics."*

"I didn't realize..." She hadn't realized anybody in the government read it and for that matter anybody who wasn't a math professor. *Like.*

"Realize." The woman squeezed harder. "I require every engineer who wants to keep a job with me to read it. I have a copy on the right corner of my desk."

Oh yeah, it's really her, with no beauty contest make-up. *Oh my God. Oh my God.* "Nice to meet a fellow geek."

"I was like you once, Autumn. A too smart girl who couldn't wait to grow up."

"Yeah, and too skinny." In the meantime, the big, but not really so tall guy started fidgeting, like a boy who didn't want to do his math homework.

The lady took Autumn's hand. "Honey, you are so adorable and pretty and you're starting to get curves. You'll blossom into a Miss America someday."

Well, at least these two weren't here to deport her. It was also nice to hear, that a similar genius valued a balanced life. But Autumn had misplaced her tiara and completely lost her cool.

"You're Ayita Starblanket, former Miss Cherokee Nation, aren't-cha?"

"Guilty," Ayita winked, "and this powerful fellow is the director of OTTS, Colonel Carlos Petrovich." She showed her ID. He did too, whipping it by her snapshot eyes.

"Wow." Ayita's ID read, Chief Engineer, NSA. "I'm just a kid. I don't understand." She did understand. They were here to ask about what she had told Cha Cha. Somehow they figured out it was her. She was sure Cha Cha would never tell. Maybe they deduced it was her from her travel records, showing Vegas late August. The morning's strange events must have accelerated their need to discover the truth, of course. The case of the cat in the tree and the stranger hugging the police officer. Elementary, my dear kid.

Her cool—way gone, Autumn pranced toward the sofa, twirling, just once. She was still a goofy kid in everybody else's eyes. She gestured them to sit down. Her dreams crystalized; her passion soared. She'd follow in Ayita's footsteps. Certainty and direction in life made a big greeting smile easy, no, a Miss America smile, if ever. She really didn't need to be deported now.

"You know why we are here, right?" Carlos grated-out English sprinkled with a Russian accent. He spied around the apartment, lingered on the bookcases, like he would place bugs. Maybe she had bugs already. Maybe after today the place would need fumigation. No, little Miss Paranoid, no reason for bugs. All they had to do was ask her the right questions.

Autumn skipped over to the refrigerator, opened it and raised her voice.

"Yes, I know why you are here. But, would either of you like me to make a yummy sandwich of orange marmalade and crunchy all natural peanut butter on seeded rye?"

"I would—ah," Carlos started to say—but for a quick glance from his couch mate—she noticed Ayita shushing him with a finger to his lips. These two must be friends, because he could kiss her way-too-close finger.

"Just some juice or water. We can't take long. Too many headaches today." Ayita used the softest and most maternal tones. They were probably running around rounding up all sorts of people, today. Maybe talking to other predictors.

Beefy guys needed to eat. She spotted, in the back of the frig, her dinner—a leftover half sandwich of pastrami on rye with coleslaw and Russian dressing. Perfect for the Ruskie. She tidied up the plate and popped it into the microwave.

"I want to know why you guys blew it and how you figured out to visit me. And why you didn't take Detective O'Sullivan's report seriously, and who that fake reporter was." There, she had made four moves in a row, illegal in chess. Their move, but now they were lost. She put a carafe of orange juice and cups on the coffee table and then hovered by the armchair next to the two on the sofa. They barely restrained some chuckling at her remarks. Ha. Ha.

"Unfortunately, young lady, the government has received hundreds of reports predicting disasters or assassinations for various dates and times over the years," Carlos said.

He and Ayita went on to talk about the probability of any one report being true, how seriously they took their jobs, and how following Cha Cha this morning led them to her, and why they could neither confirm nor deny her suspicions about the 'fake' reporter. She, a student of just about everything, understood that "loose lips sink ships." The microwave dinged.

Carlos finished with, "When we are done talking today, this meeting never existed. You can tell no one, not even your mom, not even Detective O'Sullivan that we interrogated you, because lives depend on this."

"I understand, Sir. Just a moment." She put the sandwich on a plate, garnished it with a kosher pickle and tucked a napkin. "What's OTTS and why are you here, Colonel?" Then she ran back in and handed the food to Carlos. Ayita, half-smiling, turned to stare out the window, probably her heart was down at the disaster.

Carlos thanked Autumn with his eyes and then said, "Thank you." He took a bite. "In little while, I think you will understand what OTTS is. But first, how did you pick today's date? Unfortunately, young lady, you have won the lottery."

Ayita nodded. Oh, Autumn got it, the two government executives were playing good cop, better cop. All that could be known for sure was they needed information. Ayita seemed genuine, definitely maternal. Carlos had the intensity of something too scary to think about. He was like Halloween night fright flicks and voodoo all balled into one. In the end, all this was irrelevant; they were all on the same side.

"I knew al Qaeda has been after the Twin Towers for years because of its odd light-weight center-post construction, because of the 1993 attempt, the 1995 think tank assessments and various speculations about flying planes into buildings and the terrorists' intentions. Maybe it takes a rocket scientist to put two and two together. Duh." They sat transfixed.

"Anyway, I got lucky with the date. It seemed like an insult to Americans, as in a 911 emergency. Also, the tall sleek 11 invites images of the towers. Of all the early dates in September, it was the most likely by at least two-sigma." She went on to explain how having the terrorist teams in place meant they couldn't wait too long for fear of being rounded up or making mistakes.

"Could you elaborate on your initial report to Detective O'Sullivan about the terrorist team in Las Vegas? What triggered you?" Ayita asked.

"Well, I was in Las Vegas, on the strip, late August. I saw five young clean-shaven Middle-Eastern men, almost boys, all in the same brand and style in various colored tee shirts and slacks. What idiots. You see, men don't shop together or wear coordinated outfits. How dumb is that? And none of them were speaking." She waited for a response but they remained quiet. "But then suiciders aren't good at anything else except being brainwashed and dying." The two exchanged raised eyebrows.

"Go on, hon," Ayita said.

"Anyway, there they were at the entrance to the M&Ms store. You know, near the MGM Grand on the Las Vegas strip, near the really cool Coca Cola store... Well, they didn't have any shopping bags. Strange you know. So my aunty, who's like me, said, 'How sweet. Terrorists on vacation,' right to their faces, maybe ten feet away—except she has dementia and a goofy sense of humor and won't remember if you visit her. The terrorists pretended not to hear, but you could see they were a little deflated. I knew she was right and that it wouldn't be long before they or others would fly into the Tower or Towers."

"My brave girl. You said those words, didn't you?" Carlos asked. He must have studied body language. True, she had fidgeted and squirmed, still was squirmy, but her body always ran away from her. Maybe when she turned fifteen, she'd calm down. In any case, she couldn't fool this guy.

"Yes, Sir, you're very smart, but I didn't use those exact words. I had stood there next to the giant M&M and said, 'Well, what do you know. Terrorists on vacation.' Later, I told everybody, after those men left, not to go to Windows on the World, anytime soon…if ever. But no one list-listened to me." Her throat had lumped. Too late, she realized if her mom had really listened to her, she might be home now. Not impossible, she could walk through the door at any moment, but the probability was dropping fast. Autumn sighed. Mister smarty-pants was bound to guess she was an orphan sooner or later.

"That's fairly scant. Is there anything else," Ayita asked.

"I'm sorry, but sometimes you just know. No matter how many computers you put these facts into, the probability will hover around 93% that no other scenario fits the facts. Besides, they heard me and did not defend themselves, didn't say a word to me or each other, as if they were trained not to interact or let people hear them speak Saudi or accented English. After pretending to look around at the entrance, they slowly turned and walked away in the opposite direction. But I just knew they wanted to buy some M&Ms. My mind works like that sometimes."

"Mine too, but I had to hear it to believe it," Ayita said.

She went on to explain that she knew, at the time, the terrorists wouldn't harm her family, because getting arrested would ruin their plans, and they had been programmed to do one thing. She had hoped by speaking to them that the suspected terrorists would reconsider and stop their plans. If they hadn't been terrorists, they'd speak up for themselves, and she would apologize and claim to be a lame girl meaning no harm.

"Excuse us for a moment. Maybe you can take my dish to the kitchen, darlink," Carlos said. He and Ayita whispered back and forth, but later in their conversation, even from the kitchen, she could hear that an agent of his, reported a similar incident and had predicted an imminent attack on the Twin Towers too, minus the date. She had beat out an agent by nailing the date. But thousands of people died. What a mess.

"What? The government knew?"

"You've got good ears," Ayita said, with a broad smile. Again, Autumn felt like dancing on the ceiling, but controlled herself out of respect for the many dead, and just walked back into the living room to join them. She had to be cool like James Bond. She would make a great spy, if only she could hide her emotions or truly be stoic. *Me, the rock.*

"All any of us can do is report what we know and hope somebody takes us seriously." Carlos banged his cup a bit too hard on the glass tabletop. "Sorry, *devochka*—girl. I'm as angry as you are. Not always cool like James Bond." Did he read minds too?

"How can I help?" Autumn sat composed now, like a lady-spy at tea with 007. Dolled up in a killer dress with black pearls and a little pistol high up her leg near her pink panties with black lace. *Someday.*

Carlos leaned forward. "Do you just use deductive and inductive reasoning or is there anything—how can I say this—beyond the normal, maybe an unexplained way of thinking? Maybe something like foreseeing the future…images. Do you see images?"

"No, no weird paranormal stuff has ever happened to me. I wish—how cool would that be? No, just probability, statistics, research, and being a good observer."

Carlos and Ayita exchanged looks again.

"I do have a graphic imagination."

"My dear young lady, I want you to take my card. I want you to get a PH.D., if you want to work for me. Call me for course-of-study planning, thesis, interning, and someday a job or to chat."

It was obvious that OTTS was about paranormal activity, but Ayita at the NSA: all engineering. Her heart swelled. She felt like running all over the room, screaming—she'd get Osama bin Laden. She'd do it. Maybe, pom-poms pumping, go USA, go USA. She settled down and became again the lady at tea, Miss Mystery, maybe Miss Q, no pun intended. She got up and leaned over to hug the beautiful and brilliant woman. Carlos got a handshake.

"Maybe in a couple weeks, I will meet you at lunch for chess in Washington Square Park and teach you lesson," Carlos said, with crinkled Santa Claus eyes and watermelon smile.

"Yes to chess, but it will be you who gets a lesson," she said in Russian.

Carlos translated for Ayita and then said, "My little one, we will see."

"I'll check in on you from time to time," Ayita said, standing.

"I hope so." With star-struck eyes, she knew, someday she might get a job doing exactly what she liked with the talents God gave her. Tears formed again as they exchanged good-bye looks.

Autumn led them to the door and chased away her tears with bravado. "Bring two dollars, Sir. You know the park. You lose, you pay."

"Hum, hum, hum." He kissed her forehead. Then Ayita hugged her again. They left her alone to wait for her mom's return, a return never to be realized.

She tried her mom's phone again and heard a muffled vibrating noise this time. She located the cell wedged between two pillows on her mom's queen-sized bed. Her mom had never forgotten her phone, at least as far as she knew. She picked up the glass-covered portrait from the bed table, of her mom, dad and her on the Atlantic City boardwalk next to a water taffy store. Everybody had been happy. She liked the maple-flavored ones, but hadn't been thrilled by trips to the dentist.

What could her mom not taking her phone possibly mean? She screwed the top tighter on the Jack Daniels bottle at the computer desk.

Chapter 7

Cha Cha neatly laid out her uniform on the bed. She placed her belt and weapons under a concealed lid in her book case headboard and locked it. Naked now, just like the guy in the shower. Something caught her eye through the streaming dust and sunlight of her high windows. On her blue uniform shirt where the small of her back would be, was a perfectly matching blue swatch maybe a quarter-inch in diameter. Feeling it, she froze and withdrew her fingers.

The lump underneath was a damn, tiny transceiver. A bug. Johnny Jerk was no reporter. He had to be a government agent. He had planted it on her. Why? What had she done to deserve his attention? This might be Internal Affairs, checking into something. No, not their modus operandi. They'd have to get a court order, and she hadn't done anything remotely illegal. The worst thing she had done was allow Johnny to hug her for all of around five seconds. That would be three seconds longer than he needed.

But the feds would need a warrant too. *Something about this miserable day. Maybe the CIA.* Sometimes similar agencies bent the rules when they were hot on the trail of a saboteur or it was a national emergency. 9/11/2001. He had been down at the disaster, undoubtedly, but why?

Of course, today's event, coupled with her report of what Autumn had told her, labeled her a person of interest at a time of overburdened analysts or spies. Perhaps he had chased a terrorist today down at the disaster. This hero was still alive at least.

They wanted to know who her snitch was. She couldn't give up Autumn. She was an innocent, just a kid, well rapidly a young lady. But still, how *had* she come up with the date, the target, the method and the collapse of the buildings? She had paid little attention to the girl genius at the time, just filed the report. Her lieutenant diminished her concerns by saying they received hundreds of reports like this. That it was more people worrying than anything else. They reported assassination attempts, all sorts of things. It seems Autumn's predictions had been spot on, and now whether Cha Cha deserved it or not, she'd have to take the heat. Cha Cha would act as a conduit, if the girl offered more information, but her young friend would not have held back.

On the bed naked, she stood, plastered a Miss America smile with bottom and top front teeth touching and then wiggled into her old swim team, crimson Catalina. It offered a little bit of modesty and a lot of pay back for his calculated hugging. The man in the shower—perhaps a hero, perhaps a rogue—deserved her help. But she'd also play spy today. She'd get his attention and then find out the truth. *Two can play, mister.*

All previous assumptions aside, something other than a reporter's story drove him to risk his life today. Something related to her, perhaps. Today would be the only day to level the playing field because this secret agent would disappear after she patched up his body and he took his bug back. *So bye-bye, Mr. Soul Mate.* Not. Her mom had to be wrong about this.

She headed to the bathroom, grabbed a couple washcloths from the cupboard, and for later, a small, old bottle of iodine, some ointment and the large bottle of mercurochrome.

At the bathroom door mirror, she stopped to admire her pretty, yeah *pretty skinny* self. Who was she kidding? Some men liked her, but this guy was too gorgeous for her. She turned to show off curves, her meager weapon, and reinforce her bravery in the face of the enemy on the other side of the door.

Her heart was pounding entirely too fast. The sexual tension and/or facing a handsome spy needed some kind of relief. She'd just admit she enjoyed his potent maleness and move on. The misery downtown and his weakness would keep him in line. If he were her soul mate, then there would be some day ahead, way ahead, to fall in love. Not today.

Really, this man had no interest in her as a woman; he was just doing his job when he had caressed her, nearly making her crazy.

God what a mess she was. How could she use her wiles to get information, to break him down? Especially when he probably swore an oath to defend the country. She was a lady, wasn't she? Today, maybe half a lady and half scared to death for her Autumn. And half giddy as never before in her life.

She was a to-have-and-hold woman. A loving woman, way too good for him. She may not be the prettiest girl on the planet, or virginal, but her heart was pure, at least on the subject of true love. She could boogie like Janet Jackson. She could joke with the boys. She could drink some guys under the table. She untied her curly head of hair yearning to be free from its double-bound ponytail. The crimson-brown fluffed out and crinkled so quickly because of the steam seeping from under and around the not completely closed door. She quickly brushed, but her hair had other ideas. She was electrifying. Just what Mr. Perfect would love to wake up to every morning. Not.

Well, she loved her hair, anyway. He'd have to deal with it. This frizz was her. Besides, all men had an impossible time resisting a nearly naked woman who was halfway good-looking. Right? So said her prettier sister and confidante. However, if he were meant for her, he'd be polite. If he weren't polite, she'd kick his dangling balls.

He called for her. Let the show begin. She pushed open the bathroom door. In the highly unlikely event her soul went missing, she'd get it back—*tomorrow*.

* * *

Frank wasn't used to being naked in a shower waiting for a pretty detective—little more than a stranger—to minister his wounds. Not only was she a suspect, now it was his turn to be touched or ogled. He had hugged her without permission. Turnabout was fair play.

The shower had a bench seat, but he couldn't sit down. He kept pricking his hands on God knows what, and he felt weak all over to the point the pink travertine floor kept changing hues. The shampoo just worsened his eyes. He'd collapse soon and worried that the detective wouldn't be able to keep his head from clonking on the travertine. He leaned hard against the wall, as if he were being arrested. Then, rolling his hand over his butt, he ripped it on something. He groaned.

"I'm coming right in," Chastity said.

"Grab tweezers if you have. I've got something jagged stuck in me."

She opened and closed the door. The steam whirled as she stepped into the shower. He was afraid to look back, because she was so god damned beautiful and besides, he was body shy.

Was she naked as well? He didn't want to think about it. Instead, he imagined he was in a hospital with hydrotherapy, and maybe a three-hundred-pound therapist with pimples was about to work him over. To do otherwise would—if he weren't sick—cause a huge erection. Well, even if he were dying, he'd die hard.

"Please don't turn around," she said.

"I'm very embarrassed," he said, weakly spiting.

"Where's the splinter?" He put his finger just above the piece of whatever on the round of his cheek. Her hand touched his.

"Don't worry. I see it. Eww, glass." She pulled it out and his cheeks relaxed.

"Be careful with your hands. I have other jagged things sticking out all over."

"I've had extensive training. No worries."

She went to work on his body from head to toe as smooth as a geisha giving a sponge bath. He just hoped he'd live to thank her.

Chastity gently hand-toweled his upper thigh. "Why were you down at the disaster?"

"For the story."

"I have to say—you are like a living version of Michelangelo's David. I'm a little embarrassed too, seeing you like this."

"Please don't say anything about my body. Okay? Especially not today." He looked down, his penis had swelled slightly. Damn her. He didn't need that. He couldn't, wouldn't seduce this girl. She deserved so much more respect. Besides, today so many had passed. His girlfriend, Emily, maybe. Penises have minds of their own, so his outspoken Aunts said at every family get-together. *One-eyed monsters.*

"Sorry. I was just saying you're a beautiful male, to get that chemistry thing out of the way. I don't want to be in this situation any more than you do."

He turned sideways, and quickly snapped back to lean against the wall.

"Well, you're a beautiful woman yourself." He couldn't believe what he saw. The girl was anatomically perfect and her swimsuit left little to the imagination. Her ponytail was gone, and her flaxen brown-red hair kinked up into tiny curls, which stuck out like she had put her finger in a socket. He loved her 'look' but right now, he felt more like dying.

"Please don't flash me."

"I didn't mean to. Did you know that the statue of David had hands that were too big for the body? The hands denoted power, which was an artistic statement back then." He tried to make their conversation more clinical. Would both of them need to go to confession, because they acted profanely during a crisis? *I promise. I won't touch her,* he prayed. God made man and woman to cling together. Someday much later would be a better day. Today they'd just do their best to cope.

"Yeah, and I'd say something on you was too big for your body, right now. You're supposed to be weak."

Damn it, he was caught. He peeked down.

"I'm sorry, it's only physiological. Your one piece suit is at fault."

"I work hard on this body, and I'm sure you do too."

"Yeah, every day. Snyder's gym."

"I swim there," she said.

"We'll see each other again."

"*See?*" She half laughed.

His mind blurred. His pain was increasing due to her however-soft cleaning. He felt dizzy again. Red swirled on the travertine below and beside him. Was he dying?

Although he couldn't laugh, because it would shake his body, causing more pain, his tongue still barely worked. "Why don't they have nude aerobics classes, so uptight people like you and I could get over our fears?" Was this what they called gallows humor, practiced by surgeons and other—? His mind went blank.

"Feeling guilty are you? Catholic, are you?" *Again with the strange remarks. How unlike her dossier.*

"I have sixteen brothers and sisters." Disinformation was best and most easily served to a professional with some truth. He had five brothers and five sisters all adopted except for him.

"Going for the record?" Holding her tweezers in front of him, she showed him a quarter-inch piece of wire that she'd removed from his lower back.

"My mom and dad adopted poor children and babies from all over the world." Well, maybe he just jabbered his way into revealing his identity. Did he want to be found out by this woman? He was getting soft...and God help him, he couldn't afford to let that happen. He had a job to do. If he had made a similar mistake in Saint Petersburg, Russia, he would have been sent home in a body bag, provided they could find his scattered remains.

The United States was likely going to be attacked again, likely worse and likely soon. He'd do everything he could. Still, she was no threat. A loyal American if ever he ogled one.

"Wow...sixteen siblings," she marveled. "That must be *some* dinner table."

"That's how I learned Russian." He had tried to deflect her suspicions, but he feared it was too late. "We all help out. I love my family."

"You can sit carefully now."

"But?"

"Don't worry about what I can see or not see. Nurse's orders. Sit."

He carefully, slowly sat down on the bench. What a relief. He peered up at her caring eyes and wanted her like he had never wanted anyone before. They'd fit perfectly and not just physically.

She got up from her squat and gave him a quick light hug. She checked over his front, which didn't need much attention, but he was bleeding a little here and there.

"You should stand now."

"I'll be all right...just want to sit for a little while longer."

"As long as the pain isn't severe."

"I got a call through. I hung up on my mom, today," he said disgusted. He couldn't understand himself. He had never opened up to anybody about his family, not even Carlos. Either he was crazy or dying and needed last absolution.

She winced. Perhaps he had selected an unfortunate choice of words or maybe she was feeling his pain. His mind was beyond repair.

He repeated. "I hung up on her." Maybe he should quit talking and continue surviving.

"Don't beat yourself up. Later, if you don't have to go to the hospital, and if you are feeling fairly good, just go to your mom. Let her see that you're alright. Let her see her son."

"They live in Cardiff by the Sea. That's in San Diego." He got back on track with his disinformation campaign. His parents lived in Oradell, New Jersey, just north of the George Washington Bridge.

"As soon as you can, fly to her."

"I'm sorry, Chastity, about today. I didn't mean to steal a hug. I have, or *had*, a girlfriend." Why did he have to say that? He liked Chastity, maybe too much. Now she'll think he's unavailable. Perhaps, he really was—unavailable. He forever remained focused on his job and couldn't see how he'd ever transition into a serious relationship. His job was dangerous. He couldn't have a family and keep them safe. He had tried getting serious once only to hold her in his bloody arms while she died from a sniper's bullet. He preferred his angels alive, and he'd do everything in his power to keep Chastity safe.

"What happened to your girlfriend?" she asked, seeming a bit deflated.

"I'm not sure. She may have been...down there."

"So you went to save her," she whispered.

"No. I didn't know. The story...I went for the story."

Inhaling sharply, Cha Cha leaned over and put her face within kissing distance. This was torture. "I hope you don't mind me changing the subject."

Perhaps she was the tiniest bit jealous or just didn't believe him. Her voice changed to a higher note. He wished he knew when to stop putting his foot in his mouth.

"No, sorry for burdening you."

"I think the CIA and FBI have let us down, big time. How could they be so cavalier, unprofessional, careless as to let this happen?"

He cleared his throat. "I'm sure they were doing the best they could."

"How are you sure…are you one of them?" Oh, he could smell an interrogation. *Ah, well—one foot away, interrogator looking scrumptious. Torture effective, Sir. Don't know how much longer I can hold out. Name, rank, serial number.*

Then it hit him upside his dreary head. Chastity had to have found the bug, and around that same time, she must have figured out he wasn't a reporter. So there was no sense denying it any longer. Besides, if his hunches and plans were correct, in about a week she'd find out his true identity anyway.

He stood up, grabbed her shoulders weakly and gave her the full frontal. Her eyes inspected the ceiling. Either that or she was about to have a seizure.

"Please, don't do this," she said in a tight voice.

He turned back to the up-against-the-wall pose. "Is there anything you want to tell me, Ms. Detective?"

"I found your bug, Mister Naked Secret Agent Man. Whoever you are. It surely isn't 'Johnny Lance,' is it? As in…"

Crudely put, if what his fuzzy head was telling him was true, she'd just joked about the size of his penis and caught her tongue. No matter the size, guys always worried about that. He was no exception. He closed his legs, even though it hurt. At least she wouldn't see it anymore.

"Chastity, I know you're pissed, but listen to me—"

"Why *should* I?"

""Damn it, do I have to spell it out for you?" He blew out a harsh breath. "Thousands of innocent people have died today. Your life and the life of your informant are in danger. We don't have the time now to discuss who I am or why you were bugged."

"Were you trying to save somebody?"

"Yes and now I'm trying to save you."

Crossing her arms over her chest, she glared at him. "Listen, you broke the law with your little transceiver. The enemy has no interest in chasing after a cop with a lucky guess. Besides, the deed is done, and stopped by no one. It's done. Done. Done." Her voice rose with each done. She sat and ran her fingers through her hair. "Ouch."

She must have sat on something she had pulled out of him.

"Are you okay?"

"I'm just fine. You have got to leave me alone."

"The enemy isn't done yet. They'll kill anybody they think can stop their next operation, especially you and your snitch."

A glimmer of recognition told him she understood, and he knew deep down he shouldn't have said anything. Obviously, detective Chastity O'Sullivan had reported everything she knew because she was a patriot. Now, everybody was in the dark, but not for long. But would her informant have told her everything?

Looking like she wanted to say something more, she bit her lip. "I know nothing more. I'm so sorry."

"Who's your source? I need to clear you and I need to investigate your informant."

Instead of answering, she got up and nudged him gently sideways. "I think you should leave."

"I can't. Got no clothes, kid. And if you don't get me to your bed for a long nap now, I'm going to collapse and crack my skull on all this stone."

"Okay. But don't touch me in any perverse way."

He wouldn't dare. This wonderfully empathetic woman had to be stressed beyond belief. Yeah, he'd live, but would she recover her faith in the U.S.A. just because he bent the rules? Could she be so Pollyanna naive to misunderstand that in an emergency one had to bend the rules to save lives?

She wrapped him in a huge towel and plopped a smaller one over his head, like a prizefighter.

"Am I bleeding? Your towel will get ruined."

"Maybe a little bleeding, but the towels aren't important. When you're dry, I'll put some mercurochrome, iodine and Band-Aids on you." He slipped but somehow this slim little woman kept him from hitting the floor. They meandered to the bed like a drunk and designated driver. He fell on it, face first. Right next to her uniform and the bug. Well, if he were to kick the bucket today, at least he had met his guardian angel with frizzy hair.

As though at the end of a tunnel, she said, "Get your legs up. Straighten out." She grabbed his ankles and his mind spun. He remembered Emily pulling his ankles to get him riled up, and at that time, turned on. The room spun faster now round and round. A black curtain rose to cover his opened eyes. Shock not death, he ho-p-e...

* * *

He had passed out. She pulled down the towel and put her cheek and ear carefully on his ripped-up back, right over his heart. It beat strongly. Why couldn't she get a guy like this? She kissed an uncut portion of his back and stroked his thick, curly locks. Perfect. Desperate for this guy's loving? *Could there be heaven on a hellish day?*

Maybe her mom was right. This gorgeous man could be her soul mate. But soul mates were just mystical constructs, right?

She was just an ordinary woman. This guy was probably recruited from an Ivy League school and had never disappointed his superiors. She yearned for a guy like him but she no longer believed in fairytales. Today taught her to leave her shallow life behind, because life could so easily be stolen from you. Find a good man, get married, have kids and live happily ever after. There she said it. And so, she'd do it, she'd be that person. It wouldn't hurt if he looked like this.

She'd never touch his perfect body again because spies disappeared for a living. She'd never see his handsome face, his unusual gray eyes trimmed in charcoal. He had a dimple just like hers. She dare not touch it. She bent over his face, and listened to his strong breathing. He smelled a little of egg salad, the best perfume in the world today, this horrible day. There was no time to brush teeth, certainly not now, he might aspirate. She stole a very quick and chaste kiss, which would have to last a lifetime. Why not steal a little more? She touched his dimple.

Really girl, so what do you know of him anyway? There had to be thousands of eligible good-looking men, who'd love children and would love her. Besides, they didn't have to be perfect physically, just be easy on the eyes, a good dancer and kisser and with pure heart. Not some jaded secret agent.

She leaned near the bug. "Hello man in the black van. Your buddy's heart is strong, but he fainted and it would be good if you could come here and take him to a hospital or doctor for an exam." She tapped the mike twice. "Oh, and bring clothes."

She covered the government agent with the towel and ran to fetch an extra cover from the closet, because he was too heavy to maneuver under the covers, especially with his bruises and cuts inhibiting her ability to leverage him.

Then she peeled portions of the cover and towel back for more cleaning. She inspected every inch, hoping he wouldn't wake up yet and think she was gawking. She had missed the art class with the male nude. This was educational, nothing more. And besides, today she was a nurse. *Convincing?*

She leaned over and whispered. "I understand your life. So it's okay. It is better this way, baby." She half-believed this.

She slipped her hand over his buttocks and up his torso making sure to miss the digs with the excuse that she was feeling for embedded debris. May her hands burn in hell, but let every other part live. Then she went back to removing any remaining debris by swabbing and tweezering. Next, she applied mercurochrome and kid Band-Aids after she ran out of the adult types. She busied herself with her tender ministrations, instead of dwelling on wanting him to be hers in some fantasy world where guys like him would go for gals like her. She had to be the worst nurse, allowing impure thoughts during a national crisis. *How did nurses or doctors handle good-looking naked men, anyway?*

Cha Cha bent low and let his thick black curls tangle with her frizzy auburn locks. This unauthorized touching and cooing would simply not do. However, nowhere had she read anything about how important it was to have respect for a man's body. She chuckled quietly. Well, he had started it, when he hugged her without permission out on the street.

In front of the whole dying world.

Life not death. What would life be like for a spy? A handsome lady-killer? This James Bond lay defenseless now. She moved the top of the smaller towel from his head and then grabbed her camera. Intoxicated on pure male, she inhaled the egg salad aroma one last time. She kissed his cheek goodbye. No way would a man like this ever marry, especially not an average girl like her. Then she backed off and took pictures of his face, to ID him at the precinct. She would not snap a picture of his six-pack, or his privates, or anything else. The FBI only kept full moons on file, at least in the movie, *Grease*.

Sad, she hadn't been able to balance being in a weird situation with a naked man and her intent to interrogate him in the shower. Then she tended to his wounds, and argued, but now with him completely knocked out, she combined gaping with more nursing. So perverse. All the while, innocents were dead or dying. What a cruel joke it was to be human, too human. She couldn't stop her biology, but—

The lock to her apartment door turned.

Jumpy now because of his warning, she pictured terrorists about to kill her. She stretched for the bed's bookcase. Unlocked her gun box and pulled out her pistol. But only her sister, Faith, had a key, duh. This detective's head, she had on her shoulders, had turned into mashed potatoes.

"Is that you, Faith?"

"Thank God you're alive."

Her sister's voice trembled, sounded nearly hysterical. She was supposed to be at work, a buyer for Macy's. But who could work on a day like this?

"Just a second." Cha Cha stowed her gun properly, pulled on some NYPD sweats over her bathing suit and ran to her door just as it opened.

"Oh my God. Oh my God." Faith wrapped her arms around her littler, older sister. Tears streamed down her face. "I tried calling your cell a thousand times, but my cell and the store phones weren't always working. I walked to your precinct but everybody was too busy to help me. One kind soul said you were in the park. I went there, but no you." She was getting hysterical again, so Cha Cha kissed away her tears. "I don't know what I'd do if I lost you."

"I couldn't get ahold of Mom or Dad," Cha Cha said.

"Me neither."

She choked back a sob. "I might have lost my partner down there."

"My God, Jerome has two babies, right? A wife?"

"He'll be all right, God willing."

A moan made Faith pirouette. "You have somebody in your bedroom?"

"It's not what you might think. Come look in this."

Faith peered into the bag at the ripped, sooted clothing. "What are these filthy things? Oh? Don't you go down there again. You hear me, sis?" She looked down at the wood floor as she headed to the bedroom. "There's blood everywhere."

"No matter. I found him wondering the streets near here. Incoherent, badly in need of immediate medical, but I couldn't get anybody to come right away. So I did this." Cha Cha pulled back the blanket.

"Ran out of adult Band-Aids?"

"Around one-hundred and fifty in all, plus some stitching on his rear."

"This man is extremely good-looking, minus the drool," Faith said as she got up on the bed. Head turned and obviously staring, her eyes lingering a little on his lower body, she pulled up the cover. Tucked the blanket gently around his neck and put her ear to his mouth and then chest. "Strong heartbeat, Strong breath. Egg salad."

"A NYPD officer's duty is to serve, even if he is drop-alive gorgeous."

"Tough job, sis," Faith quipped. "No name?"

"No, he was babbling. Help me get him under the top sheet and cover."

The two girls maneuvered the man, blankets and sheets to make him warmer and more comfortable.

Faith giggled. "This guy has a huge ding-dong."

"Thank God, I didn't have to bandage that." They both laughed.

"When I was running here hoping to see you, I wondered if I'd ever be happy again, even for a moment. Thank you, sis, for this small respite on the worst day of my life."

"We'll always have each other, honey." This time Cha Cha joined her sister in a clinging hug and a good sobbing cry, where tears tangled with each other's freckles.

Someone knocked at the door.

"Who's there?" Cha Cha called out and ran to the door.

"The two of us are here to pick up injured man," said a man with a heavy Russian accent.

"Show me your ID."

Through the peephole, she read, Colonel Carlos Petrovich, Director OTTS.

OTTS? "Just a second." What the hell was OTTS? She opened the door and let Carlos and his assistant, she guessed, enter.

Carlos wore a worried smile framed by curly dark brown hair on a hulking body. His assistant, a very tall older man, was opening the stretcher. Of course, these men wouldn't acknowledge in front of her sister that they were eavesdropping or for whom they worked. Yeah, alphabet soup from Washington calling.

"Thank God, you thought on your feet, Detective O'Sullivan." He winked. "Would you two help us carefully move him to stretcher?"

After he was moved, tucked and strapped in, Carlos took a quick look around the co-op, as if he were taking photos. He lingered on the punching bag. "I am sure this is embarrassing situation for you two ladies, especially you, Detective. We don't know his name, do we?"

"No actually, we don't." Cha Cha let out a noisy breath, tiring of his cloak and dagger game.

Carlos put his head on the spy's chest. "He is stable. His heart is beating strong. Like bear. We will not need you to sign anything. We take him. He is all ours. You two did great job."

Carlos was waiting for something—the bug. His message was loud if a bit unclear. Cha Cha had too much to lose in reporting this. The government or her boss could twist screws. Fire-able offenses today were mounting: the shower incident, the cat rescue, the hugging of an officer in uniform on duty and she had not arrested him.

But, she would protect her snitch, no matter what happened.

Cha Cha shook Carlos's hand, slipping him the bug. Faith quickly slapped together two sandwiches for the men. They gladly accepted.

"Just get door for us, okay? And outside door too." Carlos and his assistant wheeled the thorn-in-her-side spy out her door, up the short steps and out of her life.

Carlos waved with a polite dipping of the head; the sly devil knew his craft. The girls waved back.

Then they went back in the co-op. "They don't look much like medics and that barrel chested man doesn't sound like one. I hope that poor guy will be all right." Faith said. Carlos wore a grimy gray tee shirt ruined by the day's events and neither wore a stethoscope or carried a medic's kit.

"The hospitals must be really shorthanded today. I think the burly guy is a doctor from Saint Luke's. I've seen him before…Russian, I think." Her sister seemed to buy it.

The sisters promised to have dinner together. Faith lived in Chelsea, just walking distance to Macy's—but she couldn't work anymore today.

After Faith left, Cha Cha collapsed onto the bed. She smelled his wetness, his blood, the sweet smell of soap and shampoo. She'd never ever have a man like that in her bed again, but hopefully someday she'd find somebody as close to his gorgeousness, quirky nature, forthright caring and manliness as possible. She was tired of being alone and life today brought home an old lesson: It could be taken away without warning.

She vowed not to waste one more precious moment in her search for happiness.

* * *

Cha Cha stopped keeping count of the various ways she could get fired for all the strange things she had done today. Instead, she bit the bullet and called into the precinct from her house phone. She wanted to come in, visit the lab and try to figure out the likely spy's true identity.

She walked the six short blocks north and west. Something *Johnny* had said bothered her. "Your lives might be in danger." Cha Cha was always in danger, but her young friend with so much to offer, so much life to live… She would never forgive herself if something happened to her. Carlos seemed concerned as well. Surely when Johnny recovered, he'd watch over her, if what he said about her and Autumn being in danger were true.

Was anything that happened today, true? A brisk mid-afternoon breeze blew away a lingering smell of dust laden with death. The smoke still rose from the funeral pyres south. Two spirits of two buildings and everybody crushed in them screamed to the living to avenge the buildings' sleek black structure and their lives.

She'd do what was asked of her if she still had a job. She leaned over and watched a tear fall to the pavement.

233 West 10th, AKA the Sixth precinct, was practically deserted. She walked by the wall of honor and stopped to salute her grandfather. Soon, too soon, there would be many more here. In the computer resource room, the tech Jake was out, but his assistant Maggie was in. Just as well.

"Who is this guy?"

"Unsub."

"Well your unknown subject is very cute, minus the drooling."

"I saved his life. He was down there and I had to patch him up. Then he blacked out."

Maggie's eyebrows rose. "This your bedroom?"

"Where else was I going to take him?"

"My place."

"A little respect for the disaster, girl." How could she blame Maggie when the same bug bit her? "Damn, now that you mention it, he is cute. I was so focused, so afraid he'd die. God Maggie." This situation, ripe for gossip, was too much for even Maggie. Cha Cha had to try to deceive her friend and colleague.

"I love our heroes, but yeah sure, like God didn't give you a pussy." She crossed herself. "Like your eyes fell out. What's with the black walls?"

"I don't have much room for a gym. You know mats." Maggie loved to gab, but Cha Cha felt at home around her.

"Oh." She gave Cha Cha that what-a-freak look. "Okay, hold on." She started the facial recognition software.

"Let it chug. Want a coffee?"

Maggie nodded, absorbed in the whirling data, while Cha Cha poured some mud, Maggie called her back.

"Sorry, Cha Cha. Nothing."

"Try stories about large families. Seventeen kids, adoption."

A little later. "No seventeens."

"Try ten or more. Can you do that?"

Maggie smirked. "Of course I can."

A half a cup of coffee later, she hit pay dirt.

"There's an 88% chance he's Frank Lancia, former Notre Dame wide receiver. All-American. Hum. His one hundred yard dash record still stands at the college as of last year. He was on the debate team, thespian, chess team, finished 7th in his class. Last known address was his parents place in Oradell, New Jersey—they have eleven kids, all adopted except for our Tony Curtis lookalike here." He didn't really look exactly like a young Tony Curtis; maybe add a dash of a tall Al Pacino without the craggy face. But his face *was* compressed a little by the mattress, and the rest of her remembrances were fleeting due to the hell of 9/11. In her stressed mind, he became unbelievably handsome, perhaps because she needed a Lancelot, who by some miracle rescues all those who died. She needed to hold onto her sanity, so she'd dream of better days, a better mankind, a better man.

"Any info since college?"

"No, he's a ghost." Maggie looked up and cocked her head. "Maybe he's running from something. Maybe he's military or a civilian ghost." Referring to spies, CIA and NSA types.

"No, I don't think he's this guy, his face is contorted. Unless he lied to me. He was babbling about his brother. I asked him about family and he said his mom and dad live in San Diego, Cardiff by the Sea. But maybe he was trying to throw me off. Could I have the link and a report and anybody else you found in the summary?"

"You've got it, Detective."

More formal now, Maggie must have felt Cha Cha pulling back, becoming deceptive, covering her tracks, in order to protect her investigation as best she could. Cha Cha needed acting lessons, but these techs working with detectives had developed a sixth sense. *So what's the use?*

"If it is him, the least I can do is call his parents and let them know he's all right."

"I'll print their file, too."

Cha Cha rubbed a weary hand over her face and sighed. "The worst day of my life."

"At least you saved a life."

"Maggie, without your help, we all would be nothing. We save lives, because we're a team, right?"

"Thanks, Cha Cha." Good, she liked the familiar Maggie better.

"I'll see you at the funerals."

"The too many." Maggie dipped her head with nothing to look at on the screen. When she looked up, a tear tumbled down her cheek. The tech raised her hands in surrender. Her professional veneer was cracking, but who would blame her or anybody today? Cha Cha waved at the door while shaking her head back and forth in acknowledgment. It was a gruesome day, but hopefully the last of its kind, if she and all the other detectives, the federal government, and all earnest citizens would have anything to say about it. If Frank Lancia would just wake up, mount his white horse and lead the charge to defeat the terrorists who might still threaten the great City of New York.

Sometimes fantasy is good for the soul.

Chapter 8

Walking north away from the devastation, all the smoke and dust, Mahmoud Ali Abunayyan glanced back at the carnage for what felt like the hundredth time. Picturing the hell of buildings falling, he remained certain someone had tried to kill him. They didn't want to be found out. Somehow, he threatened them. If he were to create successfully a new identity and hide, he'd need to be more gregarious, no matter the hell downtown. He might need a place to stay, so he dreamed of salvation with every pretty woman he saw. But, he'd need to act.

Luckily, on his meandering walk, strangers engaged him in conversation. He got the names, and sometimes the phone numbers or cards of the pretty ones. The strangers' eyes invariably dropped to the bottom of his black trousers and its sooty spots. He couldn't remove the stains and the strangers worried for him. He had washed his shoes in the Saint John's Park fountain, but drew the line on soaking and cleaning his pants. Nobody had seemed upset by the probably illegal or at least unsanitary act. Today would forever be the strangest and saddest of all days.

"Are you all right?" another young lady asked, adorned with mascara streaks like Alice Cooper's.

His sad eyes betrayed his inner conflict. "Petros Papadopoulos," he answered, saving a flourish for the prettier ones. "At your service."

They had a short commiseration, before she left him—with her name and number.

Why was it, mostly cute young women stopped to show they cared? He wasn't that good looking. Maybe his sad eyes also projected a harmless and cuddly puppy dog look. A young woman professionally dressed in hay-colored tweed staggered a bit on her heels, nearly falling in front of him.

He steadied her arms and after inquiring if she were okay, he asked, "Do you know any barber or beauty shops open? I have to get this soot out of my hair." He too had been crisscrossing streets like many of these seemingly aimless New Yorkers today. In his case, he hoped to get his hair styled as a disguise. Too soon, he'd be up to Spring Street and a block away from his co-op.

She stood straight, now. "Are *you* okay?"

"My soul has been ripped to shreds as I am sure yours as well, but my body is in one piece."

She hesitated. "Try *Up Your Image* on Spring. It's just down there a block or two." She pointed and then bent her arm and pointed again to suggest a right at the corner then quick left.

"Thanks ma'am." Without him prompting her, she dug through her purse and then handed him her card. "I want to know you are all right." He swore she winked before they parted, but that was probably the glint of sun on her face. What in hell was happening to him? Perhaps, Allah was providing a path.

He flicked the card on his fingers. Hum, a high school teacher and tutor, Ms. Jody Marks. He stuck it in his back pocket. Blonde, shapely, and on any other day—a happy ending.

He could take a chance, but the people at *Up Your Image* knew him, better the pharmacy down the block, for a do-it-himself dye kit.

Once inside the store, he grabbed some Clairol blond dye for men.

As he walked up and down the aisles, a nice alternative presented itself. He could buy a wig, but then, using his credit card would show he was alive.

Cash, $27.53. He'd choose wisely.

He tried on a blond wig, just for the heck of it, but it made him look gay. Maybe people would give up bashing gays to focus on Muslims. Maybe gays would bash Muslims.

No wig suited him so he just bought the hair coloring kit— $3.99 plus tax. If only he could sneak into his apartment unseen and grab some essentials and more money, he'd be fine for a while. He focused skyward through the gathering of fine dust against a blue sky and then he dropped his head to street level and felt a ray of Allah's grace beset him, as an old rabbi walked near.

"Rabbi."

"Yes, my son." He looked like Moses with a long flowing white beard; all he needed was a staff.

"I'm going to meet my girlfriend's parents. They're orthodox, and I left my yarmulke at home. Could I please buy yours?"

The holy man seemed perplexed, but pulled out an extra from his pocket. They both twisted south and shook their heads.

"A contribution, son." Moses waved away his digging for change. "Invite me to your wedding—" The rabbi, face cocked, awaited his name, no doubt.

"Jacob, Jacob Bronstein, at your service."

The rabbi's brow furrowed. "You're not really Jewish, are you, son?"

"I don't practice. I don't believe." How did he know or was it merely a guess?

"No Jew offers a rabbi money for his yarmulke. Besides, it's Rabb-ee and-we always carry a spare and you don't know how to put it on."

The rabb-ee had seen right through him as if he had no soul. Perhaps he had lost it when the towers fell. For a moment, the useless murder of an old Jew for no rational reason except to protect his identity leapt into his head. Then was immediately rejected. He rubbed his eyes, surprised by his desperate barbarity.

"Sorry."

"God is always over your head and today especially there should be a constant prayer on your lips. Put it on, son." He reached for the yarmulke to help.

"I can do it, Rabbi." It had a hair clip, and he, like the Rabbi, grew too much hair.

The rabbi walked away, leaving him with a useless disguise, unless he hid his face with the yarmulke. He put it on without effort.

Wearing a yarmulke did somehow make him feel closer to Allah. A week ago, no yesterday, he would have reviled at the thought. Not that he hated the children of the book or the almighty. Politics, damn politics. He looked south again. The hell flamed on.

Near his co-op, he stopped and waited at the corner by the black granite façade of a Citi Bank. His co-op neighbor, Mrs.

Greenspan, stopped at every tree with her two tall black poodles. She shuffled down the street and turned the corner.

Nobody at the door.

Now.

Inside, he avoided the elevator and took five flights up on the narrow and dark back steps. He had had practice today, but his legs burned, nonetheless.

Outside his door, he reached for his keys, but stopped, key hovering then shaking over the lock. Men conversed in Arabic. He froze. His heart banged so loud, surely they'd hear. He touched his yarmulke, but no God or disguise would rescue him. The door had been jimmied. He backed off. A moment later, the elevator dinged. He ran then walked away from the elevator toward the opposite stairwell.

"Is that you? Professor Abunayyan—Mahmoud?"

He didn't answer. He was far enough away from his neighbor, Mr. Hennessey, to leave doubt as to whom he was. Plus the yarmulke would confuse the man. He rushed down the stairs. Still the people inside his apartment probably heard that. They might look out the window or leave via the fire escape. The men in his apartment would either kill Mr. Hennessey or leave. Killing his neighbor would compromise their mission. *They came for my computers.*

Now outside, he squinted up at his window but couldn't see at this sharp angle. He cut over to the first tree, then ran across the street, and jumped down steps that took him below ground level to a little used and filthy door. He could hide here. Someone had urinated. He held his nose as he stretched out to peek over the ground level ledge under the iron fence to try to see his window. But obstructing his view, right in front of him, was a black van with black tinted windows marked 'The Geek Team.' He pressed himself against the bottom of the stairs. He'd be caught. He bowed his head and stayed motionless except for the heart attack he was having and the stench making him want to retch. Would his heart burst?

Men in a rush spoke Arabic and opened the van's doors.

"Got everything?" a man said, with an out of breath voice. He too was having a heart attack.

"Let's look at it, to be certain." The van sped away. Mahmoud was confused by these words. Look at what? Did it mean they would come back to look at something else?

He'd take a chance, hoping they didn't see him and that they wouldn't be back. He'd rush into his apartment. They weren't one-on-one murderers anyway, or so he hoped. Inside his place, he found all his computer equipment stolen. Not something he could report. He checked for disks but everything electronic was gone. His day planners were gone, as well. All the years were taken. Even his whiteboard had been erased. Surely they left fingerprints, or maybe not. Besides, what could he do? These people erased his connection to them. All he had ever suspected was they probably lived in Brooklyn. Good, they could take his little microchips across the river, and would not likely be back today or any day as long as he stayed dead.

He collapsed into his sofa. He could not stay here long. Maybe they wouldn't be able to leave Manhattan and they'd come back to have a place to stay, until the bridges were open. Had to be open. Duh. People wanted to leave the island.

They got what they wanted. He was useless. Whether he was dead or alive, it mattered no more. But they were idiots. They might kill out of fear that somehow, someway he'd remember something that would lead the police to them and ruin their cushy lives. They probably weren't murderers, probably students, although one sounded older. He couldn't take the chance on staying. *Buy time to think.* Teaching architecture at Pratt was now impossible. Survival 101 was not, but it would have to be self-taught.

Yet he needed his job as an architectural consultant and professor to survive, but then it would only be a matter of time before they'd come for him. The police were out of the question, because they'd be looking for a scapegoat and their organization might have been infiltrated. He'd be shipped off to some prison for interrogation and it might be years before it was all straightened out. Too many movies influenced him. All he did was take pictures of the Twin Towers and other landmarks. So what? Crazy suiciders didn't need quaint pictures to fly into two unmistakable buildings but his family needed to stay alive.

77

Fishing into his back pocket, he pulled out the high school teacher's card. Perhaps she'd consider letting him stay with her for a while.

Jody Marks became his mark.

Mahmoud would call her from a payphone. But first he'd shower and change clothes, forget about the hair dye but keep the receipt for a return. Then he'd pack a suitcase and grab all his hidden cash—should be around nine hundred to a grand—and get the hell out of there.

He ran around the apartment like a mad man, emptying flowerpots, opening a scooped book, and looking between the cardboard sheaths of his family's portrait. It was all there, $1,056. He'd meet the lovely teacher for dinner and convince her to let him sleep at her place. Maybe even help with lesson planning. Petros Papadopoulos at your service. He liked teachers, and she was very pretty. Maybe he'd get laid.

He recalled the old movie *The Jackal* and fantasized about killing his lovers as he got closer to General De Gaulle. But he wasn't a killer.

He shuddered at his selfish, ghoulish feelings. *This is not me.*

What had happened to his life? What had he done to these faceless jihadists who should leave the country? Maybe they had to stay like him, or maybe they planned something else. He didn't know and he didn't care. He needed to stay alive.

Chapter 9

September 11, 6:01 p.m.

Autumn Breeze paced back and forth between the windows and door of her co-op apartment. She dropped her head, mimicking her Human Society and Culture professor's weight-of-the-world-on-his-shoulders pose. She had to pick up some of his wisdom, but all she got was a headache. She wanted to spit at the line-up of whiskey and rum bottles her mom had left. A shrine to death. Mom had a boyfriend all right, Jack Daniels.

If her mom hadn't died today, she would have died from the booze.

She went back to the computers and got on her mom's matchmaking website.

It had no graphics and less content. She'd have to figure out how to fire her mom's two employees. She couldn't afford them. Maybe her mom would show up. She'd wait a little longer.

More pacing. She checked the air-conditioning vents to see if they were still holding back the crud from the disaster. They were on inside circulate for two reasons. The toxic dust outside and the devil. The devil to take her soul, the dust to take her body. She shouldn't be alone.

She clicked on the TV: buildings fell, people jumped, planes crashed over and over. Nothing got her crying until she pictured her dad, a bank security guard. He had stood up to the bank robbers and got a hole in his head. She pictured him in a faint mournful goodbye. *I love you so much, my little sweetie.*

Wiping her eyes, she picked up the phone and called Joey. She needed somebody to keep her human. Miss Smarty Pants had to come down to earth and learn to see the beauty in people, like she saw in Detective Chastity O'Sullivan, cha cha cha.

"Joey. Hi."

"Yeah, baby."

Was this remark cute or rude? Well, whatever. Time to show a little empathy about the disaster. Somehow, with Joey on the line she broke out in tears.

"Oh Joey, did you lose anybody?"

"You know, I prayed you would cry. It's good for you." He choked and started crying too. "My uncle Antony is a fireman, but we don't know yet."

She wiped her nose on her sleeve. "I'll pray for you and your family."

"What about you? Your family, baby?"

"My mom," she took a Pinocchio, nose getting longer, breath, "is putting herself into rehab to try to be a better mom for me." Maybe she should have pushed Monique to rehab, put her foot down. Then she'd have a mom today, a real mom to hug. "She's going to leave me alone here to run her business for a couple weeks. She's asked me to make some changes, but I'll tell you later." She couldn't tell anybody her mom might have died. Otherwise, she'd be on the first boat to Trinidad.

"What's her job?"

"Matchmaking."

"My mom does hair."

"So, you want physics tutoring and maybe other sciences' lessons, right?

"Yep."

"Well you won't have to pay a dime, if you double our time here and help me straighten out my mom's business and whatever." He didn't know the top secret *whatever* she planned. Never in a million years would he figure out she was cooking up a love match, or at least cultivating her crush on him. Maybe he'd wait for her to grow up. Maybe he'd marry her someday as long as he encouraged her to become the world's greatest scientist or engineer.

"That's a great idea. I'll try to help you, baby."

"Call me Autumn, okay?"

"I know you're not a baby. But I—"

"That's right. I know I'm a kid, but I have a name. So, let's see what happens."

"But I want to make sure you know I—I'm like a big brother to you."

"Of course. I've always wanted one of those." She slipped a finger down her throat, but turned her head away from the phone when she gagged.

"I'm thinking about enlisting."

"Don't do it. You need to get a degree. Study and help that way."

"We'll see."

They agreed on Friday. "I'll cook some dinner, or maybe buy a bucket of chicken."

Could she trust this boy? Oh yeah, he was the good church going type, but he also flirted with the older girls, never Miss Scrawny-No-Boobs. They said their good byes.

She paced over to the mirror in her mom's bedroom. Twirled. What could she wear Friday? Maybe she'd wear one of these push up bras, with the foam. She didn't have to sneak a squeeze of the fluffy bra anymore, with no one but her here.

Mamma, come home.

She put it on. It slipped down to her belly button. Her mom was no Dolly Parton, but still. No, she wouldn't fool Joey.

Hey, Joey. Guess what? All of a sudden, in three days, I grew tits.

I didn't know girls grew that fast. Now I want to kiss you.

No way Joey. Well, one on the cheek.

Then he'd want to see these little knobs. Besides, her hips needed to spread out.

She had been told by her grandmother she had a perfect face. Her grandfather, the mathematician, had ignited in her a love for math and told her she was the perfect representation of the Creator's intent for beauty. Later, she became the only person on the planet to show the relationship between the golden ratio, God's number, and how to use it in the more mundane field of probability and statistics. This was what Ayita, the NSA's Chief Engineer, had probably referred to when complimenting Autumn on her thesis.

God, it turned out, was simple minded. He designed every living thing's parts and angles from nautilus shell to human, using one proportion for harmony or beauty in nature. Phi—his building block, 1.6180339887 etc.—would show up in more pleasant detail all over her body someday. They'd call her Miss Golden Ratio because every curve would conform to what people perceived as beautiful. She'd beat out Audrey Hepburn for near perfect face. God, she hoped so, because Joey just wasn't into her...yet.

Well, for now she wore an award-winning smile on a pretty face, so said grandpa. She'd practice her smile and dress up on Friday. All her mom's clothes were too big, but she could wear some of Mom's long shirts as nightgowns. She rummaged around; all her clothes were jeans of different colors with plenty of cutie-pie shirts and two jackets. *This will work*, a Yankees Subway Series Championship shirt. *Yo Joey, can you say first base?* She closed her tee-shirt drawer.

Somehow, she'd have to get used to being alone. She had to show strength or Satan, who's very busy right now, might get her.

That night, over and over again, she awakened in a sweat-filled nightshirt. Each time the nightmare was the same, she jumped from Tower 1 holding her mom's hand.

After changing her shirt for the bazzillianth time, she grabbed her plush sheepdog, and snuggled him under the covers. Hoped to hug life into him. Like Doctor Frankenstein. She fell asleep chanting, "No more falling." Julius said nothing, but he was very affectionate.

Chapter 10

Frank found himself in his own bed with a note pinned to his—this wasn't his shirt.

It said.

I got a doctor to check you over. Detective O'Sullivan gave me the bug and did good job on your back if you like Smurfs. The doctor said you would be all right. He gave you a shot. I had to leave, but if I do not hear from you by 10 p.m., I will come up to check on you.

Carlos.

P.S. I delivered an intro letter of recommendation for you to the Mayor, personally.

Frank checked the time, 9:33 p.m. He called Carlos and then freshened up in the bathroom. Nice to know his plumbing was still working. With all the holes in him, he sprung no leaks while peeing. He grabbed a Ginger Ale from the frig. The smell of ginger root off the fizz woke him up fully and sharpened his mind. The day's horrible and unusual events came into focus.

After a morbid review of one of the worst days in American History, he gladly moved on to his last conscious moments. They flashed out of order like an odd dance. He was showering. His back, butt and legs ached like hell. Chastity administered to him with loving kindness. He had passed out on her bed, frickin' naked. He smiled. She had to have enjoyed that. Nah, she was doing her public duty. She played nurse. He played dead. He pictured her taking the temperature of his penis. When he laughed, his body hurt. Good that he could joke. He hadn't lost his soul today, his sense that life must go on. This hardnosed spy needed to cry more often. He needed to feel more often. He needed a life, before the whole damn city was blown up. He'd stop the threats with all the talent God gave him.

Somewhere along the way he'd learn to live. At the least, he'd avenge the dead. The dead he and others had failed to save.

Again, with effort, he stood and went over to a south facing window of his penthouse in his building. He pressed a button for the privacy systems to turn off so that he could see better through the bomb and bulletproof glass. Whatever the doc had given him made him a little dizzy, but his eyes took in the horror. The work-lights, haze and the lack of Towers made an eerie and gloomy sight. Somewhere down there in the mangled steel lay the remains of his lover, Emily Livaudais. He banged his fist against the glass.

In front of the mirror, he took off his shirt and dropped his pants to inspect his wounds. The shirt's pattern, not something he'd pick out, but nonetheless appealing: Thin crisscrossing stripes of tan, yellow and blue with a breast pocket. He'd keep it, but wouldn't wear it. He liked gray and he had plenty of Dockers. The silly Smurf Band-Aids all over his back made him picture Chastity applying them. *God, what a woman.*

He'd have to get some non-drug induced sleep and lots of it. With OTTS folding faster than a lawn chair, he'd need to secure a new gig so he'd meet with the mayor soon with a proposal, thanks to Carlos smoothing the way. The mayor would sign on because Frank had the money to fund an anti-terrorist campaign and the know-how. Who else could keep what he pictured secret and out of the press? Certainly not the dysfunctional city, state and federal governments.

He turned to look at his back again. Chastity had colored him red all over with mercurochrome. No wounds were leaking. She had sewn up a small gash on his butt. Oh yeah, the glass. She had pulled it out. God bless her. He had put her through the wringer, and once again, he owed her, big time. However, remembering her seeing him in the buff, forced a familiar twinge of shame. He knew his athlete's body and Italian face tempted some women, but he was still sensitive about strangers seeing his equipment. Of course, today couldn't be helped. Just a fact of life.

Next, he went to a couch, sat on a towel and watched the unending horror on TV. Having enough, he voice-controlled the TV to turn off.

Then he practiced his pitch aloud for the mayor until he tired.

Exhausted, he finished with a prayer for Emily, slid carefully back into bed and commanded "lights out", but being asleep all day he let his mind wonder until it would conk out.

Emily Livaudais was a good woman, caught in the grinder. They shouldn't have asked her to help with his projects, but soon Carlos would have fired her anyway. No budget, and in her case, no production.

Her sad face confronted him, one of thousands of victims. He'd forever cherish her memory, smooth skin, her funny inverted nipples, which he had peaked until plump cherries, her voodoo ways. Although they had a working relationship, one of convenience, and yes, hot sex, both knew they weren't each other's match. Well, at least that's the way he still felt, and she had known that. No sense kicking himself; he had been honest with her. Nonetheless, he'd miss her goofy sexiness and strange superstitions. She did believe in ghosts, and all the other things people from New Orleans practiced.

He fell asleep remembering her Cajun songs. He didn't understand them, but they felt wonderful. In his dream, she sat on the end of the bed sobbing.

He sat up. "Why are you crying, dear?"

"I'll miss you."

"I miss you already," he said.

"I hadn't signed up for this and I make a lousy spy."

"On top of that your ghosts and voodoo never helped OTTS, not once."

"I'm going to leave you with all the ghosts of 9/11 as a going away gift."

"That's okay, as long as you're one of them."

"How cruel you are? Wake up shit-head."

He blinked his eyes, "Is that you?" A shadowy, ghostly figure sat at the end of his bed, but he was no longer dreaming. Right?

"You never loved me."

He lifted up but fell back down in pain. "No, baby. Is that you? Really you? Thank God, you're alive. I'm sorry for what I said about you being a ghost. I thought I was dreaming and that you had died and your ghost would stay with me in consolation."

"I'm going back to New Orleans as soon as the airports open again."

"Well, Carlos's agency is falling apart. I quit today. I went down to the disaster today and nearly got killed trying to save you."

"You see. That's the first thing you think of. The job. Not, I'll miss you. Not, come over here, baby."

"Come over here, baby."

She hesitated then took her blouse off and unsnapped her bra. She shrugged, but he knew she couldn't resist him. God she was so exotic, with her French, black, and American Indian skin. Her hair, well Chastity's, was kinkier. Funny thing. Chastity seemed embarrassed about her hair. God made her that way and it was fantastic. He hadn't thought much about women, especially nearly naked ones, in skimpy bathing suits.

"Pay attention." Emily pressed her boobs into his chest.

"I haven't stopped mourning," he said.

"I need relief. I need to ride your waves. Fall away. Lose myself in our ecstasy. Take me. Take me for the last time."

"Look at my back." He flicked on the bed table light and got up on his knees.

"What happened?" She looked horrified.

"I outran the Tower. You see, I really was looking for you, my sweet candy."

She started crying. He embraced her as best as he could.

She pulled away and peeked at his back again. "This fix-up job is amateurish. No doctor puts Smurf Band-Aids on an adult."

"Oh, the nurse ran out of normal Band-Aids, I guess."

"At least this stitching on your rump looks expert. Does it hurt, honey?"

"Not too much, I'll be okay. I'm sorry. I spoiled your mood." Actually, he had hoped her mood was spoiled. He just couldn't do it the way she liked with him on the bottom, because it would hurt when he lay on his back with her straddling him.

"You can't spoil my mood. The fastest way to recover is with orgasm, for me and you. I'll let you take me anyway you can."

"I don't know if I can. The doctor drugged me." He had thought her gone and had dealt with it. Although ecstatic she was alive, he liked the idea of being alone to concentrate on a fuller future. To reassess his life. And to help protect New York City from another attack coming soon. Although he cared about her, he just couldn't or wouldn't give her a fair shake.

She reached around from his back and fondled his penis. There was only so much torture a man could take.

"We better call Carlos," she said and then yanked him.

She stopped playing with him and he started aching again. "I already did. Wait." He texted Carlos that Emily was alive and well. "I just texted him about you."

Her squeezing had felt so good, he couldn't help but get hard. Still he would have liked to return the favor. No, he had to return the favor. That's the way it always was with Emily. His neck ached, nonetheless, he settled in between her legs.

She would have none of it. "Take me now." She was wetter than a swimming pool, anyway.

"I need you not to touch my back and I need to stay on top."

"Yes, yes, hurry."

Oh he hurried. He was racing again. Running away from a building, from the reality of a love affair without the love. He did care. He did. The stroking became deeper. Suddenly he pictured the mayor, the president, the governors, the police commissioner and lost it.

"Come on, baby." She wiggled.

He had never failed in his life. He settled on an image of Chastity touching his hand, of Chastity's small perky breasts, not really hidden by her crimson swimsuit. He became all man.

Later, and completely satisfied, she started crying. "You'll never love me, will you?"

"I don't think I can love anybody."

"Why?"

"I don't know." The truth was he did know or thought he knew. He couldn't take on the responsibility of a family because of his dangerous line of work. Someday he'd get a bullet in his head and some wonderful children and a wife would miss him. "Maybe I'm running away from the idea of marriage, kids."

"Why?"

"Listen, Emily, I don't know."

"You do know. Say it."

"Maybe… No. I *just* don't know." He was about to make up some reason without knowing what he would say next. Yes, his life was too dangerous. But not much, since he joined OTTS. Was what he was about to do too dangerous to have a wife? He doubted this premise too. But until plans were crystalized with the mayor, he wouldn't know for sure.

"You don't want me, because I'm not white. Right?"

"Don't you ever say that. My brothers and sisters came from all over the world. You are just as beautiful as any other woman."

"But?"

"I, I, I thought we had a deal. Have fun. No strings."

"There's not many men who can make love like you, even tonight."

"Oh that's ridiculous. You just train them to do what you want."

"I've grown accustomed to your prick, you prick."

"It hurts when I laugh."

"Just give good ole Emily some thought. I don't have a job now. I'll have to go back to New Orleans if you don't consider an engagement ring."

They had been too close for too long. "Just give me a little time." He needed time to figure out why he couldn't—wouldn't—marry her. Maybe he needed a shrink. Maybe a drink. No-o-o, not with unknown drugs floating about in his body.

"I'm going to New Orleans sometime this week to see my family. Maybe, if I can't stand being without you, I'll come back after two weeks, if you'll have me back."

Certain now. He didn't care where she lived, just not with him anymore. Damn his attitude. Damn her flip-flopping. Damn his flip-flopping over a woman he had feelings for. She just wasn't right for him. For one thing, she didn't challenge him intellectually. She had no love of sports. Her belief in ghosts was ridiculous. Goofy. Her figure—voluptuous, her exotic face—pretty, pretty amazing. He preferred the Sandra Bullock, Lucy Liu or Cha Cha O'Sullivan type of figures much better. Cha Cha's face sucked him in like falling into a volcano. He didn't know what to do or say, so he shut up until the right path struck him.

He had such great times with Emily. They made love on Jones Beach, languishing naked. Cracking crabs open on the rocks at Montauk Point. Her jambalaya. A hundred ways to cook shrimp. Her cute upturned nose, humorous ghost stories. The smell of her.

He leaned on his elbow and twiddled her ringlets. "You had better not leave your ghosts with me."

"If I do, then maybe you'll respect me more. Did you call your family?"

"Oh shit." Even though it was late, he called home and his mom answered on the first ring. She sounded fully awake. He profusely apologized, explained what happened, and gave her the details he could tell her. He promised to come home on Saturday night. Saturday was better, because he'd be mostly healed, with the red bruises and the Band-Aids probably gone. She'd surely ask him to take off his shirt. That was Mom: always needing to see for herself, a doubting Thomas-ina.

Frank fell asleep with Emily in a sweet and sour lingering of two souls not meant to be together. They both loved the sex. They both loved each other. Her love had turned to being in love while his was running away in the opposite direction. He loved her kindness, but in the end, it wasn't enough. If he proposed to her to do the honorable thing, she'd eventually hate him for not matching her feelings. One thing about Emily, she was great at reading emotion. He'd not fool her for a microsecond. Probably the only reason she didn't pick up on Chastity O'Sullivan through her sixth sense or woman's intuition, was the two buildings that had crushed his soul today. His face couldn't run away from misery over the loss of countless brothers and sisters and hatred for the terrorists. But who could?

She whimpered, her naked body lightly against his arm. Another thing about her, she sure knew how to help a fellow sleep.

Chapter 11

Thursday, September 13, 8:59 a.m., Sixth precinct

"O'Sullivan. In here now." Cha Cha's lieutenant's gravelly voice blared over the loudspeaker.

He was always brusque with her. Seemed to delight in humiliating her. Whatever happened to chastise in private, praise in public? Praise from him was like hell freezing over. As if Satan sat on cold ground lamenting forgetting to pay the heating bill.

She gripped the sides of her chair and sat as far away from his huge conference table/desk as possible. He had bought this phallic symbol—his greatest fantasy—with his own money. The mayor, no the president, didn't even sport a desk this big.

"All these funerals, Sir. I haven't stopped crying." She knew this to be a good opening line. Everybody, men and women alike, had been weeping and with good cause. Over twenty NYPD police, near forty Port Authority police and over three-hundred firemen and paramedics had died. These large families were close and now more than ever—brothers and sisters.

"What have you been doing these past two days? What have you been doing for the last year?"

"I—" She tried to emulate her grandpapa, took to heart all his lessons, and had produced results, but somehow Mr. Sexist ignored her talents. Like a bean counter, he could only see arrest records. She solved problems by mediating or talking them through. Numerous ex-thugs had her to thank for an honest job, because they could tell she cared and understood them. Her biggest turn-around: a major drug dealer with a mathematical mind, now hedge-fund manager. Although sometimes she wondered, which career was morally superior. Crime had dropped in Washington Park and surrounds. She had cited her accomplishments, but the lieutenant gave the data no value during her advancement reviews.

"You've been hugging strangers."

"Let me explain."

He pushed the Daily News her way. "Go ahead. Explain. No better yet, why don't you just transfer to Staten Island?"

He could have said Siberia. She loved Manhattan and would find a way to stay.

"I—"

"Here, they're forming a new taskforce." He pushed across a paper about signing up to fight terrorism.

"I was rescuing a cat."

"I don't see a cat in this picture. I see you, like you're having a fucking orgasm with your hands up. As if he were arresting you or feeling you up." She could have filed a complaint long ago against her boss, but she was trained to work with all types. Even over the hill, sexist bozos.

"I—"

"You know, O'Sullivan, it's the perp who's supposed to hold up his hands."

"Let me see that." The Daily News or the unnamed photographer who sent this in must have photo-shopped out Autumn's legs. Cha Cha did look happy to be hugged and she could also use one right now. She wondered if the lieutenant's wife loved hugging him, if he were the same pain-in-the-ass at home. Stay on point, Cha Cha, for grandpapa's sake and honor.

"This photo was manipulated. It never happened, Sir. I can take it to forensics and prove it to you."

"That won't be necessary. Look, O'Sullivan, we may not have agreed much in the past, but I think it's time you consider checking out this taskforce. Maybe we'll both be happier…and I'm sure you'll fit in. They need a diplomat among horse thieves. There's a call in here somewhere for a mediator and, ah, detective with mediation skills. I'll grant you have that quality in spades."

Diplomats and horse thieves, one of those strange analogies she doubted her lieutenant would ever understand. Come to think of it, right at this moment, neither did she. Not completely. But she'd figure it out soon enough.

She stood allowing her chair to scrape the floor. "I will, Sir." Unfazed by the chair noise, he smiled strangely. Not like him, not like him at all. He was up to something. He had never complimented her before even if delivered left-handed. Still, she felt like shit. This had never happened to her grandpapa. Even when she was merely five years old, he started teaching her the straight and narrow path an officer of the law should walk. He encouraged her to choose law enforcement and do it right.

Now he was gone and she missed him so much, especially today. He would have never allowed her lieutenant to treat her this way. When dismissed, she'd leave his office and head for a little privacy in the ladies room.

Her lieutenant's suggestion to apply for a job with the terrorism taskforce caused an anguish to erupt once again over the Twin Towers disaster and how she had wanted to help more directly. Would she get her chance, now? Floating in her brain were all the lost souls, her lieutenant's contempt for her. In times of nearly overwhelming stress she—feeling guilty—recalled the day her grandpapa was murdered.

She was in the creepy closet, only seven years old. There was one bad conversation. Some sort of lecture about right and wrong. Her grandpapa was giving the lecture to the man with the gun. Grandpapa had put her in the closet, told her to be quiet, to stand like a statue. She watched through a stream of tears and the closet slats as her grandpapa was shot in the head. She avenged him bravely at the trial and put away a dirty cop. She promised her family and her personal saint: grandfather Captain Michael O'Sullivan, NYPD, she'd right wrongs someday, tip the balance in favor of the good guys.

Grounded once again, in knowing she'd do the right thing, take the right path, she broke away from the vivid memory to rejoin the hellish present of 9/11 and the purgatory of having to work for an unfair and unenlightened boss. If she could, she'd leave the precinct, but she'd always find time for her best friend, Autumn and her sister. They'd be just a subway hop away, probably.

Still… Even with her boss not counting some of her techniques, her performance reviews were above average. What the hell was her lieutenant up to? But she had to take him at face value. She reassured him she'd look into the taskforce and grabbed the proffered notice, but he—as if he weren't letting her in on a joke—

said through a smirk something about the taskforce being a good fit for her.

"Get out of here." He finally waved her out of his office. "O'Malley, Rosenblatt, both of you, right now," he barked into the intercom.

Oh, he was in a good mood. She needed to sign-out a vehicle to visit with her now deceased partner's family. Detective Jerome Price, a great guy, with a pure heart had left behind a boy seven, a four-year old girl, his wife and their families. She only knew one way to handle the situation. She'd speak from the heart and show Jerome's grieving family how much she loved him. It should have been her down there in Tower 1.

On her ride out to Staten Island, images of Frank Lancia nude in her shower and on her bed plagued her. She *mostly* stayed square in the lanes. She'd have to forget God's gift to women, probably women everywhere. Likely, his body was nearly healed and right now he'd be fucking somebody's brains out. *A page from the secret agent handbook.*

Perhaps her lieutenant knew something about the personnel on the taskforce and how she'd fit well with them or one of them. A man she could love in a heartbeat. But that man, her very own secret agent, was Federal, was probably part of the mysterious OTTS.

No way was Johnny Wad or whatever his name was, oh Lance, yeah, Lance, would join the NYPD. Her boss just wanted her out of his hair.

Her fantasy man's curly locks needed combing with her fingers. Perhaps, after all the funerals were over and NYC life took on some semblance of normal, she'd ask around and try to find him. Even if he ran from her because of his profession and fast legs, she suspected he'd deliberately slow just enough for her to catch him.

Chapter 12

Friday, September 14, 5:17 p.m.

It had rained all morning and into the afternoon, but it cleared for Joey's walk over to Autumn's apartment. The late sun streamed through the windows. God had cleansed the city of 9/11's dust. He took back to the earth tiny pieces of bodies, ashes to ashes. Every one of them—minus the terrorists—a saint.

With no mom at home, she had almost gotten used to living alone. Almost used to Satan not rounding her up. This childish fear diminished by the moment. God would always win in the long run. She knew He blessed her with a glimmer of His eternity.

However, being unloved was such a drag. She just couldn't keep squeezing her plush dog, Julius. If her plan worked, Joey would stay with her for two weeks tops. She'd have to lie to him about her mom. Since she was an illegal alien, she couldn't tell anybody her mom would never come home. The crazy talk shows went on and on about kicking everybody out of the country. Renting the Queen Mary and shipping them off. Of course, the evil "them" were mainly Muslims, but talk-show hosts' unchristian attitudes slipped over to everybody else who wasn't white. Cha Cha no doubt hated these fear mongers. At least the president had spoken up for the Muslim community.

Joey arrived. His raincoat slid off his broad shoulders to the floor. He gave her one look, picked it up and hung it in the closet. They got right into his lesson. He absorbed everything she threw at him. He was smart. He just didn't like physics or maybe he liked being with her. She hoped so, not that this would end up in a crazy-kissing-for-hours session. Like it had been with her cousin William, when they were eight.

Joey, please have pity on me.

After the lesson, her very big-eyed-crush stuffed himself with her spaghetti and meatballs.

"This tastes weird, but good in a weird way." Yeah, right.

"I put some Caribbean spices, kind of peppery, in the meatballs."

"Where's your mom?" Joey talked with his mouth full like he didn't know whether to chomp or spit the glob out.

"Like I said, rehab over in New Jersey. She'll be back in two weeks. I can get Mr. Hillbrant next door, if you think we need a chaperone." God she hardly knew the pervert next door who always had some swift remark for her mom, 'your pink dress goes great with your long legs, Miss Monique.' Puke.

"Don't be a dorkette. I'm practically a man now. I am my own chaperone."

"We're both teenagers."

"This teenager could get thrown in jail for, for…"

He shouldn't have gone there.

"That's if you're eighteen. You're sixteen, right?"

All she wanted was a kiss anyway and not a sloppy one with all the yucky slobber, just a peck, just for friendship. He could thank her for the meal or the lesson with a brotherly kiss, on the cheek even.

"I'm seventeen on March 2. Are you sure about that law?"

"Kids are doing all kinds of things in high school in case you hadn't noticed. How'd you get into NYU so young?"

"You're not the only *wunderkind*. True, I'm not your caliber, especially in physics, which I hate. I have musical and other artistic gifts, plus a perfect GPA, but I almost burnt down my school. They concluded I was bored and here I am."

He told her of his ability to pick up and play any instrument, how he hated chem lab too, how he managed to visit the principal's office regularly over issues with the way the teacher conducted class. He had always had a better idea, to hear him tell it. They either had to send him to reform school or kick him up a grade. She couldn't believe this sweet boy could be so naughty.

"Okay. Here's my problems. One, I'm supposed to run my mom's business. She has two employees. I need to fire them because the business is losing money. Two, you need to sleep over here for two weeks instead of the dorm." She threw that in.

"Um, what?" Joey stuffed in another wad of spaghetti.

"They're all doable."

"No, I can't sleep with you."

"Not me, dummy. That would be so stupid. You can sleep in my mom's room or I can. I don't care." It would have been nice to hug him.

"If your mom finds out I was sleeping here?"

"I'll bake you a cake and get you two presents."

"I'm not sure you have your facts right about the law. There are laws against minors fooling around." He stared at the ceiling as if trying to believe what he'd just said, or searching for his source.

"Yo, Joey. Give me a break."

"Well, I just want you to know I'm a good boy. I won't go all the way until I'm married."

He'd want nothing from a girl with not-yet-out-all-the-way hips and electron microscope boobs, anyway. *Just an adorable face and curly brown locks.* "The nuns got to you, huh?"

"Didn't they strike the fear of the Lord into you, too?"

"I'm too young for sex. Plain and simple. When I want a penis inside me," his eyebrows kneaded. "I'll be careful not to catch AIDS and all the other diseases."

"You're so worldly." He covered his mouth to hide a broad smile.

"I watch some *NYPD Blue.* I know all kinds of weird things."

"I thought you were just book smart," he said.

"If you don't stay over, I won't tutor you."

"That's not fair. You made a promise." Joey walked over to the fridge and opened the freezer door. "Can I have some ice cream?"

"*May I.* Listen Joey, all I want is for you to stay. I'm scared alone." Maybe she could withhold the ice cream, but he was too quick. *Boys, when they want stuff, they move fast, except for Joey wanting sex.* She stood up to run over and help, but he already found the scooper and a bowl.

"I can't think without a little ice cream." He had pulled out cherry vanilla and was going through the drawers for a normal spoon when she placed her hand over his. Her breathing jumped to short wisps of something like asthmatic breaths. He felt so good, so strong. There was some sort of charge zinging between them.

"I'll get the spoon. Please close the freezer door."

"You sound funny."

"Yeah and you smell weird, but good—just in a weird way."

"What kind of rum is that?" He spotted a bottle of Puncheon Rum in the middle of all the Jack Daniels.

"That comes from Trinidad. But my mom doesn't allow it. I'm sorry, Joey, I don't drink."

"If ever, you can take a little taste and fill it back with water."

"Alcohol kills brain cells until you're an adult." She didn't want to say until you are eighteen like the study claimed. He'd drink soon enough if not already. She didn't believe the study that somehow when your brain stopped growing, the alcohol would stop harming. She wanted to protect her 210 IQ and Joey needed to be protected from himself.

Joey sniffed his armpits. "I don't smell weird. I use Lifebuoy soap. It's maybe too stinky, you think?" Okay Joey was going back to his smell, which was manly, yummy.

"Forget it. You smell—nice."

He opened the freezer again and just stared like he was solving a gig-saw puzzle.

"I want a new dad and I want a way to figure out if he's legitimate. I want to find a new husband for my mom. My dad died years ago and now mom's trying to get sober…"

"Sorry about your dad. But looking for a guy for your mom could be fun. I'm in." Joey licked the ice cream off his spoon and smacked his lips. They were shaped like a bow with a nice kissable puff on the upper one.

"Joey?" He had some kind of attention deficit, or he was avoiding her question.

"I'm no expert."

"Please stay over."

"No. Can't. Wait a minute... I do owe you some time tonight." Smiling boyishly, he gave her a curious look. "So what would you want in a father and what would your mom want in a husband? No wait, your mom's more important on this issue. He has just got to treat you fairly and love you like a daughter."

"Yes. He has to love me and mom. He should be maybe around six-feet-two, maybe black curly hair like yours. Maybe Italian."

"I'm not going to be your daddy."

She giggled. She had pictured Cha Cha's mystery man. Although the detective wouldn't say so, from her googly eyes, she liked that guy. Probably wanted him to bite her ass. That might feel pleasant. Someday she'd study nerve endings in the Gluteus Maximus and how a possible small pain could be pleasurable and why.

"Sit down, you dummy. I'm not talking about you, even if you are very extremely handsome. You're five-foot-eleven, not six-two. See?" Well Joey mustn't know she had probably lost hope over finding her mom alive and that actually this search was about spending time with him and finding a man fitting Autumn's specifications which were really Cha Cha's specifications. If Autumn couldn't land the mystery agent Cha Cha was gaga for, maybe she'd like an alternative guy. And then, Autumn desperately needed, no matter who, a husband and father. *If only her beautiful Cha Cha felt the same way now that life had gotten so real. She'd find out.*

"You got a crush on me, kid?" This Italian just wouldn't give up his silly, egocentric idea, even if he were right on the nose.

"Come-on Joey, all Italians are handsome. And noooo, you're too old for me. You're ready for the old farts home." They both giggled this time. He seemed off his high horse.

"Come-on. I need more categories," Joey said, pounding away on the computer.

"Okay, he needs to play chess, maybe scrabble. He should like walks in the park. Telling stories. He should like real dogs, not that fake dog over there. He should like cops. You know, be patriotic. Bagels are very important."

"Seeded?" Joey displayed the greatest white-toothed smile.

"And rye," she said and gave back her best feature. A big fat ear-to-ear smile to complement her creamy smooth face. Hoped he appreciated it.

"Are we talking about you or your mom?"

"No, my mom loves all those qualities and bread products."

"There's no bagel category."

"Let's add it in the general remarks section."

"Let's stop at chess for now, and the Italian looks if your mom is lucky. Let the rest of it be an education for him. He'll want to please you and your mom. You know."

"Oh? Okay. Let's try it."

A little later, without finding anybody yet, she sprung another problem on him.

"I want you to come with me when I fire her two worthless good-for-nothing employees."

After a while at the computer Joey said, "You don't have to visit them." He showed her that they worked out of their homes. They went into her mom's desk and pulled out the contracts. Joey was quick at reading them. Pretty impressive for a lessor prodigy. The employees had no severance pay, no notice. No nothing. They composed a Dear John letter—Joey had called it—and hit send. All done. Next problem.

"Come on, Joey. Mr. Hillbrant has looked at me kind of funny lately like he, well, ah…" Scrunching up her face, she tried some acting tears.

Joey got up from the computer desk, lifted her up into his arms and hugged her silly. *Oh my God, for sure. Never let go.* He liked her, couldn't resist her, really wanted to kiss her.

He grabbed her hand and pulled her out through the family room and kitchen area to the apartment door.

"You have to grow up. Look at that door." The door had four locks on it. She knew she was safe from everybody but the CIA. Besides, her mom had a pepper spray around here somewhere.

"All right. Just leave." She pointed at the door, but she felt like blowing up into a million pieces.

"I can't stay." After a couple more proddings, he finally said, "Because I have a girlfriend."

Yeah sure. He didn't have a girlfriend; he just hated staying with a teeny-bopper.

She grabbed his sleeve. "Do you sleep with her?"

He pulled away gently and touched her cheek. "I already told you. I'm a virgin."

"You mean a jerk. Leave now."

"Come on, Autumn." He cocked his head and pouted.

"There's the door." She pointed.

He checked his watch. "We have seven minutes left."

"Okay—is your main squeeze, Marcie?"

"She's too lumpy."

Seven minutes went by discussing what Joey liked and disliked about various parts of a girl's anatomy, although he seemed fixated on the size of the derriere. *The mass of the ass is inversely proportional to the heat of the meat and the angle of the dangle,* but she would not dare say that to him, on their first half-derriere date. He'd thought of her as a kid. But in reality a future Miss America, well maybe Miss Trinidad was waiting to break out of her cocoon. Besides, he didn't know physics equations and he'd be back.

He left. She stayed frozen at the door staring at four deadbolts locked. She was through with love. It just disappointed. Love wasted time, big time.

At least her ass wasn't big. Not at all, not yet, not ever if she could help it. She ran into the bedroom to the full-length mirror to make sure her bottom hadn't grown in the last two hours. Because of all those hormones making her crazy, she couldn't be sure.

But crazy, well it wasn't such a bad thing.

A little later, Joey knocked on her door again and she pictured them feeling each other up.

He hauled a backpack. "I can only stay tonight. That's it."

"Thank you. I was really scared." She hugged him without so much as a squeeze back. Well, thank God he was here.

"I know. Your mom should not have left you. My mom and dad said you can stay with them in Brooklyn tomorrow night until—"

"I'll be all right. I really like my place."

"It's cool." He looked around until he fell in love with her TV. So went the night. They watch some old movie, *The Parent*

Trap, until he fell asleep with popcorn on his lap. The film, although syrupy sweet, presented some sound ideas. Her job would be four times more complex. Make two people fall in love and then get them to love her. All this without the help of an identical twin.

She brought out an extra blanket and tucked Joey in. He had a girl's eyelashes, but everything else was all man-boy. She kissed her finger and touched his lip. It would have to do and it would have to stick.

Autumn fell asleep dreaming of accepting the Nobel Prize and thanking her husband Joey Demarco for his support and encouragement.

Chapter 13

Saturday, September 15, 10:52 a.m.

The mayor's office looked like ground zero. Emergency cables, TVs, computers secure and otherwise overlapped in an impossible tangle. *Five coffee makers.* The mayor was obviously hands on. Besides, Disaster Preparedness Headquarters had been housed in the now collapsed WTC 7.

Frank would see which way the wind blew in this meeting. In any case, a little help from the NSA and the mayor's field office could actually turn into a thing of beauty or at least not laden with tripping hazards. The phones would not stop ringing.

The Chief of Police was dribbling coffee on the green rug. "Shit."

"It's usually not like this," the mayor said with his famous half smile.

Frank displayed a warm grin. "You should see my house— I'm going to need both of your permissions to archive Detective O'Sullivan's report in a secure vault." He had already explained in his proposal the possible threat to the detective, her snitch and the embarrassment to the department this could cause. Yes, bad press could be blunted by laying out a litany of crazy reports over the days, months and years. However, some of these reports were highly classified. They'd have to be manipulated. There was a better way.

The police commissioner took the corner of the desk and tossed a tied binder at Frank.

"The files are all yours."

The mayor stood, stretched, walked over to the window and came back. "I can only give you eight weeks. If I don't see this city cleared of all threats by then, I'll have no choice but to hire a new team." Frank had offered his newly and provisionally assembled team for free, thanks to inheritances, smart stock buys, and some money from his parents after he graduated from Notre Dame.

"I'll clean up our city in less than eight weeks, provided I'm given carte blanche."

The police commissioner spoke up. "That's a problem. We believe in you, but we have many qualified managers who have risen through the ranks, who dearly love this city, who have great talent."

The phones continued to ring.

"I'm just going to matrix with them," Frank said. "You set up your channels for me to use and I'll use them to disseminate commands. That way, the cream of NYPD will rise to the top when it's time for me to leave. I just want to help."

"We don't want you to leave, son," the mayor interjected.

What Rudy didn't say was that the city surely needed some plausible deniability when—not if—some rights under the constitution were temporarily diminished to save thousands if not millions of lives. The city needed ghosts and he had a building full of them. Not the kind Emily believed in. HOS, the name of his bank, stood for house of spies.

A day would soon arrive. The debate would soon be joined. Citizens would have to balance their right to live versus other temporarily diminished rights. Unfortunately, a choice would have to be made on their behalf. He and others would sacrifice their lives, if necessary, so that the people of New York could live on.

"I more than understand, your Honor, Commissioner."

The mayor spoke first. "We can't afford to have the public perceive us as a police state. So, we'll agree to your plan, if you'll take one of eleven candidates into your inner circle." The mayor twiddled a pencil until it left his hand and smacked into the window. Frank smiled and the commissioner nodded.

The commissioner appeared conflicted over the mayor's statement.

"Sir?" Frank prodded. *Provisions, always provisions.*

The mayor looked at the ceiling. "The president is already talking about how important it is to respect the Muslim community. We can't miss our chance to infiltrate and work with them. Now. Right now. Before it's too late."

"I agree, Sir." Sometimes rights are enhanced when they're diminished." This received knowing nods.

"The eleven candidates are known to be what the psychologists call peacemakers. Just look over the list, their interviews, if you like, but I think you'll find somebody on there you'll want to embrace," Rudy said, and then he and the police commissioner chuckled. The mayor picked up another pencil. Frank was tempted to duck.

"Sir, Detective Chastity O'Sullivan wouldn't be on this list, would she?"

The mayor and commissioner laughed, so Frank joined in. It was funny, they were setting him up as if they had nothing better to do. Yes, she was extremely qualified, as a peacemaker, but not as a warrior or spy.

"This is the first time I've done anything but cry," Rudy confessed. "Go make us proud."

"I'll need her promoted to lieutenant to give her more legitimacy with her fellow officers." This would pay her back, for her kindnesses. The city and the police could and should afford one tiny bump in their expenses for O'Sullivan, while Frank provided private entrepreneurship—money, blood, expertise, sweat—without regret. O'Sullivan's job was big and deserved the boost in rank.

"I'll let you know over the weekend," the police commissioner said, but his grin gave away a likely yes.

They discussed her possible roles, how she might be available to run the taskforce if he had to leave at the end of eight weeks. The Commissioner insisted they'd both be fired at the end of eight weeks if they didn't save civilization as they knew it. Likely trying to employ carrot and stick management. The carrot, defeating terrorism, was unrealistic, based on thousands of years of history alone. The stick being the firing. Frank and his team would stop the threats on the table today, and let the politicians and scientists decide the rest.

Frank became assertive. "I have an engineer on loan from the NSA. With your permissions, he'll be issuing you both better and completely secure phones, and maybe Bud can do something about your office."

The mayor flipped a pencil over his shoulder. "What, you don't like my spaghetti?"

The mayor and police commissioner stood, signaling the end of the meeting. Frank, very much enjoying himself, couldn't resist a Lieutenant Colombo close.

He stood, and half turning at the door, said, "One other thing…I'll need somebody untouchable, hardnosed, preferably Internal Affairs, to look for a mole in the NYPD."

The police commissioner protested but relented when the debate was won by referring to the art of war by Sun Tzu and other sages. The point, a harsh one, when planning a war one must know the enemy and weaken them from within if possible. Frank would soon have enough evidence to prove his allegation.

The meeting adjourned. Walking out, Frank and the police commissioner addressed some lingering details of a necessary recruiting speech Frank had planned and gotten permission for, on Monday. Some of the sensitive disclosures would be disseminated via the management team, on a need to know basis. And some of it would be purposefully leaked to the press, to get the right spin. They discussed an Ivan as known in spy trade—a mole, to police—in their midst again. A mole existed because wars were planned and the enemy were not idiots. This war started the day Osama bin Laden took his last rifle from the CIA.

With a moderator like O'Sullivan on the team—and with the proper spin—the public perception would remain supportive, in theory. *If she could handle the task.*

He sure hoped she could because Frank was now stoked by the idea.

* * *

Later that night, Frank relaxed in the penthouse suite in his Thompson Street corner building. To the south, Ground Zero smoldered, not willing to die out, serving as a purifying fire for the thousands dead.

He noticed one of Emily's suitcases. Emily was packing. Just as well. He had wished she'd be gone already. She'd no longer linger over the hopeless idea that he would fall in love with her. Right now and for the foreseeable future, all he could think of was to protect New York City. Manhattan was his demanding mistress.

He would not disappoint. The city swirled with the noises of people living, returning to normal as best they could, even though scarred for life. On Monday, a new normal would secretly take over the everyday lives of every living soul in New York. Unfortunately, there was no other way to keep the city safe.

With hot cocoa in hand, he locked the door to his office and relaxed into his posh executive leather chair with lumbar support and vibrator controls. His back felt good.

He sipped and opened O'Sullivan's file. It read in part:

Younger sister Faith. *Hah.*

Faith and Charity, if they had one more sister, she'd be Hope.

Mother and father, now Montgomery County/Philadelphia City Line.

If he understood this need-to-know report, Chastity was an infrequent devil, typically at bars, infrequently in dance halls—*a bad girl with a great heart*. She liked her kicks once in a while with no *be backs* to the same guy. Hum, worse than he was. His angel fluttered scarlet wings. Good, because he liked the color red. First in class, Saint Joseph's University, Philadelphia—Jesuit education. Great basketball school. Scored high with firearms, superb with martial arts. He'd squash her, maybe wrestle her into a figure-four head-lock. He'd avoid boxing. Scored highest NYPD on community service and negotiator traits. Undervalued by an overbearing sexist boss.

A picture of her sister fell to the floor. He picked it up, blew off any dust and absorbed the long-legged beauty. Possibly six-feet. Too tall for him, maybe. Well, maybe he'd meet her and see for himself. Didn't matter, Cha Cha was his ideal. Not only did she have out-of-this-world looks, perhaps too pretty for him to resist, she, like he, was dedicated to saving lives and quite good at it and a good nurse temp. She had such a sweet nature, which complemented his sour. He wanted to get to know her better to see if he was merely smitten or if it was something worse. For the first time in his life, he felt in free fall. Back to the file: sister lives in Chelsea, Macy's buyer, closest friend is sister.

Wavering, he wasn't sure if he really wanted a moderating influence on his team, but the mayor's political instincts were stronger than his. It couldn't do him harm to have a counterbalance.

Also, there was a chance she could become the target of the terrorist cell or cells remaining in New York City. What better way to protect her?

He worked on two speeches on his NSA laptop, until Emily knocked on the office door. He encrypted and secured his data and then opened the door. Emily stood naked before him. His flesh was weak and there were worse things he could do? He decided to comfort her and hoped she would soon leave.

He hated the idea of telling someone he cared about as a fellow human being, ex-coworker and sweet lover, to please leave. He didn't love her the way she desperately needed. He was a cad. Makeovers of his approach to women would have to wait, except for Chastity. She had him tied up with a pretty bow. All COMINT and other intercepts led to the conclusion a possible holocaust needed to be stopped. Emily would not slow him down in his quest to help make the City of New York safe.

Something nagged, grabbed his subconscious. That adorable frizzy-haired cop kept gnawing at his psyche.

Chapter 14

Monday morning, September 17, 2001, Police headquarters

Hundreds of officers in full dress uniforms assembled in the basement auditorium. The crowd buzzed with talk about funerals and the new direction the police force was going to take. Some apologized to Cha Cha for not being able to make her partner, Detective Jerome Price's funeral with her on Sunday. These protestations only saddened her. Jerry was so great the whole world should have known him. His loving wife and two young children were holding it together with the help of both sets of grandparents. *God bless them and may my partner be with grandpapa in heaven.*

This gathering, more of men than women all seemed to be struggling. The mood was turning to upbeat as they discussed helping the people of the City of New York. Cha Cha had put in her request for transfer contingent on being accepted by the taskforce. She could easily picture leaving her lieutenant behind.

She wasn't quite sure she'd be suitable fighting terrorist threats, but it beat being canned. Maybe she could get into her sister's business with Macy's if she didn't receive an invitation to help. She certainly did not look forward to returning to her lieutenant for as long as he kept her. No, not Macy's, she was a cop from the top hair on her head to her toes. She had an enlightened approach to offer and the track record to prove it, if she could present her full resume and not use the expurgated version on file.

Instead of engaging in more small talk with the detectives around her, she dove into her favorite daydream, the naked man in her shower. It dawned on her now. Johnny Lance, AKA Frank Lancia, rushed by the disaster and a chance to tag her with an electronic listening device, made up a last name similar to his real one. He lacked planning, at least on that day.

She should have handcuffed him before he went down to ground zero. He almost died. No, he had the freedom to be a foolish, ill-equipped first responder. He had admitted to being a spy looking for terrorists, one innocent cop at a time, but had botched his assignment when he got caught red handed. Thank God he wasn't running this show or all of New York City would flush down the toilet. Gurgle, swoosh.

She'd never see him again unless he wanted to ravish her. Never in a million years would she allow him. She had to start looking, maybe in a month or two, for her very own hunk, once her career choice solidified and she settled in. Somewhere out there her man waited to meet her. Someone to love and treasure only her, not legions of femme fatales. Someone to marry, make babies with, grow old together. Someone so in love with her, he'd go crazy without her, lay down his life for her. She wouldn't let him die. She'd save him, saving her. She was a damn good cop.

Being in the milling crowd of hopefuls was just what she needed. No sexist lieutenant was going to talk her out of her vision of a good cop. And today, she'd take her first step away from him.

No one she knew was privy to who was going to lead the taskforce or the direction they'd plot. She assumed a massive increase in NYPD force was coming to protect the city from terrorist threats. Maybe one of the precinct chiefs or inspectors would step up.

The mayor and the police commissioner entered the room and ascended the steps to the stage. The room quieted. Cell phones were turned to vibrate or off. A moment of silence was asked for to honor the heroes. Cha Cha, head bowed, prayed for the soul of her hero partner. Everybody was called to attention and got up from their folding chairs. A portly Bronx detective on her right must have been nervous. Slow to stand, his opened bag of potato chips slipped off his lap all over the linoleum floor; and then oblivious, he stomped on them while applauding the mayor's intro.

The mayor started the body of his speech. He relayed a message from the president and governor about how the entire world stood to lose thousands of years of civilized advances. He promised that Republicans and Democrats would close ranks around a common cause, something already happening.

"Now is the time to forge alliances with your supposed political enemies. Cement friendships one at a time. Your lives and those you serve will depend upon it."

Then the commissioner talked about duty and vengeance and balanced it with the need to help every citizen of New York, striking much the same themes as the mayor had.

"The president, three governors, the mayor and I are all in agreement as to whom will co-lead this taskforce, at least for the next couple of months. The job of helping the people of New York thwart terrorist attacks must be tied directly to performance. Everybody here today, every cop on the beat, everybody who is getting or will get this message will be the taskforce co-leaders' judge."

"We keep the peace. Others prepare for war. We decided we needed an edge, so we hired somebody from the National Clandestine Service. His co-leader, who will remain secret, is one of our own. That person will represent us, the keepers of the peace and our public trust."

Her stomach twisted like a New York pretzel.

"To best describe his resume, consider a cross between the NCS and Sherlock Holmes."

Oh no. Maybe Frank was investigating her for a job. This would explain her lieutenant's laughter while kicking her out of his office. Nah, that could be chalked up to every good detective's gift—paranoia. On the other hand...

"We needed a spy and we needed a detective. Please welcome from out of the cold, and I'm afraid into the hot—you may know him as the former wide receiver, Notre Dame, NCAA All-American. We know him for his unsurpassed service. Give a warm welcome to Frank Lancia."

Cha Cha remained in her seat as everybody else stood and cheered.

She sat—pickled and turning as red as a turnip. He had best not frisk her before a possible interview or he would learn just how good a New York City cop was with her body. She turned redder as she realized her own unintended double entendre. And maybe she had been pulling her own leg.

Then, at the encouragement of the potato chip crunching detective, she rose and clapped enthusiastically just like everybody else.

For God's sake.

Frank, on crutches, hobbled onto the stage with bandages covering part of his face, like a mummy undressing. He had to be hamming it up for the troops. All she did was Band-Aid him. She swore to herself. Had she messed up with the antiseptics? Her eyes bugged. Could she work for this man? Would he consider her over the hundreds assembled? How many would he choose? Who here would stop him from screwing up like he did with her?

He tapped the mike and motioned everybody down.

He got right to the point. "I got into a little scrape with some buildings."

The crowd rose again for the dead, all the innocents. Damn him, there he stood playing on their emotions. Spy, detective, actor, dangerous…very dangerous. She looked around for someone who might know what secret separated her from the crowd, if there were one. Running to the exit wouldn't be prudent.

He waved his arms and attempted to settle the crowd. "Good morning, good morning. I'm honored to be here among all of you today."

He spoke over the applause, "New York—the City of New York—is *at war*. We can no longer rely on the federal government alone to protect us." The crowd quieted. "We are too big, too proud, too great. We need to stand up and take control of our destiny for the sake of our citizens, the citizens of New York City. We will work with the federal and surrounding state governments, but it's our show. Who better to protect New Yorkers than their own and I live here and if necessary I will die here defending the city we love."

Again, everybody jumped out of their seats. The yelling and thunderous applause could have blown the roof off if it weren't for all the floors above them.

"If someone were to attack your family, you'd call for help, but you'd fight to save them. We'll start with simple things. Now's the time to form alliances. We need to make friends with anybody and everybody who can help. And right about now, most of them are inclined. They all hurt, whether they're some street gang, the mafia, hate groups, drug pushers. I want eyes everywhere and I want your hearts along for the ride."

He was on a roll. "We'll develop and integrate our electronic eyes, cameras, and other devices over the city. We'll upgrade our communications so that what happened to your phones last week will never happen again."

He spoke of more strategies before wrapping up to allow people to attend funerals. The potato chip smashing detective handed her an envelope and asked her to open it later in private. It had the mayor's seal on it. She quickly buried it in her hip pocket and nodded. What a twist. The slob played the spy courier. She most likely had a new position in her pocket. She thanked God and her grandpapa for looking out for her. If she could just scream with delight or run up on the stage, she would. Decorum. She could run up on the stage and grab him in a hug to steady him. Turnabout was fair play. She could take in his scent one more time. She'd know how he felt about her once she got close enough to peer into his gray eyes.

But there was a remote chance it was nothing or worse, a layoff notice. No, not from the mayor. She noticed Detective Percy Bainwater in the next row being served a similar envelope.

The commissioner spoke. "Some of you will shortly receive or already have received orders. For now, the rest of you will continue along through your command and control to help our city's defense. You'll hear from the taskforce through us. You are to treat every command from their team as top priority. All our lives depend upon you. Some of you will be transitioning to a full time position with the taskforce as numbers and replacements are decided by me and their group. The taskforce starts tomorrow, Tuesday, September 18th, 2001. Dismissed."

Could she work for Frank Lancia?
Without drooling?
Could she get any work done?
Open the damn papers, girl.

Chapter 15

HOS Import/Export Bank

The mayor's sealed note was handwritten, hcartfelt, congratulatory and signed by both he and the commissioner. They asked her to meet with Frank.

The building on the corner of Thompson and Spring had never caught her attention before, almost as though it had just appeared today. Cha Cha was supposed to have powers of observation. She must have walked by this place hundreds of times. Its black granite façade and smoky black windows weren't inviting and said blah, blah, boring, move along.

Her text message from Frank instructed her to dress undercover, to hide her weapons. Plainclothes. She didn't mind blending in, but she did love her uniform and the looks of admiration she received for protecting and serving. She had pulled out of the closet an all blue dress, rejected it as too form-fitting, too attractive to a certain male. So instead, she wiggled into blue jeans and a daisy on blue cotton blouse and stuck three weapons into a large purse. That, along with pepper spray, a Taser and a snub nose .38, ought to be more than enough for today. Besides, the likelihood she'd have to use them was extremely small, at least in the investigative phase.

She stopped before double glass doors. No matter how she pushed or pulled or what Irish or Highland jig she performed on possible electronic pads, the doors wouldn't open. Nobody threw quarters for her performance. Then they finally slid open on their own. *Well.* She noticed a camera above the entrance.

Inside the tall ceilinged marble building, a lone bank teller was covering another for lunchtime duty, since there were two teller windows. The only other person present, an armed security guard, followed Cha Cha's every move. He smiled.

She approached the pretty blond teller who dressed in pinstriped business slacks and a white, silk blouse with white roses. "I may have entered the wrong building," her nametag read Colleen Rourke, "Colleen."

"Detective O'Sullivan, I'd just guess?"

"That's me."

"Please follow the guard—Jacob." The teller swiveled back to her computer.

Jacob approached and remained silent until they entered the back room, which resembled a bank vault without the large spinner. "We have to register your voice, finger and eye print so you'll be able to come and go whenever you want. It won't take long."

Elated, Cha Cha realized the effort to digitize her for entry to this building was most likely a prima-facie job offer. She wasn't sure she'd take a job with Frank. She could manage and be part owner of an indoor mini-golf franchise like her father had suggested. But she knew that was just her father's way of saying he was worried about her. Besides, it didn't inspire her.

No matter how much of a player Frank was with the ladies, she loved police work, real work. She wasn't here to join a harem. Her family's DNA burrowed into every cell in her body. Her grandfather would be so proud that one of his granddaughters made detective. She'd give Frank's terrorism taskforce a go. She couldn't go back to her lieutenant, not that he'd want her. Or did he know this was coming down? He had smiled while dismissing her. A very rare event. He knew something.

Jacob finished a retinal scan. "You're already cleared to secret. Your polygraph and background checks have been given the express lane. Tomorrow some time you'll clear to top secret. The taskforce starts officially tomorrow, so relax tonight. Life as a spy and cop at war will be no piece of cake."

"Thank you, Jacob."

"When you get to know me better, call me Jake." Jake, maybe in his fifties, still had the gait and frame of a man in top shape, but the demeanor of a butler. His six-five, muscled body however would stop most scalawags.

They got into the elevator. "Mr. Lancia speaks highly of you, Detective." He lowered his voice and spared her a quick glance.

"Listen, we don't have much time. He'll never tell you this, but you should know, he owns this building and everybody living or working here is affiliated with him in some way."

"Thanks for the ropes."

"He's hired some Author Murray instructor to teach him how to dance." She taught dance at LATIN FROM MANHATTAN, part-time, generally on Wednesday nights when her NYPD job allowed. She could replace Frank's teacher and they'd both have more fun. *Nope, better not. I'm here to work, nothing more.*

"How much do I owe you for that piece of intelligence, Jake?"

"Just a smile once in a while." The elevator door opened. Jake, eyes to the ceiling, looked like he had just recalled an old joke. "The penthouse and Frank await. Enjoy yourself, Detective."

"Thanks, Jake. I didn't hear a thing." They winked. She stepped out onto cherry wood flooring which stretched across a long wide hallway to a northern view of the Empire State Building. Her pulse raced when she took in his GQ pose, flattering his physique, as Frank leaned on the top of a huge Turkish vase half way across the expansive room. He wasn't on crutches or all wrapped up in bandages anymore. He wore a duplicate of the same clothing he ruined on 9/11. *He must like gray.*

"So you didn't hear a thing?" he asked, with a cocked eyebrow and half smile.

Hum, he picked up the end of the elevator conversation.

"Jake and I shared secrets," she said demurely.

"There are no secrets in this building and he knows it." He turned toward the wall. "Screen on." Next to a knockoff of the Mona Lisa, a TV screen displayed her every movement and word. "You're going to tell me that's illegal, right?" he asked over his shoulder.

"It's your building, Frank. It's your show and it is not against code."

"Not exactly my show. In this little world, you have just entered; we try to speak our minds."

Out a bedroom door walked a lovely mixed race girl in a bathrobe.

"Hello. I'm Emily, Frank's girlfriend."

"I'm Cha Cha," she said, instead of Chastity. If she were a robin, her crest would have fallen. This pretty girl was all the explanation she needed. She should have known better than to think there was something between Frank and her. She'd keep her relationship with Frank strictly business, just as she really wanted and had decided, right? His "girlfriend", coming out of his bedroom in a robe no less. *Refer to harem, Cha Cha. Get real, Cha Cha.*

Still Frank, his jaw clenched, seemed irritated.

"Emily, the feds are going to take over the building, and they have no job for you. I'll have a ticket for you to New Orleans leaving tonight."

"You lying bastard. This is your place. You call the shots. You just don't love me."

And Frank had spoken about truth telling. This little skit belonged on a daytime soap.

"Yeah, and he doesn't love me either," Cha Cha added and immediately regretted her jealous-for-no-reason remark. *Why did I say that? Wash my mouth out.*

"Listen, sister. Don't make light of me. You don't know me."

"I'm sorry. I didn't mean…"

"He'll break your heart if you let him get close." She walked off and slammed the bedroom door. "I'm packing, chure." She screamed through the door.

"Chure means asshole in Creole or Cajun. Let's get out of here. I need your eyes and wisdom at a crime scene."

They took the elevator to a parking garage. A black van smaller than the other she had seen the week before, took up the parking spot right next to the door. It bleeped to Frank's key.

Frank opened the door and she peeked inside. This one sported all kinds of electronic surveillance gear in the back and a swivel computer between the driver and front passenger.

"Don't get in. We're going to walk," he said as he grabbed a knife and a Glock and put them in his cargo pants, which he explained were lined with straps to hold the weapons securely.

"How about a little truth." Cha Cha said. Part of a concrete wall moved, revealing stairs. They ascended one flight and entered a closed dress shop.

"Fair enough, but later. We have a funeral after we see this place and then drinks and dinner at O'Malley's, where I'll explain everything. Okay?"

A date. They walked a half block to a co-op. "You're pretty much insufferable."

"True. But, we don't officially start until tomorrow and I thought it would be nice to go out tonight and get away, for even a moment, from all this death and horror."

She now regretted her words. He seemed very comfortable with her. He had a warm, maybe too warm smile, alternating with his forehead kneading. She was apparently a problem he'd like to solve.

She did love O'Malley's. "We'll discuss the job, tonight. Okay?"

"That's my intention."

They took the elevator to the sixth floor of the co-op and entered into somebody's apartment. Frank used a key, but the door had been jimmied.

"First of all, do you mind me putting you on the spot, blind, for a little while?" Frank asked.

"I love the challenge."

His sharp gray eyes zeroed in on her. "What do you see?"

"The door was jimmied. Computers and disks have been taken." Feeling a bit flustered but trying not to show it, she opened the fridge and inspected the contents. "This yogurt was bought on September eleventh."

"Wait, how did you get that?"

"I shop at the same grocery. They get new yogurt every Tuesday, early. The use-by date advances every week, so he was alive on 9/11."

"What else do you see?" he pressed.

Her breath caught in her throat as she glanced over at him. Did he have *any* clue how attracted to him she was? "Could you, uh, give me a hint of what's going down here?"

"Hold on a little more," he said, a smile twitching at the corner of his lips. He too seemed attracted, but that could describe half the human race. She needed to get to know him better, before she could narrow his interest down from attracted to the opposite sex, to I'm crazy about you, Cha Cha.

"Okay, this guy's associated with the 9/11 hijackers in some way. That's obvious because that's your job."

"Our job."

Her heart jumped once again. She was needed and he allowed her the most unusual of job interviews. She walked into the bedroom, opened the closet doors and then inspected the bed.

"A suitcase is gone. The safe is empty. Picture frames are askew, clothes are missing, four pair of shoes gone, just impressions remain. Maybe the type of suitcase can be determined from receipts or fiber and wheel tracks. He's going to do a lot of walking." She got down on her hands and knees and reached for evidence gloves.

"This time the gloves won't be necessary," he said, before dropping down on the floor and sitting cross-legged next to her. "Since we are at war, stopping the next attack will trump building a case for the City Attorney."

"Okay, if we're in a rush… Here's some specks of gray dust, likely from the Towers, and I strongly recommend we analyze trace to help find this guy. This suspect returned from the Twin Towers on the same day."

"Excellent and point taken, partner." She was holding her own. It felt good, this give and take. Apparently she wasn't there because he thought she was cute or a replacement for Emily.

She walked over to the fire escape. "This has been opened and then closed recently, perhaps on 9/11. Nobody exited or entered by the window. Well maybe not. It did rain a lot on Friday. Yet no dirt, dust or sill grime was disturbed. I'm nearly certain the perps— or perp—considered leaving by the fire escape but then decided to exit by the front door. Which means we should talk to the people in this building, especially this floor. The owner or renter of this co-op probably had money in his picture frames." Spotting a book out of place—in an otherwise neat, meticulously dusted bookcase—meant the owner was distressed. She reached up to the top shelf for a hardback copy of Tom Clancy's Patriot Games and opened the book. "And hidden in this scooped-out book."

"Amazing. You managed to pick up and surmise a touch more than the FBI forensics team had. I could use a partner like you."

That's the second time he said partner. Could it be she would be the partner the mayor and commissioner had talked about? She over all others? Had Frank gone mad? Or did he let his penis do his thinking? She had never had a management job and was therefore uncertain she qualified to run the taskforce with him. Or maybe they'd be involved in lessor roles and the mayor had misdirected the crowd of candidates.

"Just tell me what's going on, Frank."

After waving his hand in surrender, he went into a long story about how Emily had followed Professor Mahmoud Ali Abunayyan into Tower 1. How she worked for Carlos, head of OTTS. Her only talent, as yet unproven, get this, was communing with ghosts. She escaped the building and spent the day in a hospital. That he and Emily had a practical agreement that had run its course and that he had been trying to let her go.

"So what do you surmise from all I've told you?"

"That you and Emily have nothing in common." They both suppressed a laugh, something of an acknowledgement of 'true like' passed between them. "That you both went through hell. We'll find the professor, if that's what you want me to do." He shivered and shook his head.

"Frank…are you okay?"

"Yes. I just wish what we are about to do were that easy." HShe gave a half smile, patted his chest and moved on to inspect a lampshade.

"I've been trying to gently persuade her to go home since I discovered she was alive last Tuesday."

"There's no gentle way to say it's over."

"She'll leave tonight."

She got in his face. "You couldn't refuse her needs, either."

"How the hell did you know that?"

"Bathrobes tell tales." She crinkled her nose.

"Of course. We did have a good relationship, but…"

"But?"

"She was not suited to spy or police work as I'm sure you are and will be. I need a woman who…"

This time she wouldn't prompt him, because he'd have to retreat from, "I need a woman like you." *I'll have way too much fun with this man. For a top spy he is too easy to read. Obviously and for some as yet unknown reason, he had let his guard down around her. Perhaps he was smitten too.*

Her spirits lifted once again. Frank appreciated her. Her lieutenant hated her. Nobody had been able to take her out of her funk over her partner's death and all those souls lost, until Frank. She had to thank him in some small way for rescuing her from a job with little prospect. For suggesting a working date tonight. Sure, tomorrow they'd be involved in a life and death struggle for the citizens of New York, now complicated by anthrax attacks. They would not fail. But tonight, she needed to cultivate a new relationship.

Thank you, Frank, for believing in me. I won't let you down.

"Seriously, what did you mean—asking me to be your partner?"

"Let me save it for dinner."

She lifted her chin and gave him a pointed look. "All right. It's your show, Frank."

"*Our* show," he teased once again.

Frank explained how the anthrax attacks were the FBI's baby, not theirs, and then he ticked off their immediate responsibilities. Basically, find any remnants of 9/11 conspirators, stop any terrorist plot they can uncover and improve NYPD's intelligence gathering capabilities.

They took a walk. *It's our show.* He repeatedly smiled, lingering on her face, catching her eye. She caught herself poking him like she had done to her deceased partner and immediately stopped it. She blocked his way to try to pump him for more information. *Tonight.* He picked her up and moved her to the side, and dusted off his hands. This easy familiarity must have sprung from a combination of his huge family and her huge loss. In any case, she needed a new friend and colleague, and from his body language and jocularity, a girl could get the wrong idea. The right idea—from *a tell* in the way he wrinkled his eyes when she did something funny—he wanted her romantically. Her imagination had to be running wild. *This girl had a right to dream.*

They arrived outside her co-op.

He bowed and said, "See you tonight," and walked off. She waited to see if he'd peek back. Guys did that to gals they liked. He did. Her heart skipped when he waved and then he sprinted across the street. Slowly, she walked inside, savoring the moment, absentmindedly looking at the street.

She had three hours to compose herself. Her mind went into overdrive about what partners meant as she absentmindedly laid out one dress after another.

They mixed like brother and sister. Not necessarily a good thing. They mixed like soul mates. Not necessarily a good thing, either. She believed that one earns a job through keen intuition and hard work, not friendship. Friendship and/or whatever else would come along for the ride, if it were meant to be.

Something had gone wacky within her around him. When she was twelve, a boy with Frank's mischievous smile had chased her everywhere, trying to steal a kiss. Once in a while, she let the boy catch her. Frank had to show integrity in his reasoning about being partners before he'd ever get so much as a peck. Was it too soon to confess her conflicts to Faith? At least she needed to tell her sister, she had new employment. No, not yet. Wait until she understood the terms of her employment.

Chapter 16

Flickering candles danced a ballet with the shimmering tones of Cha Cha's red-brown hair. Frank had asked and tipped the maître d for the table nestled in the back corner, well behind the piano. O'Malley's restaurant had garishly decorated with muted red and dark green wallpaper, pictures of leprechauns and fairy kings. Ms. O'Sullivan, although half Scot, claimed to love his choice of restaurant and seemed taken by his choice of meal. He enjoyed his spaghetti and meatballs, damn it. Most of the restaurants in Manhattan were eclectic to a degree and pragmatic if they wanted to make a buck. He couldn't stand an entire meal of potatoes and corn beef, although the savory scent of her lamb stew was wreaking havoc with his nose.

"Do you mind if I try a little of your stew?" Okay, he wanted to dive into it.

"Fine, as long as I can taste yours."

They spooned each other a taste. God she was easygoing, affectionate, not stuck on propriety. Not since one of his sisters, Rhana, had fed him escargot while his brother, Dejon, held him down, did he have such a revelation in taste. Though, he still wouldn't eat Brussels sprouts.

"You being my boss dooms us as a couple. You know that?" she said while ripping off a piece of bread.

She was right and read him too easily. If he were her supervisor, there'd be the appearance of sexual harassment. More importantly, how would he know if she really liked him or was just being diplomatic? Now was the time to let her in on his agreement with the mayor and commissioner.

"I'm glad you brought that up. The mayor and commissioner drove a devil's bargain with me." Her eyes widened. "I had to pick one detective from eleven to balance my lack of NYPD procedural knowledge." That was a bit of a stretch. He hadn't wanted to tell her he originally needed no help or that they considered her a peacemaker and she was there to keep him from embarrassing the city.

She guzzled Irish Stout, leaving a foamy moustache. He wanted to kiss the suds off her pouted lips. Her peekaboo dimple drove him mad. Everything about her from heart to toes made him ache with desire.

"I chose you to run this show with me. I suggested you be given a lieutenant's commission after your top-secret clearance comes in. They jumped at the idea." He sat back, watching her confused reaction. Then Cha Cha choked on her beer. He patted her bare back, lingering on the touch of her soft skin until she gave him that no-no, too-soon look. A half no and half wanton stare that rummaged his soul.

"They jumped at the idea?" she gasped. "Come on, Frank."

He shook his head. In truth, he had threatened to quit before he began, if they hadn't met his two tweaks to their counter-proposal. He won the argument. He also suggested, after his two-month trial period, they could consider letting him go and installing her as the head of the taskforce, because she'd be well trained. Of course, she'd have to prove herself and he hoped to secure an indefinite extension and stay partners with her, if she'd pan out.

His device with the mayor and commissioner was merely to agree to their terms, set up worse case scenarios and get them thinking he'd easily work with her. But today, she impressed. Beyond good, she had a flair for deductive and inductive reasoning, like a real life Sherlock Holmes. She was so good she probably saw right through him. He'd need to be as honest as possible with her, if he had any chance of deserving her love. If he really knew what he wanted. If. If, those damn ifs. His life was simple before Cha Cha, before 9/11.

Cha Cha dabbed at her mouth with a napkin, and then leaned forward. "I know I'm a peacemaker…"

How the hell? Had she been hiding in the mayor's closet?

"On top of your promotion, if I don't perform in eight weeks, I'll be out and you might take over. That is, if I groom you properly…" He pictured his comb's teeth breaking in her hair and suppressed a chuckle, "if I teach you enough of my world."

She remained cool, unfazed by her potential second promotion. Possibly the detective had considered some other scenarios.

"I look at your face and I see something unsaid. So listen carefully…" Cha Cha looked him straight in the eye "We don't have time to date, and we can't lose our focus." She said this with seeming resolve.

He twirled some spaghetti and again her hair came to mind. She was extremely perceptive, but now she seemed to relax and just take in the moment. Her neck and head arched back to the wall, with a languid, relaxed demeanor, she was more ready for his bed than work. A little contented smile slipped out, showing she'd likely accepted becoming his partner.

"Let's get the physical attraction problem out of the way," he said, trying to take the higher ground.

"That's the problem—I don't want to be your next Emily."

The attraction between them was so obvious he couldn't avoid answering her questions by making that lame suggestion. Because the truth was, Cha Cha misunderstood his intentions. So he sidestepped and explained in fuller detail that although Emily was beautiful, she was too undisciplined for the kind of government work they did. In short, he reinforced, she didn't have the mind of a cop or spy. They had been in lust and good friends, nothing more. Whenever Emily tried to help out, he felt like she was auditioning for the part of the bungling Inspector Clouseau.

She placed her hand over his. "Most girls would take you home. Right now. But it would just be lust. I don't want to second-guess our working together. It's wrong."

He flipped his hand around to hold hers and tightened. It felt so right. Something electric traveled up his body and stopped somewhere in his soul.

He had to agree though. He wasn't ready for a committed relationship, especially not eventual marriage, kids. Her looks devastated him—her heart also a ten. This left him wondering what he could say next. He wanted their relationship, if ever, to be as perfect as fate would allow. He realized his mind was breaking apart and heading in two opposite directions. *A new feeling, and not wanted, not yet.*

She couldn't be more alluring. Gone were the blue jeans or blue uniforms. In its place, a low cut emerald green dress matching her doe eyes, a simple string of pink pearls teasing the tops of her small breasts with her hair tousled about her shoulders. Something primal shouted *caress her.*

She went back to talking shop. He wanted to—well, he wanted her, period. Considering all the funerals and the seriousness of their job, he was ashamed of himself. For a half-second. Living is what people who were alive did. To honor his fallen brothers and sisters, he would live. If only he knew how. Tonight might be the last time they'd have to relax.

"When exactly will I get my clearance?" she asked.

"Tomorrow at 1 p.m. Then I'll introduce you around to some ghosts and spooks. So are you sold on being a dynamic duo?" His cell rang; he checked the number. "It's important."

She nodded and sipped more beer.

"Yes, Mr. Mayor." The mayor wanted to know if all was well and if he needed any more manpower.

"In fact, Sir, my new partner is here with me now. We're ironing things out…Yes, of course— Lieutenant Chastity O'Sullivan, Sir…" Glancing over at her, he covered the mouthpiece with his hand. "He wants to talk with you."

Now her eyes were bugging out, and he felt a smile tug at his lips. He just loved the shape of her almond eyes. Passing his cell phone over, he just gawked while she busied herself entertaining the mayor. She winked, unfazed, acknowledging Frank's admiration. The call ended.

"He said I needed to civilize you." She punctuated her words with pursed lips and then broke out into a huge smile, once again complete with adorable peekaboo dimple. She had to have been sold on the concept of them as partners, which worked for him, especially after her display of sleuthing talent earlier in the afternoon. As a bonus, her playfulness and heartfelt caring fit him well. He adored this woman, but she was right, they had a job to do.

Frank went for the official close. "So we're a team?"

"Well, I'm a Democrat, although Giuliani had cleaned up the city. He's a little rough around the edges for my taste." She cocked her head, feigning worry. But really, this was a test and he'd pass easily.

Her fears of political intrigue might be unfounded. The mayor seemed enthusiastic about her involvement but the commissioner had expressed reservations. In two months, there would be little reason for a changing of the guard. No, Giuliani had great working relationships with anybody he felt was capable, no matter their affiliation and he said so to Cha Cha. It was the commissioner who seemed to have a problem and it probably stemmed from him wanting someone else instead of the last minute Cha Cha, a fit the mayor and commissioner felt Frank would easily accept allowing them the opportunity to move on to other problems. Besides, politics could be played in both directions. There'd come a day when Frank would play his cards if necessary.

Frank prefaced his own political leanings by explaining in more detail this time how his liberal, adopt-from-all-over-the-world, parents influenced him. "I'm for the little guy. The poor, the weary, the people who died last week. But, I'm an independent."

"The French gave us the Statue of Liberty so they wouldn't have to take in the weary, tired, and poor," she said, obviously pleased with her French joke.

Their green skirted, red-topped waitress came up, so they both held in their laughter at her absurd thought. "Can I get you anything more? Cha Cha...?"

"Thanks for asking, Molly. Could I have another Murphy's?"

"I'd like to try some, too." Cha Cha leaned over with her mug and offered it to him.

"You should taste it first." He had been drinking a lager. He wasn't much of a drinker, but he could do one more, especially with dessert coming. He knew the taste of Guinness but not Murphy's stout. She held onto the mug, not so much to control his drinking but he guessed to show affection. The aroma and its bitter taste made him adventurous and it might balance the soon to be ordered dessert. The aroma of lotion from her hand enticed him to want to volunteer a massage.

Cha Cha held up two fingers to the waitress. He pictured the two of them, not the waitress, drinking each other under the table and rolling around in an outright brawl, which turned into ripping off clothes. And then…

He had to show her respect and take this slowly, if he wanted in on her delights. Cha Cha had been crying for a week now, so she admitted. He had his misery mixed with anger bouts, but tonight was about a guy and a gal and a job. They both needed to live and live fully.

The flickering light dancing on her wavy hair brought to mind one subject he wanted to talk about. Her tresses had intrigued him ever since she stepped into the shower to help heal him. He couldn't bring up the subject. She might think him more effeminate that manly.

If he said there was nothing wrong with her wearing her hair au natural in his opinion, she'd think him presumptive with a hidden desire to become a hairdresser. *Is that possible?* Well whether her hair was brushed out or treated with whatever she did to it, it framed her incredible face. He wasn't effeminate. From his parents' effort to raise renaissance boys and girls to his many experiences in Europe, he had gained a fine perspective for art in any form. This girl before him was a true masterpiece.

"So what are we doing about Mahmoud?"

"We're going to find him," Frank said.

"We had better disseminate this."

"We will soon," he replied. "You'll understand the problem better tomorrow when you have your clearance."

He couldn't trust the NYPD command structure just yet. What he had done was just preliminary legwork. He had asked every detective in the five Burroughs to reconsider any arrest or report that didn't quite add up since 9/11 and send it through their command and control.

"Prior to you jumping on board, I had asked all involved in the accounting for the victims to report anything strange or unresolved to the taskforce. You and I will find Mahmoud."

She agreed, although she now seemed a little drunk. On beer? Nonetheless, they ably discussed Mahmoud's likely M.O.

He interrupted a dicing of Mahmoud's motivations, since they could only go so far without her Top Secret clearance. "I'd like to change the subject to something more personal since we'll start our work in earnest tomorrow. This has been bugging me. What do you do to straighten out your wavy hair?" She twisted her lips into a smile. *Damn, she must find me strange.*

"I use what they call *product*—as well as a flat iron from time to time when I want a different look."

He put on his dumb face, which suited him. He'd kick himself later. "I liked what I saw in the shower. I like what I see tonight. I like you."

"Do you like my body or hair or what, Frank?"

"All of you, every kissable inch of you and your great heart." He avoided saying her great ass.

"You amaze me, Frank. I've never met a man so comfortable in his masculinity that he'd admit his likes and dislikes. A man without an eye for beauty, in my opinion, wouldn't treasure what they have. You make me feel wonderful."

She had said so much. Wow, all of it hit home. She made him comfortable too. They had both let their hair, tsk tsk, down.

"A man would have to be blind."

She grabbed his bicep and gaped at him with a heated gaze. The stout was getting to her, because she had lost her balance for a moment. Thankfully, he righted her, again with a touch that could have burnt his fingers. The poor girl was caught with too much beer and her panties in a twist. He could easily seduce her, but for the first time in his life, something not quite understandable was preventing him. *Maybe this is what a crush is like.*

"In short, any man, who'd like my Doctor Frankenstein or Einstein look, is a man after my heart." She self-consciously ran her fingers through her hair.

He bent over and stole a quick kiss. Quick, it was not. She melted into his lips, but he didn't want to take advantage of her while she was tipsy. He'd take advantage of her some other time. He broke away from her lingering needy lips with his stinging with desire. He laughed inwardly about his silly joke. Her sweet lips were like heaven. Even drunk, her passion for him was so intoxicating. He had never been kissed so sweetly, so sensually in his life.

"I'm sorry, Chastity."

"No. Please don't, Frank," she said.

A doe-in-the-headlights expression appeared on her lovely face. She looked like she'd run to the ladies room if he tried to kiss her again. He had better get her back to her place and God help him—not touch her. Why, he couldn't quite figure out at the moment. Although the kiss was dessert enough. For a lifetime. They needed to sober up. She from beer; he from her. They ordered Barmbrack, which looked like tiny bits of various fruits in cinnamon bread.

"Give me your hand." He did and she let him feel the silky but thick texture of her hair. She cupped her face into his hand and trained her deep emerald eyes onto his. He gulped. She was asking him an intimate question. Would you be mine?

Someday. Maybe someday, if he could round up his demons and figure out why he felt so alien. He understood spy craft to be his primary demon, but what else? He understood he was now for the first time in his life an alien. He loved the planet he had landed on, and knew he had turned a corner away from spying out in the cold to exploring a hot and strange new world.

Chapter 17

Cha Cha positioned her dress, which had been tucked under the pillow, over her head to steal a little more sleep and dull the ache. Instead of pure sleep, she tried to remember what had happened the night before. The last thing she recalled was running her rear end across the piano keys at O'Malley's restaurant. Before that, she had sauntered about like Salome while Santana's Black Magic Woman played on the jukebox in her head.

Now the only music left, bagpipes from endless funerals, vied with the throb. Only sleep would heal. She lay still and thanked God Frank took her away from all the horror with a sweet date last night. And what did she do? She fell down drunk. Great start girl.

She wasn't much of a drinker. She should have never, ever signaled the barmaid to drop two shots of Jameson's in her stouts. Irish whiskey was reserved for dates she hadn't wanted to be on, and one shot at that, and one stout at that. The shots were reserved for loser dates. Not that they weren't decent men, just losers in a battle for her heart. Frank was no loser, just sweet, but with a devil in his eye. She couldn't cope. All he really wanted was hot, heart-thumping sex. Somebody to replace Emily, no matter what he had said.

Why wasn't her dress folded and in the closet? *Frank.* He must have stripped her. She combed her hand up from her panties. No bra, no nightgown. *Oh, the backless gown.* He peeked at her peaks. Well, that made them even. She loved the looks of her perky ones and hoped he appreciated them, because she sure liked what she had seen of him.

I can't sleep. She shook off her fog and sat up with the dress crumpled around her head.

"Are you okay?" A female voice startled her. She groped for her gun, but, of course, it had taken a walk. The tentative sounding voice was Emily's—Frank's about to be ex-girlfriend. That girl was supposed to have left last night for New Orleans.

Clutching the thick blanket, Cha Cha removed the dress from her head. He must have taken her to his cave.

Some cave. Fine dark walnut furniture, a king sized bed, with a head-aching white, thick quilt and matching pincushion backboard, two bed tables with white driftwood bases, a separate ivory and ebony chess table with South African Zulu warriors cut out of a black and white wood. Emily sat cross-legged on the bed, looking confused and sad.

"Emily is it?"

The other woman squirmed and said with an air of insincerity, "I'm sorry I went off on you yesterday."

"It's Cha Cha. Call me Cha Cha," she said, with a touch of contempt. "I started it. I didn't mean it…I'm not the jealous type." Yesterday she had said to Emily, '*Yeah and he doesn't love me, either.*' This touched off a firestorm of emotion. Funny thing, she foggily remembered, Mr. God's Gift To Women might have kissed her. She had a job to do and passion for doing it right. That other kind of passion would have to wait. She'd love to know what had happened last night.

"I know your name, detective. Want coffee?"

The clock read 9:57 a.m. Time to catch some scalawags. "I need to get home," she said, while slipping on her dress.

"Don't worry. He placed you in the bed and asked me to undress you. He got some of your clothes from your place." Emily pointed at Cha Cha's blue-plaid suitcase, which rested next to the chest of drawers near the bathroom on a white ottoman. The aroma of French roast coffee with a hint of chicory slapped the drunk right out of her.

"The coffee is from Caffe Du Monde on Decatur Street, New Orleans." Emily handed her a cup. "Cream, sugar?"

"This is fine." Cha Cha sipped the fragrant brew. "Um, so goood."

Emily stared. Her big round eyes and lustrous mixed brown/tan skin reminded her of Autumn. Autumn had some Polynesian blood, which gave her a more exotic look.

Why wouldn't Frank want this sexy, exotic woman?

Oh yeah, Emily wasn't cut out for police work, would never get a clearance from the terrorism taskforce, etc., etc. *How'd I know this?* Vague memories from her date with Frank began emerging.

Be it resolved, Frank's ex needed to fly home. Pronto. Cha Cha decided to help her out the door for the good of the taskforce, by outright lying.

"Do you miss New Orleans, your family?"

"Yes, but I love Frank."

"This is embarrassing, Emily," she said, putting on her best poker face. "You were right. I am his new girlfriend. Or maybe he just says that to all the ladies…"

"Frank, oh Frank *darling*. Get your ass in here." Emily shouted at the wall. "He's got the whole damn place wired."

Frank didn't show his handsome face. Meanwhile, Cha Cha took the time to shower, shampoo, comb out her hair, and dress in maroon slacks with matching vest and a white business shirt with cufflinks.

Emily was nearly packed by the time Cha Cha exited the bathroom. She threw some bloomers from Bloomingdales into the suitcase and slammed the lid.

"He's hiding somewhere. He's not man enough to face me. How could he be screwing you behind my back? Excuse my French." Now that was not an inviting picture. Emily traversed the room as if she were looking for something to throw.

"You've been looking for me?" Frank asked, peeking in the door. Emily hurled a black chess queen at him. The door closed, the piece thumped the door and broke in two. Good aim.

He stuck his head in again. "That's an expensive set." This time a bishop flew at him like a dagger. He caught it and chased Emily down. Tackled her, threw her on the bed and pinned her arms with his midriff between her flailing legs, a good defensive posture to protect the family jewels.

"Maybe I should leave. This is getting weird," Cha Cha said, exasperated.

"It's not weird. I don't want my rare and *expensive* Monkey Thorn Tree set from South Africa *destroyed*."

"Get off me, you…you…capitalist." Emily spat out but he only laughed.

"Only if you calm down— Cha Cha, please stay." She was inching to the door.

"You've been screwing her, haven't you?" She pointed at Cha Cha as if there were somebody else in the room to take the blame.

"It's not true. Cha Cha and I—"

Cha Cha interrupted. "The truth, darling. Let me tell her. We haven't made love yet, Emily, because of you, but we love each other. So he *said*."

"Fine, you can have the rest of him, as soon as I get the hell out of here." She focused on Frank with anger in her eyes. "Pochaut."

"I'm sorry," he said.

"You never believed I could talk with ghosts. Well, I'm going to leave both of you the ghosts of 9/11 to torment you with questions, after endless questions, including the hijackers." Cha Cha couldn't help but turn her head to hide a smile. *Bring it on.*

Two guards escorted Emily from the penthouse with instructions to see her safely aboard a plane to New Orleans from Kennedy Airport, and this time they were told to watch the plane leave.

Frank was fiddling with the broken chess piece, trying it like a jigsaw—and then resigned, he set it down. He approached her, put his hands on her collapsing shoulders, tipped up her face and in a husky voice, asked, "Do you really love me?"

Off kilter by his intense gaze, she planted a hand on his chest and pushed him away. "If you love me respect me as a colleague. We're a team, remember?"

"Yes, but what of your feelings?"

Was this an admission that he loved her? How could that be? He only knew her for a short time. "Feelings, the terrorists stole my feelings. There's nothing between us but lust, Frank." She wondered how much longer she could use that obviously poor excuse.

"I feel so much more than lust."

"Shut up, Frank. I got you out of a jam with her. That's all it was. This is the last time I'll be in your bed."

"If you say so," he said with an infuriating smirk.

"What's Pochaut mean?"

"Cajun for pussy."

She smirked. *Right back at ya.*

"Well, Mr. Pochaut man, we have work to do. I want to keep my job and you should want me to keep it too."

"The entire NYPD, all five boroughs, is reporting suspicious activity, anything that doesn't make sense, anything out of the ordinary, and two-hundred full time detectives are dedicated to the new taskforce and tracking down those leads and what our team generates for them," Frank said. He could go no further, he explained again, until she got her top-secret clearance, hopefully by 1 p.m.

"So besides coming up with good ideas, what are we doing? Why me?"

He led her out onto his penthouse deck with a full view of the perpetually noisy city. Most of the smoke had cleared from WTC, leaving the skyline with two front teeth missing. With scattered clouds, and their confused hearts, much remained uncertain. She took off a nautical windbreaker that Frank had packed for her. The air was temperate and crisp, the wind slight. One of Frank's staff, nowhere to be seen, had set two plates of deboned flounder with garnishes and some grape juice, both under protective glass domes. They settled down and dug in.

"To keep our jobs, we'll take the big risks. We're going to crack, ah… Later, I'll show you what I think we're up against." He elaborated on what he had mentioned last night. The mayor and the police commissioner had struck a bargain with Frank. They promoted Cha Cha to lieutenant and co-leader of the taskforce as a balance. In this way, the NYPD's approach was fairly represented with their most able peacemaker: to stop a religious war, to make friends with sworn enemies, and so on, the story went. Eight weeks with no positive results and they could look forward to collecting unemployment, not that Frank would need it.

"What about the professor?" She asked about the Saudi-born, naturalized U.S. citizen, a person of interest in the collapse of the World Trade Towers.

"He's one of many leads. But my intuition tells me, he's our key to stopping any imminent threats to our city."

She'd help find the professor.

What of the key to his heart? He seemed for some reason either hell-bent on saving the planet as-we-know-it or just emotionally unavailable at the moment, maybe for the same reason. She'd get to the bottom of his psyche, no matter the mess she'd find, she was willing to help the man grow. Did she actually want him? Yes, in a very primitive and mortifying way.

Just the merest look from him sent excitement pulsing through her veins, and she wanted nothing more than to have him in her bed. To feel his hands caressing her skin, his body crushing against hers. He was too used to having what he desired. She'd not be fileted, garnished and served to him. *Teach a man to fish and he'll eat for a lifetime.*

"I know you answered this before but humor me. Why didn't you love Emily?"

He leaned forward across the cocktail table and held her gaze. "She seduced me and we just couldn't stop." His crooked grin, like that of a boy who just ate all the Easter candy, the day before Easter, was infectious. She couldn't expect him to join bachelors anonymous on day one. At least his temptation was gone, but what of the next woman to catch his eye?

Maybe she'd pretend there was nothing contagious between them. She'd treat him like a brother, for as long as possible. No. No. No. She would have liked brothers, but this man would never be a brother, not if she could help it. Still, she'd have to bait the hook properly to reel in this shark.

Chapter 18

Back on Thursday, September 14, 1:33 p.m., Brooklyn

Detective Sam Langrath took a long lunch. He read the damning email for the twentieth time. There was no other way to interpret it. Osama wasn't going to contact him anymore because the man was on the run and disappointed.

It read:

Thanks so much for the $3,000 but you promised me $30,000. So, until you come up with the rest, don't bother me. For now on, you are on your own, we're busy here. Or, you could come home and join the party. We could always use a helping hand. Basically, I don't care. You owe me one way or the other. I'm not writing any more. You disappointed me. It's on you, bro.
Jose Pasqual.

Osama (AKA Jose) was so bloodthirsty. Three thousand people died last week and he wanted more. He wanted the original estimate. If Sam ran and joined the jihad, he wouldn't live long. If he stayed and tried to deliver 27,000 more deaths, he might be found out. If he eliminated his coconspirators, he'd be investigated. If he interviewed Detective Chastity's snitch he might find out why the number was lower or how the snitch knew of his plans. But who the hell was this person? Perhaps he should interview Chastity. Perhaps he should just run.

Or perhaps, he should clean out the cell, a bunch of bungling fools anyway.

He enjoyed his job as a cop. He liked the money he made, the respect he got. If he wanted to continue this sham, he'd have to go straight, but somehow he would have to cover his tracks, because the new taskforce would eventually check him out. He was alone now, just one man against the world, including his friends in arms in Afghanistan. The taskforce would discover the day, ten years ago, when he killed and assumed the identity of the real Sam Langrath. The day he forever buried his real name, Ali Ali.

Or, wouldn't it be fantastic if there were a way of killing 27,000 people all at once? The world would never forget that. Though, to pull it off, he'd likely go out with a bang, a really big bang. Maybe the Empire State Building. He'd have to talk with the Professor, if he were still alive, for that one. Ah, so many different ways to go. Positively orgasmic. For the rest of the day, on behalf of the new taskforce, he'd interview Muslims and Jews and see if he could help them get along. To hell.

* * *

Back to the present

Autumn added finishing touches to a paper for European History and was about to head out for the short walk to NYU when someone knocked at the door.

She ran over to her plush Old English Sheepdog, Julius Caesar, and flopped down his ears again; they had been flopped up over his forehead so he could hear better, when she ranted. She had always suspected he didn't listen, anyway. Like a superhero, she rematerialized before the door. Okay, she was quick.

"Who is it?" People just don't knock on co-op doors in New York. The only time a stranger knocked in all the years was last week, on that horrible day. Carlos, Director of OTTS and Ayita Starblanket, Chief engineer of the NSA, had come calling. They promised no one would know of that meeting. Actually, they just wanted her to shut up, to keep secrets. But how could she stop them from telling their trusted associates, which could lead to a leak?

"Child Protective Services. Is this Autumn Breeze I am speaking to?" A kindly woman's voice piped up in melodic tones.

Autumn peeked out the peephole. A somewhat plump woman with quaffed hair, not too tall, stood on the other side of the door. "Yes, it is. Please hold up your credentials." The creds looked legit. "What are you here for?"

"We had a report your mother abandoned you."

"That's not true. She took a short trip and will be back tonight. Besides, I'm a University student and emancipated and have the papers to prove it." She didn't have any papers which is *so why* she didn't want to see this woman.

"Would you please let me in?"

"I'm sorry. If you care to come back tonight—I think maybe she'll be home around 6:45 p.m.—I'd feel more comfortable if my mom was here with me."

"If you insist. Just tell me you are not harmed."

"Well, aside for crying over 9/11, I'm fine. I'm tops in my class. I eat good nutritious food, aside from an occasional Nathans foot long, at Yankee Stadium, and—I love my mom." She almost said my mom loves me, but no sense in lying. Saying those words would screw-up her voice and alert the social worker outside her door that poor, skinny Autumn needed a mother's love…and how about a father's, and maybe Joey's?

"Thank you, Autumn. I'm going to stick my card on your door. Just have your mom call me. That will be enough for now."

"Thanks. Bye." She'd wait a good long time before going out in the hallway to take the lady's card. Maybe they'd throw a net over her and put her with reject bananas, back to Trinidad—no mom, no pop, *on a banana boat.*

I don't want to go home, yeah man. Tarantulas replacing her plush dog.

She flipped up Julius's ears.

"This is all your fault. You promised me you'd turn into a real dog. Make my mom love me again. Bring my daddy back." She listened to him. "Shush, I'll talk to you later. I've got to call mister hunky boy."

She caught Joey on his cell. Apparently, he was in Washington park munching on something, like usual, because she could hear dogs bark, because he liked it there.

"Joey, guess what? My mom is coming home tonight. I know you were worried about me."

"Great news, Autumn." Thank God, he stopped calling her kid.

"Something weird happened."

"What?"

"Child Protective Services just paid me a visit. I'm wondering if you think your parents called them."

"They're not the type. Mom does run the PTA and maybe she chatted. I told them you were fine, emancipated and emaciated—just joking—running your household, but that you didn't like being alone. I also told them, like you asked me, that you wanted the information about your mom in rehab kept quiet. So I dunno. Sorry."

"No, Joey, it's okay. Just ask them to satisfy my curiosity, if they said anything. And to again stress not to. Let them know my mom came home, alive and well tonight."

"You got it, kid."

"Autumn, call me Autumn."

"Sorry, Autumn." He sighed. "It's just that I always wanted a baby sister."

"Someday, Joey, when my boobs pop out and I'm eighteen, you'll want to chase me all the way to Saint Patrick's Cathedral."

"How fast can you run, kid?"

Her heart fluttered and even him saying kid worked here. Classic movies for four hundred, Humphrey Bogart, 1942, Casablanca, Ingrid Bergman. "You're sweet. Thanks for staying over last week."

"No problem. It was…fun."

"For me, too." She bit her lip. "Listen Friday for a physics lesson, right?"

"For sure. Autumn. Just know, God is looking out for you."

"And I'll need your help too."

"You got it."

They said their goodbyes. If it wasn't Joey's parents and she could rule out the Feds, the probability of her two Fed friends snitching was so close to nil, she shouldn't waste her time calculating what to do. She listed the suspects in order of probability.

Her mom's two ex-employees (49%). Numero uno.

Joey's parents (48%).

The Feds (3%).

Cha Cha (near zero).

And, of course, the Unlikely Unknown at less than $1/10^{th}$ of 1 percent probability.

She'd be late for class, but in case the City worker was lingering outside a little while, she'd have to break her rule of never ever being late for class. She jumped on the internet and checked her mom's messages.

Whoops. Twenty-three messages from her mom's ex-employees, Urma and Jannine. She'd read them later. Obviously, Joey and she had made a mistake in firing them, at least in the way they did it, because these people hardly ever wrote more than one message a day. Double oops, with a back flip. It wasn't Joey's fault; she was the precise one. He was just doing what she asked. She couldn't remember ever making a mistake in her life. Maybe as you get older you get stupider. LOL.

She'd not be late for class if she left now. She opened the door, looked both ways, grabbed the lady's card and ran down the hallway. Out on the street she blew by the lady, who looked like she wanted to ask a question, of course. Autumn turned her head, gave the biggest smile and ran like hell.

* * *

Cha Cha and Frank enjoyed a flute of Champagne while lunching out on his penthouse deck. The wind was slight, the deck warm, the sky as bright as his smile. Today they matched—he chose gray cargo pants and shirt, again. She wore gray chinos with the accent on her calves. Just for him.

"Your top secret clearance is provisional," Frank said.

She dipped a lobster tail. "How's that?"

"No big deal. After our lunch, you'll see a psychiatrist. It's normal for anybody who gets this kind of clearance."

"So what have you planned for me?" She studied his eyes for body language tells, and they told her a lot. Literally, in a twinkling, she could ascertain he wanted her in the sack for all sorts of nasty undercover work. If she were he, the read of his eyes would be more like, he wanted to profess his love and then make glorious love to her forever more.

"I'm going to show you my building. We'll see what our team has discovered and take it from there." He reached across the table with his flute. "To the start of a beautiful, ah, partnership."

"To your health." Cha Cha tapped his glass. "Have you had your lungs checked out?"

Frank nodded and then described his visits to Sloan Kettering and their cancer specialists. His lungs appeared free of 9/11 debris. His blood tested negative for irritants. A young healthy body, he told her. Yeah, a young healthy and gorgeous body, but she wanted his soul as well. *Muahaha.* Package deal or no deal at all.

Cha Cha got up to stretch her legs after finishing. He however had slowed seemingly intrigued by a vein on his lobster. So he safely munched on his side of spaghetti and meatball. She strolled over to the ledge of the building facing south. *Funny man.*

Her eyes traveled down Thompson, crossing street after street until the avenues and streets blurred in a haze. Still straight ahead were pyres of smoke, little wisps from this distance. The fire that burned in her heart for the dead would never be extinguished.

Frank raised his voice, "We cleared your girlfriend, Autumn Breeze. Well, my ex-partner who you'll meet and the chief engineer of the NSA, the famous Ayita Starblanket, who you won't meet—at least not today—cleared her. They paid her a cordial visit last week while I lay naked and knocked out on your bed."

"Your tush should be in a museum somewhere, maybe next to the statue of David." She shouted back to him to overcome the insistent din of a city never at rest, while peering over her shoulder at him still toying with his lobster. *Eat it.*

"I think you'll find I'm not a hard ass." Actually, his ass was harder than David's…and she loved him for trying to keep up with her brand of humor.

She sauntered back to him. The spaghetti and meatball were gone. He moved on from the half-eaten lobster to boyishly spitting out cherry pits one after another. She pulled her chair up to him. "Autumn hadn't said a word to me about the government visiting her. I'm seeing her tonight." She wanted to let go and share her plans because she was beginning to trust him, especially when it came to their work. "I'll be staying over. Her mom's in rehab."

Frank didn't seem surprised. "Tell her an FBI liaison to the NYPD told you she was cleared and wanted you to thank her for her cooperation. Encourage her to tell you anything else related to terrorism that's bothering her." They went on to discuss how the prodigy had figured out the day, method, and consequence of the attack on the World Trade Center.

Cha Cha and Frank rode the elevator down to the second floor and joined the psychiatrist in a cozy office with light purple walls, wainscoting and molding in gloss white, and the strangest Victorian chandelier with candles, right over the desk. Two of the walls had the requisite bookshelves full of fat hardbacks with mostly brown spines. Had to be a set-up for atmosphere because the doctor wore a visitor's badge and the books were too neatly aligned. Cha Cha tried to get comfortable in one of the posh thick chairs. She had refused to sit with Frank in the loveseat directly across from the doctor. How could he not know that the closer she got to him, the crazier she became? Not good in front of a head-shrinker.

One little detail held up her top-secret clearance from being completely signed off. The doc was sniffing around the circumstances of that horrible day when she, seven-year-old Chastity, witnessed her grandpapa's murder.

"There's something that doesn't jive here," Doctor Myron Markowitz said.

"The closet slats were too small for anybody to positively ID the killer, and yet you did," Frank chimed in.

The doctor gave him a censuring look. "I'll handle this, Frank, if you don't mind."

"Go for it, doc." It was unusual to have somebody else in the room besides doctor and patient; it fractured a number of statutes, stemming from doctor patient privilege. However, Frank had convinced her that spy teams were handled this way because they'd have to understand each other to survive. And his words certainly held a kernel of truth. Her mom and dad attended her psych sessions after Grandpapa's murder. They loved her. Her ex-partner, well, she loved him in a sisterly way. This closeness would be the same for Frank and her. She'd try to embrace their strange union and hope it all worked out. Still, she would not talk about her fantasies, unless Frank left the room.

"Why is this important? My grandfather's killer is behind bars. He confessed. End of story."

"There's something you're reluctant to talk about, or perhaps you have suppressed it into your subconscious."

"There's nothing."

Dr. Markowitz leaned back in his chair, studying her closely. "I want you to relax."

The conversation went on for nearly thirty minutes, with Frank chiming in and offering his support from time to time, despite the doctor's objections. The two men were relentless. She no less so, extracting a promise from Frank. Since they were partners, he promised she'd get the same opportunity to go over his file or sit in when Doctor Myron had the time. Good, because something held Frank back from making anything but work commitments. After his walls crumbled, she'd be there to understand him better. Maybe they'd have a chance.

The doctor's somnambulistic tones—*he has to be practicing a form of hypnosis*—were interrupted by a direct question.

"Have you ever been choked?" the doctor asked.

Memories came flooding back. He was nailing her to a cross, deducing what had happened on that horrible day.

"Stop it," she answered shakily.

"You couldn't fight back."

"I can see him, doc."

"He was too strong," the doctor continued, drawing her into a little girl's world until she spoke from a place of dolls and simple times and then about the one horrible moment that changed her life. The child within her spoke.

"The killer opened the closet door on me. I couldn't run by him. He'd catch me. Grandpapa's blood was everywhere. It was splattered on the killer's face. That ugly angry face. His hand came at me… pinned my neck against skis leaning against the back of the closet. My elbow hit one. It slid down with a thunk."

"But that's not all… is it, Chastity?"

"You're almost there, honey," Frank said softly. Tears rolled down her face as she implored him with her eyes to love her, someday. Someday soon.

Vividly, she could see everything that had happened long ago. Years of painting over the ugly peeled away. The girl and the woman answered together, now.

"He started to squeeze my neck. I can't scream, just gurgle. I'm doing what my grandpapa told me. Forgive him with my eyes, because he is one of God's children. He's crying. His tears are

143

mixing with my Grandpapa's blood. He's letting me go. He let go—he's running away. I'm calling 911." Cha Cha buried her head in her hands. "Why did you do this to me?" Frank put his arms around her; it felt so right.

Then it dawned on her what the two men wanted. Would she—if confronted by a murderer—be able to protect herself or Frank? They convinced her that she had shown courage and there was nothing to be ashamed of. On that horrible day, she had used a very sophisticated tool for a little girl. That is, she used a lesson her grandpapa had taught her to save her life. Her grandpapa had raised her to be a cop. But could she now, because of this catharsis, fire her thirty-eight if need be? She had top scores at the range. But that wasn't the problem. Apparently, she had had doubts of her abilities as a cop. She'd overcompensated by becoming the peacemaker, not that that part of her should disappear. All this because she couldn't protect her grandfather on that terrible night.

"I'm satisfied, Doc. Cha Cha will reward me as a partner and the City of New York will be safe," Frank said.

She would never compromise the lives of the people of New York or her fellow agents and especially not this man. She helped save his life once already. There was no way this man would die, if she had anything to say about it. She wasn't just a peacemaker; she could use verbal skills or any other weapon to stop evil.

She received her Top Secret Clearance without reservation and was ready for the cook's tour of the people who inhabited Frank Lancia's Building, HOS Import/Export.

HOS, house of spies. Duh, why hadn't she figured that one out? Autumn would have no problem with this puzzle. Cha Cha smiled despite herself.

First, he wanted her outside. A breath of fresh air filled her lungs as she and Frank took a short stroll around the block on a temperate day of sunny skies.

He stepped over a missing brick in the sidewalk. "We're basically directors for eight weeks."

"I've never had a managerial position."

"Your file suggests you're a natural. Anyway, I have an administrator to help both of us."

She started to say something but he put his finger on her lip, reminding her of Tom Hanks doing the same to Meg Ryan in *You've Got Mail*. "We're going to have to spend time strategizing. Say over dinner."

She grabbed his lapels. "Maybe after we're fired, we can run away to Jamaica."

"Tahiti wouldn't be far enough." He cupped his hand around the skinny tree where they first met and swung around to face her. They looked up at little Billy's window. Sneeze, the cat, flicked his tail against the window.

She couldn't tell when Frank was serious, humorous or devilish. So little time, so much man. All she knew was she loved his compassion, his wit, his incredible good looks. One thing was a constant *for sure*, he wanted to take her. She caught his eye to confirm. The man showed strength and relentless drive maybe for her, maybe for the city, hopefully both.

"I can't rest until we've stopped all the threats to our city," Frank said.

"You know they gave us an impossible task." They discussed the eternal battle against terrorism. How the human spirit has been afflicted with it for thousands of years. All they could hope for was a little luck and a lot of improvements in the city's defenses. They both assumed political machinations would decide their fate when the two months were up—not their performance, no matter the mayor's enthusiasm for them. All they could do is take away as many reasons as possible that the mayor and commissioner might have to use as an excuse for letting them go and installing their own people. *Working with the electorate must not be an enviable task.*

Cha Cha was getting used to not wearing a uniform and hoped to keep it that way.

At 2:24 p.m., they entered the supposed dress shop as part of the tour. Nice girly things really, if a bit pricey, but the changing room—right out of Maxwell Smart movie—hid another secret, a hidden entrance back into the main of the building. The silk, cotton, denim and lace all gone now, replaced by a microwave proof, sound proof, satellite proof inner building—a respite for spies.

Time to work.

Chapter 19

Frank led Cha Cha on a tour of his building. Below his two-story penthouse, a beautiful tiled pool with cedar benches on the surround and off to one far side a Jacuzzi and sauna encouraged exercise and relaxation. On the next floor down from the pool, they entered a fully equipped gym with a boxing or wrestling ring as centerpiece. "You don't really have a membership at Snyder's," Cha Cha said.

"You've got me, Detective."

She wished she 'got' this strong willed man. He'd picked her out of all the NYPD detectives. He had to have more than bedding her on his mind.

In the ring, a burly man clasped his opponent's hands and held tight the arms of a grunting, spitting, angry young woman. Built like a farm girl—Cha Cha observed—and from the steppes of northern Asia, she had been told. The young woman seemed like cold fusion in a bottle. Having a better look at the brawny boxer, she realized he was the guy who picked up Frank from her apartment on 9/11. Mr. OTTS.

"Is she all right?" Cha Cha worried over their size difference.

"Nobody knows for sure," Frank said, with an amused smirk.

"Okay, what's so funny?"

"The Red Army couldn't handle her so they gifted her to us."

She asked Frank for more information by tilting her head and raising her eyebrows. In a gym, it seemed appropriate to nail him lightly on his biceps. And so she did.

"*Ouch*." He winced, obviously faking.

She pursed her lips, her patience rapidly wearing thin. Frank finally got the hint and told her the girl's story. "Her name you might recognize—Sarantsatral—means moonlight in Mongolian. We call her Moon. It's easier. She won the Olympics last year in 10 and 25 meter pistol at the age of eighteen. Since then, her entire family was murdered in a drug war, which involved drug lords from Afghanistan and a corrupt Chinese official. She took her vengeance out in a series of shootings in which the evidence was not quite enough to convict her. Rather than execute her or let her go, Peking gave her to us as a *present* to help combat terrorism. All she wants to do is kill."

"If they're all dead, why is she still angry?"

"She hates capitalists."

"Oh great. We get *her*."

"Not exactly, that red-faced fellow is my ex-boss at OTTS. He volunteered to train her. Being ex-KGB, he knows both sides of the political fence. He'll have her feel his pain and share in hers in no time. His family was destroyed in Nazi death camps."

"Could you explain a little more now about what he does at OTTS?"

"I'll have to explain OTTS to you in private. Need to know…you know? For now, you are looking at Carlos Petrovich, better known as the most feared assassin in the clandestine world."

"Well for right now, I'd say he'd better protect his balls."

Somehow, the girl, Moon, folded her calf up, jumped up with her other leg and landed square with the ball of her folded foot on Carlos's family jewels. Carlos sprawled.

"I've never seen him fall," Frank said, mirth written all over his face.

"He should have been wearing a cup," Cha Cha said.

'Ohhhhh, I am vearing cup, Detective O'Sullivan. You Frank, you think you do better? Oww."

"Frank and I are partners. I'll handle her." Cha Cha shoved Frank aside and made her way into the ring. She wouldn't dare bare-knuckle fight the Mongolian. That would be an unfair advantage. Wrestling or Jujitsu, it would be.

Others who had been working out—FBI, maybe CIA, some cops—formed a perimeter in the ring to protect the famous, in their world, Carlos. Undaunted, the girl threw air kicks and sneered at anybody who dared look at her.

Cha Cha parted the crowd and slipped under the ropes. She tossed her heels and stepped into the inner circle, face to face. Gray chinos and a cotton blouse became her armor. Backing off after a little glaring, she raised her arms and one leg in a praying mantis pose. The girl's black eyes burned with fire.

What had Cha Cha gotten herself into?

"She's a homicidal maniac," Detective Percy Bainwater warned, with some sort of amusement written all over his face. Men loved cat fights.

Cha Cha would try reasoning, it being her trademark after all. She'd show all these present the way it's done right. "The girl had lost her parents. Who here wouldn't feel vengeful?" She stared at the Mongolian. "Do you want a home? Do you want to help?"

"She doesn't speak English," a slight woman with FBI emblazoned on her sweat top said.

The girl laughed. And while Cha Cha hesitated, trying to understand the joke, the girl dropkicked her out of the ring. Where was the spirit and skill of her great-great uncle—boxing world champ John L. Sullivan—when she needed him? She resisted the urge to jump up and raise her dukes. One on Moon's jaw and she'd laugh no more. She shrugged and lifted to one elbow, signaling defeat. She stared at the ball-of-fire girl who bested her with trickery. Although she could try again, she preferred the role of peacemaker.

"You a pussay."

Oh boy.

Composing herself came naturally and from tons of practice dealing with scalawags in Washington Square Park.

"It's pussy," Cha Cha said, correcting her English. She closed her eyes to regroup, but not before noticing Prince Charming coming to her side.

Frank bent over and nestled his head to her breast. Probably listening to her heart would be his poor excuse.

"You'd do anything to get your hands on these girls."

She sat up. The Mongolian pedaled her legs at the ropes like Mohammad Ali, including holding one taunting arm up. A tiny smile cracked Moon's façade. Cha Cha knew in an instant the girl took a liking to her and all would be well—eventually. So instead of beating up on the foreigner, as if, she was easily persuaded to move on.

Next stop, a conversation with Detective Percy Bainwater in a sound proof office in the far corner of the gym. His job included liaison with the British MI 5 and 6. It seems the British started spying on people residing in the USA whether they were citizens or not. No court order necessary. The only criteria, some investigative agency in the U.S. had to suspect the person or persons of plotting terrorist activities. Percy, through the help of the NSA, would return the favor on suspicious characters in Britain. As if that weren't enough work for him. Frank made him interim administrator and liaison to New York City's finest. Frank and Cha Cha would provide direction to Percy who then would issue orders down the line, and it started now.

Frank mentioned that they would not likely see Moon again because she still wasn't cleared for the street, but she was slated to be Carlos's partner if he could retrieve his nuts from abdomen. Carlos intended a relationship that would last.

* * *

After a short break, next stop was engineering. A young engineer on loan from the NSA named Bud was busy setting up computer systems and surveillance screens. The city was just beginning to spy on their own citizens, one street corner camera at a time. For the most part, the people of Manhattan wanted it.

"I watched you get your ass kicked in the ring Detective O'Sullivan. Better than watching FLOW. You know, Fabulous Ladies of Wrestling," Bud said. He looked Sicilian, a little like Buddy Holly, with a baby face and coke-bottle glasses.

"I kno—"

Bud interrupted her. "But I think you wanted to lose, and by losing you won. I mean, you are amazing." Bud's eyebrows went way up to make his point. "The reason I know this—is—it's the first time that girl, Moonlight or whatever, you know, has said anything or smiled. She doesn't even speak in Han or any other dialect. Not since she arrived. She's like Jesus before Pilot or the Sanhedrin."

"Interesting."

"No, Jesus said, truth."

"The truth is, Bud, you're funny."

"Yeah, but I've got something for the two of you. I'd love to see you fight for real, some other time, but we have a war on. I

149

intercepted an email. Pretty clear. It came from Osama bin Laden and it landed in Brooklyn at an internet café, but it turned out the server belongs to the manager of the coffee house. His laptop was hacked, had a back door for two years now."

"A back door."

"Yeah, somebody was using his computer without him knowing it."

"I'll check him out," Frank said.

"You do that, but this guy is too smart."

"So what did the message—" Cha Cha asked.

"Here…read this."

Thanks so much for the $3,000 but you promised me $30,000. So, until you come up with the rest, don't bother me. For now on, you are on your own, we're busy here. Or, you could come home and join the party. We could always use a helping hand. Basically, I don't care. You owe me one way or the other. I'm not writing any more. You disappointed me. It's on you, bro.

Jose Pasqual. [COMINT channel redacted.]

"Okay, I'm working on a program that picks the best fit if you're looking for a hidden message. You see it's cool, because someday Cyclops—that's our beast computer, Detective—will do this for us."

Frank inspected the message. "So, what does it say?"

"Oh come on you two. You tell me. Cha Cha, is it? You're the detective. So what's your best guess?"

"Three thousand people died last week, approximately. Somebody named Pasqual wanted thirty-thousand but I'll venture his name is Osama—"

Bud interrupted again. "That's right on the money. Frank, you've got a winner here. Never let this one go, like you did all the other women you've ah dated." Cha Cha was getting suspicious that Bud was everywhere.

"Are you spying on us?" she asked.

"Yeah Bud, I'll ship you back to Ayita."

"No, you won't. First of all, I'm the best. Secondly, it's my business to protect the two of you so you can do your jobs. Yes, I was spying and if you have a problem with that talk to Ayita or better yet give the President a ring-a-ding-ding. So I stole from you and I give you something back. I have a girlfriend. She's a baker and working on her master's, MF, Masters in Foodie. She wants—"

"Bud. You don't know shit. We're professional and becoming good friends in the process," Frank said.

Cha Cha saw her chance to win this round as well. She was having a good day. She grabbed Bud's pocket protector. "Listen to me, little man. Just because you can tell that men and women are attracted to each other, happens every f-in day, doesn't mean Frank and I will act on it. We have a war on. Stick to the point. Do your real job or I'll find your girlfriend and tell her what a schmuck you are."

"I." She pulled harder on his pocket protector threatening to rip his shirt.

"You've a got a winner, her, Frank." She let go.

Bud had been bitten by the same genius bug that infected Autumn. A know-it-all who, even in his early twenties, refused to grow up. His unbridled and brilliant mind could be toyed with but not buttoned down, if they wanted to keep him productive. Or so went her initial assessment. In the meantime, just like Howard Stern, you'd never knew what he'd say next.

"There's something else." Unflappable.

Frank leaned back in his chair and laced his fingers behind his head. "What's up?" He was obviously enjoying Cha Cha's manhandling Bud.

"Two elses. There somebody inside NYU's library that is trying to hack into the NSA's mainframe and every other government agency. We get tons of this kind of stuff. We set traps to find them. This one's different because the hacker is looking for you, Frank."

"Okay, thanks. Cha Cha and I will investigate that. And the other *else*?"

"There will be some nuclear waste coming across the border from Canada through Washington State then intending to make its way to New York. The FBI is all over this one and will keep us informed in case they are tricked or it gets by them. This means, somebody here—likely a lone wolf—thinks his job isn't done and let's say, wants to see twenty-seven thousand more deaths."

"Damn ugly," Frank said.

"Well the good news is, if we read that letter correctly, and of course we have, the guy is orphaned from Osama. He will fail miserably. He will put himself on a platter and hand himself over to you, because alone or nearly alone he is bound to make a mistake, a deadly mistake. Whereas, we have an army searching for him. It may sound like he should be your main focus, but he in the end will come across as a footnote."

Cha Cha patted Frank's shoulder. "Thank you so much, Bud. We'll find the bastard, I can assure you."

"You two feel like a good team to me." Bud smiled. "And oh yes, my whole family grew up like this. We're a bunch of busy bodies. You want me on your team."

"You're the best, according to Ayita. I have every faith in you."

"I agree," Cha Cha said.

They parted from Bud and all his computers and geek helpers. The main library at NYU next stop.

Chapter 20

Frank and Cha Cha had enough time for a snack in Washington Square Park. It was good to be out on this temperate and sunny day in her old haunt.

They relaxed on a bench facing their target, the NYU library. Cha Cha munched on a soft pretzel with deli mustard and Frank had a Nathan's hotdog.

She teased him. "I thought you only ate spaghetti and meatballs." He had admitted to the strange diet the night before.

"I vary once in a while. A hotdog here, a bite of your beautiful derriere there." Frank nudged her shoulder with his.

"No calories in that."

"I've been meaning to apologize. It's you I like, not just your rear end." Said with a blissful smile.

He leaned over and kissed off the mustard from her lips. She was more than ready for a make-out session, even if the whole world watched. "Is Bud a nosy guy?"

Frank stretched. "Nah. He's too busy to gawk at us. Besides, once he makes his point, he moves on. Like most engineers, once the problem is solved to his satisfaction, he's on to the next puzzle."

"Are we solved?"

"The more time I spend with you, the more…"

"We'll find out." She rested her head on his shoulder. Could she be falling in love, so soon? One or both of them had to keep their eyes on the reason they were together. Or had some Divine Force placed them in a job so that they would find each other?

"I want to cha cha with you, my dear Cha Cha."

"Anytime you want, lessons will be free."

"Okay, soon I hope."

"You know, Autumn had translated your Russian. It probably traumatized the baby to think men bite women on the rump."

"That girl, from all I've heard, is amazing. Imagine the leaps her mind went through to deduce first the terrorist team, then the date, then the effect."

"Blows my mind."

He twirled her curls. "Are we falling in love?"

"I can't... Not yet, Frank. Give me a little time to get my legs."

He held her hand. "Your legs are runway perfect and drive me insane. Have you ever modeled?"

"No, honey. You know, your legs aren't bad either along with the rest of you."

"My turn to get embarrassed." He turned red as if to prove his point.

She touched his ruddy cheeks. "Why is it that you're body shy?"

"Can we shelf that for a while?" He leaned back and looked up.

"If you insist. But not for long."

He leveled his head and wantonly stared at her. "I want you naked. It's only fair."

Now it was her turn for embarrassment. His expression turned resolute. At the same time, she felt determined to do her job.

As if reading each other's minds, they stood. She was so proud to be with him, share his fervor for helping the people of New York. No little romance would get in the way of their doing their jobs. Their reward would come later in the form of a kiss lavishly given as only lovers do.

What had Rick said to Ilsa in *Casablanca*? *"The problems of two people don't amount to a hill of beans in this crazy world"* or something like that.

A subtle wind whisked up Thompson to join their resolve. God's breath entreated them to use their talents.

He took her hand when they crossed the street to the library. *How incredibly sweet my born-again boy scout is.*

* * *

"The problem with library computers is they're all over the campus in various buildings, basically as satellites," Cha Cha said.

"Bud thinks this is our best starting point."

154

Of course, the NYU library was huge with over twenty-eight miles of open stacks on twelve stories. This is where his partner's intuition could come in handy.

Cha Cha pinned on her badge. "We'll need an early dinner. I'm worried about Autumn and getting to her place," Cha Cha said.

Frank had half hoped Cha Cha would stay the night with him. Only half, because she was too sweet a girl to trifle with. Yes, her dossier had disclosed her devilish side. So he'd sign up if it were her idea. No problem. In the meantime, he'd try to figure out why he just couldn't get her off his mind.

For the NCS, he had tangled with many a pretty spy from Moscow to Berlin. Never gave the femme fatales much thought. They bedded each other to relieve a lonely existence where one errant word meant annihilation.

Cha Cha was different. Not only was she the most alluring and attractive woman he had ever met, she was both exasperating and comforting at once. This occasional bad girl had turned virginal around him. This mom and apple pie American was willing to join forces with the devil—being Frank—to stop another disaster from happening. Why should he second-guess her? Besides, they just issued her a top-secret clearance. *Trust her.*

Cha Cha could be giving him lip service to keep him happy and hold onto her job, but it never felt that way. They were equal partners and she had no trouble speaking her mind.

She could be waiting for the right moment to spring her likely agenda of full civil rights and procedures for terrorists. Whatever happened, they'd be together. They'd work it out. *One could only hope.*

Funny thing, librarians, especially liberal NYU librarians, could be a good test for Cha Cha's skills. Behind the counter sat a comely middle-aged woman who looked like Cyndi Lauper without the orange hair. Her tag read Marian Depardieu. Cha Cha's read, Detective NYPD, and his read nothing because he didn't have one.

"Frank is it? Pleased to meet you." She spoke with hushed voice. They shook hands and he applied a little charm.

"How can I help you two?" She fished some paperwork, little doubt obsessed with cataloguing a book.

"I've asked Frank for some help, but he's at a loss."

"Yeah, I'm only a visiting professor from Quinnipiac but considering what happened last week. Well, the detective has been so kind."

"What is it you want?"

"Someone has been using the library's computers to plan another terrorist attack worse than last week's, and we were hoping to figure out who that might be."

"Besides me being too busy," she shuffled some more papers, "do you have a court order?"

"That's what I was telling Frank. I said nobody wants to break the law, even if it meant the nuclear destruction of Manhattan."

Frank nodded at Cha Cha. "Come on, detective, I'll find a patriot."

"I'm a patriot. Our forefathers—"

"Marian?" Frank interrupted what was likely to be a most excellent lecture.

"Yes?" Marian put on that librarian air, that look where the accused was held in high esteem, right up there with serial killers. To break her funk he needed to unleash his "A" game.

"Excuse me, Detective. Some private NYU talk here," Frank said. Cha Cha backed off a few paces. He leaned over and whispered to the librarian, "I've been trying to impress the detective but now that I've met you, maybe we could get together for dinner."

"And?" she whispered back, uncertain, but definitely breaking his way.

"Well, I'll just pretend to look up stuff on that back computer. I don't know a thing. I don't have your pass code. Then I'll tell her I found nothing here. I'll send her away and meet you later."

"Six, no, better seven-thirty. Pick me up." She wrote down her address, phone number, email, fax. She'd write down her family history and the name of her dog if he hadn't put his hand on hers. She withdrew it, handed him the paper and started pulling her curls.

She squeaked loudly. "Okay, Detective, I'll let the professor poke around for a bit. There's some regular or decaf over there." She pointed with a Cross pen, then she tried to twirl it. The pen hit the floor and she instinctively went, "Shhhh."

After a little while, Frank was done—he had embedded an NSA link to Bud and also found a possible suspect.

Standing, he stretched. "I'm sorry, Detective, I couldn't find a thing. Maybe a court order and a more complete search would be better. We wouldn't want to do things halfway, would we? You know, Miss Depardieu and I are only too happy to help the cause of freedom." Marian beamed.

Cha Cha played at being dejected, pretty convincing, although Broadway wouldn't give her a call anytime soon. "I'm only trying to save lives. I can see you two are a team." She spun around and headed for the elevator. "Have a *nice day*." A nice touch of snittiness.

After a little more flirting, he excused himself, said he was looking forward to hooking up with Marian tonight and having a deep conversation. She flipped her curls again while her knees bobbed. She whispered. "Don't be late or there'll be a fine." She sat up straight and put on her stone face, ready for her students again.

He gave a bow and trotted over to the elevator. She leaned to see him better. As the door closed, he winked for good measure.

* * *

At the prearranged chess table in the park, no pieces yet, Cha Cha let off some steam. She kept looking up at the library a couple hundred yards away.

"She can't see us. The maple trees are still too thick with leaves," Frank said, while looking over his shoulder.

For not the first nor the last time did they wrestle with what was an acceptable and legal approach to their job. Today, it came down to the U.S. constitution and how it related to war. They found no stumbling block. Frank could work with her sensitivities and she could work with his tactics.

Frank leaned forward over the table. "I trust you with my life. You know this."

She put her hand over his. "We'll stop them."

"Something is bothering you. I can see it in your gorgeous emerald eyes. We have no secrets, right?" Frank asked.

"It's nothing."

"Please tell me. We should have no secrets."

"I'm worried about the librarian. I know...dumb." She'd have to get used to deception as an aspect of the job, but with her heart on the line as well as her job she wouldn't, couldn't tolerate him deceiving her over another woman.

He looked over his shoulder at the library, probably trying to figure out why God made women so different than men.

"You mean the date I set up tonight with Marian?"

Folding her arms over her chest, she gave him a dirty look. She just didn't want to come across as jealous so she decided on a sideways approach to her emotions. "I don't think it's fair to stand-up somebody."

"He won't have to," Carlos appeared as if from nowhere, per usual. How he did that with nothing but trees starting ten feet away, chess players at other tables, and, right now, not much of a crowd, never ceased to amaze Frank. The ex-KGB agent placed a long skinny canvas chess bag between them.

"Here is your prop."

"I don't know what is worse— Frank going on a date or not." Cha Cha mocked sulking, but surely truth lurked in this angel's heart—she liked him, very much. Her peacemaker ways were showing. Perhaps there was merit in her approach. Besides, if handled right, the librarian would not report suspicious behavior to the police or worse, the newspapers.

Carlos laid the cloth chessboard on the table. "No, no. Frank will not see her again. I am going to see this Marian, the librarian. I can be psychiatrist trying to chase down patient, or another detective searching for drug dealer masquerading as professor or maybe today's special, the brother of Frank's imaginary wife. Take your pick."

Cha Cha could not contain her laughter, which drew attention to their table. She unzipped the chess bag, opened the velvet chess pouches, dropping both white and black pieces on the center of the board. People went back to what they were doing, with exceptions. Some men just kept staring. Cha Cha radiated beauty, the way the speckled tree and sunlight danced with her red-brown hair. Especially pretty when laughing showed off her dimple.

"Go save your brother-in-law," she said glibly.

"Before I do, I want you two to know I will literally have your backs." He went on to explain that although he was director of OTTS, a not much doin' agency these days, he would remain on loan to the terrorism taskforce for their two-month trial period. Carlos also explained to Cha Cha how important it was to cover their tracks and that her instincts about the librarian were correct.

"That detective approaching, get his name." Carlos withdrew and promptly joined Anatoly, a chess hustler two tables over, and started talking chess with the old man. Frank had learned long ago to never question Carlos's gut instincts. Carlos had immediately moved on to the chess hustler, before their conversation had finished. He was a careful man, who needed to remain in the shadows.

Frank would, of course, get the NYPD detective's name.

Chapter 21

Hanging around NYC detectives forced Ali Ali to convince himself long ago he was Brooklyn, NYPD detective, Sam Langrath. To be otherwise—around sharp eyes—would be suicide. He couldn't help but feel trepidation over his appointment with the sixth precinct's lieutenant in charge of detectives. He had applied for Detective Chastity O'Sullivan's old job.

No matter what path he chose to avenge his family's deaths at the hands of the Israelis in Gaza so many years before, he'd likely get caught. He was orphaned by Osama and up against countless numbers of Allied spies, police, nosy citizens and backstabbing comrades.

He could do nothing but be Sam and hope. Just live with these Americans, but it wouldn't slacken the eternal fire that burned his soul.

Every morning when he woke up he remained convinced. Americans weren't human. Yet, every night he had to argue with himself why he should avenge his family. He liked the Yankees, not the Mets. He loved the Jets not the Giants. He loved hotdogs with the works. He wasn't religious, but he surely knew hell was real.

Later, he'd have to interview Detective O'Sullivan and/or her source. Find out how they knew of the attacks. Plug the leak by eliminating the traitor to Jihad, yet execute in such a way that it would not lead back to him so he could be forever more, Sam.

Then he would construct a dirty bomb, as soon as the materials arrived. Maybe, with a flourish, he'd make it look like Detective O'Sullivan was the prime suspect. *What a laugh.*

Sam entered the hallowed halls of the sixth precinct. Couldn't help but notice Detective Chastity O'Sullivan's grandfather's picture. The man was a legend.

The lieutenant motioned him into his office and pointed to a chair while he finished a phone conversation.

"I'm impressed with your creds, Detective," the lieutenant said.

"I worry that Detective O'Sullivan will want her old job back, Sir."

"Don't get me wrong, Sam. She was a good cop. A little unorthodox for my blood, but she won't be coming back."

"Well, I read as much as I could. I don't want to make the same mistakes she did, if any."

"Yeah, yeah. I need arrests, not the happy birthday parties she used to throw."

"Still, I should talk to her. Don't you think I might learn a trick or two?" He had never learned a thing in his life from a woman. He did however need to find her snitch unless O'Sullivan was the unlikely source of her report on the glorious attacks. And if so, why?

The lieutenant, head buried, paged through Sam's files and avoided answering his question. "I see you have the highest ratio and, oh, use of lethal force on record for any detective in the five boroughs. Care to explain yourself?"

"Yes, Sir. I don't care whether I live or die, so maybe I take too many chances."

"Sorry, Sam. I read about your family's unfortunate demise, but you need to live in the present. I'd like the detectives who work for me to stay alive. Okay?"

"Don't worry, Sir, I'm not suicidal. When I shoot, I never miss. And I only shoot when it's absolutely necessary—when my life or innocent civilians are involved."

Suddenly, sirens sounded. Three officers ran by the lieutenant's office in the direction of the back entrance.

"Just a normal day in Manhattan, Sam."

"Same in Brooklyn."

The lieutenant flipped a page on his planner, looked up at Sam and raised his eyebrows. "O'Sullivan managed to clean up the park without firing her weapon."

"I'd love to interview her, to get a take on her magic."

"No, that won't be necessary. Be yourself. Just don't embarrass me, Dirty Harry style. Tone it down a little, at least until you get the lay of the park and environs thereof." The lieutenant rose and extended his hand. Sam took it and put on his grateful and proud look.

"Welcome aboard, Detective First Class, Samuel Langrath. Report tomorrow, 0800. I'll have a desk ready for you, a new password, and some files to read, 0800. Dismissed."

"Yes, Sir."

After a short tour of the facilities and the use of the facilities, Sam took a walk over to Washington Square Park. He worried about his lieutenant's unwillingness to set up an interview with Detective O'Sullivan. The fat prick knew something and soon Sam would know what that was.

At the park, "soon" smacked him in the face. There she sat setting up chess pieces, prettier than her pictures, with Frank Lancia, head of the terrorism taskforce. It would be a *two-for-one* to send these two to hell.

He halted for a moment, his sixth sense drummed into him from years of training. *Yes, thank you, NYPD.* Something felt wrong, out of place. He knew that rich playboy Frank was armed to the teeth with people. If Sam went too far, he'd do nothing but get himself killed or arrested. Two Russians talked chess, seemed natural. The hotdog vendor, the antiwar kids on soap boxes, the dogs in the pen, all normal, but the hairs on the back of his neck stood on end.

Don't do anything foolish. He'd stick to his goal. Find the snitch, wait for the dirty bomb materials and then make his move.

Gathering his wits about him, he put on a happy face and slowly made his approach. It hurt to smile, so he focused on happy times in his childhood, of his father's nurturing love, of his mother's smile, her hugs. This revisiting his pass only made it impossible for him to be Sam. He stopped and pretended to observe an anti-war harangue. For years, he wore a perfect face, but the disappointment of insufficient loss on 9/11 and his subsequent estrangement from bin Laden brought to the surface his seething hatred. Simmer down. Ali Ali was a dead man walking. Sam had a chance.

He was Sam. He was Sam, the tough cop, with a witty style, a fair-minded attitude. He was Sam.

"Could I bother you for a second, Detective?"

"Sure. Take a load off," Chastity said, patting the bench next to her.

"I'm Detective Sam Langrath. I just took over your job and was hoping to get some pointers on who the players are." He shook hands and looked over at Frank, who wore a game face to match his own. *Too pro for a read.* Chastity however seemed conflicted by something.

"I know you. Mr. Lancia, right?"

"Ya got me." They talked a little about what Sam used to be doing in the Muslim and Jewish communities before his transfer. Frank insisted he keep his eyes open. Frank seemed to be proprietary around Cha Cha. Perhaps the taskforce was being run by somebody who let his dick do his thinking.

"This park is like heaven, why would you ever leave it?" He speculated the answer to this question. She joined the taskforce; either that or she had a thing for Frank. Maybe both. Unfortunately, because they sat opposite each other over a chess table and seemed focused on keeping it short with him, the lack of body language on their parts led him to assume the obvious. She was in his employ.

"I haven't. I'm taking some time off before I join my pop's business. Actually, I don't know, Sam. I keep going back and forth. Maybe I'll stay. But the job is yours. I'm not going back to the NYPD, at least not to bump you from your new job." She moved a chess piece and Frank buried his head. A little too cute, this time. He didn't know much about chess, but they had just set up the board. With a couple of moves played, they probably could not have engaged in anything pithy. He would also try to check the NYPD payroll records to see if she was still being paid.

Sam said, "I'd like to learn chess, sometime." Playing a game of Russian roulette would suit his mood better.

"I'm sorry, Sam." She put her piece down and focused on him instead. "Chess is addicting and distracting me. How about tomorrow, here, at lunch for a talk?" Okay, she wanted time with Frank. He was the interloper. Now was not the time to push it.

Although there were no cues to suggest Frank and Chastity were an item, he would for now assume they were. Yet, he'd have to act dense. "As long as I can buy you a frank or something."

"Deal." The three shook hands. Sam waved and walked off.

I am one cool customer. I am Sam Langrath.

But second thoughts followed him. *Entirely too cute.* How could he have fucked up more? Rule one of Detective 101: suspect everybody you come into contact with of being your assassin, if in that type of situation. Fine, he'd be as nice to her as a man with the hots. Considering her wavy reddish-brown hair, long legs, beguiling smile, that dimple thing, he could play the part. Swallow his pride. Pretend a woman could offer him peace. Anyway, they'd all be dead soon.

Allah Akbar.

Chapter 22

Frank and Cha Cha dined on his penthouse deck again. The city lights reminded Cha Cha of the Christmas to come. The work lights from ground zero seared the sky and reminded her of just how far off Christmas really was.

This evening arrived too quickly for Cha Cha. So far, they had learned little from their bleeding of NYU's administrative computer. Frank had a name, a graduate student in physics—James Boone—big in the vibrant NYU antiwar movement. They interviewed him and discovered that not only was he helpful but that his password was hacked.

This infuriated James, something to do with the pride this math whiz had in making unbreakable passwords. She concluded that whomever hacked this genius had to have outclassed him or watched him type in his password. He claimed he had been careful. Carlos had personally vouched for him since they played chess in the park from time to time and were becoming friends.

Whipped by a brisk evening breeze, they downed a quick and simple lasagna dinner up in Frank's penthouse, with a side of spaghetti and meatballs, which for Frank was his main course.

Cha Cha felt warmed by Frank's smile. He seemed the schoolboy around her. How this hard-bitten clandestine warrior came to fall for her was hard to understand. Perhaps he was merely smitten. She knew she had a cute face, a slim figure, but there were plenty of girls who were prettier. Frank loved her personality their common interests and her looks. If he would settle down and live in New York rather than chase spies overseas, maybe they'd have something long term. Maybe. All she knew was that just looking at him made her swoon, her heart patter and other parts smolder. But jump him, she would not. Not yet. New York City was their demanding master and mistress.

One of Frank's servants, who appeared more like a ninja then a waiter, presented a list of beers, wines, spirits and mixed drinks.

"Not tonight, thank you, just a lemon-water please." Cha Cha knew Autumn's mom drank too much so Cha Cha would not visit the young girl under the influence. Autumn wanted real company while her mom took a short trip. With a little luck, she'd get to the bottom of Autumn's troubled demeanor of late and just maybe be able to help.

After the ninja left, she asked, "Are your servants, spies as well?"

"No, he, who wishes to remain nameless, is also a body guard with considerable skills in the martial arts."

"Fascinating. Someday I'll get him to talk." She put on her most beguiling smile.

He reached out and twined her curls. "Knowing you, he'll spill the beans."

"I'm sorry I can't stay later, tonight," she said with the sultriest and promising voice she could muster.

"Baby, there's no denying our physical attraction, is there?"

She batted her eyes flirtatiously. "A guy would try anything to get into these panties."

"I'd bust them."

"Oh that I *know.*"

"Come on sweetheart, stroke my ego." That's not all she'd like to stroke. Look at him, so smug and expectant—of a hand or blow job. He knew exactly what was going through her mind.

"Of course, Frank. You know it. You're a doll."

"But?" he asked huskily.

"But, no. I won't sleep with you." She regretted her words immediately. His lips quivered like Sean Connery's when he knew the girl was his. "Listen to me, Frank." She tried to regain her composure.

He grasped her hand, lifting it to his lips and brushing a soft kiss over her knuckles. "Yes?"

Time to change tact. "I want to know what makes you tick. I want time to review your dossier. You had promised I could do to you what you and Doctor Myron did to me."

"Yes, I suppose I did." He kissed her hand again. "But I already have my clearance."

"You have a license to kill, but do you have a license to live life to the fullest?" She got up and sat on his lap, a most dangerous game.

"Cha Cha. Right now with you, I feel very much alive."

"Maybe now with me in your arms, but after my novelty wears thin, what then?" The man was so hard and big beneath her bottom.

"You'll never wear thin."

"I want to know everything about you. We can't afford to make mistakes." She squirmed almost too deliciously.

He pulled her head to his broad shoulder. "Let's do it." But luckily for her or not he didn't mean what she felt. He seemed determined to respect her, but could have taken her immediately.

After dinner and right before Cha Cha was to leave for Autumn's, Frank surprised her.

"I swear, even after I wake up and am sitting in bed, the ghosts are still talking to me." Frank's ex-girlfriend, Emily, had put a hex on him and beset him with ghosts who ruined his sleep.

"She hexed me too, remember? But I'm not getting any visitations. I don't believe in ghosts. You're just impressionable," Cha Cha said. This gorgeous hunk of fighting frenzy had conjured up ghosts. He had a flaw. Thank God, he was human which made him more adorable. Maybe he was just pulling her leg—or wanted to.

"I don't believe in ghosts either." He protested too much. He seemed perplexed. Beset with demons?

"Maybe I need to call Doctor Myron sooner than I planned. I can't go running around New York with a partner who's crazy."

"Scoff all you want, you brat. Surely there's something in that Joan of Arc armor of yours that makes you itch." He pulled her into a hug that left her breathless.

But she managed to speak after a moment or two. "Well you itch me, sweetie, but that doesn't mean you'll get to scratch what is aching me right now," she lowered her voice, "anytime *soon*."

She pushed him away.

"Don't you dare." Now was not the time to melt at the application of his lethal kisses. He could seduce her with a simple touch. He could seduce her with one look. He'd hardly have to try. She needed to get over to Autumn's and if they were going to play, she'd want the whole night.

With the object of his affection now *forboden* he got back to his story. "Okay, so Mohammed Atta says to me, 'so where did Emily go?'"

"I say, 'She moved back to New Orleans and she's not a virgin. You can't have her anyway. She hates you.'"

'Let me be the judge of that. Which airport flies to New Orleans?'

'You dumb shit, the skies aren't safe. You're dead, there are no virgins waiting for you. Why don't you leave and go to hell. I'm sure someone down there will take you in.'

'I can see we're getting nowhere. I'll walk,' Atta said.

Frank couldn't fully face Cha Cha when telling the story. He fidgeted and stared skyward. She started a back massage, which led to groans during his telling. She couldn't wait to strip him, but this time she'd smother his entire body with kisses instead of Band-Aids.

"You are so full of the finest quality BS. My sweet spy."

"No my dearest partner, I'm telling the truth, although on the telling I don't even believe it."

She turned him all the way to face her and held his bulging biceps. "First thing you do is call Emily, ask for her forgiveness. Explain why you can't get married and I'd like to listen in. Ask her to remove her hex, her gris gris right?"

"What about the gris gris she put on you?"

"She can give them all to me."

They walked over to a side table. He split a banana in half—using both hands—without peeling it. Cute trick.

"You wanted a light dessert." He handed her half but lingered with his hand long enough to touch her. Her heart pounded again. He was and would always be her dessert.

She peeled the half-banana and teased him by kissing it before she chomped which made him smile then flinch. She waivered on leaving but her girlfriend needed her. Their sexual needs could hold, although...

"I think you visiting the girl is sweet."

"Thanks Frank. Tomorrow, okay babe?"

"I'll dream of you tonight instead."

She went up on her toes and kissed his cheek. His stubble tasted all man. It had been too long, well never with a hunk like this. Yet his heart remained his shining and best feature. They locked eyes when they stood outside the elevator. His eyes harbored a haunted but hopeful look, more a longing for her, little doubt, than worries about imaginary ghosts he had no trouble telling off.

* * *

Autumn skipped about her apartment, stopped at the kitchen table, balanced on one leg while holding the other behind her, leaned over and turned a few pages of some NYU library business textbooks. Resistance was futile, the books were assimilated. John Nash's Nobel thesis made for dessert. Mom's fired independent contractors were complaining about how they were treated and now she understood better how to handle them.

She had juggled Nash's Nobel formulas with other authors. Why hadn't every business used Nash? His ideas were way overkill for what she needed, but it fired her imagination. She'd catch the movie, *A Beautiful Mind*, due out at Christmas time.

Nash's formulas, after tweaking, could work for government bureaucracies as well as business, specifically for the NSA. A place she'd someday run if only she could get over her contractor problem, make two people fall in love, have them get married and adopt her before she got kicked out of this beautiful country. Small problems, really?

How long would she maintain her "beautiful mind?" Nash, Bobby Fischer and many other geniuses went crazy in one way or another.

She was healthy and would stay that way.

I will live a balanced life and learn to tolerate and accept others less fortunate. Besides, love is a human's and dog's best quality. She hopped over to Julius, bent down, the same foot in hand pose and delivered a kiss to his forehead. "Are you listening to my thoughts, Julius? I said I love you."

Now armed to her curly-topped head with knowledge, she could address her mom's business. She'd have to act more like a young girl with her words, perhaps mangle the word contractor, ala contracture, etc. Shouldn't be too hard—seeming the mistake prone girl, since she was one. And yes, she made mistakes, especially when it came to focus. Her mind often jumped from the sublime of equations to talking to her plush dog, to going goofy over the impossibility of smooching with Joey, but she knew how to write for results.

She composed and sent her letter.

Dear Ms. Urma and Ms. Jannine,

You got me. I'm Autumn, Monique's daughter. She's been so drunk lately she asked me to help with the business. I worried that we couldn't afford you two, but she scolded me. Told me you two are commissioned independent contractures and were no drain on the business.

So, I hope you won't mind working with a kid until my mom gets better. I want to find a new daddy and if you know of anybody she would like and is willing to wait until she gets better and she will get better and then they could go out on a date and he needs to love dogs that's all I want.

Thank you so very much,
Autumn Breeze

Maybe she had overdone it with all the *ands*. But what did they know? Nothin'. Their noses were glued to society pages, not her treatises or her run on Jeopardy. Besides, normal girls, even geniuses, liked to let their locks down. *Besides, using 'ands' lets me breathe.*

Lately, she felt alienated. She used to spend nearly every day at lunch or on short shopping trips and other fun things like Cha Cha's community events with Cha Cha. She knew her detective friend was so busy since the disaster. If only she had a magic wand. Whatever. Autumn would make every precious moment count.

If only she could con Cha Cha into becoming her mom. Not that she didn't love her big-hearted friend. No, she loved Cha Cha like crazy, but worried if her disappointment with and loss of her mom was pushing her to see the beautiful, sweet woman as her savior. She remained lonely and wished her daddy could hug her one more time. Even wished her mom could have stopped blaming herself for her dad's death. Stopped closing the door on love long enough to notice her daughter.

Funny, Autumn had done the same on 9/11 when, on a tirade, she blamed her mom for all that was wrong with her life. The truth, she was her own person, and a damn smart one too.

She had read enough psychology textbooks to know all the terms and that she was a handful, but lovable. She did need a mom. A dad too, and she knew just the couple. She had spied on Frank and Cha Cha in the park. They were so flirty, it was embarrassing but sweet. She knew Cha Cha liked Frank and Frank was smitten a little like Joey felt about her, although he'd deny it. From the government records she was able to pull about Frank, he had so far been into monogamous relationships, but when without a steady, he'd play the field.

Cha Cha was a big girl and often taught her how to handle boys. All Autumn needed to do was help Frank see Cha Cha was the best girl in the whole world for him and then just a few more technical difficulties and voila, her plans would fall into place. Fingers crossed.

She did the one leg lean over thing again to flop Julius's ears over his head.

"Listen to me."

No response.

"Listen to me, Julius Caesar. Cha Cha is coming over. I need a mom. I want her to be my mom. Got it?"

She jumped on Julius and put her head upside down in front of his plastic eyes. But she swore she caught a glimmer of life and love.

"How can I get her to be my mom?"

She got up, went into her mom's bedroom, took out a pocketbook Monique used while shopping and plopped it on the kitchen table to give the appearance to a detective that her mom was still alive. The co-op was always neat; thanks to her having followed slob mom all over, but a misplaced pocketbook would be a nice touch. She unzipped it, and pulled out a Bloomingdale's receipt part way and let it hang. She zipped it half-closed, catching the receipt on the edge of the zipper.

"What's that, Julius?" She ran over to her stuffed friend. *Maybe I should ask Joey, even Marcie, cause, well, I love you, Julius, but come on.*

She sat on Julius backwards and played with his bushy tail.

"You think Cha Cha should marry Frank Lancia, first? Hmm?" He wasn't telling her anything she didn't already know.

She smacked herself in the face with the tail.

"And just how am I going to make that happen?"

Frank and Cha Cha had the hot sauce for each other. This much was obvious, but to recap for Julius, Frank, according to his hacked top-secret government files, had long-term commitment issues. He was not a bad man. He kept his floozy count to around one-on-one, totally righteous with a pinch of naughty.

Frank liked having a steady girlfriend with no cheating and lots of you know what. "Got that thought, Julius? If so, help me."

Autumn turned off her Walkman, barely hearing Cha Cha's expected knock.

How is it these CIA, NCS/OTTS operatives, NSA engineers, NYPD detectives and Child Protective Services people get around the intercom at the front of the building? "Magic, right Julius?"

* * *

Autumn had always met Cha Cha somewhere other than her home, because she was ashamed that her mom would drink. Cha Cha could have handled it, but her frenetic friend was too fragile.

Cha Cha stepped inside and gave Autumn an exuberant hug. "Nice digs."

Obviously excited, Autumn played tour guide. Clean windows, two bedrooms, wainscoting, nutmeg walls, red maple floors. Ikea pieces prevailed with some Saturday Evening Post covers framed on the walls. The entire place was spotless, nothing out of order, except Autumn's mom's purse on the kitchen table with a receipt dangling out the half-zipped top.

Autumn followed Cha Cha's gaze. "She's like that with her purses. Actually, I do all the housework, plus write her checks, and lately I've been tending to her business, too. She drinks and runs off with her boyfriend. I don't touch her purses, though, unless I want to make room for a friend and dinner."

"I'm sorry, baby."

Autumn gave her that cross-eyed look like she had just uttered a swear word.

"I'm sorry, *Autumn*."

"Joey does that *baby* thing too."

"Who is Jo-*ey*?" *A boyfriend at her age?* Well, Autumn was so fresh faced beautiful and her figure was changing. So, maybe.

"I'll tell you all about him," Autumn promised. "But first…did you have dessert? I made an upside down cake and have some Chamomile tea brewing."

Cha Cha pulled out a kitchen chair. "No, just half a banana. Cake and tea sound great."

Autumn brought over the cake and poured the tea, and tucked up her chair alongside Cha Cha.

"Joey will be seventeen in March. He's a hunky freshman at NYU and I give him science tutoring on Friday nights. I'd like a kiss from him but he's very religious, scared I'm too young, and he might have a girlfriend."

Cha Cha leaned toward Autumn and bumped shoulders. "When I was fourteen, I had a crush on an older man. He was fifteen—Bill. He wouldn't look at me and treated me like a little sister."

"Yeah, Joey does that."

"They're good boys, the ones who treat you with respect." She gave her a sage look. "You never know what the future holds."

"So what happened to Bill?"

"He got some girl pregnant," Cha Cha said with a shrug while hiding a mischievous grin.

Autumn covered her mouth then giggled. "A bad boy."

"Yeah, a real bad boy. The problem with boys starts in their pants," Cha Cha replied. "Anyway, someday baby—sorry, *Autumn*—you are going to be even more famous than you are now. You are going to do great things and boys will fall at your feet."

"As long as they kiss my toes."

Their kitchen chat continued for some time. Yet, something bothered Autumn, who wore her emotions on her sleeves.

"I decided I like it when you call me baby, like as if you are both my girlfriend and honorary mom."

"Someday I'd love to have a daughter just like you."

Her young girlfriend turned red.

Cha Cha changed the subject—perhaps Autumn wasn't getting along with her mom. She hadn't when she was fourteen, not until her mom started cooking macadamia nut brownies with her, that was her breaking point.

"Who's that big guy over there snoozing?" A huge plush sheepdog took up the entire loveseat with his fat head and droopy ears, over the armrest, poised to watch the Animal Planet on TV. *Could he see through all that fur?*

"Oh, he's Julius, Julius Caesar. I wish I had a real dog, who'd listen to me— My family is in trouble, Cha Cha." Autumn explained how her mom's business was going downhill because of her drinking, how her mom only had a work visa, which stopped them from being deported back to Trinidad. She asked for Cha Cha to keep a confidence.

"I'll do more than keep a secret; I'll help you in whatever way I can."

"Well, my mom's matchmaking business, which by the way, I'm doing lately, is struggling. The clients don't pay unless they get engaged. Nobody is getting engaged or they're lying. So we need more clients."

"Sounds to me like you need to charge them up front."

"Can you do that?" Autumn asked.

"Of course, if your service is attractive. My sister is good at marketing. I'll ask her for some pointers."

"Is she married?"

Cha Cha shook her head. "She's too busy playing the field."

"Then do you think you two, and everybody else you know, could join? It would be free for you and your sister."

"Of course, baby. Let me write down our emails and make sure to say you talked to me but please charge us."

"You're just being nice, right?" Autumn queried "You're not looking for somebody to marry, right?"

It was Cha Cha's turn to try and hide a betraying face, flushed with her innermost secrets. Autumn wasn't a mind reader, was she? Cha Cha tilted and patted her face, as if getting water out of her ear, in an effort to hide her blush. But Autumn didn't seem to notice or said nothing out of politeness.

"I was swimming today," she said lamely. Naturally, she didn't want to talk about Frank. Not because she couldn't share this with her young girlfriend, but because he seemed like such an iffy case. Their working relationship was also top secret, although somehow she got the feeling Autumn would figure it out— eventually.

"So, it wouldn't be a total waste, if my mom or I found somebody for you to date."

In order to be diplomatic, she responded, "No, I'd go out for one date, anyway. And so would my sister."

"And maybe the entire police department."

Nodding slowly, Cha Cha turned toward her young friend. "You know, you should offer a hero's discount."

"Wow, totally cool. Are you still crying over 9/11? I balled for two hours straight today."

Yes, she was still crying. Everybody with a heart was.

They talked for hours until David Letterman came on. So there they sat, Autumn leaning into Cha Cha on the couch with David reporting somberly on New York from his CBS studio. It was that way, everywhere you went. People didn't know how to act. The mayor was going to jumpstart Saturday Night Live, signaling the upbeat for the city. The sports teams would resume their seasons. People would go on living. Yet, this young girl cuddling next to her was all that mattered, now.

She'd date whomever Autumn picked for her, well, once anyway, but really, she just wanted Frank and possibly marriage. Was it too much to hope for Frank to wake up and notice a good woman? Be willing to change his life? He too probably wanted to marry someone, someday, but something was holding him back. With a little luck and a lot of perseverance, she'd soon get to the bottom of his psyche.

"Please Autumn, try not to get me anybody who looks like that guy who hugged me, you know, Johnny Lance." The girl looked perplexed—but she didn't want Autumn to knock herself out trying to find Frank. Besides, she had the man just where she wanted him. By her side.

* * *

NYPD Detective Sam Langrath blended into the dark shades of evening in a poorly lit Soho bistro. His mission, destroy America. Osama basically told him to go to hell for a job not done well enough. Osama and his friends were now running like rats.

He'd been abandoned. He should have surrendered, because they'd catch him sooner or later. The problem: he preferred not being stuffed into some CIA hole, never to be seen again. He wasn't brave or stupid enough to blow himself up. He wasn't smart enough to turn an interrogation into a collaboration. After all, he was the one who transmitted the bright idea to 'knock down these buildings' to quote a structure-obsessed president.

He felt the lacquered wood of his table and bristled as he imagined feeling his own coffin.

Each day he lived, he morphed more and more into an American, more Godless. Who'd understand that? No, it was best he'd try to cover his tracks and move to some cabin in the mountains out west or some tropical isle. Didn't know, just a pipe dream. He enjoyed killing too much to leave just yet and he had his candidates.

He slouched in the below-the-street-level bistro across from the co-op ex-Detective O'Sullivan was visiting. Rapidly getting bored, he hurried his fragrant espresso, and tried to finish off the fried plantain. Too much sugar paste, too much caffeine.

For a while, his neck hairs stood, his face reddened. A sure sign he was being watched, but it was too soon for the terrorism taskforce to hone in on him. They were good, *but give me a break.* Well, he spotted nobody and noticed no new street cameras. *Just paranoia.*

He had had the perfect excuse at lunchtime, hadn't he? He wanted to introduce himself to the pretty woman and learn a little about her old job, normal protocol for a changing of the guard. They'd have to be *paranoid* to consider him a threat. However, O'Sullivan lived as a detective and possibly a spy now. Both the bane and strength of all detectives: Doctor Freud forgot to categorize institutionalized neuroses such as paranoia as psychosomatic illnesses. He played through his meeting in the park with Miss Gorgeous, over-and-over again. Nothing but normal chit-chat. He had not betrayed his complicated inner feelings and thoughts.

When it came to the way he worked, he preferred analytical. Something too cool for body language experts like O'Sullivan or even lie detectors.

This mawkish get together enfolding through the kid's window was like a soap on TV. The mixed-race young teen couldn't be her snitch. Chances were small. The girl who twirled by the window from time to time had to be a beginning dancer O'Sullivan was teaching. O'Sullivan was moonlighting for two to four hours a week, as a dance instructor. One of her outreach services. Nonetheless, he was thorough; he'd find out who the kid was. Priorities, and said kid was low on his possible payback list. Lunch tomorrow, perhaps O'Sullivan would through some miracle give him a clue who the 9/11 snitch was. No, she'd consider that too risky even if he were NYPD. He'd need to make friends first.

That's how the first bombing in 1993 had worked. They— Osama and cutthroats—asked him to form a team and carry out his idea. He linked everybody here through pager codes. They had never met him. The innocent and naive professor's all too helpful in person information led to nothing but some smoke and arrests. Professor Mahmoud Ali Abunayyan really needed to be punished. Besides, he was the only one in America who could positively ID him. If the taskforce found him and they would, he'd sing.

Sam tipped the waiter. Asked for a doggie bag. Ascended the steps to cobblestoned Thompson and headed to Spring Street for the subway. Still, the evening air and the dark shadows didn't feel right, didn't smell right. He must be tailed, but someone or something was too good to be spotted.

He'd have to act in some way soon, yet he relied on idiots to deliver him a dirty bomb. Perhaps he should move on, not wait for something that would never happen. Give up on a stupid idea sure to kill him in the process. A long agonizing death or a bullet if caught. Kill off all those who knew of him and his involvement in the first attack eight years ago. He might need to liquidate the detective's snitch, but not Cha Cha, as they called her. It couldn't be O'Sullivan, the peacemaker. But, if he had to take her out along the way to the truth he would and maybe Frank just for fun.

He smacked his face for idiotic sentimental thinking. No one, not even Cha Cha, was innocent. He put out a hastily lit cigarette into a face on a poster tacked to the tree.

"Nasty habit."

One of those many missing who were crushed when the buildings fell, or performed a swan dive. He had ground the cig into the man's nose. If anybody spotted him, he'd be the subject of an emergency call, 911, ha ha on him. He scanned: a panel truck to his side, a new moon somewhere above, a robust treed portion of Thompson and nobody nearby, just the same, he peeled off the missing person flyer. Ripped it into shreds and deposited it little by little into each trashcan he encountered.

He had to act on the assumption that somehow the terrorism taskforce, the phantom following him, would find him out or find the professor or one or all of his idiot helpers. He needed a plan with some small hope of success, some way to save his last remaining family member. Him.

In 1991, his parents, baby sister and brother died in Gaza while he studied at Princeton. The Israelis' just blew up their home, acting like kids jumping on sand castles. Like his family weren't children of the book, weren't really human. Without America's protection of Israel, they'd still be alive.

He had put together a proposal to Osama after attending a lecture from the visiting Professor Abunayyan on skyscraper structures. The Twin Towers, the professor went on, was a marvel of modern engineering. He read between his lines. Displaying a know-it-all ego, the professor projected disdain for the cheap construction on the excuse of sway or something like that. He demonstrated what would happen if one took out the center post. Collapse. Too simplistic as it turned out in 1993.

Ali, Sam's real name, conveniently died on the same day Sam Langrath was offed. The Trenton forensic examiner allowed a vagrant, assumed to be Ali, to be cremated.

Today Sam, yes he was Sam, knew what to do, and quickly. He stopped, held onto a tree, leaned backward and peered down the street. He'd remember the kid's home.

"Let the games begin."

He dropped down into the subway station on Spring, got off at Broadway and doubled back down Spring to visit the pretty detective's co-op on Sullivan.

Now or never.

Chapter 23

Wednesday, September 19, 11:45 a.m.

Cha Cha arrived early for her appointment with Detective Sam Langrath in Washington Square Park so she stepped up to the chapel at the corner of Thompson across from the park. The tall heavy door closed behind her. A musty mix of old wood and votive candles assaulted her and carried her to a holy world, a world greater than herself. She dug past her snub-nose .38 to the bottom of her purse for a couple quarters and lit one more, adding to the prayers for the faithfully departed. Little doubt these flames were for the victims of 9/11. She knelt and prayed for the repose of their souls and especially for her loving partner.

Daymares of faces from posters of the missing plastered the walls of her brain. Each one created a why. The whys broke apart and became a crazy soup. Thousands of whys pressed against her larynx. She had to cry out to release the pressure.

"Why, Lord?"

Her despair never vanquished its faithful companion—hope. The sisters and priests who had taught her wouldn't allow hate or despair. Hate, a mortal sin, had to be downgraded to dislike against the action of evil in the world. She raised her head and imagined her grandfather on the altar, asking her to arm herself. She confronted the irony of being a peacemaker among warriors. In a blink, her partner, Detective Jerome Price, chastised her in the same way.

"I will, Grandpapa. I will, Jerome." The huge door to the chapel creaked; she used her peripheral vision to spot a figure taking a kneeler. Another soul searching for answers, perhaps?

The tears streamed down her face. The man who had just come in had taken a pew a couple rows behind her. She turned to acknowledge him. She didn't wear much makeup and wasn't ashamed of her tears. People knew. She no longer wore a uniform, just simple jeans, pink blouse and a Jets' windbreaker today. Besides, she loved the Jets. Her grandpapa had never hesitated changing the subject to the Joe Namath miracle. Although the temperature was still moderate, a breezy day was predicted making the jacket a smart choice. The man wearing NYPD blue shocked her. Detective Sam Langrath presented a twisted smile then quickly buried his face in prayer. She had studied his dossier precedent to their meeting. He was Jewish, but God awaited those who wanted to find him in this church. Anywhere a man prayed became a chapel.

On the way out, silent, both raised their hands to block the light. They blinked away the intense noon sun. Across the street in the park, the dogs were playing and beyond them and to the left chess, to the right the frantic antiwar students spoke loudly on their soapboxes mostly to other NYU students, the vendors sold roasted chestnuts, hotdogs, giant soft pretzels. God, she already missed this place; her hidden ministry were the souls who frequented the park and nearby. Well Sam, if he toned it down a little, would do a great job with or without a partner.

"I hope I didn't disturb you."

"No, detective. It's no secret the city has cried a river to rival the Hudson."

"My condolences on your partner, a good family man." Sam, too, did his homework. He was probably an excellent detective with a bad rap as a Dirty Harry wannabe. *Make my day, say a prayer, or else I'll break your legs and make you pray.*

"Did you lose anybody?" she asked softly.

"Besides our brothers and sisters, I lost everybody I didn't know." He looked up into the maples as if blinking back tears but there were none. A cool customer. They approached the chess tables for a good place to sit and talk about her old job.

After settling in, Sam opened his briefcase and offered a wrapped pastrami on rye, with pickle; took out two cups, his thermos and placed them on the chess table. He poured two hot coffees.

"Sorry. Is black okay?"

"That's fine, Sam. I'm in a black mood. Don't feel much like eating."

He smiled kindly at her. "The people who died would be the first to want you to stay healthy."

"It's not that—"

"May I be so bold?" he interrupted. "You are a beautiful woman. And it is times like these that make me think—why the hell am I not following God's plan?"

A strange way of putting a wonderful thought.

"How's that?"

"I should start thinking about marriage, nothing personal, although I would have died and gone to heaven if a gal like you thought twice about a guy like me."

He paused, but instead of words, she just gave him the big-eyed stare she so often reserved for annoying boys in school.

Flustered, he continued, "We are in the same profession. You pray. I don't usually. I'm just a little older than *your normal admirer*?" He ticked off all the reasons she wouldn't consider him.

Got to hand him credit for honesty.

Confidence likely waning under her intense scrutiny, he ended his upside down pitch for romance, turning a statement of fact into a question. He was no Frank, but who could hold a candle? His hair was a little kinky like hers when she let it go. His jaw strong, good complexion, a muscular build, a slightly crooked nose and piercing black eyes would pass most girls' tests. So here he sat, plying her with meager gifts, flirting in an awkward way. Talking about reassessing his life after the tragedy, when Frank, most likely, just wanted to dive into her panties. Perhaps she should open her eyes and close her legs. Find a man who would love her forever. If she were smart, she'd take Autumn's mom's matchmaking more seriously. Maybe she'd even date Sam.

Elbow on the table, she propped her chin with her palm and said pointedly, "I'm no longer on the force."

"You know what I mean, Chastity." He lowered his voice. "Besides, it's pretty obvious you are working for the terrorism taskforce."

"Please call me, Cha Cha. And Frank is just a good friend." Yep, so far Frank was just a friend. *Damn it. With such friends—who needs anybody else.* As for Sam's insinuation…well, Sam didn't need to be a detective to figure this out. After all, she had left NYPD the day the taskforce started.

He raised a finger and meekly extended it a few inches from her lips. "Don't say anything. Loose lips topple buildings." His way with words sent a chill through her. "Just give me some pointers about this job, if you don't mind, and maybe someday consider a date. A *real* date at a nice restaurant. If you're interested, that is..." God, this guy was catching the Cha Cha choo choo. If he danced half as well as he sweet-talked her, he'd get that date.

She filled him in on the various characters he'd run into, the snitches, the players, the rowdy students and kind ones, the perverts, and the no longer present gangs. Thanks to her, Washington Square Park was neutral territory.

Although no Tonys and Marias died here yet, there were also no murders and hardly any drugs in the park. She went over what she did to maintain the peace and how to handle her open cases that her ex-lieutenant would likely have assigned to him.

"Give me a couple weeks to recover and then ask me again about dating. Okay, Sam?"

With a slight nod, he screwed the cap back on his thermos.

"I think I'll have that sandwich for later, if you're still offering. Okay?" she asked, a little hungry.

He popped his briefcase open and retrieved the sandwich. "I am happy you will take my little offering."

Strange language, unless he's smitten.

He hesitated as he stood. "I asked for Russian dressing on the side, so this will keep fresh until you regain your appetite." He took her hand, bowed and kissed it. This tickled her. She twisted and squirmed a little. The tough cop had a soft spot and she felt, well, not lusted after so much as idolized.

"Another time." He walked away whistling, but it didn't seem natural. He was likely confused by something. Perhaps he wondered what his chances were with her.

Before she rejoined the taskforce this afternoon, she decided to freshen up in her own home. Everything was a walk for her, most days. About a block away from her place, she tossed his sandwich into the trash. Something about Sam, no matter his charm, had put her on edge.

Inside her co-op, she noticed her bedroom closet door was buckled out slightly. She never did that. Not ever. She drew her snub-nose .38 and aimed at the closet door. She blinked as she remembered the scared little girl on the inside of grandpapa's closet the day he was murdered.

* * *

Frank and Carlos dropped what they were doing and responded to Cha Cha's call for help. Her co-op was just a block and a half away.

They ran. Well Carlos, ambled like a bear, but slightly older bears could run very fast when provoked. Carlos ended only a couple seconds behind the taller, ex-college-sprinter, Frank.

"Damn, I didn't know you had it in you," Frank expelled.

Cha Cha burst out of the building, apologizing for what she felt might be a false alarm. But stating she was certain she hadn't left the closet door ajar. Considering her trauma when seven years old, and her top-secret psych file which stated, "Detective O'Sullivan had developed a compulsion to keep things in their proper place or position, notably starting with closet doors."

"We'll get forensics over here. I have no doubt somebody was or is in your flat," Frank said. They entered the co-op knowing there was no way out, since the windows were too small, too high and barred. Carlos had drawn his gun and clasped a dagger in his other hand ready for anything. Frank leveled his Glock. They swept the co-op until they arrived at the bedroom. Cha Cha, from the sidewall position, snub-nose .38 already in hand, opened her folding closet door with her other hand pushing a mop against the crease. Nobody was in the closet, but the more they inspected the more it became obvious somebody well trained at surreptitious activity paid her place a visit.

Whomever the intruder, he or she probably tailed her to Autumn's place, surmised he had little time to check out her place. They'd scour the likely co-op entry routes he took for clues. Her home computer told the main tale. It was used from 8:59 p.m. to 9:06 p.m. the night before. Bud, from the NSA, would discover what it was used for when the computer was carted over to his lab.

Frank put his arms around Cha Cha. "We'll get our team over here, but in the meantime I want you to stay in my building."

"This is what Frank says to all the girls," Carlos grunted.

"Is this true, Frank?" She poked Frank hard on his pecks to accent her point, but didn't hurt his proud sprinter's body.

"The perp was probably interested in who your snitch was," Frank said.

"Since the CIA has the snitch in protective custody, it will do them little good." She used sign language to suggest a bug was left behind. Cha Cha was becoming a spy. The idea of her snitch under wraps at some black site was appealing misinformation. However, she either hadn't considered the possibility of a hidden camera or would talk of it, once outside. It was also good to acknowledge a snitch, because Cha Cha could have been thought of by the mole as the possible direct and only precise source of the information about the 9/11 attacks.

"Let us not talk here. We may have said too much already," Carlos snarled, obviously on board with the lady's plan of deception. "That is classified."

"Pack your bags, pretty lady, some lacy things too, the nights are starting to get cool," Frank said with his patented boyish charm, so he wouldn't get kicked or punched into her bizarre black rubber walls. Cha Cha simmered just this side of tame. He lost focus for a moment as his imagination ran rampant all over her tensing but scrumptious body, face, and well yes, the girl's heart. He became sappy around her.

Her fault really, she had started the language of familiarity. She teased, therefore he could tease back. Right? He loved to tangle with her someday, but now they needed to get her out of her breached home and into his impregnable castle. *Impregnating.*

He understood her really well at this point. What was love without commitment? Didn't they both have to leave their old fears behind, jettison their loose lifestyles and embrace change no matter where it led if they wanted more meaningful lives?

* * *

In Frank's building, outside Cha Cha's new bedroom, Frank said, "there's a starlight switch on the book board behind the bed, if you like that sort of thing." He had installed the northern hemisphere star scape on the recommendation of his interior decorator, because it fit the décor she designed: moon lamps, Milky Way drifts and twilight blue to deep purple throw rugs and walls. For an idealistic dreamer like Cha Cha, it might be attractive. Her face seemed curious ranging from girlish wonder to scientific discovery.

While Cha Cha was settling into her suite in Frank's building, Carlos cranked up the espresso machine. Waiting for the brew for two, Frank, with his hand, bowled the seven ball down the length of a nine-foot pool table. The ball rolled into the pocket.

Carlos raised his tiny cup and tapped Frank's. "Here is to your new love."

"She's amazing. But not so fast, my dear friend."

"Mark my words, Frank. You two will be dancing down center aisle of Saint Patrick's Cathedral someday."

Aside from it not being his parish, he respected Carlos's ability to predict. "What makes you think so?"

"I have never seen you cross-eyed before, and you have never encountered a woman with that much compassion."

Frank huffed out a breath. "You want the god's honest truth? I've thought about marriage in general, but each time, I think I don't want the responsibility of kids or being stuck with one woman for my whole life."

"What if this responsibility were also pleasure?" he asked slyly.

"You should talk."

"You should know better." Carlos jogged Frank's memory. The former KGB operative had been married while working and living in the now defunct USSR as their equivalent of James Bond. His wife, Natasha, was poisoned to death to punish him. She had been an innocent who thought he sold vacuum cleaner parts. Actually, he had vacuumed people. He also vacuumed up everybody who had a hand in her death. By the time he left the USSR, he had no living enemies.

"I am sorry, comrade, but your wife would have wanted you to carry on." Frank knew Carlos to be nonpolitical except when it came to Nazis. Using 'comrade' had no sting. Not that he wasn't happy when the Soviet Union fell apart. One less dictatorship. Much of his father's side of his mixed Jewish family were murdered in the Third Reich's gas chambers.

"Maybe someday when I stop this crazy business."

"What do you think of the Mongolian girl?"

"Nyet." At first, Carlos looked shocked then the corners of his mouth went up, probably he imagined schtooping the wild cat. "Perhaps, someday she will be better than I ever was because her looks are disarming. People run when they see me coming." The world's most feared assassin and/or spy was being modest. Somehow, Carlos, over the years was never linked by evidence to any of his legendary 'jobs.' Many ascribed to him bizarre deaths surrounding a number of Nazis who had been in hiding. He hadn't minded the notoricty.

"You're avoiding my idea."

"All right, Frank, she is beautiful in wholesome farm girl way. But to use an American expression, *way* too young for me. If she is anything like her lightning strikes in the ring, she would not pay me second thought anyway." He sighed. "Besides, I think your ex, Emily, is more my type. How is she doing? How are the ghosts she left you with?"

"I'm surprised. You never said anything about her."

"She was your girl. You are my friend. But now, I would fuck her in a minute."

"What about Cha Cha?" Frank asked.

"She is too beautiful for me. She is made for you. *Eah*, too tall for what I like to do." Frank could only imagine.

"I haven't heard from Emily. The ghosts are a different matter. Cha Cha tells me Emily's curse on me and her is all about the power of suggestion."

"Of course, Cha Cha is immune."

"Maybe so. Last night, Mohammad Atta told me something has gone wrong. The idiot finally figured out he hadn't ended up in paradise. Then, he enlists me in reliving the flight. I kill all his terrorist buddies, put a hole in his head. Commandeer the rapidly dropping 767, clip the torch off the Statue of Liberty and limp into Newark Airport."

"Then what?"

"Nothing. I wake up in a sweat."

"This paranormal stuff is tricky. It is as if the ghosts play tricks."

"You believe?"

Carlos picked up a cue stick, aimed the cue and sunk the three ball.

"I am skeptic. But I will use anything that will get me results. These ghosts are useless to you, unless they know who the mole is, or perhaps how many teams are left behind." He glanced up at him "If you get Atta in another dream or any of his team, ask them for information. Be friendly. Tell him you know where the virgins are. Be on their side. Say, it might help to know which one of his conspirators is keeping him from paradise because he did not do what he was told to do."

Frank grabbed a different cue stick and chalked the tip. "Interesting. Cha Cha recommended dialogue without being specific. She suggested that my subconscious could be unleashed to help solve the city's problems and that I was doing nothing more than hashing over a problem in my sleep."

"She is probably right. I will tell you what, make Cha Cha a good spy and I will do similar for Sarantsatral. Let nature take its course." Carlos sunk the six ball and Frank couldn't help but grin. The Mongolian was a handful. It would be quite enjoyable to take a front row seat and watch how he'd accomplish her transformation.

Cha Cha was gifted in a different way. Sometimes he felt like Watson to her Holmes when they were at crime scenes. *A very pretty Holmes.*

"Deal." The two shook hands, downed the dregs of the espresso, and racked the pool balls for a future game.

He rehashed how Cha Cha's chance at becoming a 'good' spy revolved around how willing she'd actually be to allow her police training to take a back seat. At least, she hadn't plugged her closet full of holes and ruined some pretty amazing outfits, or shot through to the restaurant and ruined the maître d's day.

The girl looked good in anything. Tall, skinny, but shapely. A perfect face. Her face fascinated him. A bit like Mona Lisa, except truly beautiful in a twenty-first century way. She looked like she kept some secret, disguised by broad smiles and a truly caring, empathetic nature. She put up with him. More than that, in his humbled opinion, it was entirely possible she loved him. Given that insight, he damn well should treat her with respect. Love of country drove his life. Love of one woman? Well, maybe that was possible.

Something to strive for. In the meantime, a very real threat to Cha Cha existed. Whomever it was, wouldn't live long or at least keep his freedom. Something the constitution guaranteed every citizen, but not terrorists.

Human beings were endowed with rights, true, and no matter the country. So they'd read the mole his rights, if possible.

Some countries had not received the memo on human rights. Some countries preferred harboring terrorists. Some countries treated women like cattle. Unfortunately, for one country, wake up calls would likcly be delivered by Tomahawk missiles and some very brave souls. Soon.

Osama bin Laden, soon.

Chapter 24

Each stretching stroke, hard pull, kick and flip turn in Frank's blue and pearl tiled two lane lap pool created a rhythm of quick thoughts transporting Cha Cha back to her high school and college swim teams. Endless laps and memories of happy times turned into endless lust and confused times as she imagined her rich benefactor, Frank, swimming alongside her.

She had never been driven by material things. Her happiness sprung from the heart. She blew out some air and water and paused at the wall for a breath. A riff from the Faith Hill song floated through her mind, "*Cause I can hear you breathe, It's washing over me…*"

Severely tested to stay focused and finish her laps, dripping, she could run up the spiral staircase into his arms. Not going to happen. Who'd miss a tear in this pool?

Then through the slant of her goggles, she caught Frank watching her. She pushed off the wall. She'd finish. He'd enjoy her sleek body, although she felt too skinny. Not that her ribs stuck out. Her martial arts and swimming built up harp string muscles.

Normally a guy's stare would bother her, but he could dream all he wanted. He'd ravish her, jump in, palm her waist to help her with stroke mechanics. His hand would accidently slip downward. She flipped on the wall and pushed off hard, trying to swim away from her body. Failing that, she changed from freestyle to breaststroke, just to tease him.

How am I supposed to complete a workout with my sea nymph raging?

Somehow, she had to get to her suite. She loved her temporary quarters, complete with a huge bath, therapy jets, make-up table, two walk-in closets, office, kitchen and living room. The other half of her floor was dedicated to executive offices that couldn't be entered from her suite. An onyx and white marble staircase with leather foot grips spiraled up to his penthouse. An elevator ride down one floor to the pool completed her little oasis. He stressed that she could go anywhere her heart desired.

Desire. *Desire...*

Quitting two laps early, she swam lazily to the railing steps.

He opened a huge towel and a big smile. "This pool is private to me and you and no one can see what goes on in here. So, ah, if you want to even the score, you can swim nude." This had to be a bluff because he was wearing a speedo, which on *him* with his six pack and lean, chiseled body was a piece of sugary bliss.

She played the coquette. "Wrap me up, sweetie."

He did and then draped his arms around her for extra security, ostensibly, so she wouldn't slip on the floor.

"I adore you," he said huskily.

"I know you do. The same here."

He quirked a brow and a slow, sexy smile tugged at his lips. "But...?"

"But, I want to meet your family." She had read his top-secret file and suspected his commitment problems stemmed from being ignored by his parents, even though he was their only biological child. Baby of the family, you'd think he'd be pampered. The opposite was likely true—according to her favorite government psychiatrist, Myron Markowitz, 'to put it in layman's terms, they were worn out.'

"I want to visit your parents, too."

"Deal."

She noticed the drawstring for the speedo was loose on the outside and couldn't resist the antsy thought from the devil sitting on her shoulder.

"This swimming nude idea is interesting," she said in baby doll fashion and flitting eyes. She feathered her fingers along his ripped six-pack right at the top of the speedo and loosened the string some more. His breathing heavied...his body changed. She held his waist and stretched—like the dancer she was—around him to peek at his back. He was healing nicely, but what of her stitches on his hard ass? Back in front of him, she delicately played with his drawstrings. Her head tilted. She stared into his eyes.

She fingered one of her top straps on her crimson Catalina and let it slip off her shoulder but her nipple stayed hidden. "Turn around a second. I need to see your scar."

Too willing, he did as she asked. "I don't have one, thanks to your sewing."

"I'm just going to peek." To see, she loosened the draw string some more to the point that his erection was pushing out the front of his suit. *Nice to know I'm wanted.*

His slightly turned face revealed a half smile getting broader, but still he took no action, probably because he was faced the wrong way.

"Turn around, sweetie. Your butt is fine, mighty fine."

She pulled the drawstring a little more. He licked his lips, his gray eyes dilated, and he drew in a quick breath.

God, he's cute.

Then she pulled his speedo down to his knees and ran like hell.

"Hey." He did the tangled danced and nearly fell into the pool.

"Your muscle is bulging," she shouted back.

He put both hands over his crotch and that slowed him down some more.

She smirked, putting herself in his mindset: *Pull the speedo up or drop it down? Excited to get Cha Cha. Don't want to fall on my face.* He had a problem. He stepped out of it calmly and ran after her, nude. Perhaps he was getting over his shyness—around her—and that would be a good thing.

"I'll get you." His yelp echoed off the tile walls.

"Too late, Johnny Lance. Don't forget the meeting." She jumped on the elevator afraid he'd get some part of himself caught in the door as it sliced shut. She pushed her floor button and started fanning herself. Big girls do try. She'd have to read a romance novel tonight—because there was no way he'd take her without a profession of love. Maybe a ring and a date. Maybe not.

* * *

Unless Frank and Cha Cha were out on a field trip, checking on some leads, they conducted afternoon meetings seven days a week, two floors down from his penthouse. After a week and half of meetings, their current gathering bore the most fruit. Frank, Carlos, Bud from the NSA, Percy their admin and liaison to British intelligence, and Cha Cha all sat around a glassy black table. Thanks to Bud's ingenuity, the table's center had been imbedded with a real time Satellite view of Manhattan.

Frank and Cha Cha took turns chairing. Today was Cha Cha's turn.

"How's our progress on a possible NYPD mole or the person following me, Percy?" she asked.

"We have nothing yet. We've installed cameras, not even a pro could spot, outside Autumn's place and in and out at your abode."

In a previous report, Bud had discussed a meeting with the police commissioner. New York City government intended to wire the entire city with cameras. When technology caught up in the hopefully not too distant future, all the cameras would feed into a master computer in real time, which in turn would make real sense out of what it watched.

She understood better than anybody else present—except perhaps Percy—that this was the beginning of *Big Brother*. But the City under duress had to erode individual liberty and privacy as a matter of survival.

Percy continued. "There was no physical evidence left behind in your apartment. A complaint of a smell from in your building caused a hazmat-suited perp to gain entry that night."

"Thanks, Percy. Keep on it. What happened to the Saudi adjunct who funneled monies to the hijackers, Carlos?" Cha Cha asked. The low-level consulate officer working at the United Nations was also a spy. He left the U.S. under immunity on September 17th. Unfortunately for the Saudi royal family, he had gone rogue when he funded airplane lessons and handed spending money to the hijackers. The CIA recommended applying leverage to the Saudis and the U.S. State department signed off.

"The wayward Saudi met up with an ill-fated accident while in Dubai yesterday," Carlos replied. "He was inspecting the build site of Shangri-La Tower when he caught his foot in how do you say, a rut, and watched helplessly as steel beam fell on him."

It seemed the secret threat by the U.S. to take over Saudi Arabia and their oil fields was too much for the Saudis, but she had to ask. "Did the Saudis have a hand in this?"

Carlos, a veteran of many a meeting and many a curious novice—like herself, no doubt—just gave her a big smile and continued on. "I have heard South African team won construction contract for this hotel, legitimately. Maybe the Saudis should have gotten job. However, South Africans are extremely good at what they do. Before his unfortunate accident, the Saudi had things to say."

After getting over the shock brought on by her moral backbone, police training and especially her grandfather's philosophical talks, she asked about the information. She couldn't rustle any pity for the perp. All she saw was the hell of people screaming, burning, jumping as two Towers fell.

"You guys might think I'm still a cop at heart…but not this time gentlemen." Despite herself, she couldn't shake images of another victim and hero—her deceased partner, Jerome. She allowed a faint and momentary smile for a beautiful man who—and now in her memories forever—wagged French-fries in her face.

"You're too skinny, kid. You need a little more grease in your life."

"Go ahead, kill yourself, Jerome."

"What with these fries? What will kill me is a partner too weak to help me when I get in trouble."

If her lieutenant hadn't been down on her abilities so much. If he hadn't recommended her for community service on 9/11…she might have kept her partner safe. Perhaps she was weak.

Was.

Whatever happened would never repeat itself, with her new friends, and especially her new partner, Frank.

Blinking back tears, she regained her thread. "So…what do you have for us today, Bud?"

"Well one…there are reports surfacing about a suitcase Romeo we believe to be the professor, who loves them and leaves them, the girls, mostly teachers—generally wanting more education." The NSA engineer bent over the table and flicked open his hand over lower Manhattan. "He was last seen leaving this Canal

Street location, presumably to pick up another woman. His excuse is wearing thin. That is, he claimed his apartment was evacuated being too close to ground zero. Unfortunately, one love sick woman recognized his supposed home address as a commercial building." He paused for a moment. "So number two, Percy's team has his place completely wired for sound and video. So far he hasn't come home."

"He schtoops teachers?" Carlos seemed tickled. He must have had some 'bad' teachers growing up.

"Or visa versa. Number three, the person who has done the impossible, who is ripping through random crypto secure impregnable firewalls, getting by and into Cyclops, breaking into secure top secret sites and is interested in everything Frank including texting and emailing him to offer assistance to our taskforce. Would you like to know my chief suspect's name?"

"I have a suspicion," Cha Cha said. A one girl wrecking crew...

"The smartest person on the planet, no not Lex Luther, more like Albert Einstein on steroids."

"Yes, Bud," she said, prompting him to continue.

"Autumn Breeze. And I'm not talking the windy cold we had today."

"I've got to meet this kid," Frank said. "Set it up, Carlos." His pal, Carlos, had promised Autumn a chess game in Washington Square Park.

Cha Cha was intrigued. "She's probably planning to see you, Frank, with or without the park meet. What has she been saying?"

Frank said, "Sorry, I didn't confide. I wanted to find out who, before I shared, since it's only been less than a week. Basically, she writes down ideas for strengthening the city's defenses, nothing we haven't already considered. Claims she has more and wants a one-on-one."

"Why is she doing this, Bud?" Cha Cha asked.

"The kid has been lying to all of you—well Carlos, Frank, Ayita, my chief at the NSA, and you, Cha Cha. Her mom went missing on 9/11. Hasn't come home yet. The girl fears deportation, and get this, she thinks you two," Bud swept his hand at Cha Cha and Frank, "should fall in love, get married and adopt her. Presto magico. So she doesn't get deported and she thinks the world of you, Cha Cha, and thinks Frank is the ideal man for Cha Cha."

"If I'm going to adopt her, I better meet her, but marry Cha Cha? Oh, come on," Frank said, with a deadpan delivery.

"Let's stay on point," Cha Cha, lips pursed, retorted, not missing a beat. Frank would pay later for that catty remark. "Bud, find out how she's doing it. Percy, get your British friends to light up her apartment. Frank, you and I are going to tangle." The light touch at the end was her way of adjourning the meeting.

"Do you want to meet in our gym, in sweats?" Frank asked innocently as if he weren't the bad boy. Yet the jock probably did want to wrestle her at some point. She'd pick the time and place and without warning, but today she just wanted to kick his ass—literally. She had become convinced that she would make him the best wife and lover he could ever hope for.

"I think we should be leaving these two. Their roofs have slid off," Carlos said with a smirk. He stood and the others did as well. She interpreted Carlos's meaning by tone and the visual of roofs sliding off: Carlos suggested Frank and Cha Cha were crazy. Maybe plain crazy or maybe just crazy for each other.

"One last thing, Percy. No, better yet, Frank and I will find out what happened to Autumn's mom, because that kid needs a mother before Autumn brings down the entire government."

"I'll assign Autumn's tail an additional duty," Percy said. Although Autumn didn't know she was being tailed, more for her safety, Cha Cha and probably the others at the meeting wouldn't be surprised if she did know. Her tail was more her out-of-sight bodyguard. This was necessary on the remote chance that the NYPD mole would figure out her involvement in the 9/11 report and come after her. The tail was a total pro. Unspottable—to all but the prescient.

After they all left the conference room, Frank opened the liquor cabinet behind the wet bar and then the fridge below the bar. He pulled out some Jamaican coconut rum crème. He would not get her drunk to get out of this one. She wouldn't let him.

"What's your pleasure, doll?"

"You're my pleasure, Frank, and you feel the same way or I wouldn't bring it up."

"Yes. Guilty." He poured two shots and brought them over. "This isn't to get you into bed. This is to celebrate."

She sipped the smooth, delicious drink. "What are we celebrating?" She licked her lips slowly. He groaned.

"Well, plenty of couples—and we are almost a couple—have to do a tiresome amount of fucking to make a kid."

He was a regular comedian. She cracked up, got up and crawled onto his lap. So much for berating him. "Say that again."

Instead of saying something, he lingered with a kiss. This kiss was not one of those rip-your-clothes-off, pressing wantonness or a hello I-really-like-you peck.

This kiss was different than any kiss she enjoyed in her life.

His lips parted slightly. His happy dancing eyes, the way he caressed her cheeks, the way his lips formed a smile. He adored her, like a man in love. Joyfully, she felt no less. She surrendered to him. Someday soon, she'd share every intimacy. After a while, she lay her head on his chest, content with listening to his heartbeat.

She wasn't quite ready for making love. Had to hear him say it, show her.

He had said so much already with his comment implying marriage and adoption. To reach this point in their relationship so soon pushed way past her hopes. His heart beat the message. But the question dangled, did she understand him correctly? Was he earnest or had his profession of domestication to her been another flippant joke?

As if to answer her, "I love your lips, kid."

"I've never been kissed like that by anybody ever."

"Is that good?" he murmured.

"I'd say at least one of us was falling in love."

Frank kissed her nose. "You make a great detective."

"And you take my breath away."

"I've been fighting for the USA all my adult years, never knowing if I'd live another day."

"I know, sweetie. If we can find a way to stay together…"

"The terrorist threats may never end."

"There are far more of us sane people. We will never lose."

They embraced and stayed that way until she, a little dizzy, felt like taking him to the conference room floor.

He knew. He cupped her shoulders, calming her. "We'll figure all this out soon. And there will be heaven."

They had to get going to interview one of the ladies jilted by the suitcase Romeo.

* * *

Frank and Cha Cha had to put their feelings on hold. Working 24/7 over the next two weeks, Frank and Cha Cha then took point investigating a bunch of strange deaths, seemingly hate crimes against Muslims.

FDNY had left the scene. A small computer repair shop in Brooklyn, just off Flatbush, burnt to the ground, with every employee inside. Cha Cha thought of Detective Sam Langrath, who used to work in this precinct. She quickly dismissed the association as too easy. There were plenty of cops in Brooklyn.

Two days before the fire, the owner had blown himself up in what was being reported as a boating accident. The accident occurred in a bay channel between Jones Beach and Nassau Shores, Massapequa.

The reporters were being misled about the repair shop fire. The terrorist taskforce, through their NYPD network, leaked stories of the owner's financial troubles. The story implied he probably paid somebody to torch the place. The stories speculated that the arsonist probably had no idea the "Geek Team" would be working late. The dead owner certainly had no way of stopping the ill-timed torch and the manslaughter that resulted from it.

All the deceased were Muslims with middle eastern origins. The press did not know some of their computers harbored terrorism links.

The U.S. Attorney General had ordered all agencies to try to keep a lid on hate crimes as long as possible, to avoid a race or religious war. Some crimes might go unreported or underreported but the perps would be caught and prosecuted. Cha Cha, having a detective's panache, led this investigation.

"It's the NYPD mole," Frank said. Some damaged hard drives and disks at the crime scene belonged to the Suitcase Romeo, the architecture professor who might be able to ID the alleged mole. No usable data was found on this material.

"Yes, the mole is covering his tracks, destroying all possible paths that might lead to him." Unfortunately, Cha Cha was either a curiosity or a target. There were no links yet to Autumn, as far as they could judge. The taskforce remained vigilant.

Autumn's deep surveillance tail had tales to tell. Autumn had a boyfriend, of sorts, named Joey, just as Autumn had mentioned. A good boy, who had a soft heart for the girl, but remained hands off. They exchanged lessons on Fridays. He helped her do her mom's business and she helped him with science. They cooked up a storm each Friday night, and apparently, this was enough for the boy, thank God. They made a cute if unlikely couple.

The investigation had yet to find her mom, which prompted a phone call and a concerned visit from Cha Cha.

Autumn kept lying. "Oh, my mom is always doing the disappearing act. She knows I run the household, pay the bills. No worries. I'm good." This always brought a tear to Cha Cha. She loved the girl so much.

There wasn't a day in which Cha Cha couldn't help but worry about her unofficial kid sister. The best way to slow down her worrying involved catching the mole, before he caught Autumn.

Chapter 25

It was time to breathe a little, the air crisp with autumn breezes, the trees and ground heavy with yellow and red maple leaves. Time to live again. Play lunchtime chess in Washington Square Park for two dollars a pop. Autumn could use a little extra change and *perhaps* a change from the ridiculous notion of getting a new mom and dad to fall in love. *Idiot.* She pulled on her brown macaroni curls.

Well okay, way ahead on all her courses, and audits of Quantum Mechanics and the History of Film, she could use this time in a bucolic setting to concoct some brilliant way out of her mess. The smell of sauerkraut on very fat hot dogs reminded her she needed to eat. Her winnings would go to lunch.

That bear of a man approached and slid into the end table opposite her.

"I will pay you twenty dollars for the pleasure of your company and game. You will try. You will lose." He leaned toward her. "No matter—Autumn Breeze, your fear of me will destroy your skills as a master," Carlos, director of OTTS and on loan to the Terrorism Taskforce said.

You will lose.

This was some sort of hypnotic suggestion he tried on her. Although scary, he'd not harm a kid. Not likely. Well, maybe 1 in 23.6753 million. *A squirrel should steal her pawn and leave behind an acorn.*

The man had those demented genius eyes, not of her caliber naturally, but dangerous as a spy and on the chessboard, no doubt.

"Talk is cheap, mister."

"Take the white pieces, devotshka."

"Just don't offer me candy and we'll get along fine, chess master Petrovich." *Put on that puckish face, girl.*

Yeah, she knew Petrovich's history. She had long since hacked into the NSA, at first primarily using Frank's phone to identify the ever-changing gatekeeper codes and then front door into the NSA mainframe. She used an intermittent and tiny parasitic hop onto Frank's transmissions—thanks to NYU's labs. The parasite or virus she had devised opened a hole for her as wide as the grand canyon, but it wouldn't last long because the engineers at the NSA were trying to stop her. Those men and women must think of this as a game, but to her it was survival.

So she kept reinventing her approach using new viruses and also dropping Frank's phone for others including Cha Cha's. Being embedded within the NSA mainframe and satellite computers also helped. She opened up so many portals the engineers would have to play hide and seek with her for maybe a couple more weeks and that would be all she needed to find a way to stay in the USA, by proving to them she was a national treasure. Hacking Frank's and Cha Cha's phones also allowed her to keep tabs on them. The surveillance led her to realize they liked each other. All they needed was a little push *and baby makes three.*

Soon there would be another way to ingratiate herself. She almost had it nailed down. All she needed was Joey's help to pull it off.

Carlos had been Leningrad's junior champion and placed third in the USSR Championship Prelim, one year. He never took it any further than the coveted soviet master's title, which was close to senior master in U.S. chess. He preferred working for the KGB full time doing what, she couldn't find out, but had a hunch he installed air-conditioning in peoples' heads. He now played chess with friends as entertainment. She'd entertain him alright.

No psych-out today. She'd skip the normal kibitzing with him because he'd chew her up and spit out the bones. No one, not even her fat pockmarked uncle, had looked this scary. She half expected him to ground up her king in his hand. It wasn't his stocky body or bushy eyebrows, many guys were built that way; it was that secret killer look in his eyes, right through to his fake *smiling mouth.*

She twisted her nose and pushed her e-pawn two squares. He responded with the double-edged Sicilian, her favorite defense to crush. Soon he played to restrain her bishop's mobility on the queenside, so she wouldn't be able to saddle him with doubled pawns. He smirked like he just thought up a new way to kill somebody.

The game was even until a squirrel showed up to watch by balancing itself on the top bench slat behind her. He got up and fed the furry fan a peanut. Okay, so maybe he wasn't all-evil or maybe he was trying to distract her.

"Got a girlfriend, mister?" *Every Boris needs a Natasha.*

"Always be prepared." He ignored her, his none-answer being too cool.

Then he sacked his rook normally worth five points for her knight worth three. She had seen this before. In this position, black wasn't supposed to have enough compensation for the sacrifice in power. She knew the lines, all the lines, but he uncorked a novelty and she found herself rooting for him without blabbing the correct variations, of course. She found all his moves right down to her being mated in six.

"I resign, Sir," she said, tipping her king, trying to appear cool. She hated losing.

In master chess, it wasn't necessary to watch the last few moves; she gave up with three to go. The chances, after his brilliancy and his mating attack, left no doubt. Still the man displayed a courteous poker face and a slight fatherly smile directed at penetrating her eyes like a vampire. *Got to be a joke, right?*

"I came today to ask your help. I am sure in long run you would beat me maybe 30% of the time."

"Maybe 36.24%. I grow when I devote time to learning more about the game but I want to do more with my life, like get Osama bin Laden. I'll remember this, Sicilian. If you try your novelty again we'll be testing a different variation."

Carlos fished in his pocket.

"Keep your twenty bucks. I'd rather have a pretzel. I'm hungry. Please." She tried her Little Orphan Annie smile on him.

"You will have both. I support the arts and your art, my little Judit Polgar. I will be right back." He walked off. She replayed the game in her head. No holes were found. Avoid the variation, next time.

"Deli-mustard," she shouted.

"Do not let anybody take my place."

"No way," she said quietly.

After he came back and they munched a bit, he started smiling.

"You're not here to hire me as a spy?"

He burst out into a bellowing laugh. "Nooo. Mind your tongue. Someday my little *chudo*, someday." He called her a little miracle. How sweet. She hoped so. "Ms. Ayita Starblanket and me too, we think very highly of you. I am here to fulfill your wish, maybe a fool's journey. You want to get Frank and Cha Cha to fall in love and get married and adopt you, yes?"

"Ah."

"But I am afraid at the moment they will not adopt you, for many reasons... Wait, wait a minute." He put up his hand to silence her pending verbal deluge. She wanted to find out how he knew her plan. "I am also here to warn you about somebody's *cyber-attacks on the NSA* and one other item." He whispered some of the important spy words. Of course, she was that somebody. *Caught. Go to your room.*

This bear had stepped into her fantasy world and now acknowledged her deepest desires. Who was hacking who? She should have known better. But, at least, there was an upside. No longer alone—Carlos her unlikely friend— and maybe, just maybe she had a chance at a mom and a dad. *Stay cool.* "Have you been spying on me? Why do you think I want Frank and Cha Cha to get married?" Tears tickled down her cheeks, she knew he knew. Her fantasy world crumbled. She dipped down as if studying a chess move for the post mortem of their game and swiped her tears away.

"Let me answer your second question first. Frank is brother to me. I have known him for years. He never makes his heart completely available. But, around her, he is like puppy. His eyes get very big. He is very happy each day. Cha Cha is special. She has the intellect of a great detective, heart of Mother Theresa. She is a gifted athlete with the bod—" Carlos shut-up for a moment. "So maybe you have a chance."

"Hey, I'm fourteen, I know. She's very pretty—beautiful and super sexy."

"Is your homework done for the day?"

"Yes, but Master Carlos, please answer my first question."

A strong cool breeze whipped west to east through the park causing little dirt devils to dance in the speckled sunlight on the hexagonal-block concrete walk. Hopefully a good omen but usually bad, *So what Carlos is going to say has to be good, right? Think positive.*

"I told you the first time I met you that you might be *target of terrorist forces*." He lowered his voice for the last four words once again, and wiped his mouth at the same time, even though no one was walking by and the nearest chess game was six tables down. Barny-the-drunk was closer but passed out behind his table, not sleeping. Carlos might have been covering his mouth to throw off lip readers. She too could be a detective.

"So let us say we have been watching you and why would we not? You are driving a team of the *NSA engineers meshuga* and, of course, Frank and his people. Nobody knows of your report yet, we are hoping. So we watch you for these many reasons." He obviously didn't want to mention—she could get killed by one of Osama bin Laden's lackeys—because she was a defenseless and *tender child. Snick.*

"I'm a big girl. I understand. I'll explain. But there's something else, isn't there?"

"You don't need to explain—you want a new mom and dad."

"You have something else to tell me."

"Yes. Whatever you do, try not to react. Always assume you are being watched. Your mother is alive. I cannot take you to her but do not look because I feel an evil presence near. Frank's black van is in front of library. You know this van?"

She'd be brave. "Oh yes and I understand." Carlos needed to pretend to be a civilian to maintain his cover. She had the hardest time holding back tears and rage. Her fantasies were crumbling again, but mom was alive. Inwardly, she screamed for her mom and most of all her dad. She felt like falling into his grave. Why couldn't Dad be raised from the dead? They could have a real family again. The three of them had run down Seaside Height's boardwalk, happy. The cotton candy. The hugs. The doll he won for her. He spent $10.75 to get a doll that could be made in Thailand and sold in bulk for 76 cents. But it was hers. It meant her daddy loved her. Her mom too, jumped up and down when he won. Gave her the best kisses and hugs.

Carlos had to know, she had no incentive to put Frank and Cha Cha together now that he told her they wouldn't adopt her. She'd do it anyway, because they, dah, were in love. Yeah, she'd do it for their own good; they belonged together. She knew because on top of hacking, she had been spying and just loved it.

She'd do it for herself. Cha Cha was her BFF, best friend forever. Besides, she would not give up, just because some know-it-all spy told her it couldn't be done.

"Walk over like you are going to library, and Frank and Cha Cha will do the rest. They will answer all your questions. I want you to have this phone. You can call me using it," Carlos said. She fingered and studied it. Sleek black plastic, Sprint, but its feel was different, maybe the weight, maybe smoother."

"Is this, a 'you know,' phone?"

"This one will not get you into 'you know,' *NSA*," he whispered into her ear, "like you do. It is special phone. I will tell you more about it on phone later."

She picked herself up, took his twenty bucks, thanked him for the game and pretzel and double-timed her steps. She slowed down. *Natural. Look natural.* She blew her nose and quickly wiped her eyes to stem the about-to-be flood.

She turned to him and walked back seemingly to shake his hand but really for a little more information.

"I'm sorry about my hacking."

"Eh. You break down their walls. They build them bigger and stronger."

Shit, she could go to jail for hacking into government sites and maybe she'd get no books in her tiny grimy, smelly, moldy cell. Maybe, just to torture her, they'd make her share her cell with a stinky three-hundred pound child molester. She wouldn't be able to go to the bathroom. But her hacking was for one reason only and maybe the judge or Ayita would understand. She wanted a mom and a dad. At least now, she would get her mom back.

* * *

Standing proud in NYPD blue, with one foot on the fountain bench in Washington Square Park, Detective Sam Langrath munched on a Nathans with the works. His job today was to mix with the antiwar protestors. He had always thought that odd—protesting war. With war came change, but the attacks on 9/11 had backfired. The United States killed Muslins, wholesale. They'd catch Osama. They'd infiltrate the cells. They'd find him, someday soon. He knew he had days to live, if he didn't turn himself in. He couldn't do it. He'd rather go to hell.

A dirty or real nuclear weapon would have had teeth, might still. He gave encouraging glances and smiled to the kids who stood around antiwar speakers. That's right, kid. Stay weak and die. This country was ninety-nine percent behind the war on his freedom fighters. Fat chance, waiting for America to go asleep again would not work. He flashed the peace symbol, but some of the kids he hadn't already befriended on previous occasions, regarded him with suspicion.

He observed the pretty, mixed-race kid. First, she played chess with a Russian chess master. He had seen this man before in the park, heard of his prowess. He played chess with a grad student and another Russian. Seemed to be harmless.

She, looking a little upset, left the chess nut. Perhaps she lost. Then she walked across the street to the library where an SUV, reeking U.S. government issue, whisked her away. Unfortunately, the SUV was faced the wrong way and was too low from the mirrored entrance to the library for him to see anything. Besides, the doors and full-length windows were all up steps and just missed reflecting the inside of the van.

Why did this kid get so much attention from law enforcement, both local and national? Only one explanation fit all the facts. Cha Cha met with this kid. The government had an interest. As ridiculous as it seemed, she had to be Cha Cha's snitch.

She leaked information about 9/11. Cha Cha's report now nowhere to be found had read something like, *One or two planes will fly into the Twin Towers on September 11, 2001 and one or both buildings will collapse.* Simple and damning. Damning, because he was heading to hell, sent by a girl. Somebody screwed up royally and the idiot would pay with his life.

Or she might have overheard something from somebody who knew of the plot. Perhaps there was a redundant or separate cell he wasn't aware of. Maybe the kid's parents or parents of her friends knew something somehow. No matter—it would only be a matter of time before they'd get to him. The professor was still running loose or the girl might recall some new tidbit. The only thing that slowed them down from discovering him was the diversion of resources to investigate the Anthrax threats. In his opinion, some domestic idiot thought that one up.

He'd use the NYU library to research this kid, not the precinct, and make sure he hadn't jumped to false conclusions. Kids died in the attacks of 9/11, collateral damage. One more wouldn't make a difference.

* * *

Autumn's head simmered to a fast boil. Of course, she loved her mom; of course, she hated her mom. No, she resented her for not loving her back. She stumbled off the curb across from the library. Maybe there in that blackness of the SUV lurked all the answers. She hoped her conclusions would be proven wrong. Nobody was perfect. Least of all, her. She had been an obnoxious piece of work. Every day her mom lived with her, Autumn said something to try to upset her. She was getting fat. Her hair was dirty. She couldn't do her job. She hated Autumn, for sure. She wanted her mom back, sober and loving. She'd fix their relationship. Another chance, just another chance. Please, God. She wanted her daddy back. She wanted love.

Her logic failed her. She couldn't attach stupid probabilities to explain the sudden resurrection of her mom. *Not today, brain fog setting in.*

Still she tried to rev up her neurons. Her mom disappeared on the same day the Towers fell. The same day she had told her mom not to go to the Towers. All she could think was her mom ran off ashamed to admit to being a lousy mom. She got married maybe, and was here to tell Autumn her goodbye. She was moving to, ah, any damn place. Philadelphia. The SUV door slid open and in she hopped.

* * *

The kid surprised Frank when she threw her arms around him and then climbed over his thighs to get to Cha Cha. Autumn sobbed. They drove off. He was intrigued by her familiarity. He reached out and patted her curly hair to show back to her that he too could be an instant friend although his cell phone had already played host to her.

She wore the same black denim jacket she had on the day they rescued the cat. 9/11. God, they, all of New York—all the world, he speculated—had gone through so much over this insane act of killing innocents.

Through sobs and a blowing nose, Autumn said, "Why didn't my mom call me? I thought she died on 9/11 in the Towers. In the Windows on the World. I've followed the survivor lists. I've checked the hospitals. All of them." She waited.

"Let me," Frank said to Cha Cha. He wanted to get to know this teenaged force of nature a lot better, this hurricane. Cha Cha nodded while she held the girl tight to her bosom.

"Your mom wrote a note that should explain everything." He dug into his Dockers pocket and pulled out an eight-and-a-half-by-eleven ruled white paper her mom's nurse had given him.

She glanced at his hand holding the paper. Cha Cha pushed the girl's curls away from her eyes.

"I'm going to see her, right?"

"Yes, dear," Cha Cha said.

"Then I want to wait to see her before I read this. How long?"

"Maybe five minutes."

"You're wearing the same pants you wore on 9/11, Mr. Lancia."

"Same brand, same color, different pants. Those had to…" He trailed off, not wanting to speak of toxic waste or being naked with a thousand tiny knives in his back in front of Cha Cha in her shower.

The girl picked up the slack. "Do you love Cha Cha?" She buried her head into Cha Cha's shoulder as if afraid of his answer.

He hesitated, looked out the opposite window. Did he? He certainly acted like a lovesick schoolboy around her. He loved her. But Autumn might get her hopes up before the two adults in the back seat could work things out. He caught the kid's dark brown penetrating eyes and knew he couldn't lie.

"Little Miss Hacker, I think you know the answer."

Cha Cha raised one eyebrow and exchanged exasperated looks with Autumn. Now he had two women sniffling. Luckily, they arrived at the hospice at Warren and West Broadway.

Autumn's mom had written WW on a whiteboard the day she disappeared. Autumn jumped to the conclusion—it stood for, Windows on the World, atop the North Tower of the World Trade Center. The kid snapped her head as she noticed the street sign, obviously putting two and two together—Warren and West Broadway—shook her head, and then sunk again into her unofficial big sister.

They climbed the steps in the apartment building being used as a hospice. The dingy hallways were only matched by threadbare brown carpets, worn drapes. This place was little better than a flop house. It's beautiful but grayed outside façade recalled a bygone era.

"Is this a hospice?" Autumn asked. "And how did you find her?"

Cha Cha explained how this converted co-operative helped those who had no insurance to die with dignity. The nonprofit running the place didn't have the money to spend on cosmetic improvements. Instead, they took contributions from the dying to pay for communal nursing and one doctor who made daily rounds. Frank felt uncomfortable in answering her question about how they found her mom and mentioned how they'd address it later in a more private setting. Autumn knew anyway a lot about the way the NSA used probability and how detectives followed leads.

She suggested, once again, Autumn read the note before she saw her mom, but Autumn explained she wanted her head free of preconceptions. The kid was fighting for her sanity. She intimated, the moment her mind put together what happened, she'd be at peace with whatever had happened to her mother.

Frank gave the kid a hug.

"Autumn," Cha Cha prompted, but the girl said nothing.

Frank jumped in, trying a different tact. "Sorry, Autumn. We are with you. You are loved." The girl roused from her funk and displayed a small smile drooped by her sad eyes.

She turned away and grabbed the handle to her mom's shared room.

Monique Breeze lay still in her bed, eyes closed. Her hair was combed out onto the pillow, obviously by somebody else. Monique had fine Asian mixed with South American Indian, maybe some French, some black—all giving her a deep bronze hue to her beautiful skin.

"Mom?" She didn't respond. Cha Cha went out the door and came back in with a nurse.

"She comes in and out of consciousness," the nurse said.

"Are you the one who combed my mom's hair?"

"Yes, dear."

"Thank you." Autumn picked up a washcloth, dipped it in a bowl of water and wiped her mother's forehead.

"Frank, let's leave Autumn alone." He had gone to the window and peered, through the grime, south toward where the Twin Towers used to be.

"Please stay." Autumn wiped her eyes. "I can't read this."

Cha Cha picked up the letter and read it aloud.

Dearest Autumn,
I'm so sorry, my sweetie,
We lost your daddy,
And it killed me.
I started drinking.
Then, I found out I had liver cancer.
My chances were dim and the operations were too much
money.
Funny thing.
I lived all this time.
I know you think you hate me.
But I never stopped loving you.
Once I started drinking I went crazy.
When I lost my hold on reality I lost you.
I'm sorry. I spent most of your Jeopardy winnings on this
place.
I knew you'd find a way to pay the bills.
You are so incredibly smart.
I wanted you to keep studying, not take care of me.
Although you shouldn't just study.

210

Have a little fun.
Make friends.
Someday you will do great things.
You tried to help this great country.
Someday you will.
I love you with what is left of me,
Your mom,
Monique Breeze

On the way out, the administrator of the hospice called out.

"Your Grand mom is on my line, Miss Autumn."

Shoulders slouched and miserable looking, Autumn entered the front office next to the exit. After about five minutes, she ran right by Cha Cha and Frank and started up West Broadway. Frank gave chase with Cha Cha trying to keep up.

Frank grabbed the kid a half block later. She turned and beat his chest. He held her closer. She stopped and didn't speak until Cha Cha caught up.

"You two have ruined my life. Leave me alone. Let me go."

"What is it, honey?" Cha Cha asked, just as Frank was beginning to put a scenario together. Autumn's grand mom was going to take her out of New York or move in with her. The reality was far more shocking.

"My granny is going to take me back to Trinidad when mom dies." She tried to break loose but Frank grabbed her wrist.

"Not yet sweetie," he said.

"You want to be my friends, help me stay here. I want to help my mom too."

"We're so sorry about your mom." Cha Cha gently extricated Frank's hand from Autumn's wrist and gathered the sobbing girl into her arms.

Frank added soothingly, "We'll escort you down here, anytime. Our prayers are with you."

Once Autumn had calmed down, they all sat on a co-op stoop. Cha Cha and Frank both promised to see what they could do about Trinidad, but since her mom was here on an expired work permit and about to die, their hands might be tied. Autumn left unsaid her feelings about being adopted. Frank—through the taskforce's surveillance, Autumn's texts and emails and observing her antics—had become attached to this girl of simple heart and complex mind.

But, Cha Cha and he had to negotiate a life together without confusing their love with anything else. After they were solid, and only then, could they seriously address fighting to keep Autumn in New York as their daughter. With a mole out there somewhere showing interest in Cha Cha's 9/11 prediction report, perhaps the safest thing Autumn could do was move to Trinidad.

Chapter 26

After nearly a week of tending to her comatose mom with either Frank, Cha Cha or both by her side, Autumn came to the surface to breathe, at least for this Friday night.

Friday night rivaled classes at NYU as Autumn's favorite time, anyway. Although Joey and she weren't a real couple, she enjoyed his attention. She had something to look forward to. He had said he'd kiss her when her boobs plumped and she curved out more.

Like a stick, now. She pranced in front of the mirror on the bathroom door.

He cautioned her that a kiss was just a kiss and they agreed—well, more him than her—to the proposition that neither of them knew who they'd like when they grew up. He treated her with respect and that laid the foundation for a great friendship. Even though he was probably growing up faster with lots of girls to tempt him, she'd enjoy these little sessions in the kitchen and at the study table for her business and his studies.

Joey and Autumn were trying to figure out how to make from scratch a Stromboli without it burning or exploding. She wouldn't resort to deep frying, which was unhealthy. Besides, she didn't have a fryer.

Basically you fold up a pizza—chock full of your favorite stuff—until you have a small football and hope it doesn't burn or blow up. Interesting problem of gaseous pressure being inversely proportional to heat rising. Kaboom. She calculated the safe cross-over of time, pressure and heat.

They were also trying to cook up a way to turn her sly promise to Frank and Cha Cha that she would supply them meaningful dates into something more. Of course, it looked way more like—they were doing her the double favor.

Frank played along with Autumn's matchmaking because he had promised to help support her mom's failing business and he needed to change his ways from dysfunctional and meaningless relationships to something more fulfilling. If city politics played out, he and Cha Cha would soon be fired. Autumn hadn't figured this one out. She could discern only so much from hacking and sometimes felt as though she was being deliberately misled. Probably, Bud was there on the other end of her hack laughing at her.

Frank and Cha Cha had supervised and performed beyond expectations their Taskforce responsibilities, according to some emails between the mayor and the police commissioner. *So why the talk of firing?* Although she couldn't breakdown the encrypted messages that actually said what Frank and Cha Cha did, she was happy because this meant they were careful and this in turn would protect all the people of New York including herself.

Her best guess: Unfortunately, no matter how good a job Frank and Cha Cha were doing, the mayor, the commissioner and even the president could move the goal posts if it suited their strange political worlds often dedicated to whom you know, not how much you know.

Autumn cared, she followed through with her promises and she needed to make money to pay the bills until her affairs were in order. Thanks to Cha Cha's suggestions, especially about charging up front, Autumn had money coming in.

She and Joey set both Frank and Cha Cha up for dates, with a double twist, tonight, and Joey all excited wanted to get a table in the same restaurant, just to see their twists work-out and eat some yummy Chinese food. Hey, it was her first date, too.

* * *

Frank reluctantly took the subway to Chinatown to meet a sharp looking Chinese-American girl at the Platinum Palace, Lilly Wang. Since he had met Cha Cha and with Emily back in New Orleans he hadn't enjoyed a sexual interlude. Moments with Cha Cha—from a tease to a smile—fulfilled him. Almost. But, you never know about Chinese food. If he was hungry after the meal, he will have failed his first test. Was he in love? Doing this favor for Autumn would help clarify these feelings he had for Cha Cha.

His date approached being directed by their waitress. Taller than he expected, perhaps six-two, his height. This was fine. One rule of online dating: no matter what, they'd lie about some facet of their lives or their age and other physical characteristics. He just wasn't very attracted to really tall girls—in general.

"You are, ah, Johnny Riccardi?" He insisted in staying out in the cold, as a spy, as much as he could, thus a better fake name this time.

"Yep. You are taller than you wrote, Lilly." They shook hands. Best get the awkward gorilla in the room stuff out of the way, up front.

"Don't you like how my outfit fits?" She twirled and showed off a most infectious smile.

This was not likely a come-on, just a display of girl tease, good spirits, and a pinch of feisty. What a challenge had been thrown at him, but it was fair considering he wasn't very polite with his first words. He should have known she'd be bold. She listed herself as an unrepentant tomboy who loved to wrestle guys. He pictured her strong upper thighs squeezing some poor fellow. But Cha Cha was also a tomboy, just a more delicate one.

"Yes, you are elegantly beautiful and sorry. I believe in getting the awkward stuff out of the way first."

She slipped into the seat with a little butt wiggle. Erotic. He poured two fingers of plum wine from a decanter designed with peacocks on white porcelain.

"So many guys are insecure. They think they can't satisfy a woman my height." She took his hand and inspected it. "I hope we can find out someday." She paused and cocked her head back a little. "You look like you are hiding something from me or maybe you're just uncomfortable."

As an attorney, Lilly's experience reading juries and her job in general, meant she'd pick at his psyche and confront him with verbal acuity, until he answered her honestly or she could read him. She had or would soon have his number.

"I'm only uncomfortable because, after we corresponded, I had developed a crush on a fellow worker." Partially true—Cha Cha came first, but no sense in making Lilly feel tricked. "But she has let every guy know she wants marriage. I'm trying to work through my fears of committing with her or anybody else. I wrote that on the profile, right?"

"Yes, it's all right. In order for me to find a decent man, I start with honesty and integrity. I sense, you've got it, Johnny." This time she leaned in and focused eye to eye.

If only she knew the lies he used to protect and develop his life as a spy. But he loved his country. He would never tell anyone, not even Cha Cha, of the horrors he had seen or even the funny stories. He forced images away of the spy Dimitri's last breath. Of the double agent Olga hanging from the roof. He replaced them with easier ones. The mirror that had transmitted an illegal transaction, saving the bank of Denmark. The listening device he put in the countess's dildo. He remembered its hum and her hum. She had used that thing far too often. Secrets.

In the now, they exchanged tidbits not already disclosed on the online profile while eating. He enjoyed Chow Mein with tiny pork meatballs. She devoured a roasted duck with veggies. She wanted to save the whales. He wanted to divorce his siblings.

She described her current job as an attorney for the city's child welfare department. He stayed undercover, pretending to be a freelance reporter. He asked, without disclosing the facts, about Autumn, which Lilly found endearing.

"I'd love to help you. He sounds like a very special boy."

"His mom is sick. If she dies, she was on a work visa you see. Maybe the young teen could be deported?"

"Usually not, we'd take them in as a ward of the State. But you can't be certain these days, because of all the shouting about people being here illegally after 9/11. He might need a protagonist or sponsor/guardian. If the teen is from a Muslim country he might have a hard time."

"No, Tahitian."

"I might have an out service pro-bono attorney willing to take this on. You let me know."

Then, they talked about the possibility of an 'us.' He loved that she'd like to wrestle, but she wasn't Cha Cha. He'd have to project an open mind in order to be a good dinner partner. But the more the evening wore on, the more guilt over Cha Cha grabbed him.

* * *

Across the grand dining room at a table, tucked out of sight, Cha Cha was out with her date, a semi-retired professional wrestler, Lance Longer. *Oh sure.* He was more obsessed than Frank with the idea of wrestling her. Although professional wrestlers choreographed their moves, they damn well knew how to wrestle.

"If we wrestled, how would you keep from hurting me?"

"It's not like I'd take a chair to your head or power slam you. No, we'd be having fun, rockin'-an-rollin'. You know what I mean?"

His professional wrestling moniker was the "Doctor of Death." He had sported white tear away cotton jacket, pants and a stethoscope. When he won, he'd listen to his opponent's heartbeat. Then, he'd stomp on his opponent's chest. The hapless loser was carted from the ring with a sheet over his entire body.

"In real life, I'm a good guy." Oh, he was all right. Maybe too tall for her, six-six. He had one of those cartoon faces like square-jawed superman but with blond hair. Besides some cameo performances in the ring, he currently sold real estate and was trying to break into show business.

Frank was cuter, by far. More importantly, Frank had stolen her heart. It took every cell in her body to stay focused on the man across from her.

"You're in love with somebody who you aren't sure loves you. Aren't you?" The Doctor of Death was no dummy. The Brown University graduate could read body language or was it in her eyes? He went on to explain. "When growing up and before I beefed up, I was bullied, for being geeky smart. I developed an ability to read people and turn the bullying into friendships, most of the time."

"What you said—I think I finally realized it, myself. Nothing against you. You're quite a mountain of manliness and you have a good heart."

* * *

Cha Cha's Terrorism Taskforce text message beeped. Every other incoming message or call was kept in silent mode out of polite consideration.

The message read: *Yo Cha Cha, You're so pretty. I'm five tables away tucked around the corner. Why don't we end this sham, switch dates, and blow this joint?*

* * *

Frank's Terrorism Taskforce text message beeped. All incoming was kept in silent mode except for the terrorism channel.

The message read: *Yoo-hoo Frank, I'm five tables away tucked around the corner. Why don't we end this sham and switch partners?*

* * *

Cha Cha introduced everybody.

It must have been fate that drove the two couples together.

Not.

Actually, the fate of the four adults resided in the devious hands of Autumn Breeze and… In the corner of her eye, she spied two kids drooling noodles and so-into-each-other with funny faces and giggles. She recognized Autumn. Her sidekick had to be Joey. What a handsome boy. No wonder the teen spent time with him. He was very Italian, zit free, his face still a little babyish. Joey's dossier showed a lazy boy with a brilliant mind. Although no one could ever match Autumn. Joey's mix of good looks, good heart from what Cha Cha heard from Autumn and smarts made him a good friend, at least for her.

Lilly and the Doctor of Death hit it off immediately after they realized wrestling was such a strong bond between them. The atmosphere between Lilly and her soon-to-be wrestling partner was electric. Those two were going to do the dirty for sure, but not until they knocked each other out wrestling, probably nude and oiled up. Hum. Cha Cha and Frank settled with the waiter who was confused over the two bills and why Frank was paying both. Frank upped the ante by paying Autumn and Joey's bill, but the handsome tip went a long way to clearing things up.

Having witnessed the other couple's instant attraction and Frank's passionate argument for switching dates, Cha Cha's libido took over. She needed an outlet for this foggy steam heat swirling about her psyche. *Pull Frank into the nearest hat and coat check?* In the past, dancing had worked wonders. But Frank had claimed to be a beginner. Well, Jacob, one of his security people said Frank would be taking dance lessons to get ready for her, lessons never taken due to the exhausting work for the Terrorism Taskforce.

If she could talk him into trying dance tonight, she'd put on her teacher's cap and assume the gifted athlete had rhythm. To be the fastest wide receiver in Notre Dame history had to account for something. Receivers demonstrated surefootedness and certainly good hands...*all over my body.* If he proved incorrigible, the mambo could be practiced horizontally. *Stop it, girl.*

Cha Cha turned to Frank's ear. "Catch the kids at the corner table."

"I noticed them when I first walked in but decided to play ignorant of whatever they were up to. That's her friend, Joey, right?" Frank asked.

"Yep. Give her a year to fill out and we'll have to sit on him."

"It's Wednesday right? What about their homework?"

"They're in college, NYU, remember?"

"I stuck my head in the books all the time."

It wasn't the plum wine influencing her disbelief again. Being a handsome athlete from Notre Dame, captain of the football team, star sprinter, homecoming king, president of his junior class, meant he worked in a few more activities and probably a number of coeds than he wanted her to believe. His face gave away no signs of irony or understatement. Well—he was a spy—where one wrong look could be fatal. But why did he tease her? She presented him with her incredulous face, accented by killer emerald green eyes. A look meant to slay him or the lies he rode in on.

"All right, I did get out regularly, but my studies were number one with me. I had always prepared for class." She handed out a pass for now, not because she believed him entirely, but because he was so damn cute.

They were getting ready to leave. "I'd love to go dancing, Frank."

"Well, I'll give it a try. Where to?" Her pulse quickened. She needed to dance and would finally partner with somebody her own age.

They left the Platinum Palace and drove to LATIN FROM MANHATTAN in Chelsea. The dance studio and nightclub's quiet second floor would be a good place to teach her novice partner.

Temporarily, she had given up part-time teaching there, after 9/11 for the same reasons. She hoped her showing up wouldn't cause a sensation. No doubt, her students would love to see her again.

She decided to take Frank through the nightclub and up the back instead of using the separate back entrance to gauge his feelings to the scene. His eyes widened. Wall-to-wall bodies undulated to Latin sway. A Samba dominated. Hot. The black lights, strobes, pulsating beats, free flowing drinks and all the grinding allowed by law were not conducive to learning dance *down here*.

Twisting and turning their way through the crowd, in which both of them were bumped by leering opposites, they barely slipped through to the back steps with no one getting pregnant.

Taking a breath half way up. "What would you like to learn?"

"What do you have?"

"All Latin, ball room like foxtrot, tango, bebop, rock-n-roll."

"A little of everything," he said with a boy's bewilderment but a man's conscientious resolve. She really had to dress him for dancing the next time. He always wore gray Dockers and a matching gray shirt. Today he bundled up with a gray bomber jacket. Really appealing if she wasn't sick of seeing him dress this way every day. At least his patent leather shoes would let him slide on the dance floor.

"We'll see how fast you learn. Okay?"

They entered onto a large squared yellowed oak dance floor with windows on two sides, mirrors with ballet bars on one side, and offices and bathrooms in the back. The place hadn't changed. Half full with various levels of dancers, ideal for lessons.

Maurice, the manager, ran out of the office to greet them and some of the dancers and wallflowers gathered around the school's favorite part-time teacher.

"Your students are missing you so badly, Cha Cha. Her proper name is Chastity, boys. Make a note of it." Maurice said that for the benefit of any newcomers who might get the wrong idea. He had never liked—no, he was appalled by—the infrequent maulings she received by some dirty old men. Maurice, with white hair, was much younger than most of the grizzled guys surrounding Cha Cha and Frank.

Cha Cha could handle herself. In a proprietary way, Frank wrapped his arm around her waist, supposedly to put his feeble rivals on notice. *Just blow on them, Frank.*

"Are you going to teach, tonight?" Winston, who was never shy, asked. The portly Englishman only needed a cigar.

"A dance with Cha Cha, and I'm in heaven," Irving said. So much for Frank's movie star looks and body. Irving couldn't care less, since he had often said, "you can't get enough wisdom."

"Maurice, boys. I'm thinking maybe December and I'll come back when time permits. Tonight, I'll be giving private lessons to Frank." She pulled him through the circle of old men who had elbowed him to the outside. Some women had gathered near Frank and nudged their way closer. She introduced him. She could have named him Dick Upyourbutt because they weren't listening to her.

It would be nice to be properly propositioned by somebody her own age for a change if his name was Frank. Frankly, he could do just about anything with her and it would be about time.

"Okay. Everybody give the lady and her matinee idol some room," Maurice said, playing to the crowd. They backed off.

She took Frank's hand. "So let's start by walking side by side— One, two, three; one, two, three." She twirled to repeat but he spun to the floor like a deflating doll, nearly pulling her down.

"I only have eyes for you," he said huskily.

The women nearby swooned on that charming remark. She forgave him. After all, he fell, the poor dear. Maybe later she'd kiss his boo-boo; she was good at that—had some experience with his boo-boos. The constant eight beat of a merengue, piped into the room in low enough volume to allow any variation in music or beats.

He fell again. "Teacher, won't you teach me?" What a devil Frank was. Blaming her. *This, this, impish ego maniacal…*

She recovered quickly because out of respect for the art of dancing, that's all that counted. *Honor the dance.* "The foxtrot is akin to walking cheek to cheek." This time, with his hands properly placed, he avoided falling immediately, but on the second turn, he twisted and spiraled down with her nearly on top of him. What a klutz, but falling with her was probably something he liked. How could this gifted athlete be so horrible? A baby learning to walk could do a better job.

"I'll pick myself up, dust myself off and start all over again."

No.

Cha Cha burst into a round of suspicious thoughts, set in motion by years of detective training. All his words seemed so familiar, choreographed. Just what? A song? Famous songs? She thought she had left her detective's head at the Chinese restaurant. Now her dreamy six-two dessert stood straight, tempting her to break her diet. Only dampened by his two left feet. Not appetizing. She however was aroused by his unflappable demeanor. Something didn't fit. He was way too smug.

They tried again but this time legs tangled and they both ended up on their fannies.

Exasperated.

"I couldn't teach you in a million years." She couldn't believe she just said that. Her sweetest memory of the greatest dance team to grace the earth flashed in so many elegant movements. The words, all the words were too *too* familiar. Her childhood obsession with the dancing and charm of Fred Astaire and Ginger Rogers had been breathed life, accidently on her part, when she mouthed words from one of their movies.

Her being a damn fine detective: what did he know and when did he know it?

Maurice came over. "Cha Cha, how are we going to keep our doors open with an attitude like that?"

Frank rose to his feet. "Oh, it's always like that with me, Maurice. I get nervous in front of people, especially when she shows me a dance for the first time. She always says that and then we get it. Let me show you." Frank took Cha Cha by her waist. "Oh teacher, won't you teach me?" He kissed her neck. She quivered like Jell-O, a very red Jell-O. Would be nice if he could dance. Please.

She got it, completely. Frank was acting out the 1936 classic, *Swing Time*, starring Fred Astaire and Ginger Rogers. Frank repeated or paraphrased Astaire's lines. He was no Astaire and tonight she was a detective caught with her pants down. How could she have missed this?

He took her in his arms and danced the foxtrot as if they were competing at nationals. The entire room, after the onlookers stopped laughing, applauded. The normally serious Maurice appeared to get the joke and the references to Astaire/Rogers. He wore a tickled grin.

But what a bastard Frank was. He had set her up, since the first day she visited his building. This had to be some sort of male campaign to win her heart and drop her drawers.

With every twirl, every tug of his sure hands, she fell deeper and more madly in love with him. Could it get any better than this? Yes, he could really love her back. *What is love when it isn't given back? Foolishness, incomplete, juvenile, untrue, useless.* Yet, she had loved him from the day she met him. A little less hopeless, today, but still universes apart.

Would she still have loved him if he couldn't dance? Yes. In sickness, health, and two left feet.

He whispered, "I played the great Astaire in *Swing Time* at Notre Dame."

She cocked her head to the proper angle for the dance. "I read your records."

"They were expurgated, modified." They twirled. The beat changed to a rumba and so did they.

"Jacob, your building guard told me—"

"He works for me."

"You want me, don't you?"

"With all my heart."

"Can you, cha cha cha?" She batted her eyes.

"Does a bear tinkle in the woods?"

"Anywhere he wants."

They danced for hours. She lost all perception, dangerous for a cop, but she was among friends and having a ridiculous day. She literally saw no one else but Frank. The oak floors faded leaving wisps or clouds. She felt weightless in his arms. They danced on and on, madly. She stole a quick look at her hopeful future: children, and a home on Long Island or in Bergen County. This man by her side, who'd love her forever. They'd dance.

Wait a moment, Miss I've-Got-My-Whole-Life-Planned-Out. She needed to attack his prejudices against marriage and children with the same gusto he embraced dance. And soon, very soon. She wanted to scandalize the dancers and make love right there and then. If that happened, she really would get fired. She needed her sister's advice, before she made a huge mistake and became his latest conquest. The Visigoths were about to pillage Rome. Frank, the barbarian, had ridden off with her heart.

So this was love and it hurt. She peeked up at him. He brimmed with confidence and gave her the kindest smile. Those gray eyes trimmed in charcoal could have hypnotized Dracula.

"Take me home," she panted. His eyebrows went up and they hurriedly exited, waving to the remaining dancers. Maurice waved back with a beaming smile, which could have helped Con-Ed light the city.

Chapter 27

Usually, Joey came over on Friday nights, but Halloween fell on Wednesday and Autumn would like to fall on Joey. So she had talked him into switching days. She had much planned for tonight.

She found an old *What's New Pussycat* outfit in her mom's closet. On her, it looked like a giant red and pink prune. After stuffing two toilet paper rolls where her breasts might be larger someday, and three couch pillows for hips and ass, she was ready to knock him dead. Or maybe he'd die laughing. She used a black mascara pencil to paint on four-inch whiskers and a piece of burnt toast for a round spot on her nose. Voila. She was so damn cute—and a little silly.

She was a kitten not a cat. This, Joey had told her with his eyes every moment they spent together.

She buzzed Joey into the co-op.

She peeked through the peephole at the Headless Horseman, with pumpkin in arms.

"Is that you, Joey?"

"Whatdaya think?"

She opened the door. "I never told you that some people are trying to get me, because I'm a national treasure." She couldn't very well tell him, she had predicted 9/11. Could she? Nope. But just in case she was killed, she had to say something. Yet his face, peeking out from the now opened portion of his costume, screamed 'I don't believe you.' He looked like he was about to give her another one of those lectures on growing up and being real.

"I thought we could carve up the pumpkin, put it in the window or bake pumpkin pie," Joey said. "And, oh yeah, you look like ah, like ah, you've got a cat under there with cancer bumps." He rolled his eyes and chuckled.

"That's not nice." He had a weird mind. Maybe his cat had died. Sad.

"Sorry, more like a bag of potatoes. Listen, I've told you this before and I mean it—someday you are going to be a complete knock out. I want to be there when that happens. I want you to knock me out, if you'll even think of me, then." She didn't know how to tell him that her days were numbered. Not by the idiot trying to kill her, but by her nothing-will-stop-me Granny from Trinidad. And her kindly Pappy, who pictured beating her at cards at their Matelot beach cottage. And he could, because he was a professor of mathematics and physics.

"My mom is dying of cancer and my grandparents want to take me back to Trinidad when she goes to heaven. They want to take me away from all this terrorism, buildings falling, anthrax in the mail, planes falling out of the sky, people hating immigrants."

Joey's face drooped, actually drooped. He loved her?

"I'm sorry about your mom. That's terrible. I'm sorry about you leaving, really sorry."

She filled him in on the hospice. Except she forgot to mention that mom had never been home at all, since 9/11. That would take too much explaining.

Joey sipped a little cocoa. "What about NYU? I can learn on my own, but I'll miss you, Autumn, and so will all the people you could help with an American education." He looked like he was going to cry. Some tough guy, some headless horseman, more like Ichabod Crane.

She walked to the window and peered at the outdoor thermometer. "Forty-two degrees now, I don't want to go out Joey. Would you stay with me? We'll cook and talk."

"Yes, baby cakes. But yo, genius," he knuckled the top of her head, "what about NYU?"

"Sorry. I'm distracted by all this," she said, wiggling her pussycat whiskers. His face changed from flat as a portrait to animated by hope or maybe by how cute she was.

She dropped her head a little, letting her curls tickle her face. "My grandmother is negotiating with NYU's dean for undergrads and getting them to talk with The University of the West Indies, St. Augustine's campus, Trinidad. They're including the department head of the school of Electrical and Computer Engineering who wants me real bad." She took a deep breath. *Here goes.* "It's a great school, but I, well…ah, I love you, Joey."

"Oh, my sweet little—kitty. You are not only pretty, yeah pretty beautiful, but you're heart has grown faster than your IQ. Ah. You know what I mean?"

She wrapped her arms around his broad shoulders. "Why won't you kiss me?"

Joey changed the subject. "Tell me more about what's bothering you." They both knew the answer to the first subject. She was still a girl-child in his eyes, but her body was whispering different things to her. She couldn't hurry love or her body. As a couple, they were doomed like Romeo and Juliet without the poison, of course. But life and its choices could be poison, right? If they split with her going to Trinidad, that would be a sort of lights out, right?

"You helped me put Frank and Cha Cha together. Now comes the easy part. Ha. Ha—Not. We are going to get them to marry each other. And then, they're going to adopt me."

He sank into the couch, which made his head disappear into his costume. In a muffled voice, he said, "That's almost impossible, you're a lot crazy. But kid, I'm in, because I…"

Love? Whether he liked it or not she jumped on him, found his head and planted a wet one right on his big Tom Cruise nose.

"Yuck. I need a hankie. I've been slimed." His head slipped back down into the costume.

Chapter 28

Frank tossed and turned. It was All Souls night. Many of the ghosts of 9/11 asked him how their families were doing. He needed his head examined. Emily needed to stop her gris gris curse. But, ghosts couldn't be real. Cha Cha was fond of saying this. They hadn't bothered her. Absolutely: He needed his head examined.

But staying in this real world, not some amusement park of odd ghostly characters, was easy during the day. He made each one promise to leave him alone until November 13th. In return, he'd get more information on their families.

On November 13th, he and Cha Cha would meet with the commissioner and mayor, and if the political wind blew away from them, they would be fired. He blinked his eyes a couple times and peered at the digital clock: 3:18 a.m. He took a pillow, put it over his face and wished he could knock himself out.

They needed to trap Professor, AKA the Suitcase Romeo. Or as his string of jilted lovers knew him, Petros Papadopoulos. They had already theorized how the professor became entangled with terrorists. Through pressure from his Saudi family, big in the Wahhabi movement, and/or his lectures on how buildings were constructed, he might have unwittingly crossed some line. His and Cha Cha's staff opinions varied but most felt he was not guilty of anything more than vanity or lying to get laid. It would be so much easier to find the student or students turned terrorists if they could interview the professor and narrow down the lecture or lectures that inspired someone to suggest mass murder, or so the theory went.

He checked the time again, but the clock was not lit. He tossed the pillow balanced on his head and dropped his hand to where the clock was supposed to be. Yep, still there. Yawning, he fastened his black terrycloth robe. The backup generators were supposed to take over smoothly. Halfway to the bathroom to pee, Stars and Stripes Forever began playing over his intercom. Only certain members of his team would hear this. No need waking up the entire building. They had no outside alarm or connection to the police department, since they comprised their own army. He flicked on the bathroom lights. Jacob entered the bedroom with two guards. They wore nothing more than Uzis and underwear. They all moved to the living room.

"The building is secure, Frank. As far as we know now, somebody was testing our defenses, but hadn't breached them."

"Let's go to the sit room." Cha Cha came up the spiral steps, seemed embarrassed by the underweared men and apparently her sleepwear. Frank had spent a chaste as-could-be time in bed with her not wanting to take her until she was one-hundred percent sure. He loved her and would soon prove it. She started running back to the steps, no doubt embarrassed.

"Cha Cha," he shouted, "Situation room in one minute." He wanted to say her boobs were perfect. Through her silky, filmy and backlighted nightie, he spied a perfectly constructed angel.

"Will do," she shouted back. "Nice choice of music." She tossed her hands up as she descended, as if conducting a brass band.

Down one flight, Frank's men followed procedure and opened the locked door to the situation room.

"Sir, I think you should see this," Jacob said, while backing out of the left side of two doors.

Frank walked in followed closely by Cha Cha. Frank rubbed his eyes, and then took Cha Cha's hand. There at the head of the table sat that devilish girl, Autumn Breeze.

"I bet you are wondering why I called this meeting." She said, then pushed back on the high back leather, which didn't recline an iota. "Nice place you've got here." She had cat whiskers and a black spot on her nose. This was not a good time for trick or treat.

Frank needed his NSA engineer, Bud, to relate to this little genius regarding the breach. He cleared his head and eyed the coffee pot. "Get Bud. Dismissed and thank you. Thank them all," Frank said. "Now you, my sweet little pain in the…"

"Tush."

He couldn't help feeling like a dad about to ground his daughter. He was pissed in a fatherly way and it felt wonderful. He never wanted nor thought he'd be a good dad. Yet, this possessive emotion was as good as anything in his life. Cha Cha had been civilizing him. He was the man behind the curtain in Oz. Perhaps he should make sure his old ball and chain mentality was dead before Cha Cha tired of the chase. He peeked at Autumn's big wide eyes. How could he crush her in a fatherly way?

"Are you all right, honey?" Cha Cha asked.

"I'll know for sure when Daddy War Bucks stops his scowling and says something." Poor little about to be orphaned, Autumn, with her hard-knock life. He braced. Heartless he wasn't. The kid was hopping and skipping through hell. Her tough but at the same time pleading eyes made him grab the nearest chair for support.

"This better be good, girl." He couldn't figure out how a fourteen-year-old got into his impregnable fortress. According to the engineering team, she had wreaked havoc with the NSA computers, especially the mainframe, Cyclops. She had hacked every government site except the Farm Bureau, and that was a matter of time. She spoofed Cha Cha's and his NSA cell phones, etc. etc. As a joke, he speculated she knew more about the government than the President.

Carlos and he assumed they had been safe all those years in the field using the NSA's double crypto mumbo jumbo, codes touted as unbreakable. Yet some girl broke them like a piggy bank.

"I think I know how to catch the Suitcase Romeo, but I want a job," said the kid with the cat smile and smudgy nose.

* * *

Before the NSA engineer, Bud, joined them in the situation room, Cha Cha's young girlfriend admitted that she borrowed and deciphered Cha Cha's NSA cell phone when she had slept over. She used cell phone data as one of her tricks to get into the HOS building. Frank asked that she share the remaining details with Bud. Engineering would secure the building.

"How's some hot chocolate, hmm?" Frank asked.

They both said yes.

A few moments later Bud opened the door and pranced in, looking rather chipper for three in the morning. The Sicilian version of Buddy Holly, complete with big plastic glasses, sported a wizard's cap and Harry Potter pajamas. Cha Cha was unsure if he dressed that way for their stowaway, Autumn, or if he was always so stuck in adolescence. In any case, this young and brilliant engineer was Autumn's perfect match for the wonky, geeky, techy electronic world. He danced up to Autumn, who started laughing. Ever want to win over a fourteen-year-old girl, well?

"What's so funny, kid?" He put out his hand and she grabbed it with both.

"So the NSA's Chief Engineer, Ms. Ayita Starblanket, put you in charge up here?" She snickered.

"What of it? Listen kid," he became more serious, "you should study up on me and Ayita and then compare our backgrounds to yours. Hackers and crypto-conjurers are three dollars and sixty-seven cents a dozen. We need great, innovative engineers slash scientists, especially physicists." He pulled out of his deep wizard pocket a five-by-five Rubik's Cube and a stopwatch and placed them on the table. "If you want a job with us, you should buy your way in. You can buy in... Hey, can I have some cocoa too?" He had taken the leather chair next to Autumn. Frank and Cha Cha relaxed on Autumn's other side.

Frank got up. "You got it, Bud."

"This won't take long to solve," Autumn said, fingering the Cube. "Maybe under a minute." But Bud didn't pick up the stopwatch.

"This cube fights back, kid." Autumn studied it, fascinated as only a kid or Peter Pan here, would be. "Like I was saying, kiddo. You can buy into a temporary job because you're still too young. *And...* Your education is number one with me. Ayita's contingent promise to hire you someday and loving your family should also be top priorities on your list— Shush up, kid." He put up his hand. "After you tell us your plan to catch the suitcase Romeo, me and you are going to have a long talk in the engineering room. Is that okay, Cha Cha? I mean, she's a kid. Ah, someday I'll be a father and this kid might help us improve our defenses."

A bead of sweat formed on Bud's brow. Was his bravado cracking? He was obviously juggling Cha Cha's close ties to the kid with his role as educator of the moment. Once and perhaps still a kid, judging by his cute wizard garb, he'd morph into genius speak with the girl. Being a temporary father slash mentor shouldn't be too hard for Bud.

"That's fine, Bud. Okay sweetie, tell us what you've got. Just remember you are talking to adults. One's a great detective, *moi*. Another, America's sexiest spy—this guy next to me. And then there's Bud, Ayita's most brilliant engineer. You play nice with him."

After sipping steaming cocoa, Autumn smiled broadly. "I'd be delighted." She reached into her backpack, pulled out her laptop and flipped it open. "The Suitcase Romeo, Mahmoud Ali Abunayyan, is a lonesome guy running out of money. He can't go back to his job teaching architecture at Pratt until the mole in the NYPD is caught. He has to find a long-term relationship. Now, nobody laugh." She waited for somebody to say something.

Cha Cha winked. "Go ahead, sweetie."

"Okay. Think like a kid. My first idea might be goofy." She went on to describe a suitors' ball by a young beauty who wants someone to be her guy Friday with the possibility of more. She finished her idea. "All living expenses plus after she comes back from a two week business trip, there would be a more formal interview—then maybe a job, room and board. The winner must stay in her New York City apartment during her two-week trip. The ad should say he was needed immediately.

"His longevity would also be based on how he kept her apartment while she was gone. Alter Cha Cha's face with makeup, colored eye lens, and a wig. Give her a background like his victims. In this way, the terrorist mole who wants to kill Mahmoud won't pay any attention to it. Should be safe."

"The old princess bride trap. I like it," Frank said, then yawned. "Sorry."

Cha Cha guessed Frank decided not to tell Autumn they had tried a comparable tactic. But, perhaps Mahmoud's psyche was in a different place right now and they could try something similar, again.

"But how do you keep Mahmoud from worrying about presenting his resume?" Cha Cha asked, more to see how her young friend would handle the answer.

"I'm thinking he'll at least visit the party, because he has a big ego and a history of successfully fooling women. His ego should be huge by now and maybe he's wearing out his welcome."

Wise beyond her years.

"What's your backup idea?" Frank asked, with a twinkle in his eyes and a closed mouth smile.

Autumn hesitated.

Bud got up and put his wizard's hat on Autumn. "Sounds good to me, too. Let's see what other magic you can conjure up." The adults in the room were obviously enjoying and engaging their visitor. Considering the bleary eyes around the table, not bad.

Autumn, hesitation gone, continued. "Well, another idea I had, ah," she hesitated and scrutinized her listeners' faces, "was to get the girl he carried down the steps to put an ad in all the papers and TV. She could ask Petros Papadopoulos, his alias, to meet her. She misses him and wants to thank him by treating him to dinner." She pushed back on the chair. "My third idea, you probably tried already. Posting female cops in the parks he trolls."

Bud spoke up first, "I like the rescued girl idea. Maybe we could do the princess ball trick as a backup and dress up Cha Cha."

Since Bud was on a need-to-know basis, he might not have been up to speed on what they had already tried.

"Are you suggesting I don't have nice clothes?" Cha Cha asked, faking haughtiness.

"Oh no, not me."

"I forgive you. Actually, Autumn, we have tried all of these ideas in slightly different ways. I think it's time to set the traps again," she said.

Deeper into the night, on and on, they refined their plans. In this short time, the kid had found a home with kindred spirits. Nearly an hour passed, washed down by a second hot cocoa.

Cha Cha stood and stretched. "Bud, Frank, do you mind if I take Autumn to my bedroom? She'll see you in the morning." She tightened her nightgown's belt and peered at the clock, 4:03 a.m.

Autumn reached up and put Bud's hat back on his head. He bowed. Frank kissed her cheek and then turned to lay one on Cha Cha. The girls giggled and ran out the door.

A little later in Cha Cha's king-sized bed, she said, "I've got a surprise for you, baby."

"You're getting married?"

"Well, I'm not sure if Frank is ready just yet. But for now, we can dream. Can't we?"

"Hard head?"

"Softening."

"I just don't want any more nightmares." She cuddled up against her substitute mom. Cha Cha reached back and flipped on Autumn's surprise, the northern hemisphere star scape.

"Wow. They're all in the right places and luminescence from the relative prospective of our position in bed. My favorite is Sagittarius, The Archer."

"The artist used a convex ceiling," Cha Cha said. They chatted for a while.

"Do you think there's another me and you up there on some planet? Maybe on that planet, you are my mom?" Autumn's voice cracked.

"Oh honey, scoot yourself a little closer."

"I love you."

"I love you, too." Cha Cha choked. They spoke of Autumn's mom until they could push out no more words through the girl's sobs. Anything more she could say would only further disturb the girl.

Someday impossible dreams could come true, but she had no husband, and Autumn had a very influential family in Trinidad waiting to take her when her mom passed on. She only hoped someday, she'd have a wonderful young lady like this one. Autumn was even, in spite of her sassiness, a pretty good representative of the wild North American teenager species.

She patted Autumn's curls. They fell asleep, just a dream or two or three away from Cha Cha's happily ever after. For Autumn, bitter reality proved a cruel master.

Chapter 29

Skipping across from the NYU library to Washington Square Park, Autumn slipped onto the wooden bench at a chess table, prepared for lunch and readied her fighting spirit for a possible game. Barny-the-wino sat at the table next to her, waiting to watch her play. She smiled. He wobbled.

An officer she recognized approached. She was about to call Joey, but instead she put her cell phone next to the chess clock and looked warily over at the curly-haired cop.

"Hi Autumn. You don't know me. I took over Cha Cha's job here in the park." His badge read Detective Sam Langrath, and it was true that Washington Square Park was Cha Cha's old beat.

"The antiwar kids and druggies know you, Sir." Of what possible interest could she be to this man? She emptied her chess bag of pieces into the middle of the vinyl board.

"I'm not here for a chess game. I don't know how to play."

She'd play along. "I give cheap lessons."

He sat down across from her and picked up the white queen. "Maybe, but first I want to be honest with you."

She bit her lip. This was getting a little spooky. Why wouldn't he be honest? "Go ahead, Sir." Her lips twitched involuntarily, which would be a bad sign that she's hiding something, especially if interpreted by a trained detective. Disaster was one twitch away. *I'm over the top with paranoia.*

"Cha Cha is, or *was*, a great detective. I'm trying to follow in her footsteps, but I'm no dummy. Her shoes don't fit." He jutted one leg out and wiggled his polished boot. "She hasn't helped much because she's been busy with whatever her new job is. I saw you with her, right here at this table in fact. I want to know everybody she knows. That's all."

"How did you know my name?"

"Are you kidding, kid? The youngest winner of a huge pot of bucks on Jeopardy. Huh? With a name like Autumn Breeze?"

So maybe this guy was on the level. "You saw me on TV?"

"Yep. The show, the news, the magazines. You're famous."

He twiddled the white queen until it was upside down in his fingers. For some reason, she imagined him smashing it on the stone table. Carlos's admonition struck her hard: *'If any adult strangers approach you, squeeze this special NSA cell phone. We will come to your rescue immediately. There is likely only one reason a non-chess playing adult, especially NYPD, would approach you. He'd want to know if you're the 9/11 snitch.'* But she'd have to make an exception for this detective who took Cha Cha's place in the park. Wouldn't she?

He did look uncomfortable, fidgety for a big man. Perhaps he didn't have a good memory of her time on Jeopardy and was afraid she'd ask a question about the show. She'd drop the subject, for now. Not many people had a perfect memory like hers.

The warm noon sun speckled the board and his NYPD cap. Naked branches twisted in the breeze and little dust devils danced. She hated these whirlies. They signaled something horrible would happen.

"You must be a very good detective. I mean people look differently on TV."

"I am. So listen, Autumn. I want to know if you guys were just friends or if you can snitch for me… Think of it as your way to help the City."

She knew better than to admit that she was the one who predicted the day and the method of the 9/11 attack. No brainer. She had to throw him off. If he hung out in the park, he might have seen her with the spies or getting into their SUV.

"Cha Cha and I are great—no, *super*—friends. It all started when she came to me for chess lessons, like maybe you will. She knows my mom, somehow, too." This time her lip overruled her self-control and twitched. This guy was too smart. He eyed her. Like he knew she was the 9/11 informant.

"Okay, too bad. I'd thought I'd solve the world's problems. Maybe not today for a lesson, but if you'd like a hotdog, I'll get you one."

"No, Sir. But thank you."

He hesitated getting up, patted his pockets, felt over his gun and stuff. "I left my cell phone at the precinct. Do you mind if I borrow yours to make a quick call?" She saw him glance down at it, so she didn't have a choice here. *Play it cool.* He might be able to tell it was a custom spy phone from the NSA, but probably not. Worried, very worried, she squeezed the phone just like Carlos asked her to do and then handed it to him. He inspected its outside casing a little too long, then flipped it open. He seemed to know this phone was not store bought.

The detective shrugged. "This phone…isn't Sprint. Did you get it from some street vendor?"

She knew by the horror in his eyes and the way the phone seemed to burn his hand figuratively that he knew this to be an NSA issued piece of equipment. This guy was not at all interested in busting some street vendor over a phone that was two generations ahead of anything in any store and not buildable in some garage.

There was no sense in lying to him. He had got her number. So she would just have to intrigue him for a little while longer. "I'm not afraid of you just because you're a big guy. You're a detective. Most of the kids here would come running if you got all weird on me."

"I have no interest in young girls. I'm married." He was so lying—about the married part, anyway. She could tell. He had an interest in one girl, her.

"How about all the young girls who died on 9/11 or those who lost their dads and moms?" Oh shit, she bit her tongue, he seemed infuriated.

"I—I. Of course, the NYPD…we lost so many, so many died and are dying. I'm sorry if I gave you some kind of misimpression. I have to take off now. Maybe a lesson next week. Okay?"

She had blown her cover and his as the mole. The chance that he was the NYPD mole was exceeding 76% to her way of calculating. As she continued to sift through all his odd reactions, the percentage kept going up. At least he wasn't going to shoot her today in front of all the chess players nearby and Barny-the-wino, who sat entranced by their conversation. Barny's head swiveled back and forth like a Ping-Pong ball. Her student friends protesting the war would come running if he made a move against her. Right? Or would they pee in their pants?

"I'm sorry, Detective. I go nuts regularly when I think about 9/11." Her elbow knocked over a pawn. "You know, irrational. There was nothing you could have done. Nothing any of us could have done."

Frank shouted as he and Carlos were running to Autumn's defense. "Detective Samuel Langrath, we need to talk."

* * *

Cha Cha pulled up the rear, as hastily planned. She approached from the north side of the park and planted herself on the grass five feet behind the chained fence, wooden benches and Autumn, while Frank and Carlos had run up to the table from the opposite direction on the concrete walkway. Detective Sam Langrath had whirled around the table and lifted Autumn by her hair. He pulled out a Sig-Sauer and planted the tip above Autumn's ear. The chess players ran like rats.

Barny took a swig and slurred, "This is gettin' gooood."

Don't be a hero, Barny.

"I'm done talking. You people have destroyed my family. You let the Israelis do what they want. To enslave the Palestinians. It's time you pay." She thought she had made eye contact with Sam before he twirled to face Frank and Carlos. Could he be losing his senses? She took aim.

"Maybe we can work together to try to change the world. You'll never know unless you try," Cha Cha said calmly.

The detective glanced over his shoulder. "You'd never shoot me, when there's a chance I'd surrender." He kept his eyes on the two men, a fatal mistake.

"Put the gun down or I will shoot." Cha Cha warned.

He shook his head and laughed.

"You're outrenumerated," Barny said, spitting out words.

"Shut up," Sam said.

"Yes, shut up," Carlos growled.

Autumn twisted her head but Sam had grabbed her, with his free hand, by the neck and tightened until she went passive. "My mom's a psychic—she works with the police, not me."

"You're a bad liar, kid." He pressed the trigger. "I don't really care." This was said with a scary rise in octave as if he had suffered a psychotic break with reality. In his demented world, the only thing that made sense was to execute Autumn as his last act of revenge. He was going to shoot Autumn and then go to hell by firing squad.

Cha Cha had a split second to save Autumn's life. She pushed aside the nagging image of her grandpapa's execution. She would let no one down today or any other day.

Sam wore a bulletproof vest. Then she shot Sam Langrath square in the center of the back of his head. Autumn twisted away from the dying man. He fell, smashing the chess pieces. The chess clock went flying. Only half his torso had hit the table. He slid off and landed on his back. A pool of blood formed a halo around his head. An angel of death. Yet he was still convulsing.

"Hey Choo Choo, you shot a defensillisless man in hizz back of hizz head." Barny said something irrational. Someone needed to take him to rehab. For now, anywhere but here.

Carlos leaned over, pressed his Waltham's nozzle between the perp's eyes but observed the man was already dead. Then he turned to the drunk and waved his pistol. "You, sir, stink. Get out of here, now." The drunk banged his hip on the stone chess table, fell once and ran out of the park as fast as his rum-soaked legs could take him.

Carlos threatening a civilian did scare off remaining witnesses who scattered like cockroaches. Cha Cha no longer cared about Carlos's style; her sweet friend was safe. For now, she'd let the men figure out what to do with the police reports and media.

Frank approached Autumn. "Hold still, child." Frank took out his hankie and wiped some blood splatter from her face and hair.

After he was done, Cha Cha wrapped Autumn in her arms.

Autumn peered down at the bloodied dead man and sobbed. "Is it over?"

"We think so," Cha Cha said. "Let me get you safe." In moments, she would lead Autumn south with her arm around her. "We're going to your place, Frank. Somebody collect her pieces, board, phone and clock. Better yet, let's buy her new." Carlos took the NSA cell phone and pocketed it. Frank grabbed the rest. Bent over too long, Frank had to be hiding a joyful tear for Autumn.

Their team's fake ambulance hopped the curb and stopped on the enlarged walkway just before the table. Cleaners passed for medics with a stretcher. Frank got down, retrieved Sam's NYPD cap that had rolled and put it back, pulling it down just enough to cover his face.

The ambulance took off with the body of Sam Langrath or whomever he was. No way, this wouldn't make the papers. One of the kids was on his cell phone and kept looking back.

Later, after she settled Autumn, the team would stop by the sixth precinct to talk with her ex-lieutenant. After all, one of his detectives was shot. They'd have to brief him on the why of it.

Frank would call the Mayor and the Police Commissioner to report they found the mole, but they needed proof. A team would be dispatched to Sam's home and his locker and desk at the precinct. A story would be manufactured for the press. Or perhaps some small dose of the truth. The mayor and the commissioner would decide this one.

In spite of all this, one question remained.

Although Sam was orphaned by Osama bin Laden, likely alone in the city—he killed his confederates—was up against the Taskforce, the NYPD, CIA, FBI and NSA, he managed to last a couple months. The taskforce's job was still nowhere near done and might never be finished until the day when all men were at peace.

But who was Sam Langrath and what drove him mad? Perhaps only the Professor could answer this last question. It was time to spring the next and hopefully more effective trap on the Suitcase Romeo. Only then could Frank, Cha Cha and a certain young lady—who had been through too much—consider a life together.

Chapter 30

Saturday night, November 10th

Frank had borrowed a friend's penthouse on Delancy to set the trap and snag the Suitcase Romeo. The trap's centerpiece, Cha Cha, played bait like the mythic Sirens had sung songs. Both Frank and Carlos stared, nothing better to do. They were like brothers; otherwise, Frank would have to kill him for the way he squinted in her direction.

Cha Cha—tonight Mata Hendricks, not Mata Hari—lounged demurely, long, bare arms spread outward on both sides of the red velvet couch as if to say: *"Here I am...you can't have me."*

Frank wanted her right then, well always, no matter what she was wearing or the state of her hairdo.

She had crossed her long exquisite legs, accented at the bottom by delicate toes tucked into thinly strapped white-leather high heels. Her gown, a simple drape of white gossamer silk, flowed straight down from her upper thighs to the marble floor revealing more leg than any man could stand. The silk continued up in two flimsy triangles from her midriff to nearly invisible straps that kissed her shoulders. He preferred to do the kissing. The lighting was subdued. A fog machine splattered out about an inch of cloud on the milky white floor.

The lady was drop dead gorgeous, and she would be his.

To think this woman had just killed a man two days earlier, to think this thin slip of a gal was both deadly in martial arts and with her heart, forced a swell of pride in Frank mixed with a dose of lust. He longed to caress her, to have her completely.

To possess her.

To love her.

Soon.

"You love her, you do?" Carlos asked but really said. He fixed two more Vodka martinis. Those Russians loved their vodka.

Frank sipped the potent drink and paused until he caught Carlos's eye. "This is my first time. I never thought it would happen to me." He noticed his friend seemed ready to start a debate, again. It was time to end the argument they had been having over Cha Cha for the last two months. "To be more precise, my dearest friend, I love her with my whole heart and soul."

"Then why is it, you are not telling her?"

"Shush. Observe the lady do her thing." They both turned slightly to watch her reject one more applicant with such aplomb, you'd think the guy just won the lottery.

Their mark, the Suitcase Romeo, had not yet made an appearance. "I want to be able to back love up, because the moment I say I love her, she'll want a proposal. And I can't give her a proposal until I overcome some reservations about marriage that you know too well." Frank had long since shared his story with Carlos. His philanthropic parents, worn out by ten adoptions before they conceived him by some miracle, gave him little attention. Truly a cruel twist of fate. His siblings, acting like babysitters from hell had put him outside naked in the winter, until he acted properly and promised to be their willing slave. Was it any wonder he was shy about his body? Although he loved them, they played too often the jealous adopted sisters and brothers.

Too many slings and arrows.

Frank resolved: although abandoned emotionally by his parents he would try his best to help a girl physically abandoned by her parents, Autumn Breeze.

Frank knew his childhood was not the main factor in his previous inability to commit to a woman. His profession as a spy did that in his opinion. Now that he was assuming a leadership position in a job in which the antagonists were badly outgunned, maybe he could settle down. Oddly, the moment his life changed over 9/11, in marched the love of his life.

Frank took another sip, stopped a waiter and grabbed some beluga on rye wafers.

"I do believe she is most beautiful woman I have seen," Carlos offered, testing him no doubt.

"It's not that. Emily is just as beautiful."

"She is knockout, too, only different. How is that voodoo princess, by the way?"

"I don't know. All I have are her ghosts." Surely by now, Emily would have found somebody in New Orleans to get her mind off Frank, and maybe in turn forgive him.

"You do not really believe this, do you?" Rehashing old conversations, he'd let Carlos's remark pass. Carlos had, after all, hired Emily for the purpose of exploiting her paranormal gifts, which came to naught.

"I've finally decided they were a figment of my imagination, so I don't pay any attention to them anymore, especially not Mohammed Atta. I haven't mentioned this to Cha Cha. I want to play with her. She thinks I'm weak, imperfect. Gives her something to fix—besides my immaturity about marriage."

"But you are perfect—for her, my friend. But, of course, you are not me."

Ignore him. "I want somebody who's a perfect fit, mentally, spiritually, physically, emotionally. She should have a great sense of humor."

"What do you think her best quality is?"

Frank wrinkled his nose, a sure sign to his friend he was about to deliver a joke. "In the morning, before she brushes out and calms her hair, she looks like a wild woman, like she stuck her finger in a socket. That drives me nuts with desire."

Carlos, as always, played along. "This, this is what you like?" He scratched his head and twisted his bushy eyebrows.

"Yeah, I do. I love an infinite amount of things about her."

Autumn walked up to them. The blossoming fourteen-year-old wore a pretty island smock with satin butterflies, complements from Frank's dress shop. Once in a while, he moved product out of his front store, not storefront. Not only was the business illegitimate, so were the prices.

"Are you feeling okay, sweetie?" Frank asked, showing worry for the *wunderkind* he had come to care for. The kid was an impossible mix of contradictions, who could out think anybody, anytime. She'd act like a baby one moment, a spoiled brat the next, and then solve problems as if an Einstein.

"Yep, I'm good. Frank, would you make me another black cherry float? They're so yummy, the way you make them." Frank had not only ordered his staff to pamper the girl now that she was living in his building and his heart, but he personally doted on her every chance he got. Yes, he understood he was making up for the way his parents treated him, but so what. Did one need a reason to love somebody?

Autumn seemed at peace, tonight. The kid had taken in stride being held at gunpoint and almost shot. Even though she was a super-genius, she was still just fourteen, a baby really. Her emotional IQ still needed nurturing to grow. Frank's dearest friends and staff had all taken to the task. Someday this cute girl would contribute immensely to the U.S. war on terror. NSA bound, without a doubt.

"You look lovely, Autumn. Someday some young man—" Carlos said, but the kid interrupted.

"His name is Joey."

"Someday Joey will fall down on his knees and worship you."

"Hope so." She pointed indelicately at Cha Cha. "God, she's so pretty."

"Agreed."

"Ditto," seconded Frank.

"So when are you going to get down on your knees, Mister Spymaster?"

Frank drained his drink. "I'm thinking about it, kid. Seriously—thinking about it."

He could imagine the wheels of her mind whirling. She sipped the float he had just concocted. The secret: a touch of ginger.

"Actually if you were thinking about proposing to her, you would know that, statistically speaking, a girl like her was made for you and God only made one. If you wait too long, let's say 3.6 years, your chances of marrying your soul mate will drop to less than 27%. God tattooed your name on her behind. It's time to collect what is yours."

Both men laughed. Frank sputtered his drink back into the glass. Autumn had never as far as he knew just made numbers up. Her head was full of statistics and a calculator ready to use them.

"Young lady," Carlos said, "I need to teach you some manners."

"Yes, Sir."

Frank cracked a wicked smile. "Oh, come on. Who are you kidding, kid? Well, maybe God does do tattoos. Maybe I *should* have a look at her behind."

Autumn appeared dreamy eyed. She had plans for them, he knew. Poor thing. Apparently, unless some legal miracle came along, they'd be friends, not parents, especially when her grandparents took her to Trinidad. He'd always watch over her as long as she was in New York. He'd also give her more pretty gifts, earnest conversations and sage advice. He and Cha Cha had a place in their hearts for this girl who brought them together when she predicted 9/11. Her leaving would not change Frank's surprisingly strong paternal instincts. Guess he loved the team of Autumn and Cha Cha. Whatever broke Cha Cha's heart would do the same to him, because he did not want to see his woman unhappy. Besides, the whimsical Autumn had grown on him.

Carlos's kidding admonishment and Frank's blue remark didn't faze Autumn, who found a chicken wing with her name on it. "I don't know how the three of us are going to get into high society," she said, nose in air and with a deadpan delivery.

Got to squeeze this kid. So he did.

Just then, 8:38 p.m., the outside surveillance team, namely the doorman, let the mark into the co-op. The game was afoot.

The elevator exited into the suite. In walked Professor Mahmoud Ali Abunayyan. He wore a tweed suit—a collegial outfit—a red, power tie and a frightened look. He couldn't take his eyes off tonight's prize. Cha Cha played her part, ignoring the newest arrival, smiling at another man who brought her a drink. Mahmoud scanned the large room. He partook of one hors d'oeuvre after another, probably building his courage but definitely filling his belly. He looked famished, but he was on the run. Not much longer. He looked around at the others gathered, maybe for someone to talk with, and then he withdrew into himself and another hors d'oeuvre, glancing around furtively.

He swallowed, hesitated and turned to leave. If they had to, they'd arrest him.

"The lady would love to see you now, sir," Frank said closing the distance between him and Mahmoud.

* * *

Mahmoud turned and approached Mata Hendricks, AKA Cha Cha. She had always wanted to play spy, ever since some kid stole her hamster and she went under her covers with a telescope focused on the home next door. The cute kid, yep next door, was the culprit. A fine romance had been ruined before it started. She refused the impulse to take his Starship Enterprise model. She forgave him, but he never ever got a kiss from her.

The coffee table to her left had numerous drinks left by unsuitable suitors. Various magazines fanned out on the center of the table with issues of Architectural Digest at the top of the fan. He bent over and picked up an issue, then bowed using the magazine like a fan. "Petros Papadopoulos, at your service. May I say how lovely you are, Mata?" Why did she let the boys talk her into using the moniker, Mata? This guy was no fool.

In their defense, they had suggested that the absurd and obvious use of a spy name would help produce a calm in the perp. He'd calculate that no one trying to capture him would be so stupid as to use a spy reference. Therefore, in the perp's confused mind, it was safe if not humorous. She was learning.

"Have a seat, sweetheart. You're the only man here who picked up the magazine. That was my little trap. I didn't say so in the ad, but I love architecture. Not only that, you showed me the balance of a Renaissance man. The lady or the magazine."

He hesitated.

"You've been snared."

"I must be gay." They laughed. "Seriously Mata, I've taught architecture. I miss it. I hope someday to get back to it. Sabbatical, you know." He saddened as any actor would, but his body language suggested he meant it. He picked up with both hands more hors d'oeuvres from a passing waiter. The guy could pack it away.

"You've got a big appetite." She straightened her gown and patted her hair. Feigning a sign of interest to a man who acted outclassed and a bit nervous because of it. She too felt the tiniest bit uncomfortable in a gown too vampish for a tomboy. Oh, he was good looking enough to try to date her, with his crazy curls but, in the end, he stood a bit too tall and a bit skinny. His personality charmed, though. She could see how all those ladies fell for his bullshit.

"When you go on your trip, I'll eat you out of house and home. However, when you come back, I'd humbly apply to be your most willing teacher—of architecture."

"I like you, Petros. I think we'll do just fine. But before we seal the deal, I have a couple questions."

"Anything for you. Your bewitching charm is holding me hostage."

Enjoying her femme fatale role, she clicked her fingers and Carlos brought over a folder containing pictures of the deceased Detective Sam Langrath. She pulled out his younger pictures from when he first entered the force. She'd save the gruesome ones for later.

"Do you recognize this man?"

He started to rise, but Carlos put his meaty hand on Mahmoud's skinny shoulder. They exchanged looks. He sank back down. His face said it all: severe disappointment with just a glimmer of hope. All his running and scamming might finally be over.

Frank issued orders to his staff. "The party is over." Mahmoud looked up at Frank as if he too wanted to leave, but Frank just shook his head with a closed lip smile.

Shortly all the remaining suitors were ushered into the elevator. Cha Cha started her interrogation as soon as the door closed. "We aren't going to harm you, Mahmoud. In fact, if you help us, it is entirely likely you can resume your life, get back to your students, because as you will soon learn, it is entirely safe now."

His mouth drooped; his eyes searched the expansive flat as if looking for an escape route. Cha Cha began to calm him with soothing tones, but—

Mahmoud stood. "I'm a free man. I've done nothing wrong." Carlos resisted reseating him.

"Could you fetch my badge, Frank? I have nowhere to put my NYPD detective's badge, Mahmoud," she said, demurely.

Frank ran up with her badge and showed it to him. "I want a lawyer, Detective, O'Sullivan."

"Yes, you can have a lawyer, but I hope you'll think differently after we tell you what we can do for you and how it is better to keep this away from the press and a trial revolving around terrorism and a few beguiled women."

"I am not a terrorist."

"Make no mistake, if you want to be arrested we will oblige you." Carlos said.

"Tell me your story and then I'll decide if I need a phone call."

"The picture I showed you—this one—is of the man who was pursuing you. He is dead as well as all his helpers," Cha Cha said. "Who is he?"

At first, Mahmoud hesitated and then he collapsed onto the sofa without Carlos's help. "I've never forgotten him. He was unusually interested in the Twin Towers from an architectural point of view. At the time, I thought he was merely precocious, but later… He was a student of mine at Princeton in 1991."

First, she showed pictures of his students from that year. After he identified the deceased as Ali Ali, all the pieces fell into place. Ten years ago, Ali had killed Sam Langrath, an applicant to the police force. Ali was a loner with no friends and a mom and dad who had, now suspiciously, died when their home burnt down. Mahmoud was told in detail of the Geek Team's murders by Ali Ali and how all traces of the terrorist cell in New York were now gone along with most of his files. She offered Ali Ali's death shots as final proof.

"The bastard." Mahmoud exclaimed as he turned over the gruesome images.

After Frank, Carlos and Cha Cha were satisfied that Mahmoud's lectures on the structure of the Twin Towers and other buildings were nothing more than an in depth study of the strengths and weaknesses of NYC architecture, mixed with a slight overdose of ego, they decided to tentatively clear him of all wrongdoing. They, of course, would interview all the students who had heard his lectures.

"So here's your choice, Mahmoud, besides a lawyer. We'll offer you a new identity or we can give you a cover story for your dean at Pratt."

"I love my students. I miss them. I want to teach, again." He blew his nose.

Frank handed him a medical file for his review.

Mahmoud poured over the documents. He lifted his head. His eyes twinkled, his grin broadened. The file showed him released from New York University Hospital. Apparently, Mahmoud had recovered from amnesia, a victim of the Twin Tower attacks. After his memory returned, his attending physician gave him a clean bill of health.

"So Miss Chastity. I don't suppose, you're not taken." Mahmoud started laughing and it became infectious with the entire team.

"I am very taken, thank you for your flattery. But don't be so forlorn." She rose and took his hand. "There's someone out on the deck who has been hoping to see you again. Do you remember the lovely young woman you gallantly carried down the stairs of Tower 1 and on to safety? She's been wanting to meet the real you."

Chapter 31

Tuesday, November 13, 9:02 a.m.

Frank and Cha Cha waited in the mayor's anteroom, while the police commissioner and the mayor finished up some other business before the axe fell, or so their intelligence led them to believe. It never ceased to amaze him that they could get fired for saving the city from a dirty bomb attack and eliminating the idea man behind 9/11. Being fired would mean taking NCS or CIA assignments overseas. He doubted Cha Cha would want that life. He had hoped to build his courage, ask her to marry him. Perhaps, the mayor had something else in mind today.

Frank touched the cold glass of the tall window. Optimistic about not getting fired, he wondered if Cha Cha would like to go shopping on this gray day for a brilliant diamond. She dressed as a *cool-cat* in form-fitting black jeans, a James Dean-like black leather jacket, and black pearl earrings. She could melt away the morning cold. Had already melted him into mush. Now too crazy in love with her, what would he or could he do to keep her in his life?

They were motioned in by the commissioner. Rudy seemed in a festive mood as he paced back and forth talking on his cell.

"No baby, she's getting, ah, ah..." He muffled his voice but old bat-eared secret agents can hear very well indeed. He coughed. "Ah testy. I gotta go. See ya— No...people are waiting. No...not her. Don't be silly. I'll call you back." He hung up. "It's a fundraiser."

Yeah, right. The mayor had a very public affair and dissolving marriage going on, which single-handedly kept all the city newspapers busy chopping down more trees. Besides, since when did a mayor, any mayor, make excuses for talking on the phone?

The police commissioner chimed in. "Just some details to iron out." *Bosom buddies.*

Looking a bit flustered, the mayor dispensed with the chitchat and got right down to business, but first he flicked on a desk switch which started a low-pitched hum to deconstruct voice in case of intercept equipment. The equipment was best left on all the time. "Tom Rich is forming a Homeland Security Department to oversee everything, but I want this city to have an independent but cooperative force.

Things were looking up for Cha Cha staying in his life.

"I want the City of New York to have its own CIA for here and overseas." He flicked off the voice disruption equipment. The humming stopped. "We'll *share.* But nobody, and I mean nobody, is going to take away our right to defend ourselves."

He turned the equipment back on.

"That equipment should not make a noise and should always be on. I'll have Bud visit you again."

"That would be nice. I thought I had ear wax build-up."

They went on to discuss how the anti- and counterterrorist force would not all be housed at 1 Police Plaza except for their mini NSA engineering arm. The city would borrow Bud and others from the NSA to set up and train the City's team. What they were about to do was absolutely necessary to keep the citizens of New York as safe as possible. They were about to establish an under the table, invisible to audits, invisible to chain of command arm of the NYPD. 1 Police Plaza would have its terrorism taskforce and then somewhere, or many somewhere else's in the city, there would be ghosts, sometimes called spooks.

Frank hoped the mayor and the commissioner were about to give him a chance to help his city and country in a way most pleasing and meaningful to him and Cha Cha. And then, with a little bit of luck—and a lot of dedication—they could stay together. His HOS building occupants could rededicate for the foreseeable future to fight terrorism in a way they knew best. His eclectic mix of ex-CIA, NCS, FBI, and current assassins, rogues, and foreign agents would continue, but with renewed purpose. This added punch would work. It was obvious now the mayor was heading down a well thought out path. But he needed Rudy to say the words, almost as important as 'I do.'

The commissioner poured another cup of coffee. He seemed worried. He asked Cha Cha if she'd like a refill. "So Cha Cha... Unfortunately, because of bad press and some in the department who cared about the mole and who haven't quite bought the story, I have had to approve an Internal Affairs investigation of you. You'll have to take a leave of absence with pay. You'll need to plan regular visits with the NYPD shrink and might as well see that guy Frank uses."

Time for a honeymoon?

"Doctor Myron Markowitz, Sir," Cha Cha offered.

The commissioner continued, "You *did* kill one of our detectives."

"Sham detective," Rudy corrected, cracking a crooked smile. He squashed a peanut shell and popped the nuts. The debris fell to the floor.

"So all this has to take time, maybe two months." The commissioner now focused on Frank.

Frank fidgeted in his chair then spoke up rather loudly. "We've linked the deceased Ali Ali to a dirty bomb plot. The nuclear material will be ferreted across from Canada somewhere in the northwest and soon. We are also working on other possibilities."

"Let's throw the Attorney General a bone," Rudy suggested.

"He's already in the loop, Sir. But this IA investigation—she should be getting an NYPD award instead." He took a breath, let it out slowly. "She *will* be getting an Intelligence Star." Such things were rarely handed out and because of secrecy immediately taken back after the ceremony, because the award was secret. Both Frank and Carlos had received these ephemeral awards for their service in Berlin and Oslo foiling two heads of state assassinations. But Cha Cha needed a resurrection, not some secret ceremony.

"There's another problem." The police commissioner walked over to the window and then coming back said, "Child Protective Services, who read the newspaper, are also launching an investigation of Cha Cha, claiming possible reckless endangerment and corruption of Autumn Breeze. The source for this inquiry is very interesting. The U.N. Ambassador of Trinidad and Winnebago at the behest of Autumn's grandparents, Professors Eustace and Amber La Badie."

"That's Granada," Frank said, but he knew the correct name. A tiny grin erupted for just a moment.

"That's Tobago," Rudy added, same grin.

"Yes, that's what I said. Autumn's grandparents have a strong influence in the political scene of Trinidad. Half their family is in public service. I'm sorry. They're not too happy with you, Cha Cha. They're coming here personally to escort Autumn and her mom's body back to Trinidad."

Autumn's mom had died two days before on Sunday afternoon in her arms after whispering 'I love you' to her distraught daughter. This prompted Cha Cha to file papers yesterday for custody of Autumn.

"But I applied—"

The mayor interrupted. "That application to become her guardian and a cup of coffee will get you nowhere. Sorry, kid. Listen, we know you both love this girl and that Autumn wants to stay at NYU and with you two. We also know she is a tremendous asset to our country and city. I'll do everything I can to smooth out the IA investigation and Child Protective, but no legitimate force on earth can stop the rightful guardians—her family—from taking this young lady." He cleared his throat. "Besides, Monique Breeze's last will and testament is clear on this point. And really, what right do we have to steal talent from another country? We play by the rules in the USA. Well, mostly. Make your case of what you think is best for the child and we'll take our chances."

Not knowing the Mayor better, Frank couldn't tell if this particular moral argument was believed, just mouthed, or somewhere in between. Frank would assume, for now, Rudy was earnest. Maybe Frank could bend life in Trinidad, a little.

Had he been a spy too long? What right did they have, indeed? Heady thoughts, he'd discuss this soon with his beloved Cha Cha. She complemented and balanced him. They'd devise a strategy.

Although the will was written a year ago, Frank saw no legal way to hurdle all these obstacles. He loved the kid too. He could be a great dad, but what was best for Autumn?

"Maybe I could talk to her grandparents," Cha Cha said.

"You could try, but their flight with Autumn back to Trinidad is arranged, the documents are in order and a foreign government and ally is involved. The Bush admin will not rock this sinking ship." Rudy sat on the corner of his desk, perplexed. *Got to give the mayor and commissioner much credit for working this problem.* "Thank Bud for cleaning up and rewiring my office and I hope to see him soon."

Frank had his answer. The two governments would work together to develop Autumn's talents, if the status quo remained.

Frank could also recognize in the mayor's words a *good-bye and good-luck* when he heard one. He stood. "I understand, Sirs. Cha Cha and I will see what we can do through our contacts. I can't guarantee we may not make our case in person, but we won't break any laws or step on anybody's toes." Frank assumed for now Autumn would very much want his help and didn't give a damn about *rules* in this case.

The mayor picked up his cell and then put it down again. "So, I'm not saying our relationship won't still go forward. We've both reviewed your joint proposal and with a little modification—" The mayor broke out into a wide smile. "Cha Cha, after her administrative leave will be given city-wide roving status as a lieutenant directing the Terrorism Taskforce assets. You, Frank, and your crazy group over at HOS, will neither be confirmed or denied by us. You read me?"

Yes.

But Frank's mind wandered. He'd propose. Before answering the mayor, Frank caught Cha Cha's gorgeous emerald eyes. If he knew how to say I love you with his eyes, he just did. Cha Cha smiled and her dimple appeared. Message received.

Cha Cha spoke up. "Yes, Sir, for both of us, and thank you very much. But what about our staff, Percy and the others?"

The commissioner spoke up. "Allow me, Rudy. I think we need to find a way to keep Percy with you. The others, on a case-by-case basis, will filter back to 1 Police or their previous precincts.

"I recommend you weave your webs very quietly until January. Then we'll have your visible-to-the-public counterpart, former CIA head of operations and analytics, David Cohen, take over the operation here at the Plaza. I understand, both that Russian, Colonel Carlos Petrovich and you have worked with him," Rudy said. Both Carlos and Frank had dealt with the hard-nosed Cohen before. A marriage made in heaven, with all the trimmings of hell, meant to keep the faint of heart out and the patriots in. David kept people on their toes. Cha Cha would be the go-between for the official taskforce headed by Cohen and the ghost team headed by Frank.

The stage was set for him to get down on one knee and the City was set on the right path.

"Frank and I will make sure we don't miss a beat until the official kick-off."

The mayor said, "Frank and Cha Cha, also consider until January the moral question of what's best for Autumn Breeze. Bring that to a resolution if you can, before official kick-off. Okay?"

"We won't let anything slip, Sir," Cha Cha said.

The mayor meant, without official direction from the NYPD or Mayor's office for the next two months, Frank and Cha Cha could choose their path, judiciously. Frank had every right to pursue Cha Cha, knowing they may never have a better time. They'd station in NYC, Carlos could continue on loan from OTTS for a while, staff was ready, willing and able to assume any role. The time would never be better to get married and raise children or, if a little bit of luck came their way, Autumn Breeze would become their daughter.

"For the record, I hereby officially end the city's relationship with you," the mayor said with relish. "Frank Lancia, we owe you our eternal debt, but you're fired."

Cha Cha spoke up through the chuckles. "We are honored to have resolved this case and many others through our taskforce, Sirs. And will soon let you know how the situation with Autumn is handled."

Frank added, "In the meantime, we will transition Bud and his team to the plaza over the next two months."

The meeting adjourned. Frank snuck a peek of Cha Cha, who seemed somewhat down by all the accusations against her. He needed to brighten her day and had just the sparkly remedy. A planned trip to Tiffany's might fill her spirit with joy. They and the commissioner left the mayor's office.

"Good job, you two."

"Thanks, Sir. Cha Cha, would you wait here? I forgot my Cross pen."

After getting by the secretary, Frank approached the mayor.

"Back so soon? What can I do you for?"

"This is top secret."

Rudy smirked "Let me guess."

"Would you marry us, if she says yes?"

"That woman of yours is terrific. A looker with brains and a huge heart. The city is proud of her and what she has achieved already. You two make a great team. I give you my blessings." The mayor winked. "You bring her back here, anytime. Just give me a day's advance. Love her, right."

"I will, Sir. It's a deal." Frank couldn't help but beam.

"Hey, come here. I've got something for you."

Frank rounded the mayor's desk. The mayor stood, digging into his breast pocket. He handed Frank two orchestra seats to the new Broadway play, *Mamma Mia*. Wow, Cha Cha would love this, *and the dancing*.

"I have to wait before I can see it. So who better than the two people who saved our great city."

"Thank you so much, Sir."

"Call me, Rudy."

"Rudy."

Frank felt like flying. Their plan was basically accepted by the mayor and commissioner. He wouldn't need a catharsis session with his parents and siblings, or her family, with Cha Cha acting as a stand-in shrink. He knew what he wanted. He knew he could accept the responsibility of marriage, children, and until death do us part, but just with this one lady. His soul mate. Who'd have thunk it? He had grown up.

His only problem would be trying to convince Cha Cha that he wasn't fooling himself. That he could stay monogamous, loyal. Be willing to grow old with her, have children. *Maybe, no more than two kids, plus hopefully, Autumn.* He was getting way ahead of himself.

* * *

Cha Cha and the commissioner chatted while waiting for Frank.

"If you clear IA and Child Protective Services, I'm going to need to promote you to captain, due to the responsibility you'll be taking on."

"Thank you so much, Sir." She hugged him. This early Christmas present was totally unexpected, but still the press, a foreign government—not to mention IA—were circling above her like vultures. She remembered her dear Captain Michael O'Sullivan and knew he'd be beyond proud.

"Yes, well, there's not a better person for the job, and frankly, on a captain's salary, you'll be underpaid." He truly smiled for the first time since 9/11, which had crushed this great man.

"If everything turns out okay, I won't let you down, Sir."

"It will. Listen, I have to run," the commissioner said. "Keep my promise under your hat for now. Loose lips."

"Yes, Sir."

"Good luck." He nodded farewell, then jumped on the elevator.

Frank hurried out of the mayor's office. Cha Cha stood by the elevator waiting for him. She loved him completely. But the detective in her wondered what made him spend so much time with the mayor just to retrieve a Cross pen? A pen he had never taken from his pocket.

Chapter 32

"57th & 5th," Frank instructed the cabby. Cha Cha knew the City of New York. Tiffany & Co. and the ghost of Audrey Hepburn dominated that corner.

She should preempt where Frank seemed headed. Or maybe, she should hold off and take the ride to dreamland with him. He must have noticed her sadness, which made it unlikely today he'd pop the question.

But, what if? *Oh my God, Chastity Mary O'Sullivan— married lady—Chastity Mary O'Sullivan-Lancia.* Or maybe he just wanted to buy cufflinks.

He put his arm around her. She collapsed into his chest, trying to hide her misty reflections. But he lifted her chin and peered into her eyes and looked worried. "The University of the West Indies has won accolades."

She sighed. Okay…he had caught her. She *couldn't* hide how she was feeling about Autum. He knew her inner thoughts better than anybody and didn't need the sight of a tear or two for verification.

"I know and she'll be with family. What hurts me, Frank, is I keep getting pinned as a loser."

"We're going to launch a campaign to correct that image and stop these stupid investigations."

A guy, a gal and a fourteen-year-old genius had gotten their feelings in knots only Alexander the Great could untie.

He kissed her forehead, which sent her emotions into a freefall of breathless anticipation for the future. "Let's meet her grandparents. They'll be here this afternoon to help Autumn pack."

"Why Tiffany's?"

"I—I need to do some shopping and we could use a break." The sham firing by the mayor was just the beginning of a shadow life of ghosts or spooks or whatever the latest term for people deep undercover was.

Adam, the store manager, met them at the door.

"Good to see you, Mr. Lancia."

"Likewise. I'd like you to meet my partner, NYPD Lieutenant, Cha Cha O'Sullivan." Part of the ruse of him being fired, included her paid leave, and at a lieutenant's salary.

She whispered to Frank, "I'll be promoted to captain in January."

"Wow. You deserve it," Frank whispered back and then nuzzled her ear.

"Would you like our little breakfast at Tiffany's?"

She politely declined the gold-leafed, dark chocolates. Frank didn't even look at the confections. He was distracted by display cases, maybe a bit nervous, like a schoolboy.

They chatted on.

After the required wandering around, Frank got down on one knee next to an engagement ring case. His eyes bore into hers turning her into Jell-O. "I'm so in love with you, sweetheart. Would you consider marrying me?"

"Rise, my gallant knight." She couldn't wipe a huge grin off her face if she tried. This klutzy way of proposing was so him. Although he had a lot to learn about romance, his heart, the only important part of true love, was all hers.

Everybody in the store displayed the most ridiculous 'ah-faces.'

He rose, eyes still locked with hers, questions written all over his face. Everybody in the store watched quietly and seemed frozen—hoping for a happy beginning—so she tiptoed up and kissed him. The kiss lingered with the promise of so much more. He caressed her face then wrapped his arms around her. Wow. Talk about fireworks. Every cell in her body wanted him, every beat of her heart swelled with joy. But not here. Not now.

She whispered in his ear. "Buy me some earrings. We need to go to Macy's for a ring—that's if I say yes," Cha Cha teased. Her sister would get them a special deal. Besides, he needed to meet Faith, the more beautiful, taller and younger version of herself before she strolled down the aisle. Just a little test. Didn't want any cloakroom misadventures at the wedding. But, of course, she trusted him and her sister. Wasn't it the bane of all detectives and spies to entertain the most outlandish scenarios?

She broke away from the heady swooning embrace. Then she poked his chest.

"That's a maybe, mister. And I love you back." That stick and carrot approach won a quick peck from her hero with a happy glow and easygoing demeanor.

Her momma don' told her she'd know her soul mate when he came along. He must feel the same way, but was he really ready? His psych profile suggested a fear of commitment that ran deep. Would he tire of her? And why *her*? When he could have his pick of any woman in the world? She devised a plan. She'd discuss the simplest thing first. The easiest thing for a man to explore was physical attraction. Then, at lunch, she'd talk about matters of the heart and later, the soul. He might have questions for her, which she was beyond ready to answer. She vowed to give and take.

"For today, Adam, the lady would like to look at earrings." Which they did, since Frank Lancia had more assets than Donald Trump. Well, maybe not, but he could easily afford the two half-carat blue diamond studs set in the yellowest gold she had ever seen.

The shoppers and salespeople politely clapped as she kissed him one more time. *This is getting to be a habit with me.*

Outside, maybe 34 degrees but warming up, they hugged and agreed to walk south on 5th past all the pretty stores down to Saint Patrick's.

"How about a prayer first? Then you pick lunch." An unknowing fear or malaise was overtaking her once again. Only a conversation with her Maker would help. Still wrapped in each other's arms, she peered up at him: her five-foot-eight to his six-two, his thick black curls to her auburn frizz, his sprinter's and so yummy perfect body to her tiny-breasted, bony-assed body. Yep, what a match.

"I'm talking just physical here. Why do you want me?"

"I think men are crazy to want their women to get boob jobs."

She couldn't help but wince. "That was direct and to my little points."

"I've always loved the Lucy Liu types rather than, ah, Pamela Andersons." Cha Cha had often compared her body to Lucy's, Helen Hunt's or Sandra Bullock's when she sang *I feel pretty* in front of the mirror. Apparently, some men didn't like being smothered by breasts.

"Or Dolly Parton?" she quipped.

"Dolly's a sweetheart for sure."

"Go on. I'm liking this so far."

"I will, but first things first. Why do you want to get your ring at Macy's?"

"My sister works there and their jewelry is just as good as Tiffany's."

Shrugging affably, he smiled over at her. "Okay. After lunch, let's pay her a visit."

"Works for me." While they waited for the walk signal on the corner of 5th and 53rd, she wound her arms around his neck and peered up at him. "By the way…your gray eyes with charcoal trim, did me in, the day we met."

"I'll never forget the night you drank too much. Your emerald eyes and dress, falling on your fanny. I picked you up off the floor. You were so out of it. I had to dust off your perfect rear end." Tingles took over her body. This guy sure knew how to make a gal feel great about her rear—and later—he can work over the rest of her.

"So tell me more, I'm not convinced."

"Your complexion is creamy smooth. I love your peekaboo dimple, which shows when you smile or are up to something naughty. Your reddish brown hair."

"It's auburn."

"Whatever." He leaned in closer, inundating her with his brisk masculine scent. "I have a thing for your thick, unruly tightly curled—"

She interrupted him. "Fro?"

"Yeah, it drives me wild. It makes me crazy with desire."

"You need to see a shrink."

He chuckled as they crossed the busy intersection. "I don't want to be cured."

"Tell me more about my bony ass," she said coyly.

"You got that expression from Working Girl—Sigourney Weaver, right?"

She took his hand and put it on her bottom and practically orgasmed. God, she was horny. Horny for him. Guessed it came with the soul mate territory and his proposal. *No kidding, Sherlock.* "No, I got these yams from my mom and dad."

"We should get a room before I burst."

"Later, baby," she purred.

"Your rump and your breasts are perfectly proportioned to your body, which is also a masterpiece."

"How sweet. You still want to bite my rump." The church neared, the devil had their tongues, just as she had planned.

"Well I...It was just what overwhelmed me on the look of you the day we met."

"I can't let you do it here or in church."

"What are pews for?"

"That is so wrong."

"There is so many things I want to do to you."

She needed a breather before she jumped him. "Before we go in can we talk a moment about Autumn?" Actually, she wanted to divert his thinking about her sexually, until she sprung her surprise. There'd be plenty of time later to talk about her girlfriend.

As they ascended the steps, he glanced over at her and gave her a knowing smile. "You love that girl, don't you?"

"I feel like I'm losing a daughter. She stole my heart."

"I love her too, but we better shush now."

He nodded and opened the huge door. She recalled how the girls of Saint Mary's had teased the boys, with the nuns but feet away, right at the church door. The boys and the girls narrowed at the entrance, the perfect opportunity. The nuns supervised two lines converging. The boys entering church could do nothing but listen red-faced, but maybe a little later go to confession for impure thoughts or sit in the pews with proud boners.

She whispered into his ear just as she had to the boys. "I've been such a bad girl. I need to be spanked." She put her finger to her opened mouth to shush him and briskly walked right into the cathedral. He held the door for a moment longer to let in an elderly lady. Then he caught up in a flash, panting, but not from his quiet

Olympic walk. They slid into the back pew of the huge but sparsely seated place of God. He nudged her and sulked. The smell of too many candles mixed with his hot breath filled the air.

She peeped at his crotch. Yep, worked again. She hoped a nun wouldn't come along with a ruler.

He stayed seated, rejected for the moment, while she kneeled. Glancing back at him from time to time, well often, she prayed that if Frank really wanted to marry her, he'd be open to children, *or one instant teen.*

Somehow, Lord, please bring Autumn to us. She loves me, loves him too. She loves NYU and this city. In my humble opinion, her talents would be better developed here.

I want Autumn Breeze to be my daughter. I will love her with all my heart, always.

I love this man. Help me, help him grow. He has a great heart. He's so gorgeous. Thank you for that. I know. We'll grow old, maybe not be so attractive anymore. But our hearts, may they with your blessing and grace, stay true.

She crossed herself. *One more thing, Lord. Please let us never forget our heroes.*

Tears streamed down her face as the images flashed of her grandpapa telling jokes, her partner spilling his drink, and all those pictures tacked up and on the news of the victims of 9/11.

"We're a great team, aren't we?" she whispered but he disappeared.

He bent over behind her, lifted her coat and before she could protest or react he bit her. Deliciously sinful. She muffled a yelp as a matronly lady with blue hair walked by with barely a side glance, one raised eyebrow, but no show of disdain. Cha Cha could swear the lady walked off concealing a flicker of amusement.

Chapter 33

They prayed at Saint Patrick's for about ten minutes, he for guidance in understanding Cha Cha, a woman like no other. She most likely for a multitude of devilish thoughts. He couldn't and wouldn't blame her. He had always had this problem with women. Now, with his life-mate by his side and his feelings just as strong as hers, he'd plunge into all things Cha Cha.

They left the cathedral holding hands—stealing glances as if double-checking reality. These acts so simple and sublime. The sun had broken through to set their minds, bodies and hearts ablaze.

The sun also highlighted her emerald eyes, eyes that said *yes, I'll marry you.*

"Let's walk south on fifth. You know Little Italy Pizza at forty-third?"

"They moved from Grand Central, right?" Cha Cha said. "I love their eggplant hero."

"Yep, same company. After eating we can stretch our legs some more. Head south until 35th, cut over a block to Macy's and meet your sister."

Cha Cha hugged him tenderly. "Can't get enough exercise." She gave him a come-hither look that drove him nearly as wild as her comments at the cathedral's door. "Maybe we should swim later."

The thought of skinny-dipping lingered. A little later, she said, "I'm a little cold."

"There will never be a shortage of hugs when I'm near you."

When he tightened his arms around her, she looked up at him as if to say, *Is this really happening?* Somehow, she got it in her head that he was too handsome for her. But she had it so wrong. How could he tell her how beautiful she was, inside and out?

"I wish people could not see inside a phone booth." He suggested a sensual but illegal idea.

"Maybe they'd think you're Superman."

"I'll let you be the judge of that," he murmured.

Smiling broadly, she flipped open her cell phone.

"Got to call, sis."

While she connected on the phone, he nuzzled and kissed her neck. Her voice rose. "Hieee." Her hair's fragrance made him dizzy, made him think of Jamaican nights on the beach. Skinny-dipping. Rum Mojitos drunk from coconuts. He undressed her, well mentally, and she was perfect, down to the last freckle of her fair skin. He hadn't dated many white girls, but Cha Cha had stolen his soul and color didn't matter, anyway.

Could she live without Autumn? He too had been smitten by the brilliant, impossible teenager. His heart wrenched at the thought of the girl leaving. But, wasn't it better she be with her relatives? Was he really ready for an instant family?

But it is "we" now, and the answer is without reservation: we are ready.

Wouldn't they need a very long and private honeymoon? Everywhere in his penthouse, they'd romp. He'd find a way to adopt Autumn in her sophomore year with Cha Cha's agreement. *She would, she's crazy about the kid.*

She finished a call full of giddy sister shorthand and enough whispers to confuse him. But there remained no doubt he made her happy.

"A penny for your thoughts," she said.

He had to check his surroundings. People everywhere.

"I would like to get married while our duties are light. We could turn over most of the day-to-day to Percy. We'll oversee. Whadaya think?"

"A very big yes to Percy. But marriage later, maybe. We could make love all day long?" She stretched and pecked his cheek. She formed a cupid's bow with her lips and accentuated one naughty word, "tonight."

"I'm...ah...thinking we should get married first." He teased her because he knew her too well. Neither of them were traditional Catholics. He'd bet nearly everybody had pre-marital sex no matter their religion or lack. Yet, it was nice to offer her the option. He could wait for...

"No way, mister. If we honeymooned. You might tire of me. We'll end up either divorced or never able to take the beans out of the jar."

"You mean put a bean into a jar every time we make love the first year and then take them out after the first year?" he asked.

"Yep, one-by-one."

Her eyes sparkled with mischief. "We're going to need a very big jar."

What an upside-down crazy day. Again, the crowd they walked with came back into focus.

"I've got a better idea, Frankie boy. We hole up for two months naked. If you're not tired of me by then, I'll marry you." My God, she was young, vibrant, healthy and rearing to go. The thought of her running around his penthouse naked with him in very hot pursuit titillated him.

Aside from a now urgent erection that threatened to rip his Dockers open, her idea somehow almost made sense. They could start tonight and come again and again and again. How would it be like to make love to a woman he actually loved? Probably heaven. No place, he had ever been before.

He'd play their little game a tad longer. "No honey, I talked to the mayor. He'd marry us, tomorrow. We could get the church wedding later. You don't want to live in sin."

"I want to sin so bad." Eyebrows raised, a bit of a jump, as if she needed to pee. She perused the street scene, apparently set on ravishing him, right then and somewhere near. They could run back up to Saint Pat's and steal a confessional. No—no lightning bolts, please. Of course, getting arrested wouldn't help their cause while Cha Cha was being investigated by IA and defamed in the newspapers.

She wrapped her arms around his waist. The people disappeared again. Just like the great old song sung by many but remembered fondly through the genius of Fred Astaire, *maybe millions of people walked by.*

While she was squeezing him senseless, she wrested a tear of joy from him.

"I only have eyes for you, dear." If she were the least bit jealous of all his past conquests, now was the time to start a campaign to convince her otherwise.

"Hey, watch it, bud." A construction worker shouted at the corner of 49th before Frank nearly walked into a metal lattice. A little later, they entered, still unaware, a pedestrian pass under scaffolding.

"Can you read my mind?" she asked. Perhaps she *was* jealous, but he'd prove himself through his devotion to her. She nuzzled her face against his gray wool long coat. He stopped their walking to kiss her. Her willing lips wouldn't let the moment pass. She pressed him wantonly. They lingered in a steamy interlude of clutching and exploration, enough to turn this frigid day tropical.

Someone up above, whistled, "Whee whee-al," and then said, "That's some tomato you're squeezin'."

Frank's smile widened. The City of New York pulsed with vibrant life. No one would ever know how dire the threats had become or that this couple had saved the city.

"You don't know how crazy I am about you," he said throatily. "There will never be another woman. That's the way I was raised and how I feel." She just smiled.

They entered the nearly full restaurant, designed with simple long rows of bright square tables. They managed to find a table. Mostly everybody rubbernecked. They had to be beaming.

"Alright Frank, for some reason you think I'm the most gorgeous girl you've ever seen. Well, wait until you see my sister."

"I've seen her already," he said with a shrug.

"When was that?"

"Remember the day we had to split, after the fire in Brooklyn?" he asked. "I stopped in Macy's and checked her out in person. She didn't see me."

"And...?" Cha Cha prodded.

"Oh, she's cute alright, but you're exquisite. She's too tall. She's not you, baby."

She munched on her hero while he twirled spaghetti.

"Besides my turning you on, tell me one more time, this time in depth what is it about me that made you kick out Emily, a Miss America, if I ever saw one?"

"Emily and I were coworkers who cohabitated. We had little in common. You and I, besides outrageous chemistry, share a love for our work and country."

"Emily."

"Well, there's really not much to it. She was a sweet and honest and yes beautiful woman, but we started with a promise to each other that we would just be friends who shared a good time. It was easy for me because the more I knew her, the less likely I was to fall in love."

"For her it was the opposite."

"I'm afraid so." He took a long swig of soda but never broke eye contact with her. "I love the way you solve things, like a Sherlock Holmes. I love your compassion. I'll never forget the way you cared for me that first day, even though I had done you wrong. My heart aches for you." If he didn't stop talking, she'd weep from joy.

She offered him a bite. "I'll never forget the way you looked that day, that awful day, September eleventh. Your body bruised and cut all over like they were trying to pull your soul out of you. They didn't succeed...they never will." She got up from her side of the table, wrapped her arms around him from behind, kissed his cheek and held him tight. "That's the day I fell in love with you."

"For God's sake lady, get a room." A burly fellow with a cherub's face decided to display some New York attitude. He wore a Yankees coat over tie and pale blue dress shirt. His shoes perfectly polished. A pushover who had eaten a few too many donuts.

"Aren't you Detective O'Sullivan?" Mr. Burly's female tablemate asked. She was dressed to the nines in a wool pinstripe suit, which hugged a well-kept figure. She seemed empathetic.

"It's not true what you've read in the papers. I'll be cleared of all charges."

"But that poor girl. The genius..."

"I can't really talk about it. I saved her life. That's all."

"Well good luck. I mean it." Then she leaned forward toward their table and whispered, "You two should bottle what you have. It's making me hot under the collar. Come on, Henry, munch it down. We have to get back."

"They don't have cold showers at the library, Peona, do they?" So they worked down the block at the public library. He imagined Peona, in charge of the romance section, Henry in charge of action-adventure.

Henry came back to their table. "My brother is a priest at Saint Luke's, Father Mark. Get my drift." *So New York.* He wrote on the back of his card, and then tossed it on their table. It flipped upside, showing off the Knights of Columbus emblem. Frank could smell an inquisition coming and from Henry's person something else, library dust.

New York impertinence was back and he loved every minute of it. After they left, Frank gave one look at Cha Cha and they both burst out laughing.

Chapter 34

Cha Cha stopped Frank with a turnabout body check in Macy's menswear.

"Happy Birthday."

Having this girl in my face—heaven.

"It's not my birthday."

"Happy Ides of November, then."

"What's up?" He placed his hands on her waist and rocked her hips—a little suggestiveness seemed in order.

Obviously, she wanted to buy him something. But why?

"I can't let you meet Faith while you're dressed in gray Dockers, gray dress shirt, gray West Point coat. See a pattern here?"

His lips quirked. "You forgot my gray eyes."

"At least they're trimmed in charcoal and amazing."

"Everybody says, you get married, your wife dresses you."

"You have impeccable taste as long as it's gray," she deadpanned. "Today, blue and not Dockers."

"And why blue?"

"Because my sister has seen the tattered remains of this same outfit. Your only outfit. A copy of the one you wore on 9/11. The same fucking clothes you wear every day." Sheesh, 'fucking' was pretty strong. Not since he had ripped his Hans Solo kid shirt had he stressed so much.

Seeing his shocked expression, she rushed to add, "Look, you can wear what you want. Just not today." He smiled.

So they went on a shopping spree, until his dulled brain woke up. Oh, the clothes were okay, a signal of a changing lifestyle, just not secret agent gray. He'd vary his wardrobe because it made her happy, because he was crazy about her, because she helped him grow, but—

"I don't remember meeting your sister then."

"You lay naked on my bed, sores and Smurf Band-Aids all over your gorgeous body."

Yes, he was getting out of the shower with her help. Oh, he had passed out right before the bed. "Didn't you cover me?"

"We had to lift you to get you under the covers. She laughed at your penis. Okay, okay, she ogled you. I think your," she gulped, "equipment is very nice."

The one thing you didn't do is laugh at a guy's penis, but Cha Cha made a jealousy slip. She basically admitted to a rivalry with her sister. Millions of women could walk by, but he'd still choose Cha Cha.

He also had a thing about being naked in front of anybody— or at least he used to—stemming from being tossed outside in the freakin' cold, no clothes, as a young kid by his older siblings. Although he wasn't quite ready to streak in Yankee Stadium, he believed he owed Cha Cha one more thank you. When she ran around his penthouse nude, so would he.

"You will be spanked," he teased her back for earlier at the doors of Saint Patrick's.

Meeting her sister produced enough angst to rival spy gigs. Guess he was changing. He had grown a heart and hadn't had to walk the yellow brick road.

After a spanking, would Cha Cha's rump get as red as her freckles? A delicious thought and he needed to know.

"I hope you spank me." She smacked her romp and he ate her up with his eyes.

With her back to them, Faith, a statuesque beauty, in blue slacks and working white shirt was holding up granny panties, wide out, making some joke with another employee.

"Baby." Cha Cha ran toward her. They hugged. Both jumped up and down and turned toward him in unison.

"I bought that suit line in Hong Kong. Hi, handsome."

Faith wasn't shy. She rushed to hug him. Cha Cha appeared unfazed.

"So glad to meet you too, sis."

"Ever think about modeling?" Faith asked, giving him the once-over.

Cha Cha and he had rehearsed their professions.

"My job as a police consultant doesn't cut me much slack." Could he say it anymore lamely? Modeling might be fun, once in a while. Maybe the Sears catalogue, holding a drill.

"You look just as good with clothes on." Faith was a cut-up just like her sister. He girded himself against his diminishing fear. The ha-ha-you-were-naked tease. The price for getting back into his boyhood home had been to eat horseradish—straight. Likely, Cha Cha planned a more tasty surprise.

He decided to give both of them a dose from their own medicine cabinet. "Maybe when the weather warms up we can boat over to Jones Beach and have a nude party and drum circle."

"Frank's a wannabe nudist," Cha Cha said, smirking. He pictured—just as a future joke to spring on his gal—a blushing groom locking himself in the bathroom, insisting on lights out. He loved the girls' sass.

Faith took them down a flight to see Macy's fine jewelry. Cha Cha was torn between emerald green to match her eyes or NYPD blue. They all liked an oval blue diamond with emerald clusters around the base on a simple platinum band. Round or oval, with less jagged edges was best because this waif of a woman fancied herself a tomboy. Something he found both hilarious and alluring. Great at martial arts, game for wrestling, lethal with her fists. She had promised to attack him when he least expected it, like Kato, of Pink Panther fame. Unfortunately, this had not happened yet, probably because she had feared it would lead to sex before a promise of forever. Yes, it would have. Now, they'd take the ring off when she felt the need to mix it up with him...maybe oil up... His fantasies were running amok. *Remember, I'm in Macy's.*

Since Cha Cha was thin and preferred light, the diamond weighed one carat. She was so happy, if her loving flirty looks were any indication.

Frank decided to mirror their style with jokes of his own. He took Faith's hand. "Your sister wants to test drive me before we marry." From the look on Cha Cha's face, he had struck home. Of course, he wanted her. He had wanted to make love to her from the first moment he saw her, just not that awful day. His subconscious lust for her had blown his cover on 9/11.

He had suggested waiting to be married because he thought he could convince her to marry standing before the mayor—and quickly. Marriage, however, was about compromise or better put, about growth.

"*Chastity* O'Sullivan, I thought you were going to—wait." Faith had that severe disappointed, disillusioned look on her face. Then a twinkle in her eye signaled a return to merriment. "I don't want to hold the two of you up." She smacked her sister's rear. "And you thought you could fool your baby sister."

"My mom taught me that when a woman is done with a man's body, they're done with the man. So, I decided to save myself for marriage."

Cha Cha smacked her forehead and displayed an incredulous look.

Faith took but a moment to retort. "The O'Sullivans' have never had a divorce. We choose wisely, and I think—no I know— you're her match."

"I love her with all my heart."

The girls shared more secret sister talk, admitted he was the main topic of conversation between them—nearly every day. Frank purchased the ring, slipped it on her finger to kisses that if they kept it up much longer they'd have to close the floor or get a changing room. Maybe she would be so noisy they'd have to evacuate the building.

No doubt, Faith O'Sullivan loved her sister's choice. Now they had to prepare for Autumn's grandparents, never an easy problem to tackle.

* * *

Frank and Cha Cha discussed the situation in the penthouse before they went over to Autumn's co-op where she was packing with her grandparent's help.

"It's the *National Tattletale* we have to thank for losing Autumn," Frank said, squeezing Cha Cha's hand. This scandal rag, whose editor-in-chief claimed to be from another planet, was the most popular way some people from Trinidad got their Stateside news. This week's cover showed proof that aliens collapsed the Twin Towers with ray guns. The editor's disclaimer: the aliens weren't from his planet.

Cha Cha had worried every time a new story and its variations came out—in all its media guises—about her shooting Ali Ali and all the gossip about her life with Autumn. Each story felt like somebody was pounding a stake through her heart. Allegedly, she had used Autumn's brilliance to hunt down bad guys. Encouraged her to run a dating service. Used her as a lure to capture the idea man behind 9/11, who in another story was a patsy. Used Autumn to get even with her old boss by shooting her replacement. Taught Autumn how to be a grown up and date boys. Showed her how to escape the Earth's gravity. On and on.

"I know Autumn is doing what she can to correct this nonsense with them," Cha Cha said. Her grandparents were intellectuals who immersed themselves in University life. People who believed in reasonable argument. Professors' Amber and Eustace La Badie would present rational and passionate arguments for their granddaughter's coming home to Trinidad. They could expect to be countered by three very strong willed adversaries. The countering would be touchy, considering her grandparents' authority and obvious love of their granddaughter so Frank and Cha Cha decided to proceed carefully.

So far, they had ascertained: Amber had semi-retired as professorship in Theology and Philosophy and now looked forward to being a mom again and shepherding—or showing off—Autumn around the University. Eustace treasured his role as math and physics professor—of being Autumn's personal tutor—and the chance to beat her at cards while in their beach cottage or on the sand at Maracas Bay. Apparently, on top of loving her grandparents, Autumn missed some childhood friends, her cousins mostly. She'd visit with enthusiasm the nesting turtle site near her grandparents' cottage, but all the positives weren't enough for Autumn.

The girl had already texted them that she'd tried nearly every argument and sprinkled in sporadic tantrums. She couldn't sustain her urgings much longer, due to the way she was raised and believed. When Frank and Cha Cha arrived, Autumn promised not to interrupt the four of them, unless she couldn't stand it. She wished them luck.

"We will be respectful and see what's best for you." They texted back.

They couldn't encourage her because Autumn appreciated honesty above all.

Besides, you can't beat family.

* * *

"There's nothing like the excitement of Manhattan," Autumn said—regretfully, el lame-o style—while being squished on the couch between Granny and Pappy. They had stopped packing once again to respond to another tantrum she manufactured to twist their hearts. She loved them crazy, all right. But she belonged in New York, at NYU and with Frank and Cha Cha, who really needed her. Those two were so in love, it was only a matter of time before they figured out they should marry each other and adopt her. Right? There'd be no messy diapers to change and if they made a baby, she could help, even with diapers. Well, maybe.

Her grandparents weren't big people but they wedged her, so close, she couldn't get up. So she bobbed her head between his and her shoulder.

"Love you, both."

Her grandparents were sweet, intellectually stimulating, loving, but they were old-fashioned farty types. *Pappy must blow away his class with all the beans he loves to eat.* Now, he stunk like he had been sneaking Oreo cookies. She'd check her stash later. She had hidden the Oreos in a Wheat Chex box to slow down Joey. Maybe Pappy liked to munch on cereal without milk and was surprised to find something yummier.

Now, being mostly vegetarian was a good thing. Great, he'd live long. He still had the super sharp mind—somehow beat her at cards, 68.377% of the time. Granny was smart, too. Sneaky smart.

But still, she wanted to grow up with a mom and dad. And then, what about Joey? Sure, he wouldn't touch her. Sure, he thought of her as a baby sister, yuk. But she could tell, he thought someday, maybe someday when she grew up and out, he'd like her for sure. Love her for sure. And he'd be lucky because she was too cute for words, already.

"We have to get to JFK soon, child," Granny said.

The co-op's building door buzzed. This time Frank and Cha Cha didn't dare use their spy equipment to get by the door.

"Please Granny, Pappy, treat them nicely," Autumn pleaded while walking over to the door.

She let Cha Cha and Frank in. Resisted shouting out a *wow* when she gawked at Frank's blue suit and red tie. He was really good looking for an old man of thirty.

She played it cool and said, "Sharp." Then she noticed the rock on Cha Cha's finger and her heart blew out all its valves. Part one of her two-part plan—accomplished. Cha Cha focused on Autumn studying the ring and then showed it off, which also caught her Granny's eye.

"So you're the New York City detective who endangered our grandchild."

Oh no, please don't do this.

She had tried to explain the truth of her loving relationship with Cha Cha but Granny and Pappy hadn't listened. Especially when they wanted to take her home by right of blood and squish her on their own sofa every time she wanted to argue. She was so stuck.

"With all due respect. We saved her life. What you read in the papers isn't true."

After some back and forth, Autumn got them to exchange names at least. Horrible, would now be her super un-favorite word. *Horrible, horrible* withered her silent scream.

"May I explain, Amber and Eustace?" Frank asked.

They sat down and Autumn ran for tea. She studied her collection; maybe chamomile would calm them. Maybe Frank was good at talking people down off high horses. But Granny and Pappy stood like circus clowns atop Clydesdales.

"We don't have much time, son," Pappy told him.

What's this son stuff?

Endearing or condescending?

"I was talking with the mayor and the police commissioner earlier today. They promised me, they'd have a full and private report for you soon. The commissioner even offered to bring it to you in Trinidad." Nice touch of humor, everybody wants to go to Trinidad—for vacation. "The report will show you, not only that my partner and fiancée is innocent of all charges but that Autumn was nurtured and protected as if Cha Cha were her mother."

Pappy stood up as if to give a speech. His vest with gold pocket watch was so—Dickens. His ruddy round face with curly gray hair was so huggable, kissable. "Let's say, for the sake of argument, all you say is true. Let's say you two get married and want to adopt our grandchild."

Then Granny got up, smoothed out her carnival cotton dress and squeezed his hand. Oh no, they were going to do their tag team act.

Horrible. Horribler. Horriblest.

She said, "I have questions I don't want you to answer now, because we have to leave soon. How do we, her closest relatives, know you aren't attracted to her for her gathering fame and aren't ready to exploit her while she matures?" *Zap.*

Pappy took over still holding Granny's hand. How sweet. How deadly. "Who is better for a young lady who has come so close to death? Family or friends?" *Not totally fair. Specious.*

Granny said, "To whom will two young working adults run when they need babysitting?"

Autumn was getting Ping-Pong sickness. Besides, she didn't need babysitters, for God's sake. *How old-fashioned.*

Oh no, now Granny rested her petite self against Pappy's chest. Autumn would need an eye doctor, her eyes were so crossed.

Pappy said, "How much do you love her? As much as we do?"

Then Granny, "Who better than my husband and I to help her with her education?"

"How do we know you two will last as a couple?" Pappy asked.

The end was coming because Granny started waving her finger at them.

The death blow: "Do you really think rushing to get married instead of observing the bands of marriage in the Catholic Church is wise?"

Frank crossed his arms. This was as close as her favorite spy would get to a firing squad, no cigarette, but he seemed unfazed.

"It's better than living in sin." Frank quipped.

Everybody started laughing. Oh yay, Frank was wounded, not dead. Maybe the four of them would get closer to each other.

Pappy, still standing, arm wrapped tight around his sweetie-pie. This one coming might be the *coup-de-gras* since the last one didn't work or maybe the weight of all their ideas was enough for him to rest their case. She had seen this done so many times at their tea parties with the other professors. "We've forgotten the temptations of youth. We've been married, well forever. I'll offer you two one last query to ponder. Which island is safer, Manhattan or Trinidad? Hmmm."

Granny way beyond overkill added. "Annnnd, maybe it isn't true that you encouraged her to date an Italian boy named Joseph."

Cha Cha slumped into the sofa not quite TKO-ed. She'd get back up, but maybe she should be rescued with something witty, but Granny got to Cha Cha first, sat down and draped her arm over her.

"It's all right, Detective O'Sullivan. A young couple needs their space and private time to grow with each other when first married. You'll see I'm right." Granny caught Pappy's eye. Something passed between them. A fondness, a sweetness for times of passion and love. *Oh my God, they're still in love. I want that. Always.*

In turn, Pappy put his arm on Frank's shoulder. "Did you know that it only takes three days in Trinidad or Tobago to get married?"

"I might be able to swing a priest," Granny said.

"I'll miss you, Autumn, so much." Cha Cha gave Autumn that droopy-eyed, we-did-our-best look and then hugged Granny back.

"Maybe Autumn could be your flower girl?" Pappy suggested. Both Frank and Cha Cha nodded their heads.

Yes. Yes. Sweet, sweeter, sweeetific.

This had to be good in the long run. All the people she loved should love each other.

"We have a big family waiting for her. Especially her cousins." Well, her studies would likely cut down on playtime. She hoped her cousins and everybody else would understand.

Cha Cha relaxed, looking like she gave up. *But spies never give up. We'll see.*

The co-op entry doorbell buzzed again, three buzzes. Oh my God, Joey.

"He likes to be called, Joey. We're just friends and it isn't true. I don't like boys that way." Autumn said and then broke into crocodile tears, especially prepared for this occasion. Not quite one of her earlier tantrums, considering her promise to let the adults talk.

When he arrived, they stuck him in the middle of the couch. All four adults took turns grilling Joey like he was a sizzling hamburger. Guess they needed somebody to pick on after Frank and Cha Cha lost the Intercontinental Tag Team Belt to the Professors of Trinidad.

Joey cracked a little under the interrogation, but it was all good. He looked so cute in jeans and bomber jacket. "I might not look it, but I'm sixteen, so I feel closer to a fellow genius than the rest of our class. This skinny fourteen-year-old is just my littlest friend. Only God knows what the future holds." Joey went on to describe using in-your-face terms, how unappealing a girl with no figure is for an older boy with hunky muscles, good looks, and possibly plenty of co-eds chasing him all over the campus and city.

Thanks for rubbing it in, Joey. Of course, he never kissed the coeds. Well, at least he had told her that, showing some respect for the future Mrs. Autumn Demarco. She wished she could read thoughts; she'd start by studying body language.

He also said that the only thing he and Autumn had going besides their friendship was intellectual growth. At least he was honest and smart. He likely knew to speak in any other way about her would completely ruin his relationship with all four adults. If only she could kiss him, somehow before she left.

No. She'd have to settle for someday. It was best she didn't give Joey the goodbye smooch in front of Granny and Pappy, who secretly wanted her to be a nun anyway.

Okay, they were worried. They loved her. Life on Trinidad was fun anyway. She'd get back to New York once she turned eighteen. She could do what she wanted including marrying. *God, what a long time. A prayer would be in order here.* Something needed to change.

"Would you take Julius for us, son?" Granny asked.

"I'm sorry, ma'am. I don't have room in my dorm." He probably wouldn't be caught dead.

Frank stood and stretched. "We can take Julius for a while. Maybe someday you two will see your way to allow us to adopt her." Oh my God—times two. Frank would actually do it. She became giddy and nearly fell down with pride. She gave Julius a big kiss and hug, instead.

"You're a Manhattan dog. Stay with them. They'll love you, too. Okay?" She didn't care to study whatever looks the humans all had, because she talked to fluff and cotton. They were kids once upon a time.

But that's all she needed to know. *Going home was nice, but living in New York City, able to kill terrorists, work with spies, go to school, Joey, Frank and Cha Cha, AKA dad and mom. Well, no contest.*

She'd work on Granny and Pappy, *relentlessly*. With all due respect and lots of love, of course.

Chapter 35

Frank and Cha Cha walked holding hands, swinging them like children would. Was he real or had she just entered a fantasy? Her guy dug her for numerous reasons. He loved her looks, hair, *that's big*, detective abilities, height, sense of humor, her duality of tom-boyishness and sultry female.

I made a good—an excellent spy. And he compared her figure to Lucy Liu's. *Well, of course.*

They left Autumn and her grandparents to their packing. What a day. The mayor and commissioner had basically given them two months to get most of the initial taskforce completely underground except for her. She would become the NYPD's roving inspector, with carte Blanche. A dream job.

Part of their semi downtime until the January kickoff revolved around a strange half serious suggestion of the mayor to recruit Autumn as a national asset.

Of course she was.

But they had no right. *All men are created equal.* America and the City of New York would be stronger if they took a laissez faire attitude—celebrating the inner destinies of free men as they decided what to do with their lives even if it meant having one less genius on board.

Cha Cha was also now without her gun, with visits to the shrink, IA and Child Protective in her near future. Autumn would leave. Nothing they could or should do about it. Family was the foundation of society. Cha Cha's parents, her grandpapa taught her that.

Cha Cha was now a taken lady. She studied the diamond as it flickered in the mix of late afternoon sun and cloud wisps. She was engaged to the man of her dreams, a man she had thought she could never have.

Have.

With her passions taking over the beating of her heart, she'd wait no longer to give herself to him. She just wanted to spring one last promised trap on Frank while he least suspected it and before they made love.

She'd surprise attack and they'd wrestle.

He'd likely get the upper hand. If they boxed he'd be demolished, possibly hurt. She couldn't have his male ego or his body suffer today. Besides, her hero had physically suffered for weeks after 9/11.

So, she'd have to grit her teeth, survive her swelling needs and wait until the evening for part two—mad, passionate love.

Also, Autumn's problems left her a little hesitant and that spoiled the mood for sex. She wanted her first time with Frank to be perfect. She'd set the stage.

Eustace and Amber had been formidable in argument, which caused Frank and she to become reflective.

"Maybe Autumn will discover she really misses Trinidad, her cousins, her grandparents," Frank said.

"I'm so torn up over this," Cha Cha admitted. "That kid has been my almost daily companion for two years."

Frank swallowed hard and she could see the raw emotion on his face. "I hate seeing you like this. I will do anything I can to get her back."

A block later, a cab with a *Sex In The City* ad on top stopped to let out passengers. The banner was her perfect cue.

"Promise, Frank, until I say make love to me. Hold off. Just wait until tonight."

"I understand."

"No matter what."

"I promise."

She would attack him like Kato, as promised. He'd never suspect it. Any other time and he'd overwhelm her and she wouldn't be able to resist making love. Ha. Ha. She was leading a spy into a trap.

"Chastity."

"No baby." For a moment, she had forgotten her name, until Frank's sweet joke twisted her nose. Fuck it. There was more John L. Sullivan in her than Mother Theresa. They clinched.

"I need to stop at my place for a little while," Cha Cha said.

Her place was perfect for wrestling with its black rubber walls and floor. She was a jockette. Apparently, this turned him on, big time, and it would be her prelude. All of this would make them laugh years from now as they shared memories.

"My corporation could use this place for our undercover work." Frank said. She wished he wouldn't use the word undercover right now.

He turned her into mush every day.

"If our engagement holds."

He pursed his lips. "Yeah sure, kid. We're soul mates and I'll prove it."

What had he in mind? You couldn't prove something mystical. Well, maybe he had a surprise for her as well. She'd wait.

"We'll see." She teased him while leading him down the steps to her ground floor co-op by pulling on his tie.

"You know I wore much more than gray when overseas. I even dressed up when the occasion demanded. I still have a wardrobe."

"You just got yourself in a rut." She gazed adoringly up at him. "You look so scrumptious in your blue suit."

They clung together at her door. "Take me," he whispered into her ear. "Ah, I mean later."

What a devil. He'd be overwhelmed soon.

"Autumn is a one girl wrecking crew, Cha Cha. She'll solve this problem."

"No Autumn for a while, okay honey?" She raked her fingers through his curly thick black hair and kissed him. "So where in your place do you want to make love to me?" She knew it would be the pool area.

"On the kitchen table or maybe in the observatory."

"You don't have an observatory."

"I've wanted you everywhere all the time, relentlessly."

She kissed him passionately. "We'll talk about it tonight. Okay, babe?" She implored him. Still he didn't answer. There was a low growl rumbling from his chest that she had never heard from a man before. Oh, this was so beyond anything she had learned on the Nature channel. She couldn't outrun him. Oh no.

She broke their hug before he… "Just give me a moment to gather some things." She said with wispy breath. "Take a seat. There's some waters still in the frig."

"Oookaay." He said like a little boy who wasn't allowed his PlayStation any more. The good news was: he was respecting her subtle wish. The bad news: he was respecting her.

She pulled the curtain on her bedroom, quickly kicked off her heels so she wouldn't hurt him. And twisted off her rock.

"Take off your shoes, honey. House rules."

"They're already off." He said with a husky, naughty voice.

He was about to get the surprise of his life. "Could you help me reach something high over here?"

"Right away, babe."

He pulled the curtain back and she leapt off the bed, throwing her front, upper body sideways into his chest. God, he was quick. He was supposed to fall back through the curtain opening and onto the mat; instead, he caught her and she was suspended, body sideways and flailing in both directions. She tried for leverage. He just lowered her on the bed and kissed her lips sweetly, then her neck, then a little lower. *Oh, ah.*

She lifted her legs, wrapped them around his body and squeezed, but that wrestling hold didn't work because he was too tightly muscled. He just snickered.

"Let me go, you, you brute."

"Say Uncle, no better yet in your case say Aunt Fanny."

"Who's Aunt Fanny?"

He flipped her over, pulled up her dress and spanked her rear.

"You are so bad. Let me up so I can get out of this."

Frank immediately released his hands that were holding her thighs down. Seemed he liked the idea of her without her dress. Excitement pulsed through her as she slid the dress down her body and it pooled around her feet. All she had left now was pale-pink lace panties and a flimsy red bra.

His eyes had that hungry wanton expression of a man grown mad with desire.

She attacked again, throwing a head lock, but he just flipped her back on the bed and started all over doing the same stuff he had done before.

He was too quick, too strong, too anticipatory. Maybe she'd get him someday by finding a way to sneak attack that would be more effective. She needed to test his defenses.

"Would you mind satisfying me in the middle of the mat with a real wrestling take-down?"

"I like the satisfying you, part." He took off his pants, tossed his jacket and threw the tie, God knows where. No pants today wasn't so embarrassing, since she had bought and made him wear boxers. But there was no hiding what he displayed and it was getting bigger.

"Maybe you should put your pants back on."

"Come and get me, you tigress." He wasn't going to put his pants back on.

They shook hands. Giggling, she lowered her gaze. He grunted. Then she dropped into a leg hold. She tried to flip him to the mat but he just stood there like a tree.

"Is that all you've got?" He scoffed.

She stood up, bowed and tried a hand flip, but it was she who ended up on her rear on the mat.

"Fanny hurt?" He pounced on her and somehow she was on her back with her legs as open as a Colorado valley.

He leaned forward, pressing his chest to hers. *Will he take me like this?* It would be easy, she couldn't move. She was so wet. He'd clutch her panties, move them to the side and slide right in. *Oh, Frank.* She shivered again.

It surprised her that she orgasmed while wrestling, but why not, she was so much in love. *Tonight will be outrageous.*

"Most wrestlers worry about being pinned instead of being screwed." Her shoulder blades were flattened to the mat. She had forgotten the contest. She had lost, but had fulfilled her fantasy.

He kissed her lips sweetly, then her nose, then her eyelids, her forehead. "Later, I can't take it much longer," Frank said.

"Maybe you should try boxing with me. Helmet, gloves. I mentioned him the first day we met but you were dizzy. One of my very great uncles, John Lawrence Sullivan was the first and last world heavyweight champion of both bare knuckles and gloved boxing," she panted. "There's some family photos of him in the bookcase."

"I want to see them—later. I want a very different round two with you at our place and no bare knuckles, just a very bare you." He looked like the jock he was. The former sprinter and football star for Notre Dame. He looked like his wife had just handed him a beer.

"My mom and dad have his championship belt."

He grinned. "Wow. I want to see that and visit with them."

"We need to call our parents today and tell them the good news or they'll feel like we don't love them enough," she said.

He got up and held out his hand.

"I love you, Cha Cha O'Sullivan and will love your family."

She sprung up and wrapped her arms around him, more to cover her skimpy self than for the thrill of holding the man she loved.

"How does Cha Cha O'Sullivan-Lancia sound?"

"Like heaven on earth."

"Thank you for loving me." She didn't have to thank him for not taking her, ravishing her. It was clear he loved her with every nuance of his soul. Love and respect went together. But, chastity as a virtue was just about out the window.

They dressed. She gathered her things while he perused the World Champion's album.

They walked from Sullivan Street to the HOS building. She called her parents to break the news of their engagement. Frank talked with them for a bit.

She looked forward to moving upstairs to his penthouse and into his arms. Tonight.

"Don't think I won't try a Kato on you again," she warned.

"Never stop loving me."

She propped her hands on her hips. "Hey, that's my line."

"No it isn't."

"'Tis," she insisted.

She had never had such yearning like this in her life, and judging from his four-hour erection without the need for a pill, they were quite a match.

Tonight, over dinner, they'd fully address what to do about Autumn and the now "officially" defunct taskforce and how to handle their secret orders. And just maybe, because she could no longer stand it, make love until she could hear a rooster crow in New York City.

Chapter 36

Cha Cha had managed to come to terms with Autumn leaving. Her young girlfriend, sister, wishful daughter would join her family in Trinidad. Her grandparents presented devastating, professorial arguments, which neither Frank, Cha Cha nor Autumn could rebut. Still, Frank and her would hash it over and over. It was human nature and she was so glad he not only wanted to see her happy, but he also loved the kid. If there were some nuance they missed, they'd find it.

The cool night breeze slid over the clear glass barriers of Frank's penthouse deck. The kerosene heaters kept it toasty. Cha Cha wore an American-Indian white-beaded dress. She hoped the illusion of nakedness under the beads and symbols would capture Frank's imagination. He appeared mesmerized. Her nipples hardened at the thought of what they'd do later this evening.

He had promised they would finally track down and then break the news of their engagement to his parents. It was beyond polite to tell his mom and dad immediately. It was also necessary for her to be introduced.

The fragrance of roasting chestnuts couldn't compete with his aftershave. He shaved twice today, wonder why?

The candles flickered over the delicious flounder. He gave up his normal side order of spaghetti and meatballs tonight. Must be hungry for something else—her.

Frank recommended the Sauvignon Blanc, but she needed no aphrodisiac.

"Let's beat down Autumn's grandparents' objections while in the Jacuzzi," he said.

They'd have each other for dessert—after they called his parents.

"Are you really still that shy about taking off your clothes? Cha Cha asked.

"I'm going to let you help me turn over a new leaf."

She quirked a brow. "Maybe I should get you a fig leaf."

"Around you I feel comfortable in my skin."

"A very nice skin, with toned muscles." She saluted him with her wine glass and sipped. "Ummm."

They devised a game while sipping the wine. Whoever shot down one of Autumn's grandparent's arguments for keeping the girl in Trinidad got to strip an article of clothing off the other.

They'd probably stay dressed because the grandparents held the winning hand.

She went commando under her dress for the first time, just like he always had. Also, she had removed her bra. Her perky breasts needed no support anyway. Okay, to be honest, she wanted to be naked with him soon. Call it liberation. Adam and Eve. Tonight, she'd be freed from all her sins of the past: a past of very infrequent one-night stands—due to her dedication to the NYPD—with men she had no interest in, and worse, felt little pleasure. Her penance for these sins would be to join the man she loved with barely checked passion.

This game of striptease would be fun, but she had a dress, two high heels and nothing else unless she could convince him her new gorgeous earrings, which he had bought her, counted.

Advantage Frank. He had a long coat, belt—did that count? tie—the same question, suit jacket, dress shirt. Why did she have to dress him today? Pants, shoes, and for the first time anywhere, Frank would appear in boxers and socks, thanks to her dressing him at Macy's.

Anybody for a fan dance? True, she loved dancing, although she had never danced like Sally Rand, naked but for the feathers. She would someday dance erotically for her man. She wondered if they could dance while making love. Someday they'd experiment.

"You have more clothes on, so let me go first." She licked her lips. He gave her the sweetest approving nod, then swirled his wine.

"They say Trinidad has less crime than Manhattan. I say we study it, document it if it's not true." She faltered, realizing the unlikelihood of it. "Well, we can try."

"Better than that, my about to be dress-less lover—"

"Shoes." She countered.

He paused. "I'm a spy with years of experience, to your two plus months. The National Tattletale prints lies to entertain. Spies spread misinformation to defend their country. We could play with island press reports and statistics to call into doubt their safety premise."

"No honey, it would wreck their economy," Cha Cha said.

"Not if the grandparents don't get the same news everybody else receives."

They mulled it over, established boundaries and ways to protect Autumn's family. They discussed the ethics of lying, ends justifying the means. They finally agreed to a one-time demonstration. She took off her heels, without protest from him. Her anxious heart pattered. She knew this man would have her soon. But then, an idea struck her.

"Better than us planting stories is to use the spy we have in place. Autumn still has her NSA phone. We still email and text. She has her genius. She may find a way to solve the problem."

"That's not strictly countering her grandparents' argument, but it merits me taking off my shoes."

He had been generous with his shoes, since Autumn already said she'd do this very thing. With a glimmer of hope, she watched him unlace. Could she run the table, have him naked before she'd strip? Maybe ravish him on the *table* he had mentioned earlier in jest. Why not?

He completed her thoughts. "Who better to do this than the one person who wants so badly to have us as her parents and to live again in New York, to see Joey, to go to NYU?"

"Take off your pants."

A frown flitted across his brow. "That's not fair. I took off the shoes and I was just completing your thought."

"There's a penalty for roughing the passer of the thought. Take them off, Frank." She gave him her stern impression, then melting again bent nearer and kissed him senseless. He reluctantly took off his pants but put back on his shoes. He looked ridiculous. Like some guy in a cheap porno movie. Okay the pants were better. She'd take the penalty.

"We're going to use Autumn to disprove or call into question every argument of her grandparents," she said. "Take off your jacket."

"Not so fast, sweetheart. You are restating the previous point. But I've got a new point. You forgot the one thing Autumn can't prove. That we want to adopt her to take advantage of her fame."

"You have a point. We can only be ourselves. Rely on our own fame."

He countered. "Oh my about-to-be-dressless beauty. I can make a big deal about my holdings, maybe play up my charities, hold big events. The mayor and commissioner owe us favors. You could be awarded both national and city awards for valor."

"Okay."

"Okay nothing, off with your dress." She'd have to think fast.

"The earrings."

"No, the dress. Your rules." She was screwed and as soon as the dress came off, well, she would be screwed.

Phew. "Before we go any further, we need to call your parents. Remember?" Cha Cha's parents said in a nice chat, an hour earlier, they might be available for the wedding. Shouldn't they at least offer his parents the same courtesy?

"Okay. I grant you a temporary reprieve. Let's head down to the situation room and use the Sat TV equipment." Frank explained how his parents, Salvatore and Giulana Lancia, were traveling with INC, Independent News Corporation; presently, somewhere in the jungles of Mindanao, Philippines. Since it was 7:14 p.m. in New York, it was 8:14 a.m. in Mindanao. They should be up and about.

They entered the sit room. "My parents are a little weird, different," he cautioned. "They were flower children."

"I have some of those in my family. No problem."

They up-linked to the satellite. At first the camera came into focus, close-up on some ferns. A stick bug took center stage. Then somebody who heard their call sign beep did something to make the camera go up mechanically, since they could hear the gears whining. A beautiful early morning mist was dissipating—showing off jungle, a waterfall, caves and a bunch of people frolicking in the frothy waters—naked. Oh no, this was embarrassing, but they looked like they were having some innocent fun. She wouldn't know because she had never done it—well, her sister and her did skinny dip once in their aunt's pool. Unfortunately, Auntie caught them. End of that adventure.

His mom and dad ran out of the lake, not bothering to grab towels, and came up to the camera. Frank, who looked like he was going to roll up into a ball, whispered, "I've never seen them like this. Sorry."

"It's all right." She lowered her voice. "Your mom *is* wearing *Sampaguita* flowers in her hair." She put her hand over her mouth to hold in the giggles. If only she'd look that good when she reached sixty-something. Considering how Cha Cha was about to get naked in her fiancé's Jacuzzi, maybe this was a trend or a sign.

"What's all right? And who is this lovely lady?"

Frank looked at the bookshelf in the sit room rather than the screen. "Mom...Dad. I'd like you to meet the girl I just proposed marriage to, Lieutenant Chastity O'Sullivan, NYPD. Call her Cha Cha."

"And?" Giulana said.

"And I said yes, Mr. and Mrs. Lancia."

"You're stunning," Salvatore said, cocking his head to get a better look.

"I love your American Indian princess dress," Giulana said, pushing away a fern and showing her other breast. "I'd like your designer to make one for me."

"You two look...in shape." They were both buff, literally, and, well, literally. Despite some well-earned wrinkles. Frank's face was more like his mom's. His body was out of this world. His dad wasn't so tall and much more lean. Both men were well endowed. It was not often a girl got to "know" her family. Growing old with Frank might include a lifetime's worth of lust, if they both took care of themselves and each other.

"We can cover up. There's clothes around here somewhere."

They heard somebody call out, "Come back in."

Some news organization.

"Are we interrupting anything?" Cha Cha asked.

"No. We'll have our orgy later. Thank you for asking." Giulana said. Now she knew where Frank got his sense of humor.

Frank threw up his hands. Communicating in Italian, no doubt. "*Mommm?*"

"You're no prude, son," Giulana said.

Had they spied on a spy?

They then discussed what they were doing in the middle of the jungle. His parents had hoped to find a real stone age tribe. They had been suckered into contributing big money to the stone-age Tasaday tribe hoax, and they wanted a return on their investment, but would probably just end up naked in one waterfall after another. They were going to other remote areas of the globe over the next couple of months and didn't expect to get back home until February, 2002, or sooner if exhausted.

Their conversation meandered much like the stream in the background.

"We met when I consulted with the NYPD over the terrorist threats," Frank said.

"Show us a kiss, Frankie."

"Dad...no."

Cha Cha grabbed him by his cheeks and planted a lingering wet smooch.

"That's great. If you two kids have half the passion I still have for your mother, you'll be in great shape." Giulana yelped and pushed Salvatore's hand away, probably from her rear. "We have to get back in the water," Salvatore said. With that, the link went black.

"Sorry about them. I wish I could erase the images."

"I think we should both get naked. That'll work for me." Somehow, the time between her having to remove her dress, and the time of watching the older couple au naturale, had caused her beloved Frank to forget the bet they'd made.

"I've won the bet. But you'll still have panties, bra." *Oh, never mind. She spoke too soon...*

"I'm not wearing anything underneath this dress." A lump in his throat formed. His eyes became crazed again—he had forgotten his parents.

He grabbed her hand. "I can't take it anymore. Let's go to the Jacuzzi before I...I..."

Him exploding from a bad case of the hornies put a smile on her face.

"I feel the same way." She shook at a wild imagining of him grasping her rear and entering her for the first time.

* * *

They reached the Jacuzzi and set the stage by grabbing towels. Frank kept an immaculate and tidy home. However, tonight housekeeping would have to wait.

"Unzip me," Cha Cha gave up trying to win their strip contest. Besides, Autumn's grandparents had decimated them in debate and rightfully took the girl.

Frank fingered her beaded dress. "This beautiful dress adorns a lily." He gently and slowly unzipped her. She tried to peek over her shoulder through her bushy ponytail. His warm wet lips kissed inch by inch as he lowered the zipper. This ended at the curve of her bottom. He bit her there again. She remembered Autumn translating his bad Russian, 'I want to bite your ass.' Mission completely accomplished, mister spy. Enough of Autumn, for now.

Holding her waist, he stood up and slipped his hands around to cup her breasts.

"Oh." She purred, raggedly inhaling his heady masculine scent.

"Perfect."

No more skinny girl worries. He loved her just the way she was.

"Perky," she suggested.

"Scrumptious," he corrected. Still behind her, he nipped the nape of her neck.

Next, with some struggle, he unraveled her ponytail. He felt the texture of her thick hair, breathed her in. Arching her back, she rested her head on his shoulder. She tossed her arms and hands backwards like a ballerina and tangled her fingers into his thick locks.

He stopped. Breathed heavily.

She needed one final hint that she was okay before they... Of lusty voice, she said, "One more time, dear. Why me?" He after all was built like Michelangelo's David. She was above average, nothing more.

"The right woman for any man is a subjective thing. You nursed me, honey. You're funny, smart, talented, loving, gorgeous. You get me. I get you. You, you…" All that choppy breathing tangled his tongue, but his words made her shimmer deep inside.

She rescued him. "Make love to me, babe."

He fingered the top of her dress. It tumbled down. She stepped out of it naked and half turned, just a small tease.

"Your dress is too beautiful to get crumpled." He laid it out on the cedar bench, and then turned to her, beaming.

"Tub, or sauna—or bed?"

"Ohhhh, a little of everything." She remembered him saying the same when he pretended he couldn't dance.

Teacher won't you teach me, but I know a thing or two.

His eyes glistened with desire, his lips curled. "Strip me." They worked together to toss his jacket, tie, shoes, everything except shirt and boxers. They were hers to remove. One shirt button at a time, she kissed his very Italian upper body, giving back his loving sweetness when he had kissed her down the length of her back.

Then, his shorts. Should she? She tugged it little by a little. Her hands then raked his shoulders and feathered his body as she kneeled.

She nearly ripped his boxers down. Damn obstructions.

She had never seen a man so big before. None of her so-so lovers stuck out long and fat like this. She caressed his tip with her mouth, lips, tongue. She tasted him. He groaned. She moaned with vicarious pleasure.

"I want you so bad, and for so long. I might not last long," he said.

She squeezed his firm backside. "I've already climaxed twice. Little quakes. We have all night, honey."

She played with his magnificent shaft, enjoying what she could take in. Would they fit?

He lifted her into his arms and led her into the steam room.

"Phew." She fanned herself and laughed. "I'm already too hot." Her eyes rolled with a dreamy feel. She needed to pinch herself.

"A little of everything." *More like a lot.* He lay her on a toweled bench and spread her legs. He kissed her toes, ankles, then up her legs. He lingered at her upper thighs, close to her tangles. He sure liked to bite. *Ummmmm.* Then he licked her, there. She couldn't stop moaning. In her whole life, she had never ever made noise, until him.

Their bodies beaded with perspiration. He buried his head deep in her folds.

She raked him, while she came again. Then she remembered his just barely-healed back.

"Sorry."

"I'm not hurting," he rumbled. "I'm somewhere in Eden."

He swept her up into a hug.

"All my life I hoped to meet you. I hoped to be a real man. You gave me my life, my happiness." He kissed her again and again. "I am your soul mate." She wrapped her arms around his neck and raised her legs high, straddling him. Just like that, he slipped deep into her. Fulfillment. A perfect snug fit.

"Our bodies." They were made for each other. A funny thought, but true. She undulated her hips. He bucked her a little, then their rhythms matched, perfectly.

"Oh, God," he said.

Soon their engine couldn't stop.

He held onto her so tight about her high thighs. Writhing sensually, expectantly, they shared quick pecks. She couldn't wait and by his deep needful thrusts, neither could he. They quickened until their bodies pulsed again and again harder, together.

They hadn't made it to the Jacuzzi. He slowed down his thrusts, hoisted her and carried her toward the bubbling waters away from the steam. The grind of his thighs over her bottom as he carried her caused him to shutter and cry out. A tight feeling like she were to burst overwhelmed her. Her body pounded like she had never felt before. For these moments, they gripped tight in ecstasy and abandon.

Gasping awhile in the exquisite aftermath, he let her slide off at the Jacuzzi.

He kissed her eyelids. "I wondered what it would be like. Loving you. I've never felt much before, just quick orgasms with women I cared for as friends, but didn't love. It was all shallow before you."

"I know. My flings never quite satisfied me." She nuzzled him. "But carrying me, boy. Phew. With your total love inside me, this roller-coaster climaxing was beyond my wildest fantasies."

"In a way, we were both virgins before tonight," he said huskily.

"Do you think God made us for each other?"

"Autumn said, God put a tag on your butt with my name on it."

She stepped up onto the ledge seat, turned. "Well…?"

"Shapely." He caressed her bottom. "It says here, Soul Mate of Frank Lancia. Keepa your hands off."

"It *does* not." She pretended to try to look, but wasn't a contortionist. So she rubbed her rear into his face and started laughing.

"I can't breathe." He laughed and bit her rear again.

"I love it." She slipped down. "I adore you, Frank." She kissed him wantonly, exploring him with her tongue.

"So it's pretty much settled, then."

"Stuck with each other. I guess," she said.

Her hair had frizzed out to monster quality since the steam room. So she brushed his face with her frizz.

"Lethal."

"Can't breathe again?"

"No, someone very pretty has stolen my heart."

After some heavy petting, okay they had the whole thing backwards, he took her hand. "Let's go to bed for round number ah…"

"Four for me. The last two were endless. So I guess that adds up to a couple hundred."

"I've got some catching up to do," he crooned.

He carried her into his bedroom suite and laid her gently. "Our bed. We are becoming one. I never knew…"

Leaning over her, he stroked her hair back from her ears and cupped her cheek. Emotion welled up within her as they stared into each other's eyes. She pressed her lips to his. "My whole life, I ran from the demons of my grandpapa's murder. You cured me. I ran from believing in myself as a first rate detective. You corrected me.

I ran from men, but then I ran into you. I danced, but then you took me to heaven. I have had sex, but then you made love to me."

"You awakened in me the man I never thought I had any right to be. You abolished my body shyness. You stole my heart the first time I hugged you, the first time I laid eyes on you."

He stopped his words and replaced them with kisses. They cried joyful tears wrapped in each other's arms and legs.

Finally, they were one.

* * *

Why had Frank waited all these years?

For her. That's why.

Her bare shoulder glistened in the moonlight from his skylight over their bed. Her perfect complexion and creamy smooth skin struck him. The most beautiful woman he had ever seen was now his. He kissed her forehead. Her dimple appeared. She had to be dreaming.

He couldn't sleep much, didn't matter. The dead of 9/11 were saying their goodbyes. The gris gris curse Emily stuck him with had been broken because he was no longer simply Frank. He was part of a new and powerful entity. Frank and Cha Cha. What a wonderful ring to it. He had an urge to dance with her in the middle of the night. But, maybe tomorrow, after they took in Broadway's new play, *Mamma Mia,* they'd dance into the night, if they could control their urges.

Tears started forming on her doe eyes. She awoke and quickly wiped her face into his shoulder.

Looking up, she said hoarsely, "I was dreaming of my ex-partner."

"I'm so sorry, Cha Cha."

"He was a great guy, you would have liked him."

"We should visit his wife and children again." Over these two months, they shared each other's worlds. Learned them. Gave their all for each other, family, friends, city, country.

"It was so real. We were eating hotdogs in Washington Square Park. He teased me about being too skinny. But in a rare moment of seriousness, he said you and I were perfect for each other. He bent down, kissed my forehead, said goodbye, said he was going to heaven and then disappeared."

"Maybe there's something to the gris gris. Maybe the curse is gone because we are one, stronger," Frank said while kissing her shoulder.

"I talk with my grandpapa. Haven't you had dreams like that, too?"

"Maybe you're right. In any case, I doubt we'll be hearing from the ghosts of 9/11 anymore."

"We'll never abandon their memories." She slithered her body, like a kiss, until on top of him, spread her legs, arched up, pushing his chest with her arms. She started to move back and forth suggestively. His arousal was intense, immediate. She eased onto him. She was ready.

They slowly rocked and rolled, dancing shadows of moonlight. He filled his senses with the beauty of a woman more an angel than real. This angel had saved him from a life of denial of his own spirit. Climaxing together, he spilled his seed inside her, hoping someday for children and hoping for a long life to see them grow and their children grow.

By some fate, they found each other.

There's more to life and death than meets the eye.

Chapter 37

Every night since Autumn left, Frank and Cha Cha eagerly read together the encrypted emails of her misadventures in Trinidad. Sometimes she wrote like a poet, sometimes like a brat, sometimes like a genius, but always as the indefatigable, undefeatable Autumn.

* * *

Autumn hoped her prospective mom and dad would read the lines and in between the lines to know that although she enjoyed herself she still wanted to live with them in New York and was still searching for a way to make her grandparents think it would be their idea to let Cha Cha and Frank adopt her.

Email: I float above the sea turtles, too scared to hitch a ride, too worried I might disturb their environment. A school of Labrisomidae, you know Starksia rava, AKA Tawny Blenny whisk by taunting the sea turtle just like the rabbit does to the land turtle in the fable. Turtles are smart. They wear their own army tanks. Just like the turtle, I might have to take my time getting back to New York and you guys, but I will. Granny and Pappy are outsmarting me, taunting me. But I love them. I pout, they laugh. I screw things up, and they join in my goofiness.

Luv,
AB

Email: I like Granny and Pappy's cottage by the sea much better than their house. They said you two could honeymoon here. They said something about walking on the beach at midnight. Don't trip over driftwood. Make sure there's a moon out. I've heard and read stuff about romance, but you have to be careful.

XOXO

Email: Protected bird habitats everywhere, here. You must see them when you honeymoon, if you aren't too busy kissing. Yuk. I'm excited to be your flower girl and meet Cha Cha's sister, mom and dad.

Birds have various complicated languages, even across species. It should be easy to decode. Here, in the forest, I listen to the Piping-guan harmonize with the Motmot. I'm talking Momotus bahamensis, which should be considered distinct from the Blue-crowned Motmot. Anyway, the two species are doing their duets when upstart crows try to quash their song. The nerve.

A new singing show is starting in the spring, American Idol. But me (even though I can sing), I'm going to stick to my studies. Birds can sing and communicate, but I can solve Bud's crypto magic… Ask the wizard to write me.

TaTa XoXo

Email: Why do people say black and white? This is too stark, too much like wow, look at the big differences. It's totally opposite sides of the spectrum. White is all the visible wavelengths of color and black is invisible, to us, the nothingness of space. Totally unfair. Why not chocolate and cream? These are friendlier colors. People might not fight as much.

"Hey you, chocolate man."

"Yes, cream daddy, what's happening?"

To my NYC dreamy creamies,

AB

p.s. I dream of Joey.

Email: I say to Granny today, "I want a teenager's room. You're trying to keep me like a little girl. I'm big and getting bigger. I'm smart, and getting smarter."

She goes, "but honey, we want you to remember better times. I made your favorite cookies, oatmeal raisin."

Okay, oatmeal raisin and the smell from the oven is driving me nuts.

So I say, "I don't like oatmeal raisin that much anymore." I put on my if-I-have-to-eat-this face. "I'll take one, and thank you, Granny. Can I go to my room?"

Granny says, "I want to talk to you for just a moment. Your friend, Cha Cha, has not only been cleared of all those spurious charges but she just won the Congressional Medal of Honor and the Medal of Valor for the City of New York. She also has a promotion to an NYPD captain coming up and she's writing a book on negotiating as the way to problem solving."

Bam, "It's a safe job now, Granny. Can I go back to them *now*?" Guess what. None of those great facts worked. Not yet.

"That's nice dear," Granny just kills me. She is way too wise.

I am so out of this kitchen (before I turn into the cookie monster). "Can I go now?" I swipe another yummy cookie, quickly rearrange the pattern of the remaining cookies on Granny's pan, to make it look untouched.

C-o-o-k-eee,

AB the CM

Email: More stuff. "Be down here *now* for University," Granny says.

"I don't like my classes." I slam the door to my bedroom. But I can't stand being a brat, so I run back down the steps and hug her.

"I'm sorry, Granny." But, I really am. Sorry she won't let me go home too. BTW, they follow me everywhere, well Pappy does when he's not lecturing at University.

Granny is just strangling the life out of me.

I'm gaga for Pappy. Earlier today, he sat me down on the bench under a Mango tree and showed me some advanced tricks in calculus and differential equations.

AB

p.s. I'm sorry I haven't totally figured out their weaknesses yet.

* * *

After each email, Cha Cha cuddled with Frank. She wept a little and he looked on the verge for the girl who stole a piece of their hearts and changed their lives. They laughed more than they wept and loved more than they laughed.

"We'll see her soon," Cha Cha said, her eyelashes tickled his neck.

"Carlos reported that her family is making the flower-girl dress."

Carlos had decided to plead Frank and Cha Cha's case, ostensibly while on vacation in Trinidad. He picked up Emily in New Orleans and the two of them enjoyed Trinidad and Tobago and each other. Minus sharing secrets, he recanted what he had observed of Frank, Cha Cha and Autumn hoping for some empathy but couldn't report a glimmer of success.

However, Carlos promised Frank and Cha Cha, Emily would be back in New Orleans long before the wedding. Good, otherwise the infamous assassin might need to move to New Orleans.

Chapter 38

Trinidad, Maracas Bay, the morning of Christmas Eve

The Neem trees wanted to shed their beauty as a wedding gift.

The bride sat on a wicker chair under a stand of Neems as Autumn and Faith weaved the tiny white blossoms, falling all over, into Cha Cha's thick auburn hair. The trees would become the arbor sheltering Autumn's dearest friend on this her wedding day.

"You are so fantastic, like a sea nymph," Autumn said. Frank was *so* lucky. Would Joey be *so* lucky someday or would she forget him when chased by a thousand guys? Or would he forget her, when some co-ed pulls up her shirt and says 'I've got boobs?'

Cha Cha held Autumn's elbow. "Someday, you'll be a Miss Universe."

Autumn was five-five and figured she'd get taller, so it was possible and exotic multiracial girls were in.

"The head of the NSA, Mary Ayita Starblanket, said that to me too and she was Miss Cherokee Nation. But I'll be too busy for that."

Faith said, "Don't close any doors, sweetie. Be like Leonardo Da Vinci, diverse master of everything he chose. There's nothing wrong with a beauty contest and everything right with a liberal education and way of life." She was right. People weren't abstract blots destined to become units in a too neat and functioning society.

"I doubt I can be a master of beauty. I'd settle for the love of one boy with a true heart." Speaking of hearts, Autumn's just did a triple backflip when she imagined Joey walking out of the surf in his bathing suit. He was so hunky.

"It's every girl's wish," Cha Cha said, all *dreamy* eyed.

"Dejon, Frank's brother asked if he could show me the island later," Faith said. Dejon was an orphan from Tobago when Frank's parents adopted him. The tall and handsome Best Man for the wedding was taken by Cha Cha's sister and told Frank as much.

"He's a great guy, sis. I hope you enjoy your tour."

"Well, I won't have much time. Got to get back NYC tonight."

Autumn and Faith weaved in their last blossoms. Cha Cha's face was radiant and she smelled now, a lot like Lilac. That would drive Frank crazy and then he'd want to kiss her and all that. Autumn knew. She had read Playboy and seen an X rated film her mom had hid in the top of her closet.

In a last minute hug before the ceremony, Cha Cha said, "Know this, my precocious one. Frank and I love you so much and although your grandparents won't let us adopt you, you'll always be our daughter in our hearts."

"I don't want to cry all over your lovely gown." Her gown, all white silk, had tiny shells instead of beads. Really cool. Another brilliant island design by her granny's friend's daughter.

* * *

Love in a natural setting. An odd place to be on Christmas Eve, a perfect place for a wedding. Frank's beautiful barefoot bride wore a white Neem flowered headdress. The fragrance intoxicated him. Her white bodice cut low and tight to show off perfect proportions. Her gossamer train floated above the glistening sands, rustled by every soft breeze.

Lapping waves were now but fifteen feet from the wedding's arbor of Neems. The afternoon puckered light purple kisses on the teal waters.

Autumn's grandparents had lent their beach cottage to Frank and Cha Cha. The young couple stole many joyous runs, *au naturale*, on this deserted beach, under the moon and into warm waters. Cha Cha, an alluring mermaid, had run his bachelor ship aground. Never to be repaired. He'd have it no other way. He had never believed in soul mates. Whether mystical or just plain dumb luck, but Cha Cha was perfect for him. The way their bodies fit and moved while they made love or just hugged gave him chills and something else. His white pants were filling up. He'd have to think of something else or abduct her back to the cottage.

Over the last three days, they had been so naughty. *Cop and spy gone wild.* The worst public place they dared and bared to make love was in a confessional at Saint Michaels. Hey, nobody was using it. They both said twenty Hail Mary's and dropped a contribution in the box. Best sex ever, complete with lightning up their asses.

Autumn twirled before them, then squeezed her toes into the sand and stepped closer to the priest and family. This island doll competed with exotic birds warbling for the wedding by being her merry self. Autumn wore a rainbow of tight bows made of silk and jersey to match her mahogany curls. At the altar now, Faith was dressed simply in a three-quarter length sea-blue gown, which was the theme for the adults present. She beamed for her sister.

Autumn led the way to Faith, Dejon and the local priest with Cha Cha's parents and Autumn's grandparents in attendance.

Frank grinned when he recalled a silly disagreement he had with Cha Cha over the number of times they should kiss when the priest would say, 'You may kiss the bride.' He wanted one long one, which was traditional, maybe. She wanted two short ones. Her kisses, of all kinds, had always melted his resolve to stay sane.

"I do with all my heart," Cha Cha said, her emerald doe eyes glistening with the tiniest hint of a tear of joy.

"I am forever yours," Frank responded.

The priest pronounced them husband and wife. "You may now kiss the bride."

Frank, in this heady moment had forgotten how many times he should kiss her so they went at it. They could do this all day. No one told them to get back to the bamboo beach cottage. Autumn started to giggle and broke through his haze. So this was love.

* * *

Everybody except Faith and Dejon stayed over for Christmas at Eustace and Amber La Badie's main home in Saint Augustine's near the university. It was so nice of Autumn's grandparents putting them all up. They exchanged gifts, stories, love. Even Cha Cha's parents stopped pushing their ideas about her joining their business opportunities in Pennsylvania. They had tried to get New York out of hers and Faith's systems but the girls loved the city too much.

Frank and Cha Cha planned to host Autumn's grandparents when they flew to New York on the 27th for Eustace's interview with NYU. Eustace was attracted to their summer exchange program and Frank assured him he was a shoe-in. How sweet her man was, but more than that he loved Autumn too. Frank, although a spy by nature, couldn't hide his true colors from her.

Nobody was driving especially after Eustace poured the whole bottle of Trinidadian Angostura Rum into the eggnog. This loosened tongues.

"A toast to the newlyweds," Eustace said. They all clanked, including Autumn with her cocoa. "Amber and I want to apologize for not getting you two a more personal wedding gift, but we want to shop in New York City." Their Christmas gift, a case of Trinidadian rums and other drink was very generous. Frank's private plane and the La Badie family's political connections with Customs on the Christmas holiday insured he would have no trouble taking it all home.

"You don't have to shop, the drinks and your loving us are the greatest gift," Cha Cha said.

"No, we have something in mind we think is just perfect for you," Amber said.

"I can't wait. I want to toast you two for your gracious hosting and allowing Autumn to come with you whenever you travel to New York. This girl," he patted her shoulder, "has stolen mine and Cha Cha's hearts, so seeing her is pretty fair and as Autumn would say, totally awesome."

"I hope someday to be a grandparent with the wisdom you two have," Cha Cha added. Okay, the eggnog was strong, but her and Frank really meant what they said.

Just like the day before, everybody danced on and on. Full of energy and passion for the dance and each other, Autumn's grandparents looked like newlyweds while Frank and Cha Cha played parents, alternately teaching Autumn some Latin steps. Autumn, as in everything else, learned quickly and with unmatched enthusiasm.

* * *

The evening of December 27th

Cha Cha and Frank had invited Eustace, Amber, Faith and Autumn to dinner on their penthouse deck after Eustace's interview with the dean, which was successful, of course.

Frank had mentioned that Carlos was bringing a surprise later, but he couldn't specify because he didn't know. Or so he said. Frank and Carlos were up to something. Once again a glimmer of hope that Autumn could be theirs, flitted by Cha Cha like an Irish fairy. Later, she would have to instruct her husband on sharing secrets, since she was an equal partner in their work and marriage. Maybe tickle him with a feather or better yet give him a boxing lesson.

Amber raised her glass of Chardonnay. "Eustace and I had misjudged the two of you. You obviously love our granddaughter and for that kindness we will be forever grateful to you," Amber caught her husband's eye, raised one of her eyebrows, as if to say 'your turn,' a routine Frank and Cha had been subjected to back in mid-November. *Please, no more lectures.*

Faith was 'all in' regarding Autumn. They took to each other like best buddies from the first moment they met. Autumn excited by fashion. Faith intrigued by her outlandish brilliance. At this moment, they were having an animated discussion about what type of clothes might showcase the Golden Ratio on a woman. They designed with asparagus and carrots and drew on napkins.

After Faith's last asparagus and design disappeared, she stood and offered a toast. "To the wonderful family of a special girl and my friend, to my beautiful, big hearted and talented sister, to Frank, they don't come any more handsome or nicer. I wish us all a fantastic New Year."

A couple drinks later, Eustace reached for a stewed and wimpy carrot. "Does anybody think they know why grandparents spoil their grandchildren?"

Frank grabbed a carrot too and pointed it at Eustace. Maybe they'd duel with vegetables. "I'd say, because they only remember their successes in raising their own children and practice them."

"Pretty good answer, Frank. But no, at least not in our case."

"May I try, sir?" Cha Cha had this one down pat.

Eustace nodded, pointing at Cha Cha with what was left of his carrot. Her cue.

"Grandparents only have a limited time with their grandchildren, normally." She nodded to Eustace and Amber. "They don't want what little time they have to be full of stress creating unhappy children who won't want to visit again. Grandparents want to play, to share hugs, candies, video games, maybe some school lessons. They want to intrigue the child."

Autumn had ants in her pants. "This is true. Granny and Pappy kept me intellectually stimulated, well fed, and we explored the island's wonders. And I really do like your oatmeal cookies, Granny."

"Thank you, Autumn. We are proud of raising you." Amber said. "But, Cha Cha, although generically your answer is correct, you have all missed a unique point."

The waiters brought out rainbow sorbet and cleared the dinner plates. Cha Cha peeked south at the work lights streaming forever upward from Ground Zero and recalled the day she and Autumn met Frank, AKA Johnny Lance. 9/11.

Eustace spoke, "No, Amber and I had to take on the job of rearing a very difficult teenager. We knew why she was giving us a hard time. She loves you two so much. We love a good challenge and gave her better than she gave us. Barely." He laughed. "We had a nice long discussion with your president of overseas accounts." This was Carlos's cover story of the day: President of HOS Import/Export Bank, overseas accounts.

"Carlos?" Cha Cha asked.

Amber continued. "Yes, odd first name for a Russian. He made a case for the two of you by not trying to change our minds but by filling us in on what you have done for our granddaughter and what Autumn's life was really like here in New York City."

"We are especially interested in why Autumn thinks it's okay to talk with a plush sheepdog she named Julius Caesar," Eustace said.

"But Pappy, I know he's not real. I just needed somebody to talk to."

"Could it be, child, that since you're really talking to yourself you see yourself as a Julius Caesar?" Eustace posited.

"I admire his greatness. That's all."

"You see, child, this is what is called projecting. You want to be great. You will be great," Amber said.

"You, not the dog, are Julius Caesar," Eustace said.

"And there is no better place for you to be your very best then here in the States in its greatest city," Amber said. Tears filled her eyes and then her husband's.

"You mean it?" Autumn got up, overturning her sorbet and then hugged both grandparents. These tears being infectious, migrated to Cha Cha's eyes. She checked Frank. His intense black-rimmed gray eyes were gleaming, too. He presented them all with the biggest smile.

The group was standing now, hugging.

"We won't disappoint you," Frank said.

Amber grabbed Cha Cha's arm and whispered in her ear. "Besides, Autumn has crimped our style, if you know what I mean." Amber put on a suggestive look, which no doubt led her husband to steal a kiss.

"In November, Cha Cha, you started papers. Perfect them to full adoption with our blessings and love. We want our granddaughter to have a mom and a dad. Our granddaughter wants you two, right?" Eustace asked.

"With all my heart." She uttered that with a nearly inaudible, dreamy voice Cha Cha had never heard before.

After a little while they all sat down again to finish dessert.

About a minute after dessert was finished, Carlos appeared carrying a gift. "I am sorry I have missed your wedding and Christmas but I had job to do. You might think this present is for wedding, but it is for Autumn." Carlos put the box on Autumn's lap.

Big-eyed Autumn ripped the ribbons off the box and opened it while making gleeful squeaks. She pulled out a gray and white fur ball, a puppy, an Old English Sheepdog. She held him high. He whimpered. She lowered him to her chest.

"Now. Now. Julius. Oh, Carlos. Thank you so much. He's so great." The girl pushed back the fur from his eyes and kissed his forehead. Carlos kissed her forehead and patted the pup. The adults got up from the dinner table and gathered around, all wanting to touch the puppy. Cha Cha and Frank squeezed each other's hands while they waited just a tad longer to hug their new daughter.

Finally, the new family embraced. Then Frank picked up the pup. "Can you take orders, little guy?"

Why had Frank not told her about the pup? Possibly, he worried about Autumn going back to Trinidad. She guessed Frank wouldn't have wanted to raise a pup without Autumn's help. Although the pup was adorable, he was right to keep the gift a secret.

Now that their taskforce network was securely underground they could easily raise a daughter and an adorable pup.

Eustace raised his glass, "Hail, Caesar." They all chuckled because they were really toasting Autumn Breeze.

First Frank, then everybody turned south. A moment of silence followed except for little squeaky sounds from Julius. Cha Cha felt safe, because America nurtured greatness and out of greatness sprung the strongest will to live with the means to achieve it. While some others wallowed in destruction contributing nothing, Americans helped forge the future for free men everywhere and for every one of God's children.

The beginning.

Epilogue

Autumn's diary, 12/27/2001, 11:48 p.m.

I am a New Yorker.

Joey called me today. Told me he really enjoyed our swapping of lessons for help with the matchmaking business and wanted to get back together, starting Friday, tomorrow night. I won't have anything to swap anymore, maybe, but at least the lessons will continue and we'll cook up interesting dishes* and share life, maybe we can check in on the matchmaking business. *My new and great Mom and Dad's place has fantastic kitchens, even a walk in frig/freezer upstairs.

Joey said he missed me, YES. I pressed him and he admitted OMG that he wanted lessons true but wanted 'originally' to 'bank' me. Bank me: meaning he thought he could be on the inside track when I grew into a beautiful woman. And I've done some curvy growing. Guess I'll have to totally grow into a beautiful woman. I looked in the mirror. Okay, I'm super cute. But what an interesting prospective, he took a cool calculating approach, getting a head start on legions of suitors. Well— thing about him, besides his gorgeousity, he gets and lets me, and supports me being myself.

Tada, back to Mom and Dad. Picked up new parents today. LOL. Speaking about long range planning, I guess I was guilty of the same kind of thinking that Joey had used. I banked parents.

I'll never stop loving my original mom and dad. They raised me, loved me, helped me grow my genius, put me on TV shows, but kept it real. I have understood for some time why my mom did what she did. I forgave her. I love her.

Love is infinite, so I love my new mom
and dad, too. Well, I'm crazy about them.
Speaking of crazy. They are one wild and
strange couple. Late tonight, I refereed
a boxing match (in a ring—in a full gym)
(really a spar in Frank's case). My mom
was safe. They both wore protective
everything. God, Mom was so good at this.
I thought he was quick, star athlete and
all, but Mom—she knocked him on his butt in
thirty-three seconds. He even claimed to
have seen little tweety-birds flying around
his head. We both kissed him senseless.
Lights out for those two upstairs. They
stopped dancing, I guess. But they can't
stop kissing each other. I want that
someday. Tomorrow I'll tell Joey we have
to seal his 'banking me' with a real kiss.
He couldn't refuse that logic. We'll see.

Can't wait to have Julius sleep with
me. The pup has to stay on the penthouse
poop deck until he's house trained. He
certainly has plenty of fur and a heated

doghouse to keep him warm. In the meantime, watch where you step.

Faith, love & action.

Note to future self: Get Osama bin Laden.

Goodnight NYC.

You have just read *Autumn Breeze* and the author wants to thank you.

I need your help to succeed. Please correspond if you have questions or write a review if you have the time.

I'm at rwrichard@ymail.com or visit
http://romancetheguyspov.blogspot.com.

If you enjoyed this story, you may enjoy the author's other works:
The Carlos series (which includes this book) is offered in both paperback and e-book formats. The Carlos series have some continuing characters and related story lines. They're listed in chronological order. Each novel stands alone.

1st in series
Autumn Breeze: I am a New Yorker. You have just read this editor's choice novel. Please review it or send the author a note.

2nd in series
Angel's Eyes will be out early 2016. An Army Colonel loses her sight in battle and discovers she has an unusual talent, *blindsight*, a documented but little understood human condition. Out of the Army, she copes with a world in which she must rely on others, specifically one other.

3rd in series
A More Perfect Union - a novel in e-book and paperback. **Finalist: San Diego Book Awards.**
Former Miss Cherokee Nation, present Virginia Senator, Ayita Starblanket, is running against a former MLB slugger and present Florida Governor, Arturo Arnez. After circumstances force the unlikely pair together, she suspects her opponent is falling for her. They had a past but will they have a future. The story explores the struggle between power and love.

Let the author know if you'd like more in the Carlos series.

Other works:

The Wolves of Sherwood Forest - a novella in e-book format only. Wolves… is a lighthearted romp through Sherwood Forest with a young-adult Robin, Marian and real wolves (as opposed to werewolves). The couple band together to save the recently returned to England, King Richard (1194 AD). If you like your politics really dusty-old (before the Magna Carta), try this flashback to a time when people could just walk into your home for no particular reason (oh, you say, they're relatives and neighbors, never mind).

Double Happiness - a novel in e-book and paperback. A Stand-up comedian and his fall-down-drunk artist brother need and want to switch places secretly. The comedian is in jail and needs out to prove his innocence. His brother needs in to detox with the hope of saving his engagement. Now out, the comedian has to enlist the help of a Mafia Don to clear his name, but suspects he may end up cat food. The comedian must also live with his brother's Fiancée—a demanding psychologist—without touching her.

The comedian's attorney, a beautiful Chinese American is surprised when whom she thinks is the comedian starts flirting with her and nearly steals her heart. The twin flirts to set up the attorney, he just knows is perfect for his brother. Meanwhile, the comedian is having difficulty holding off his brother's fiancée. They must switch back, and it won't be the last time.

Through a deal with the Don, he's out of jail, but a renegade mobster still pursues him. Now the four best friends—entwined like spaghetti—must survive the chase while weighing the bonds of identical twins against the meaning and respect for an engagement and their own feelings. They'll decide—who should marry who—if they live that long or even if there is a double or single wedding.

This novel is inspired by William Shakespeare's Comedy of Errors.

Neanderthals and the Garden of Eden: Running with Wolves - a novel in e-book and paperback. This, the author's first story, is different from anything else you will have read, because multi-protagonist stories have been out of style for a 120 years. But, that's the way life was back 100,000 years ago when we, through this story, witness the intermingling of tribes and wolf packs and how they lived. Although not a romance in the traditional sense, this story includes a man traveling back in time to find his one true love. The pace is fairly quick because the tribe members usually demonstrated their thoughts with action. You may think of this novel as a scientist's rejoinder to so many well-written but scientifically incorrect pre-history stories.

Reader's notes:

_____

_____

_____

_____

_____

_____

_____

_____

_____

_____

_____

_____

_____

_____

_____

_____

_____

_____

_____

_____

www.ingramcontent.com/pod-product-compliance
Lightning Source LLC
Chambersburg PA
CBHW060400260626
47160CB00006B/2384